DILLY COURT

SUNDAY'S CHILD

Complete and Unabridged

MAGNA
Leicester

First published in Great Britain in 2022 by
HarperCollins*Publishers*
London

First Ulverscroft Edition
published 2022
by arrangement with
HarperCollins*Publishers* Ltd
London

A catalogue record for this book is available
from the British Library.

ISBN 978-0-7505-4913-4

Published by
Ulverscroft Limited
Anstey, Leicestershire

Printed and bound in Great Britain by
TJ Books Ltd., Padstow, Cornwall

This book is printed on acid-free paper

For my two beautiful great-grandchildren,
Marcy and Oakley

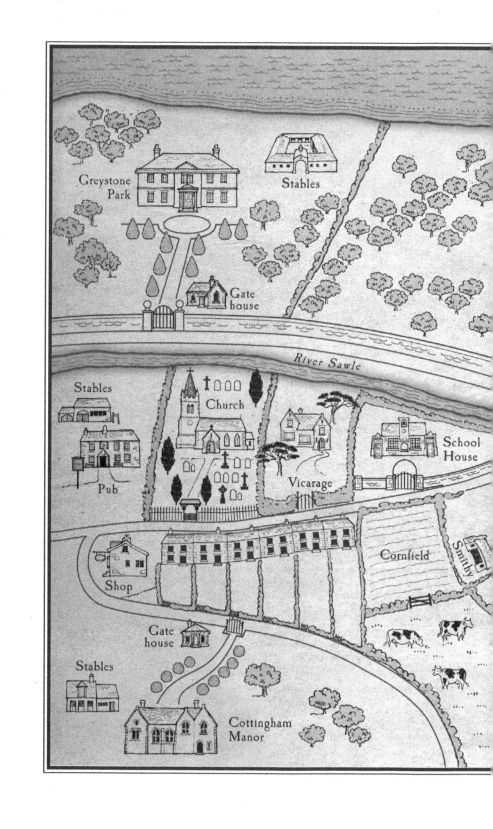

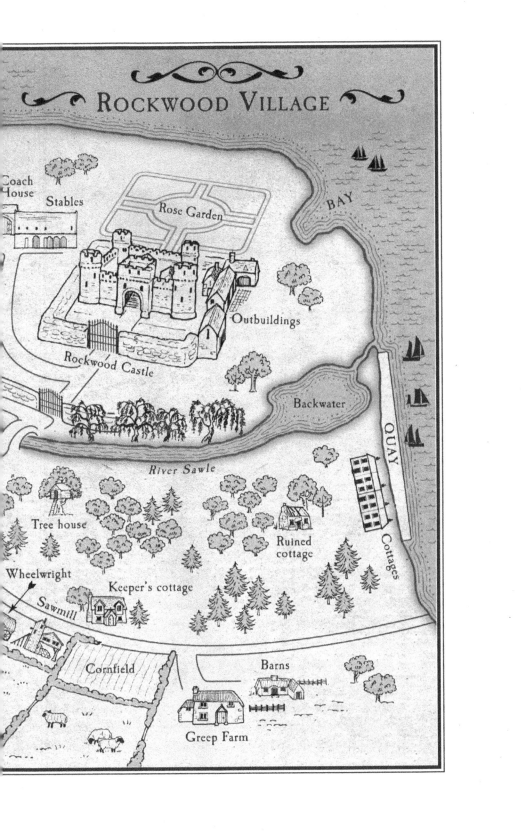

ROCKWOOD VILLAGE

Coach House
Stables
Rose Garden
BAY
Outbuildings
Rockwood Castle
Backwater
QUAY
River Sawle
Tree house
Ruined cottage
Cottages
Wheelwright
Keeper's cottage
Sawmill
Cornfield
Barns
Greep Farm

❧ THE CAREY FAMILY ❧

Lady Hester Carey m Vice–Admiral Sir Lucius Carey m Lady Prudence Carey
(Neé Dodridge)   (1776–1853)   (deceased)
(b. 1804)

Claude de Marney m Felicia Carey m Wilfred Carey
(b. 1805)   (b. 1806)   (1800–1851)

Sarah   m Bertram (Bertie)   Captain Alexander m Rosalind (Rosie)   Piers   Walter m Louise   Patricia (Patsy) m 1. Sir Michael
Farthing   Carey   Blanchard   Carey   Blanchard   Carey   Shaw   Carey   Greystone
(1829–1847)   (b. 1827)   (b. 1827)   (b. 1830)   (b. 1825)   (b. 1832) (b. 1827)   (b. 1834)   (b. 1806–1859)
                                                                                                                                 m 2. Leo Wilder
                                                                                                                                 (b. 1829)

Tommy Carey   Rory   Phoebe   Adela (Dolly)   Charlotte
(b. 1844)   Blanchard   Blanchard   Blanchard   Carey
                                      (b. 1856)   (b. 1858)   (b. 1854)   (b. 1859)

1

Rockwood Castle, June 1862

It was a hot summer day but the four-foot-thick stone walls kept the interior of the castle at an even temperature. Even so, the kitchen was not exactly cool, with a fire blazing in the black-leaded range and pans bubbling on the hob. Fanning herself with her apron, Cook slumped down on the chair she had claimed as her own. She pointed to the board on the wall where a bell was jangling frantically.

'What's going on above stairs, Molly? Tilly and Jennet have been running round all morning. That there bell hasn't stopped ringing since I came down to prepare breakfast.'

'It's Lady Carey, Mrs Jackson,' Molly said, sighing. 'She's had the girls chasing round in circles, getting Miss Nancy's things packed for her trip to London.'

Edna Jackson shook her head. 'I'll never forget the day that Nancy Sunday came to Rockwood Castle. Poor little mite, she was half-starved and skinny — all stick-like arms and legs. Nine years old and already in service at the vicarage. Mrs Blanchard took pity on the child and brought her here.'

'I don't think Lady Carey thinks much of ⟩ Blanchard's plan to send Nancy to that expʳ academy in London. She's always remindinʳ that she was a foundling left on the stʳ orphanage.'

1

'It's not for us to criticise our betters, Molly Greep.'

'Hester Dodridge was housekeeper here before the late master upped and married her. She was once a servant, just like us.'

Edna pursed her lips. 'For heaven's sake, answer that bell before it jumps off its spring.'

'I'm not a chambermaid, Mrs Jackson.'

'That's enough of your cheek. Go upstairs and see what they need or we'll have Mr Jarvis descending upon us, wanting to know what we're doing.'

'Mr Jarvis can't move so fast these days, Mrs Jackson,' Molly said, giggling. 'He must be seventy if he's a day.'

'That's neither here nor there, Molly.' Edna bristled angrily. 'I myself have reached the age of sixty and I am just as sprightly as I was when I was twenty. Now, do as you're told or you'll find yourself back on your parents' farm.'

Molly tossed her head. 'I wouldn't mind that. Or maybe Mrs Blanchard will decide to send me to London with Nancy. It would get me away from Rockwood village and all the gossips. I've never been further than Exeter.' She marched out of the kitchen.

★ ★ ★

Above stairs, in her pretty bedroom situated in one of the four turrets, Nancy sat on the window seat, watching Hester and Rosalind arguing about what a young woman would need to take to London. Who would have thought that the simple act of leaving home to attend a prestigious young ladies' academy would cause such a to-do? Nancy asked herself this dozen times a day as she tried in vain to influence

2

the choice of garments to be packed in the campaign trunk that Sir Bertram Carey had used in his army days, as well as a large valise and several hatboxes.

Hester had raised Rosalind and her three siblings during their parents' long absences from home, and Hester had set ideas as to what was proper for a young woman of eighteen to wear. She was more concerned about practicalities like pantalettes, flannel petticoats, cotton lawn chemises, and nightgowns that left everything to the imagination, with wraps to cover modesty at all times.

Rosalind Blanchard laughed at the notion of Nancy having to wear flannelette nightgowns with high necks and long sleeves in the middle of summer.

'Really, Hester. There's no need for such modesty,' Rosalind insisted. 'Nancy will most probably be sharing a room with one or two other young females anyway. Miss Maughfling, the principal, said she was very strict about such things.'

Hester sniffed. 'If you ask me, I think finishing school is a waste of time and money spent on a girl who had started life as a foundling.'

'Where she came from doesn't make any difference,' Rosalind said sharply. 'Nancy is a member of the family and as such she deserves the best chance in life.'

'Neither you nor your sister attended such an institution.'

'No, because when we were younger there wasn't the money for such luxuries.'

Nancy listened to the argument with a feeling of resignation. She had always been painfully aware that Hester did not approve of her being treated as a member of the family. Rosalind, on the other hand, insisted that although Nancy did not bear the Carey name, she was one of them nonetheless. Hester might have captured the heart of the late Sir Lucius in his final years, but Rosalind was undoubtedly the head of the family. Married to ex-army officer Alexander Blanchard, Rosalind had taken charge of the practical day-to-day running of the household after her brother Bertie had been crippled by injuries received in the Crimean War. Rosalind ruled by love and respect, whereas Hester believed in following the rules with grim determination.

'I'm quite happy to remain here and help with the housekeeping,' Nancy said, sighing. 'Please don't argue.'

'It's just a discussion, dear,' Rosalind said, smiling. 'Of course you need undergarments and nightdresses, but I think you ought to have at least three sprigged muslin afternoon gowns, apart from your plain skirts and blouses. Maybe you ought to take that charming shot-silk dinner gown.'

'She's going to school,' Hester said, frowning.

'Nancy might get invited to the other girls' homes. There might even be the chance to attend a ball. There's the cream satin creation, trimmed with lace, which Meggie Brewer made for her. That would be eminently suitable.'

'Nonsense. I thought it was too grand for her when it was made.'

'Hester, dear! The whole purpose of the Academy is to teach manners, deportment, dancing and other social graces.'

'And it's costing a small fortune. Surely that sort of money could be spent on improvements for the castle, or clothes for the children.'

4

Rosalind folded the satin ball gown and laid it in the trunk. 'Nancy has been educated to be a young lady. She will need a maid to attend her. I was thinking that Molly might be the most sensible choice.'

'Why would a schoolgirl need a lady's maid? Really, Rosie, this is getting out of hand.'

Nancy could stand it no longer. She rose from her seat, snatched up her bonnet, and escaped from her bedroom, leaving Rosalind to deal with Hester. Neither of them had thought to ask her which of the servants she would like to accompany her.

Nancy made her way down the spiral stairs leading to the main landing and the grand staircase, where ancestors of the Careys gazed down from their portraits with sightless eyes. A sound in the entrance hall drew her attention to Abel Wolfe, a giant of a man, who had lost one eye in a fight many years ago. Wolfe was never forthcoming about his past, but he was Sir Bertram's devoted personal servant and everyone treated him with a degree of respect. Wolfe pushed the Bath chair over the threshold, taking care not to jolt his master too much.

Jarvis closed the main door and stood aside, casting a surreptitious glance in Wolfe's direction. Nancy suspected that Jarvis did not approve of Wolfe, but the old butler was tight-lipped and too tactful to voice his own opinions. The hierarchy at Rockwood Castle was strict, unbending and observed by almost everyone.

'Good morning, Nancy,' Sir Bertram said cheerfully. 'It's a lovely day for a walk.'

'I'm going to visit Patsy.'

Sir Bertram winked at her. 'Getting away from the fuss upstairs, I expect. Good for you, Nancy. When in doubt, take cover.'

'Time for your medicine, Sir Bertram,' Wolfe growled. 'You've had too much sun today.'

'Balderdash, Wolfe. I'm as fit as a fiddle, even if I have to sit in this damned contraption all the time. I'll have a tot of brandy and a cigar.'

Jarvis opened the door and stood stiffly to attention, staring straight ahead as Nancy stepped outside. Putting on her straw bonnet, she headed across the cobbled bailey and out through the tall wrought-iron gates. The sun beat down with the intensity of a hot June day. The air smelled sweetly of newly mown hay, garden flowers and a tang of brine from the sea. Sunlight sparkled on the swiftly running waters of the River Sawle as Nancy crossed the bridge. The Rockwood estate covered many acres of rolling countryside and farmland, and included the whole village. The wood on her left looked cool and green, a tempting area of shade away from the blazing sun, but she ignored its siren call and walked on, past the smithy and the wheelwright's workshop. The sawmill was next, and the cottage that had once housed the manager had been completely rebuilt by Leo Wilder so that it was a home fit for him and his wife, Patricia. Nancy knew that she would miss all this more than she would have thought possible.

She quickened her pace until she reached the house, hoping that Patricia would be at home. Each time she visited there was something different to admire. The picket fence surrounding the garden had been painted white, and the flowerbeds were filled with hollyhocks and lupins. The scent from Patricia's favourite rose bushes wafted on the warm air, and the whirring of the machinery in the mill was at odds with the birdsong and the gentle rustle of the leaves ruffled by the summer breeze.

Nancy's knock on the door was answered by Fletcher, a servant with a criminal past, who had been rehabilitated and was now more protective of the family than any guard dog. Fletcher's granite features rarely broke a smile and today was no exception.

'Yes?' Fletcher's gravelly voice was not welcoming.

'Is Mrs Wilder at home?'

'I'll see.' Fletcher slammed the door, leaving Nancy standing on the step.

Nancy sighed and let herself into the house anyway. She was used to Fletcher's ways. No amount of tactful comments or out-and-out criticism seemed to make any difference. Fletcher was never going to change, but she was devoted to the family and entirely trustworthy.

'Patricia,' Nancy called, crossing the spacious hallway. She opened the parlour door and was met by Fletcher, standing arms akimbo. The tattoos on her forearms gleamed in a shaft of sunlight, and her grey hair shone like polished steel.

'Did I say the missis would see you?'

'It's all right, Fletcher,' Patricia said sharply. 'You know I am always at home to my family.'

Fletcher rolled her eyes. 'Most families in my experience avoid each other like the plague.'

'I've told you a dozen times not to close the door and leave my visitors outside, unless it's someone we really don't wish to see.' Patricia patted a space on the window seat. 'Come and sit down, Nancy. Would you like some lemonade or a cup of tea?'

'Lemonade would be lovely. It's really hot today.'

Patricia gave Fletcher a stern look. 'Lemonade for two, please, Fletcher.'

'You ain't Lady Greystone now, and I ain't no skivvy,' Fletcher grumbled as she left the room.

Patricia sighed. 'I don't know why I keep her on, except that she's really good at helping in the mill, especially if we get a difficult customer.'

'Not many people would have employed Fletcher,' Nancy said, laughing. 'Rosalind takes in all the waifs and strays.'

'My sister has a soft heart. She met Fletcher at a particularly difficult time in her life. We've all endured harrowing experiences in the past, as you well remember.'

Nancy sat down beside her. 'It was hard sometimes when we were in London, but I wouldn't have missed it for the world.'

'You were my staunch companion then, even though you were so young. We had some adventures, though, didn't we?'

Nancy giggled. 'I remember the people in Clare Market throwing rotten tomatoes at us when you sang to them.'

'That was so humiliating. The crowd on the previous day had clapped and cheered. They took a hat round and raised a few pennies to beg me to return.'

'Then there was the trip to Paris. I don't suppose I'll ever experience anything like that again.'

'I should hope not,' Patricia said, laughing. 'Being involved in a jewel robbery was not the highlight of my life.'

'But Leo rescued us and brought us safely home.'

'I'll never forget that week being tossed about in a smelly fishing boat before we docked at Rockwood Quay.' Patricia sighed. 'I have to admit it was all very exciting, but being married to Leo makes up for everything I went through in the past. I never thought I'd say so, but I'm happy being a mill owner's wife.'

'Leo is a lovely man.' Nancy nodded emphatically.

'But what brings you here today, Nancy? I thought you would be busy getting everything together for your stay in London.'

'I had to get away from the castle. Hester and Rosalind can't agree on anything, even what garments I need to take with me. I'm not allowed to choose which servant will go with me, although I don't really need a personal maid. What will the other girls think?'

'Miss Maughfling's Academy is quite select, Nancy. I dare say all the other young ladies will bring their maids. You don't want to be left out, do you?'

'No, but I'm afraid they will guess that I'm not really one of them. Hester has always told me I should know my place, and I should be below stairs with the other servants.'

Patricia's pretty forehead creased in a frown. 'Don't say things like that, Nancy. You are as good as any of us. Who knows, your papa might have been a lord or even a wealthy businessman?'

'Or a dustman or a chimney sweep,' Nancy said ruefully. 'What will happen to me when I've been polished? I don't think I'll be on the guest list for debutantes' balls and the like.'

Patricia rose to her feet. 'That's nonsense. You are as good as, or even better than, the silly young things who think of nothing but fine clothes and catching a rich husband. Come with me.'

Nancy gazed up at her, uncomprehending. 'Where are we going?'

'I was planning on visiting Sylvia at Greystone Park. I want you to accompany me.'

'But why me?'

'You are as entitled to visit the local gentry as anyone. I want you to stop thinking of yourself as a servant. You have been given a wonderful opportunity to take your place in the world, so don't throw it away.'

Nancy stood up. 'I thought Miss Sylvia was very ill.'

'She's suffering from consumption, but today is her last day in Greystone Park for a while. Her uncle and aunt are taking her to Switzerland where the mountain air is supposed to be good for people with chest complaints. I'm going to wish her well.'

'After the way she and Christina treated you when Sir Michael died, I'm surprised you want to have anything to do with them.'

'That was years ago. I don't miss being Lady Greystone. I far prefer being plain Mrs Leo Wilder.'

'You certainly seem much happier now than you ever did.'

'Can you imagine me as the Dowager Lady Greystone, living with my stepdaughter and her ghastly cousin, Martha Collins, and her companion, poor downtrodden Miss Moon?' Patricia pulled a face. 'I think there would have been blood on my hands in such circumstances. Far better to let it all go.'

Before Nancy had a chance to respond the door flew open and Fletcher barged into the parlour carrying a tray of lemonade.

'Where are you going?' Fletcher demanded crossly. 'I squeezed six lemons to make this.'

'Put it on the marble shelf in the larder, Fletcher. We'll enjoy it later.' Patricia picked up her bonnet and shawl, which lay in readiness on a chair by the door. 'We have to go to Greystone Park to see Miss Sylvia before she leaves for the clinic in Switzerland.'

'I wouldn't spit on her if she was on fire,' Fletcher said acidly. 'That one deserves all she's got.'

'Don't speak of her like that. Miss Sylvia is very ill. This is her last chance of a cure, so I think we could all be a little kinder to her.'

Fletcher shrugged and turned away. 'I got no time for her or that sister of hers. You wouldn't have been so generous to her when I first knew you.'

'I've grown more tolerant since then, Fletcher. I don't want to hear any more about it. Will you tell Robbins to harness the horse and bring the trap round?'

'You ain't thinking of driving yourself?'

'It's not far, Fletcher. I'm perfectly capable of handling the reins.'

Fletcher sniffed. 'I'll drive you. Mr Leo wouldn't like it if you was seen driving yourself.' She marched out of the room.

'She really thinks she's in charge,' Nancy said, laughing.

'And I let her. If it keeps Fletcher happy it's worth the irritation it causes. She is worth her weight in gold when it comes to dealing with difficult customers at the mill if Leo isn't there.'

'I really admire Leo. I should think he can handle anyone and anything.'

Patricia smiled. 'You missed all the excitement when Leo rescued Tommy from that awful man Ewart Blaise. I think Ewart was mad enough to torture Tommy in order to get his hands on the deeds to Rockwood Castle.'

'I know. Tommy has told me about it in detail. I think you were all very brave.'

Patricia stood in front of a wall mirror to straighten

11

her bonnet and tie the ribbons. 'Ewart will spend the rest of his life in an Australian penal colony. We won't be seeing him again.'

Nancy sighed. 'Tommy will be home from school in a day or two, and then he'll be off to university and I won't see him if I'm in London. Although last summer he spent all his time with the boys from the village. He didn't want to know me then.'

'That was a year ago and he was at an awkward age, but you'll be best friends again, I'm sure.'

Fletcher stuck her head round the door. 'Are you coming? Or are you going to spend all day gossiping?'

Patricia drew herself up to her full height. 'One day you will go too far, Cora Fletcher. Don't assume that you can get away with bad manners just because we allow you some leeway.'

Fletcher raised her skirts to expose a pair of skinny legs ending in men's boots as she executed a clumsy curtsey. 'Sorry, my lady. I forgets meself sometimes.'

Nancy giggled and Patricia's lips quivered, despite her attempt at a severe look. 'You can stay here for that, Fletcher. I will take the reins. Come, Nancy. We'll leave Fletcher to consider her future.' Patricia swept out of the room, and left the house with Nancy following her.

Leo Wilder strolled out of the mill just as Patricia was about to climb onto the driver's seat of the trap. Nancy met his friendly grin with a smile. Leo had always been her favourite, even if he did look like a corsair with a gold earring in one ear. With his rugged good looks and tanned complexion he looked his best in casual clothes, but he was an attractive man no matter whether he wore his customary open-neck shirt and leather waistcoat, or the more formal clothes he chose when visiting the castle. Leo was someone to be looked up to and admired.

'Where's Fletcher?' Leo asked bluntly. 'I thought she was going to drive you to Greystone Park?'

Patricia tossed her head. 'She was, but I left her behind because she was being objectionable. She will have to go if she can't mend her ways, Leo.'

He lifted his wife onto the seat. 'I'll give her a good talking-to. She can work in the mill for now if she's being difficult.' He helped Nancy onto the seat beside Patricia. 'When are you off to London, Nancy?'

'In a day or so. Hester and Rosie are forever arguing about what I should take with me, and which servant should accompany me.'

'That sounds like Hester,' Leo said, grinning. 'She likes to have the last word.'

2

Sylvia looked thin and fragile, but her eyes shone with vitality and her cheeks were pink, as if she was in the best of health. It was a deceptive look and Nancy was well aware that Sylvia Greystone was very ill indeed. Her aunt and uncle, Mr and Mrs Pennington, were dressed for travelling, and the servants bustled about, carrying bandboxes, trunks and valises down to the entrance hall to load onto the waiting carter's wagon, ready for the start of the journey to Switzerland.

Mr Pennington, an earnest middle-aged man with a ruddy complexion and a kindly smile, greeted Patricia warmly and extended his welcome to Nancy.

'I don't think we've met, but you remind me of someone.'

Nancy bobbed a curtsey. 'I'm Nancy Sunday, sir.'

'Are you related to the Careys, Miss Sunday?'

'No, sir. I was in service as a child. Mrs Blanchard felt sorry for me and she took me in.'

'Nancy is very much part of our family, Mr Pennington,' Patricia added hastily.

He smiled vaguely and turned to his wife. 'Does Miss Nancy remind you of anyone, Violet?'

Mrs Pennington, a small, mother-hen of a woman, gave Nancy a searching look. 'Now you come to mention it she does resemble Oliver a little. It's the eyes, I think.'

'Uncle Oliver?' Sylvia was suddenly alert. 'I remember him vaguely, although I was very young when

14

he died.'

'We don't speak of Oliver Greystone in our family,' Violet said severely. 'Every family has a black sheep and Oliver was a disgrace to the name of Greystone.'

'That's a bit harsh, Violet.' Mr Pennington took a spotted blue silk hanky from his pocket and mopped his brow. 'It was just a passing likeness. I can see now that I was mistaken.'

'Yes, my dear. Best let sleeping dogs lie, as they say.' Violet rolled her eyes expressively. 'We plan to take the journey in very easy stages. I don't think Sylvia should do too much travelling in any one day.'

'No, of course not,' Patricia said evenly. She turned to Sylvia, who was seated on a hall chair provided for her by the butler, Foster. 'How are you feeling today?'

'Not too bad. I tire easily but I'm hoping the clear air in Switzerland will cure my ills.'

'You must write to me often,' Patricia said, smiling. 'I've been to Paris but that's as far as we got. I would love to see some pictures of where you will be staying.'

'I'll write to you and send you drawings, although art isn't my best subject. I want you to keep in touch with me, too. I'll be longing to know what's happening in the village.'

Mrs Pennington placed her hand on Sylvia's arm. 'Of course Patricia will keep you informed. I'm sure Christina will, too.'

'Where is Christina?' Mr Pennington demanded crossly. 'We'll be leaving in a few minutes.'

'I think she's going to meet us at the railway station,' Sylvia said hastily. 'She has such a lot to do with her children and Ossie's parishioners.'

'Nonsense.' Mrs Pennington shook her ruffled feathers. 'Your sister hasn't taken care of you as she should. She has a nanny and a nursemaid to look after the babes. As for working in the parish, I think Christina spends more time with her modiste than she does visiting the sick and elderly.'

'That's not fair, Aunt,' Sylvia protested.

'I only speak the truth. Your sister married Oscar because he would one day inherit Cottingham Manor. She has no interest in being a parson's wife.' Mrs Pennington shook her head, frowning darkly. 'My sister would be saddened by the way her elder daughter has turned out.'

'Never mind Christina,' Patricia said hastily. 'You are more important now, Sylvie. Are you going to close the house while you're away?'

'I don't see what else I can do. Foster will stay on, of course, and Mrs Simpson will continue as housekeeper, with Mrs Banks cooking for the remaining staff.' Sylvia sighed, shaking her head. 'I wish you would come and live here to supervise them, Patsy.'

'If you'd asked me that when your papa died I would have been only too pleased, but I have my own life now, Sylvie.'

Sylvia's large pansy-brown eyes filled with tears. 'If only I had my health.'

Nancy was close to crying herself and she laid her hand on Sylvia's shoulder. 'Don't worry, I'm sure Patricia will keep an eye on the servants for you.'

Patricia frowned. 'Why doesn't Christina come and look after everything? After all, she does own half of the estate.'

'The squire is very sick. I heard that he had an apoplectic fit.' Sylvia lowered her voice. 'Dr Bulmer said another attack could be fatal. I think Christina is staking her claim to the Cottingham estate.'

'Glorina might have Romany blood in her veins, but she is still the lady of the manor.' Patricia moved closer. 'What do you know, Sylvie?'

'Glorina will lose her position in the household when Oscar inherits everything from his father,' Sylvia said breathlessly. 'Can you imagine Glorina and my sister living happily together? It's worked, in a fashion, because Squire Cottingham keeps them both under control, but when he goes it will be all-out warfare.'

Nancy turned to Patricia. 'Can you do anything?'

'No, I'm afraid not. Christina never forgave me for marrying her father, but even before that she always went her own way.' Patricia leaned over to brush Sylvia's thin cheek with a whisper of a kiss. 'Let them sort it out between them, Sylvie. Go to Switzerland and get well.'

'That's right, my dear.' Mrs Pennington bustled towards them holding out a shawl, which she wrapped around Sylvia's shoulders. 'You mustn't get cold.'

'But it's a hot day, Aunt.'

'It will be cool in the carriage with the windows open. There's no point taking chances.' Mrs Pennington turned to Patricia and Nancy with a beaming smile. 'So good of you to come and see us off.'

'Good luck, Sylvie,' Patricia said gently. 'Do remember to write.'

Mr Pennington helped his niece to her feet. 'Come along, dear. Let's start on our journey. This is the beginning of the cure you've been waiting for.'

'I hope so,' Sylvia said breathlessly. 'I won't say goodbye, Patsy. *Au revoir*, as the French say. Until we meet again.' She rose to her feet and between them her aunt and uncle helped her across the marble-tiled floor and down the steps to the waiting carriage.

'Do you really think she will get better in Switzerland?' Nancy asked anxiously.

'We can but hope.' Patricia slipped her arm around Nancy's shoulder and gave her a hug. 'Let's go home. There's nothing more we can do here.'

'It seems sad to abandon such a beautiful house,' Nancy said, gazing at their elegant surroundings. 'It's such a shame that Sir Michael didn't leave it to you in his will.'

'That's one of those strange things that happen in life. I should have been able to live here, but in a way it was the best thing that happened to me. Had I settled down to a comfortable life in Greystone Park, I might never have married Leo. That would have been the tragedy.'

They strolled across the marble-tiled floor to the door, where Foster waited patiently to see them out.

'It's a sad day, my lady,' he said softly.

'I'm sure you will look after Greystone Park as always, Foster,' Patricia said graciously.

'I will do my utmost, my lady.'

'I'm Mrs Wilder, now Foster. I have no title.'

'You will always be Lady Greystone in my eyes, if you'll forgive me saying so, my lady.'

Patricia acknowledged this with a wry smile. 'Thank you, Foster. Good day.' She stepped outside into the sunshine with Nancy close on her heels.

★ ★ ★

A strange carriage was in the castle bailey when Nancy and Patricia arrived. It could only have drawn to a halt a few minutes before them as James, the footman, was busy unloading luggage and the coach-man was still on the driver's seat.

'Tommy!' Nancy leaped to the ground and ran to hug the boy who had been her friend from the first moment he had arrived at Rockwood Castle. At seventeen, Tommy Carey looked like a younger version of his father. He had Sir Bertram's golden-brown eyes and dark blond hair that flopped over his brow. He was tall for his age, and broad shouldered from activities on the sports field at his boarding school, but the person who caught Nancy's eye, and brought her to a sudden halt, was Tommy's companion. The handsome young man leaned nonchalantly against the coach door, eyeing them all with a look of amusement in his moss-green eyes. He was fashionably dressed and he held a silver-headed cane.

'Nancy, you look wonderful,' Tommy said enthusiastically. 'I swear you get prettier every time I see you.'

She knew that this was untrue, having been told by Hester that she must have been behind the door when God handed out good looks, but praise from Tommy gave her a warm glow inside.

'It's good to see you too, Tommy.' Nancy shot a sideways glance at the stranger, but he said nothing and Tommy seemed to have forgotten his manners.

Patricia handed the reins to Pip Hudson, who had risen from stable boy to under groom. 'Aren't you going to introduce us to your guest, Tommy?'

'Of course. What was I thinking? Aunt Patricia, may I introduce my good friend, Gervase North?' Tommy turned to his friend. 'Gervase, I would like you to meet my aunt, Mrs Wilder.'

Gervase bowed from the waist. 'How do you do, ma'am?'

'And this is my adopted sister, Nancy,' Tommy added, grinning.

Nancy bobbed a curtsey, suddenly at a loss for words.

Patricia extended her hand to Gervase. 'How do you do? It's always a pleasure to meet one of Tommy's friends, but how do you know each other?'

Gervase raised Patricia's hand to his lips. 'We met at school, ma'am.'

'Surely not,' Nancy said, frowning. 'You're much older than Tommy.'

'I've led a dashed hard life, Miss Nancy. Instead of studying I spend my time gambling, attending parties and generally having a good time. I am in fact just a couple of years Tommy's senior.'

'Don't take any notice of him, Nancy,' Tommy said, laughing. 'Gervase is a tease. He was my teacher and when I first started school he saved me from the bullies.'

'Alas, it's part of school life.' Gervase shook his head. 'But Tommy put up a brave fight. You can be proud of him.'

'I'm sure we're very grateful to you,' Patricia said warily. 'But I find it rather odd that you choose to befriend a boy so much your junior. Is mentoring boys in the holidays a common practice at your school?'

'My career in the academic world was cut short when my father died. I received my inheritance, which enabled me to live like a gentleman.'

'But that doesn't explain why you are here, Mr North.'

'Really, Aunt Patsy. I thought you would be more welcoming to my friend,' Tommy protested. 'Gervase and I met again by chance at the Old Boys' cricket match. He actually remembered me. Goodness knows why.'

'I never forget a face. You are an exceptional young chap, Tommy.' Gervase slapped him on the back. 'But if my being here is inconvenient, I will put up at the village inn, which we passed on the way here.'

'Nonsense, Gervase.' Tommy clutched his friend's arm. 'Come inside and meet my papa and the rest of the family. Aunt Patricia doesn't live here anymore, so she has no say in what happens at Rockwood.' He dragged Gervase over the threshold, leaving Patricia and Nancy staring after them.

'There's something suspicious about that young man,' Patricia said darkly.

'I think he's very handsome.' Nancy knew she was blushing and she turned her head away.

'Handsome is as handsome does, as Hester would say.'

'I think you're being very unfair.' Nancy had never known Patricia to take such a sudden dislike to a person, but she was wrong. Anyone with such honest eyes, a classic profile, a winning smile, and dark hair that waved back off a high forehead must be above suspicion.

Patricia shook her head. 'Be careful, Nancy. I've met young men like Gervase before. You need to take anything he says with a pinch of salt.'

'I don't know what you mean, Patsy. He seems perfectly charming, and Tommy obviously worships him.'

'That's what I mean. I think Gervase North has an ulterior motive for coming here with a boy who was his pupil. All that luggage suggests that he has come with the intention of staying for quite a while.'

'I'm sure that Uncle Bertie will keep an eye on him.'

21

'I sincerely hope so. If not, I'll prime Wolfe and he will put a stop to any misbehaviour. Anyway, I must go home now or Leo will wonder what's become of me. If you need me, you know where I am to be found, Nancy.'

'Thank you. Of course I'll visit you. Maybe I'll bring Gervase and Tommy with me,' Nancy added with a mischievous smile.

'Just heed my warning. Tommy is gullible, but you are old enough to see through a charlatan. Remember all the trouble we went through when Ewart held Tommy hostage.'

Nancy stared at her in amazement. 'Surely you don't think that Mr North would do anything like that?'

'Tommy is the heir to Rockwood Castle and the estate and I can't help being suspicious. Gervase North has already charmed you, so what chance does Tommy have? Look after him, Nancy.' Patricia climbed onto the driver's seat and took the reins. 'Give my love to Rosie. I'll call on her tomorrow afternoon.' She drove off, leaving Nancy staring after her.

Nancy shrugged and turned away. Patsy was wrong. Gervase North was the most exciting person she had ever met and she intended to get to know him better. Nancy hurried into the house, making her way past the mountain of luggage that Jarvis and James were bringing into the great hall. She followed the sound of Tommy's voice and Gervase's lower-toned responses and caught up with them as they entered the drawing room.

Tommy rushed in first, but Gervase stopped to hold the door open for Nancy.

'Your brother has no manners, Miss Nancy,' Gervase said with a devastating smile.

'Tommy isn't my brother. We're not related, Mr North.'

'Call me Gervase, please. To be fair, Tommy talks about you as if you were related, so I don't see that it matters. I, for one, am delighted to make your acquaintance.'

'Gervase, stop chatting to Nancy,' Tommy said impatiently. 'Come and meet my aunt Rosalind and uncle Alexander.'

Nancy stood aside as the introductions were made, but she could tell from Alexander's expression that he, like Patricia, had reservations when it came to Gervase North. Rosalind, however, greeted him with her usual charm and open friendliness. Hester remained aloof at first, but Gervase bowed over her hand, treating her to a dazzling smile.

'It's an honour to meet the woman who captured the heart of such a hero, Lady Carey.'

'Sir Lucius was a great man, Mr North.'

'Indeed he was. Not that I had the honour to meet him, of course, but I know my history, Lady Carey. I've read about the battles at sea and I have huge respect for the men who sailed those gallant ships.'

'Well said, sir.' Alexander nodded in agreement.

'You are very well informed,' Tommy said admiringly. 'I hardly know anything about Great-Grandpapa Carey.'

'Then I must enlighten you, my boy.' Gervase gave him a friendly pat on the back. 'I might not be your tutor anymore, Tommy, but I can still instruct you in your family's history.'

Rosalind smiled. 'You are welcome to stay here for as long as you like, Mr North. I am sure it will be a pleasure to have diverting conversation at dinner every evening.'

'Are you saying I am boring, Rosie?' Alexander said, laughing.

'I simply meant that our conversation is always about the children, or estate matters. It will be interesting to have a fresh set of topics to discuss.' Rosalind rose from her seat. 'I promised the children that I would walk down to the cove and collect seashells. I mustn't disappoint them.'

'I have a meeting with Bayliss,' Alexander said reluctantly. 'Estate matters, you understand, Mr North.'

'Of course, Mr Blanchard. Don't let me hinder you.' Gervase turned to Hester. 'Tommy insisted that I would be welcome, but I can see how busy you are. Perhaps I should book into the village inn.'

'Certainly not,' Hester said firmly. 'You helped Tommy through a difficult time at school. The least we can do is to offer you hospitality. I will make sure that a room is made ready for you and have your luggage sent there. Perhaps the solar above Tommy's room would suit you.'

'It's a very nice room,' Nancy added hastily. 'You'll be comfortable there and it has a lovely view.'

'I don't want to put you to any trouble, Lady Carey.'

'It's no bother at all.' Hester rose from her seat and tugged at the bell pull. 'Tommy, I suggest you take Mr North on a tour of the grounds. You can help me, Nancy.'

Nancy was about to argue but she could see from Hester's expression that it would only cause an argument. She sighed. 'Yes, Hester.'

'Off you go then.' Hester shooed Tommy and his tutor out of the room. 'Don't forget that you are going to London tomorrow, Nancy.'

'I'm not sure I want to go now that Tommy is home for the summer,' Nancy said sadly. 'Couldn't I start at the Academy in the autumn, Hester?'

'Don't ask me. I wasn't in favour of you going there in the first place, but Rosie insisted and you must do as she says.'

Nancy could see that Hester was not going to champion her sudden desire to remain at Rockwood, but that made her even more determined to speak to Rosalind, who had always been her friend.

'Perhaps I should help Rosie take the children to the beach, Hester. After all, there is little I can do here. You have everything so well organised.'

Hester gave her a long look and then smiled. 'You are a minx, Nancy Sunday. But Rosie is determined to make a lady of you. Once she's made up her mind she's unlikely to change it.'

* * *

Nancy caught up with Rosalind and the three children just as they were about to climb down the cliff path to the sandy cove. Dolly, now a bright seven-year-old, had gone on ahead, followed by her six-year-old brother, Rory. This left Rosalind holding three-year-old Phoebe by the hand as they negotiated the steep slope.

'This is a nice surprise,' Rosalind said, smiling. 'I thought you would stay with Tommy and his handsome friend, or I would have asked you to come with us.'

'I wanted to talk to you in private.' Nancy stepped carefully, avoiding the large stones and the slippery patches. 'It's about the Academy.'

25

Rosalind lifted Phoebe over a boulder and set her down on the sand. 'You don't want to go?'

'Of course I really want the opportunity to better myself,' Nancy said quickly. 'But perhaps I could go there in the autumn, when Tommy goes to university.'

'And the handsome tutor has nothing to do with this request?' Rosalind's hazel eyes twinkled with merriment.

'No. Well, yes, maybe. But summer in Rockwood is always lovely, and I miss Tommy when he's away.'

'I'm sorry, but it's all arranged. Miss Maughfling runs her classes from the end of the London season in late June until Christmas, after which the young ladies are prepared for the next season.'

'I could wait until next year.'

'Nancy, by then the other young ladies will be a couple of years your junior.'

'I don't see what difference that makes.'

'It might make it difficult for you to fit in with the other girls, Nancy. They will have come straight from the schoolroom.'

'But what sense is there in paying a lot of money simply to teach me deportment?'

'It's more than that. I want you to feel confident in yourself.'

'Are you trying to marry me off to some rich lord, Rosie? I don't want that.'

'No, of course not, but you don't want to spend the rest of your life in Rockwood, surely? If you make friends with other girls your age you will get invitations to house parties and you will meet eligible young men. I want you to marry for love, not money or position.'

'Maybe I want something different for myself.'

26

Nancy bent down to pick up a particularly pretty shell.

Rosalind put her head on one side. 'Such as?'

'I don't know, Rosie. But Hester has always told me that I might have to earn my own living. I wish I could sing like Patsy, but I do know how to keep household accounts and I could cook a meal if I needed to.'

'Don't even think like that, Nancy. You will never have to earn your own living if I have any say in the matter. You are like a sister to me and Patsy. We will always love you and take care of you.'

Nancy dashed tears from her eyes with the back of her hand. 'I know you mean that, and I don't wish to sound ungrateful, but I really would like to know where I came from.'

'I understand, of course, but you are a special person, Nancy. Don't ever let anyone tell you differently, and I want you to have every opportunity in life.'

'I do know that, Rosie.'

'Then go to Miss Maughfling's Academy and take advantage of her expert knowledge of etiquette and deportment. It's only a short course and then you can come home for Christmas.'

'All right, if it means so much to you, I will.'

'Good, and now we'd better catch up with Dolly and Rory. The tide will be on the turn soon, so I don't want them to go too far.'

They walked on, stopping every now and again for Phoebe to pick up a shell or a pretty stone, which she solemnly stowed away in a canvas bag that Rosalind had brought with her. Dolly and Rory ran about, laughing as they dodged the waves washing on the shore. It was a carefree, happy scene that Nancy knew she would treasure during her lonely days in London. She was beginning to wish that she had refused to take up the offer when it was first suggested. Suddenly home and family, not to mention a certain handsome house guest, were more of a priority than acquiring the polish required to shine in society.

* * *

That evening, the family assembled in the drawing room, having enjoyed a splendid dinner. Gervase entertained them all with stories of his exploits in London and the various house parties he had enjoyed with his raffish friends. Nancy could see that Patricia was unimpressed and Hester was scowling ominously, but Tommy was obviously in awe of his former teacher's ability to hold an audience's attention. Walter, Bertie's younger brother, and his wife, Louise, sat together, their expressions guarded, while Bertie sipped a brandy, apparently enjoying the monologue. He waited until Gervase finished speaking.

'You've had some interesting experiences, Mr North. I can see why you gave up teaching.'

Wolfe made a low growling noise deep in his throat, as if voicing his disapproval.

Alexander laughed and slipped his arm round his wife's shoulders. 'You've had a colourful life, Gervase.'

'You have indeed,' Rosalind added, smiling. 'But we know nothing about you. Where did your family come from?'

Gervase stood with his back to the empty grate, brandy glass clutched in his right hand.

'My mother was Elizabeth Greystone.'

There was a stunned silence, broken by a sharp intake of breath from Hester.

'Are you telling us that your mother was Elizabeth

Greystone of Greystone Park?' Patricia eyed him suspiciously. 'Greystone never spoke about his sister, although I know she died young.'

'Precisely that. Sir Michael was my uncle, although he did precious little to support my mother after she was widowed.'

'I thought she went back to live with her husband's family in Suffolk,' Rosalind said slowly. 'I believe they were quite wealthy.'

'That is all history now, as is the fate that befell Uncle Oliver.'

'He died suddenly.' Rosalind turned to Hester. 'You must know the full story.'

Hester shook her head. 'It was a scandal that shook the whole country.'

'My uncle Sir Oliver Greystone was shot in a duel. He was murdered eighteen years ago, shot through the heart on the orders of Sir Lucius Carey.'

Hester clutched her hands to her heart. 'That's a foul lie.'

3

A murmur of consternation rippled around the room. Rosalind jumped to her feet and moved swiftly to Hester's side, giving her a comforting hug. 'I don't believe a word of it, Hester.'

Tommy's eyes widened in horror. 'You can't come here and say such things, Gervase. My great-grand-papa was a fine man.'

Bertie faced Gervase with an ominous frown. 'Why would you make such an accusation, North?'

Walter clutched his wife's hand. 'You should be ashamed of yourself, sir. The dead can't defend themselves.'

'Exactly so,' Gervase said, shrugging expressively. 'My late uncle's name has been muddied by accusations of cheating at cards. It was put about that he had an affair with Lady Prudence Carey, even though the woman was old enough to be his mother, which is why Sir Lucius arranged for his demise in a duel.'

Bertie half rose from his chair, but sank back again, panting from the effort. 'How dare you cast aspersions on our grandmother's good name?'

'I only speak the truth.' Gervase reached for the decanter and helped himself to a tot of brandy. 'I'm sure you've heard the rumours about Lady Prudence's amours while Sir Lucius was away at sea. The late Wilfred Carey's paternity has been a cause for speculation . . .'

Leo Wilder stepped forward and snatched the

decanter from Gervase's hand. 'That's enough of that. How dare you come here and abuse Sir Bertram's hospitality? You can go to hell.'

'Why would you do this to us?' Rosalind demanded angrily.

'I suggest you leave now, North.' Alexander made a move towards him, hands fisted. 'Your behaviour is shocking beyond belief.'

'I agree.' Bertie signalled to Wolfe, who was poised ready to leap in when required. He grabbed Gervase by the collar and was marching him from the room when Gervase grabbed hold of the door jamb.

'I know more about the Greystone family than I've told you, but now you'll never discover the truth.'

'Out with you,' Wolfe growled.

'Just a moment, Wolfe,' Rosalind said hastily. 'Just one thing before you are thrown out of our home, Mr North. If you are part of the Greystone family, as you claim, why are you here making trouble? Surely you ought to take your problems to your cousin Christina.'

'Don't worry, Mrs Blanchard. As the next surviving male in the family I plan to take my rightful position at Greystone Park.'

'Sir Michael left the estate to his daughters.' Patricia made a move towards him but Leo held her back.

'Ignore him, Patsy.'

'Let me go, Leo. I was part of that family. I feel responsible for what happens in Sylvia's absence.'

'Interesting,' Gervase said, curling his lip. 'Thank you for the information. I heard that Sylvia was seriously ill. As the only surviving male in the Greystone family, that will make it much easier for me to take over the estate.'

'Take him away, Wolfe,' Bertie said furiously. 'If I wasn't confined to this chair I would take pleasure in forcibly ejecting him from my home.'

'Right away, guvnor.' Wolfe tweaked Gervase's arm so that he yelped with pain and released his grip on the jamb. 'Out we go, cully.'

'I have information that you might wish to know,' Gervase called out as he was dragged from the room.

'You tricked me, Mr North,' Tommy cried passionately.

Nancy could see that Tommy was close to tears and she placed her arm around his shoulders. 'It's all right. It's not your fault. You couldn't have known what he was going to say.'

Walter rose from his seat and laid his hand on Tommy's quivering shoulder. 'Don't upset yourself, old chap. I dare say this isn't the first time that North has abused someone's hospitality. The fellow is clearly unhinged.'

'I'm all right,' Tommy said, sniffing. 'I'm not a baby. I want to punch Gervase on the nose for saying things like that.'

'Good boy,' Bertie said with a grim smile. 'The fellow is obviously out of his mind.'

'Do you think that any of it was the truth?' Rosalind asked, frowning.

Patricia shook her head. 'I don't know much about Elizabeth. Greystone never spoke about her, or his elder brother, Oliver. Their names never came up in conversation.'

'I cannot believe that this evening has turned out to be such a fiasco.' Rosalind sank back on her seat. 'That man insinuated himself into Tommy's good books with the intention of coming here and causing as much trouble as he could. Although why he would want to hurt our family is a mystery.'

'Whatever his intentions, he certainly succeeded in gaining our attention,' Alexander said drily. 'I'm going to make sure he leaves the castle right away. Are you coming, Leo? I think we need to give Wolfe a helping hand.'

'I hope he hasn't unpacked.' Hester stood up. 'To say I'm shocked is an understatement. I knew Lady Prudence for many years and she was a good and faithful wife. That man rattled off a tissue of lies.'

'I am so sorry for bringing him here,' Tommy said sadly. 'He was so nice to me when we met at the cricket match.'

'He obviously planned the whole thing.' Nancy patted him on the arm. 'Don't worry, Tommy. Leo and Alex will make sure that Gervase North goes on his way, and he won't be allowed back.'

'Why would he come here now?' Louise asked. 'He could have staked his claim on Greystone Park after Sir Michael's tragic accident.'

'Elizabeth Greystone died of consumption, so I believe,' Hester said slowly. 'Her husband succumbed to apoplexy. They only had one child, but you're right, Louise — why would Gervase leave it until now to make his presence felt? And why come here making trouble? It doesn't make sense.'

'I neither know nor care.' Bertie held up his hand for silence. 'I don't want to hear another word concerning Gervase North. From this moment onward we will have nothing to do with him.'

Tommy sighed heavily. 'He was very good to me when I first started at that school, Papa.'

'He must have had his sights set on this family for a

long time,' Bertie said firmly. 'I don't want you to see him again, Tommy. Is that understood?'

'Yes, Papa.'

'Perhaps I should stay here instead of going to London, Uncle Bertie,' Nancy said eagerly. 'I could keep Tommy company in case he gets lonely.'

'No, Nancy.' Rosalind shook her head. 'We will take good care of Tommy and you will finish your education.'

'Yes, my dear,' Patricia added, smiling. 'You will be able to spend Christmas with Tommy and the rest of us. I don't think you should miss this opportunity to get a little town polish. You might be grateful for it one day.'

★   ★   ★

Despite all her attempts to persuade the family to allow her to remain at Rockwood for the summer, Nancy arrived in London late next day, accompanied by Molly Greep. The decision as to which maid to take with her had, in the end, been the easiest of all, and Molly had accepted the offer eagerly. Perhaps because of the upset caused by Gervase North, the final arrangements for their travel had happened quickly. Ned Hudson drove them to Exeter where they caught the train bound for London.

Nancy had gained knowledge of the city when she had lived there with Patricia, and she found herself looking after Molly, who had never left the village until now. Nancy summoned a porter, who took their luggage to the cab stand and she tipped him generously before giving the cabby the address of the Academy in the Outer Circle of Regent's Park.

Molly said little and was clearly overwhelmed by the hustle and bustle of the metropolis, the noise and the different smells. She sat in the corner of the cab, half buried beneath a pile of baggage and hatboxes, which left her just enough room to stare out of the window. Nancy sat back on her seat, feeling like a seasoned traveller.

The cabby dropped them off outside the elegant, white stucco-fronted residence, set behind a formal front garden. On the opposite side of the road, Regent's Park stretched as far as the eye could see, imprisoned by iron railings. It was a balmy summer evening and the trees in the park were in full leaf. Glimpses of the lake shimmered in the evening sunlight and the air was filled with the scent of blossom from the gardens, mingled with the less pleasant odours of summer in the city. However, it was a far cry from Covent Garden and the wharfs at Puddle Dock, where Nancy had lived with Patricia during their stay in London. This was obviously a very affluent area, far removed from the poverty of the East End. Nancy felt as if she had landed in some foreign country where no one spoke her language.

'It's smart isn't it?' Molly said in a hushed voice. 'I hope they don't think we're country bumpkins.'

'Open the gate, Molly. We won't get anywhere by standing here on the pavement.' Nancy spoke with more conviction than she was feeling. The large white sign with black lettering proclaimed 'Miss Maughfling's Academy for Young Ladies', and all her doubts assailed her in one stomach-clenching blow. If Molly was apprehensive, Nancy felt as though the ground was shaking beneath her feet. She wished she had stood up to Rosie and Patsy, although they only wanted the best for her. Perhaps she should have asked Hester to intervene. Maybe her position in life was to be that of housekeeper or the wife of a humble artisan. The staff at the orphanage had told her often enough that she was a nameless nobody from goodness knows where. At this moment in time, all she wanted was to return home.

Molly picked up the two heaviest cases. 'Don't worry, miss. You'll be the top of the class in everything you do. Just think of me below stairs with them London servants. I expect they'll think I'll have corn growing out of my ears.'

Nancy took a deep breath. 'Then we'll just prove them wrong, Molly. We're here now and it's less than six months until Christmas. We'll conquer London, just like Mrs Wilder did when she sang in Clare Market. You go on and knock on the door. I'll follow you with the rest of the luggage.'

The shiny black front door with its highly polished brass furniture opened to reveal a maidservant dressed in black with a white mobcap and starched apron.

'The servants' entrance is reached through the mews at the back.' She was about to close the door when Molly put a foot over the threshold.

'Oy, you, girl. This is Miss Nancy Sunday and she's one of your young ladies, so you'd better let us in.'

'Wait there.' The door closed in their faces and there was nothing to do other than wait for the maid to return, which she did moments later. 'Come in, but leave your luggage there. The porter will take it to your room.'

Nancy stepped over the threshold, but when Molly tried to follow her, she was stopped by the maid. 'Not you. Servants' entrance is in the mews, like I said.'

Molly cast a frantic glance at Nancy, who understood immediately.

'No,' Nancy said firmly. 'My maid comes in with me. You may show her where to go below stairs, but I won't allow her to wander the streets of London on her own.'

The young maid looked as if she might argue but she jumped to attention at the sound of a stern voice. Nancy looked over the girl's shoulder and saw a tall, thin woman descending the stairs. Her dark, glossy hair was drawn back from her forehead so severely that it looked as if it had been lacquered onto her skull, and cruelly confined in a snood at the back of her neck. Her face was pale and lined, and her hooded grey eyes took in the scene with a single glance. She glided towards Nancy with the bell of her crinoline swaying from side to side as she moved.

'Welcome to the Academy, Miss Sunday. I am Miss Maughfling, proprietor and headmistress.'

'How do you do, ma'am?' Nancy bobbed a curtsey, which seemed to be the appropriate way to acknowledge such an important person. There was something almost regal in the headmistress's manner. The entrance hall echoed with silence as Miss Maughfling cast her critical gaze over Nancy, Molly and the pile of luggage.

Nancy held her breath, wondering what was coming next.

'Watkins, send for Little to deal with Miss Sunday's belongings. Take the maid to the servants' quarters and introduce her to Mrs Branson.'

Watkins hurried off with Molly following her, although Molly hesitated and turned her head to give Nancy a pleading glance. Nancy smiled encouragingly and nodded, but a sharp blast on a whistle made her turn to Miss Maughfling with a start. Molly scuttled after Watkins, leaving Nancy feeling alone and vulnerable in the presence of the strait-laced principal.

'I use the whistle to signify an order, Miss Sunday.' Miss Maughfling allowed the whistle to drop on its chain, which in turn was attached to a silver chatelaine hanging around her waist. 'Now follow me and I will show you to your room. You've missed supper, so I hope you have eaten.'

'Not really, ma'am.'

'Then you will have to wait until breakfast. Meals are served on time each day without exception. If you miss one meal you have to wait until the next one. Punctuality is paramount.'

Miss Maughfling headed back towards the staircase with Nancy following. Not a word was spoken as they climbed three flights of stairs. The room that Nancy was to share with two other young ladies was at the front of the building, with two tall windows overlooking the park. The furniture was adequate and the rugs on the polished floorboards were dun coloured. The walls were Spartan white, with nothing to mar their pristine surfaces, and there was little in the room to encourage anyone to do anything other than sleep, wash and dress. Comfort was not on the curriculum.

'That's your bed by the window.' Miss Maughfling pointed to an iron bedstead with a white coverlet. 'Your maid will be sent to unpack your things, but tidiness is one of the things about which I am most particular. You are not allowed to keep anything on top of the dressing table, or the chest of drawers. Anything left out will be confiscated. No food or drink is allowed in the bedchambers. We do not call them dormitories. You are learning to be a young lady, Miss Sunday. We train girls to be able to conduct themselves in polite society and in all matters of etiquette, deportment and genteel conversation. You will, I hope, benefit from being here.'

'Yes, Miss Maughfling.'

'Good. I'm glad you understand. I'll have your maid sent up to you. Breakfast is at eight o'clock. You will find a timetable pinned to the inside of the door.' Miss Maughfling swept from the room, leaving a faint waft of lavender cologne in her wake.

Nancy perched nervously on the edge of the bed. The spotless coverlet was stretched so tightly over the bed that she was afraid she might leave it creased, and she jumped to her feet when, minutes later, a brief knock on the door was followed by Molly peeping nervously into the room.

'Come in, please.' Nancy sighed with relief. 'Are you all right, Molly? Have they shown you where you'll sleep?'

'I'm in an attic room with six stuck-up lady's maids. They'd better not poke fun at my Devonshire accent or I'll end up clouting someone.'

'Oh dear! I'm so sorry. Maybe I should have come on my own, but they all insisted that it was right for me to have my own maid.'

'Don't fret about me. I can look after myself. I'll unpack your things and put them away. I expect things will get easier when we've been here for a while.'

Molly set to work and had just put the last garment in the clothes press when the door opened. A pretty young woman entered the room, followed by another who was not quite so attractive, but was dressed in the very latest fashion.

'Thank you, Molly,' Nancy said hurriedly. 'That will be all for now.'

'Yes, miss.' Molly bobbed a curtsey and hurried from the room.

'My goodness, we are friendly with the servants, aren't we?' The less appealing of the two raised a dainty eyebrow.

'You must be the new girl.' The pretty young woman held out her hand. 'I'm Tamara Fitzallen and this is Eleanora Smythe.'

Nancy rose to her feet. 'I'm Nancy Sunday.'

Eleanora curled her lip. 'What sort of name is that?'

'I think it's charming,' Tamara said hastily. 'I hope we're going to be good friends, Nancy.'

'You are such a ninny, Tamara.' Eleanora pulled out a drawer in the cabinet beside her bed and took out a silver case. She flicked it open and took out a small, black cigarillo, which she lit with a vesta. 'I am sick of this place already.' She slumped down on her bed and put her feet up, lying back against the pillows.

'Do you have to smoke that thing in here?' Tamara asked crossly. 'I hate the smell.'

'You are a frightful prude,' Eleanora said, sighing. 'I am so bored. I think I'll elope with Sir Jack Marshall. He's proposed to me so many times I've lost count.'

Nancy stared at her in surprise. 'Why did you refuse him?'

'Not that it's any business of yours, but my mama hopes I'll do better than a mere baronet.'

'I'm going to marry for love,' Tamara said dreamily.

Eleanora puffed blue smoke towards the ceiling. 'Why do you think your parents sent you here, you silly girl? They're grooming you for the marriage market next season.' She eyed Nancy curiously. 'What about you, girl with the strange name? Why are you here?'

'I'm here, like you, because my family sent me to learn manners,' Nancy said sharply. 'It seems that some of us need instruction more than others.'

Tamara stifled a giggle. 'That put you in your place, Eleanora.'

'I suppose you live in a draughty country parsonage, Nancy Sunday,' Eleanora said loftily. 'Only a vicar would have such a stupid last name.'

'Actually my family live in a draughty castle and they own the whole village.' Nancy was not given to boasting, but she needed to put Eleanora in her place.

'Do they really?' Tamara went to sit at the dressing table. She took a silver-backed mirror from one of the drawers and a matching hairbrush. 'We live in a mansion built in the last century, but it's hardly a castle.'

Eleanora sat up and swung her legs over the side of the bed. She walked over to the nearest window, threw up the sash and, having taken a last puff on the cigarillo, she tossed it out onto the garden below. 'If either of you tell Miss Maughfling that I smoke I will personally make your life hell.'

Nancy gave her a withering look. 'I'm not frightened of you, Eleanora. Keep your threats for those who are.'

'There's Jack. He said he would come for me and he has.' Eleanora leaned out of the window and waved. She closed it and rushed over to the dressing table, primping in the mirror. 'How do I look, Tamara?'

'As always, you are immaculate,' Tamara said reluctantly. 'But surely you aren't going out now? What will Miss Maughfling say if she finds out?'

'She won't. I've bribed Watkins to let me in through

41

the kitchen when I return. You could come with me but I know you're such a slave to the rules you won't do anything daring.'

'Leave her alone,' Nancy said sharply. 'Go out if you must, but leave Tamara alone.'

'I can speak up for myself.' Tamara unpinned her hair and allowed it to fall in a golden cascade around her shoulders. 'I think you're mad, if you want to know the truth, Eleanora. You'll be in trouble if you're found out.'

Eleanora wrapped a lace shawl around her shoulders. 'I'm too clever to be caught, and you will cover for me if anyone checks the room after lights out.' She waltzed to the door and let herself out onto the landing.

Nancy sighed. 'She's going to be found out, Tamara. I can see it coming.'

'I hope she doesn't get caught because it will reflect upon us.'

'I don't see why it should.' Nancy unfolded the nightgown that Molly had laid out for her. 'Why do you let her bully you, Tamara?'

'I don't take any notice. I probably won't be here for much longer anyway.'

Nancy unbuttoned her blouse. 'Why not?'

'I'll tell you a secret, but don't say anything to Eleanora.'

'All right, I won't.'

'I'm supposed to be doing the season next year, but I have other plans.'

'Have you got a secret lover, like Eleanora?'

'My papa is in trade and he's made a great deal of money, which is looked down upon in some circles. He sent me here because he wants me to marry well.'

Nancy slipped her nightgown over her head. 'But you have other ideas?'

Tamara turned to her and her pale cheeks flushed prettily. 'William is Papa's head clerk. He works in the shipping office. We've known each other for a couple of years and we fell in love last Christmas at a party given by Papa for his staff.'

'How romantic.'

'It was, but Papa would never allow me to marry William. He wants me to find a titled husband, just as Eleanora's family do. Is that why you're here, Nancy?'

'No. At least, I don't think so. It's quite complicated because I was a foundling. I don't know who my parents were. I was left on the steps of the orphanage and I remained in that place until I went to work for the vicar and Mrs Shaw. I was only eight years old at the time.'

'Were they good to you?'

'Mrs Shaw is a tyrant who doesn't know how to treat servants properly. I was rescued by Rosie — that's Rosalind Blanchard — whose brother owns Rockwood Castle. I've been raised like one of the family.'

'But you feel that you don't belong?'

'Yes, but how did you know that?'

'You have a sad look in your eyes, Nancy. You've obviously been used to standing up for yourself. I could tell that by the way you spoke to Eleanora. New girls usually end up in tears after five minutes in her company.'

'I'm not going to allow anyone to bully me, least of all someone like Eleanora. Have you known her long?'

'No, we met here for the first time. We both started a week ago.' Tamara undressed quickly and put on her nightgown. 'We have to be up at six o'clock and then

43

there's the march to the washroom.'

Nancy climbed into bed. 'The washroom?'

'Yes, there are no luxuries here, Nancy. We have to walk in single file to a room on the ground floor, where there are basins lined up on a shelf. The servants fill them with hot water and we have to strip down to our chemises and wash. Miss Maughfling really believes that cleanliness is next godliness. It's all part of the discipline she hopes to instil into us.'

'I don't fancy that.'

'None of us does, but we have no choice. If we don't obey the rules we aren't allowed to have breakfast, and sometimes that goes for luncheon, too.' Tamara slipped between the covers on her bed.

'If she's caught tonight, Eleanora will be going without sustenance for a week.' Nancy turned on her side and closed her eyes.

★   ★   ★

Next morning Nancy was roused by Tamara.

'It's nearly six o'clock and Eleanora hasn't returned,' Tamara said urgently.

Nancy yawned and blinked. 'Perhaps she's run off with Jack Marshall.'

'Oh, heavens! There'll be such a fuss and we'll get the blame for allowing her to go in the first place.'

Nancy sat up in bed. 'Nonsense. What could we have done?'

'I don't know. Maybe we ought to have told the mistress on duty. They patrol the corridors at night.'

'Then they weren't doing their job very well if Eleanora managed to escape from the house without being seen. I'm not taking the blame for something

44

she's done.'

'No, you're right. I must stand up for myself. Talking of which, it's time for the washroom parade. Get up now, Nancy. We need to take our own towels and soap. You did bring some with you, I hope.'

'No, we wash in the river where I come from,' Nancy said, keeping a straight face, then seeing Tamara's horrified look, she relented. 'I'm teasing you. Of course I have what I need. I can't wait to see this peculiar routine in action.'

'Put on your chemise and robe and follow me.' Tamara was already halfway to the door, and Nancy had to hurry to catch up with her.

They followed a line of their fellow students down three flights of stairs to the ground floor, where they joined another half-dozen girls, all barefoot and wearing their dressing robes. The washroom was at the back of the building and the flagstones were cold beneath Nancy's bare feet. They had to queue to take turns at the washbasins, which were filled by servants carrying pitchers of hot water. Robes were hung on wall pegs and Miss Maughfling stood on a dais at the far end of the room, together with a younger woman.

'That's Miss Franklin,' Tamara said in a low voice. 'She's Miss Maughfling's assistant. She's nice but beware of Miss Sharp. She's one to avoid.'

A blast from Miss Maughfling's whistle made Nancy jump, but it was obviously a cue for the girls at the washbasins to move on and the next in line to start their ablutions. It was only then that Nancy noticed another woman, whom she assumed must be the formidable Miss Sharp, standing at the other end of the room. As each young lady walked past her, Miss Sharp grabbed them by the shoulders and inspected behind their ears and the back of their necks as if searching for tidemarks. Nancy wanted to laugh, but she could see that everyone took the washing routine very seriously.

When it came to their turn, Tamara glanced round anxiously. 'Eleanora is going to be in so much trouble.'

Nancy turned at the sound of footsteps on the flagstone floor. All the girls were barefoot except for Eleanora, who marched into the washroom, fully dressed, but with her towel wrapped round her head like a turban and a cake of soap sticking out of the fold.

'I'm sorry I'm late, Miss Maughfling. I was out taking the air. My papa always says a good bracing early morning walk is the best medicine.'

A ripple of laughter ran round the room but was quickly stifled. Miss Maughfling stepped down from the dais and marched towards Eleanora. She snatched the towel and soap from Eleanora's head.

'You have only been in my academy for a week, Miss Smythe, but you have broken the rules for the last time. You will report to my study immediately.' Miss Maughfling allowed her gaze to fall upon Nancy and Tamara. 'And you will accompany her.'

'But we have done nothing wrong,' Nancy protested.

'We will see about that, Miss Sunday. My study, now!'

'Might they not have breakfast first, ma'am?' Miss Franklin asked nervously.

'You know better than to question Miss Maughfling, Lily,' Miss Sharp said tersely.

Lily Franklin bowed her head and one of the girls

at the washbasins sniggered. Miss Maughfling turned on her angrily.

'No breakfast for you, Lady Annabelle. The rest of you, get dressed and go to the dining room.'

Nancy fastened her robe around her and stepped forward. 'Miss Maughfling, with the greatest respect, Tamara and I had nothing to do with Miss Smythe's escapade. I suggest you look to your staff for allowing a young lady to leave the building on her own. In the meantime, I would appreciate being allowed to have breakfast, as it's many hours since I last ate and I believe my family are paying quite handsomely for my board and keep.'

A whisper of astonishment rippled through the steamy air as everyone waited for the principal to respond.

4

Miss Maughfling's study was strictly organised and almost painfully tidy. The books on the shelves were lined up in size, like disciplined rows of soldiers. There was not a paper out of place nor a speck of dust anywhere to be seen. The only patch of colour in the room was the green leather top of the desk, which was polished to such a high sheen that Nancy was certain she could see her face in it if she leaned over. However, she found herself standing to attention next to Tamara, who was visibly trembling. Eleanora stood apart, gazing out of the window with an unconcerned smile curving her full lips, while Miss Maughfling paced the floor, taking tiny steps so that the crinoline beneath her full skirts did not get caught on any of the furniture.

'I am horrified,' Miss Maughfling said at last. 'I have never had one of my young ladies behave in a similar manner to you, Miss Smythe.'

Eleanora yawned. 'Might I go to my room now, Miss Maughfling? I'm a little fatigued.'

'You will speak when I give you permission to speak, Miss Smythe. I've a good mind to expel you from the Academy right away.'

'You won't have any argument from me,' Eleanora said calmly. 'But my papa, Lord Smythe, will be most displeased. I believe you have requested that he serve on the board of governors.'

Miss Maughfling's thin cheeks paled to ashen and

her grey eyes widened. 'Are you trying to blackmail me, Miss Smythe?'

Eleanora giggled. 'Now would I do such a thing? Actually, I'm awfully hungry and I'm sure my friends are a little peckish, too.'

'You know that the punishment for disobeying the rules is to miss meals,' Miss Maughfling said faintly.

'Yes, I'm aware of that and so are my friends, but it's the only weapon you have against us, ma'am. You know that if we complain too much to our papas it will reflect badly on you.' Eleanora faced Miss Maughfling with a belligerent look that did not bode well.

Nancy stepped forward. 'Might I suggest that a warning is enough in this instance, Miss Maughfling? I am sure that Miss Smythe has learned her lesson, having been scolded in front of the other young ladies. Perhaps she will feel more amenable when she's had something to eat?'

Miss Maughfling blinked and swallowed hard. 'Precisely. You may go. All of you. But, Miss Smythe, if this behaviour is repeated I will have to report you to your papa, no matter what the consequences. I am, after all, *in loco parentis.*'

Eleanora opened her mouth to respond but Nancy could see the situation spiralling out of control and she seized her by the arm. 'Come along, Eleanora. We're very hungry and I'm sure you are, too. Thank you, Miss Maughfling. We appreciated your leniency.' She dragged Eleanora from the study.

'Thank you, Miss Maughfling.' Tamara bobbed a curtsey and hurried after them.

Nancy did not release her grip on Eleanora's arm until they reached the dining hall.

'You should have let me have my say,' Eleanora said

crossly.

'I think you said enough.' Nancy opened the door and peered into the large room where the rest of the young ladies sat at a refectory table, finishing their meal, which seemed to consist of porridge and bread smeared with butter. It was a far cry from the sideboard laden with silver serving dishes at Rockwood Castle, where crisp rashers of bacon, devilled kidneys, buttered eggs and the occasional dish of kedgeree were served each day. There was tea but no coffee, and none of the girls seemed inclined to raise any objections. Miss Sharp and Miss Franklin were presiding over the meal and they eyed the newcomers suspiciously, but Eleanora marched to her place and sat down.

'We have permission,' she said boldly. 'Ask the principal if you don't believe me.'

Miss Sharp said something under her breath to Miss Franklin, who looked round nervously but said nothing.

The pupils ate in strict silence and Nancy took a seat next to Tamara. She was too hungry to care that the porridge was salty and cooling rapidly. She finished the bowlful, going on to eat two slices of bread and butter, washed down with weak tea.

A sudden blast on Miss Sharp's whistle made the students rise and stand to attention until they were allowed to march out of the dining room.

The first lesson of the day took place in the drawing room. Miss Franklin gave each girl a heavy book to balance on her head with instructions to walk slowly up and down the large room. This seemed easy at first but there were plenty of mishaps and these resulted in bursts of laughter. Miss Franklin smiled indulgently but she made them practise until she was satisfied that they carried themselves well. Another of their exercises was being made to perch on the edge of a hard chair for twenty minutes while maintaining perfect posture. The girls who could not keep their shoulders back were strapped into a brace for the rest of the lesson, and those who could not keep their heads held in the correct position were forced to wear a cardboard collar. Tamara giggled and said that poor Lady Jane Doubleday looked like a giraffe with a sore throat, which made everyone laugh, except Lady Jane.

By the end of the morning, Nancy was stiff and sore, but she had managed to escape the embarrassing use of the back brace and the cardboard collar. Miss Franklin told her that she had naturally good deportment, but Nancy knew that it was due in part to the almost savage treatment by Mrs Shaw, who had strapped her shoulders back daily so that she was forced to hold herself upright. Even after she went to live at Rockwood Castle, the early training had never left her, and for once she was grateful to the rigorous discipline she had endured at the hands of the vicar's wife.

Luncheon was a simple meal of cold cuts and salad, followed by a dense and sticky jam suet pudding with custard, which was filling and satisfied any cravings for sweet food the young ladies might have.

'So they can cook when they try,' Nancy said as they filed out of the dining hall.

'Shh.' Tamara put her finger to her lips. 'No talking until we get to our room.'

Nancy sighed, wondering if the rules were ever going to relax just a little. The other young ladies seemed to be accustomed to the regime, although she heard them whispering to each other as soon as they were out of earshot of Miss Sharp. Nancy had seen Miss Sharp's way of dealing with anyone who stepped out of line: a spiteful pinch or a brisk nudge from her very pointed elbow, together with a menacing look that meant trouble.

When they reached their room, Tamara went to her cupboard and took out a pair of dancing slippers.

'You'll enjoy this afternoon, Nancy.'

Eleanora stretched out on her bed. 'Only if you have two left feet and no ear for music. Otherwise it will be your idea of hell. I'm not going.'

Tamara stared at her in horror. 'Eleanora, you've already been in trouble today. You won't get off so easily next time.'

'Who cares? I don't, and I am not going to walk through the park to that ghastly suburban villa so that Mr Poppleton can teach us to prance about like circus horses.'

'I think it sounds like fun,' Nancy said, smiling. 'You'll be sorry if you miss it, Eleanora.'

'Let her do as she pleases,' Tamara said, sighing. 'She will anyway, so don't waste your breath.'

Nancy sat on the edge of her bed. 'Tell me more about the dancing lessons.'

'You'll need your maidservant to accompany you. Miss Maughfling insists that we take our maids so that we are neat and tidy when we return through the park. We are supposed to represent everything that's good about the Academy.'

Eleanora gave a snort and turned on her side. 'Ridiculous. Our parents are being tricked out of their money by old Maughfling, and all we get is sore feet. Anyway, I'm meeting Jack at three o'clock. We're going for tea at Gunter's.'

Tamara rolled her eyes. 'There is no helping some people.'

'Molly won't know what to do,' Nancy said worriedly. 'She's a country girl and she's not used to city life.'

'Don't worry. My maid, Annie, will help her. She was born in Spitalfields, as I was.'

'We know your papa is in trade, Tamara.' Eleanora yawned. 'I'd keep quiet about it, if I were you. The other young ladies are frightful snobs, unlike me.'

Nancy and Tamara exchanged meaningful looks and laughed.

'I don't know why that amuses you,' Eleanora said crossly. 'You are both so childish. Go to Poppleton's dance studio and see what fools you make of yourselves then.'

★ ★ ★

The young ladies walked through the park, two by two, followed by their respective maids. Miss Sharp led the way and Miss Franklin was at the rear, encouraging stragglers to keep up.

Mr Poppleton's dance studio was a large room built onto the back of his suburban villa in a crescent close to the park. Mr Poppleton's tiny wife showed them to the changing room, where they swapped their button boots for dancing slippers. Mrs Poppleton seemed flustered, and she flitted around, begging the girls to hurry.

'Mr Poppleton is a demon for punctuality,' she said anxiously. 'We have another class at three o'clock and Mr P is very strict about starting and finishing on time.'

Miss Sharp drew herself up to her full height so that she towered above the trembling woman. 'Madam, we arrived on the dot of two o'clock. We have an hour's dancing lesson booked and we expect to have the full time, otherwise we will have to take steps.'

'Steps?' Mrs Poppleton's myopic blue eyes almost popped out of her head.

'I suggest we start as soon as the young ladies have changed their footwear,' Miss Franklin added hastily.

Mrs Poppleton shot her a grateful smile. 'I'll tell the dancing master that you are ready to begin.' She fluttered off like an agitated butterfly.

'Forward, young ladies,' Miss Sharp said loudly. 'Into the studio, quickly.'

Molly helped Nancy to fasten her satin dancing slippers and she grinned. 'What a to-do, miss. I've never seen the like.'

'Nor I,' Nancy said in a whisper. 'I'll see you in an hour.'

She followed Tamara and the other girls into the studio. Mr Poppleton was standing in the middle of the room, striking the floor rhythmically with a long silver-headed cane. The blows grew faster as if demonstrating his impatience and desire to begin the lesson. Nancy eyed him suspiciously. So this was the maestro who bullied his poor little wife to the point of turning her into a bag of nerves. Poppleton was a large man, dressed in black velvet knee breeches and white stockings, a gold satin waistcoat over a white shirt. The high points of his collar rested on his double chin, below which flowed a frilled cravat. He looked as if he had stepped out of a fashion plate for gentlemen at the beginning of the century, but he wore his apparel with such aplomb it was almost possible to forget that it was ridiculously old-fashioned.

'Young ladies, line up and we will start with the basic steps. Mrs Poppleton, music, please.' He waved the stick at his wife, who scuttled over to the piano and sat down. Her playing was so dreadful that Nancy wanted to cover her ears. An accomplished pianist herself, having been top of the class in music at her old school, Nancy could hardly bear to listen to the waltz being murdered by Mrs Poppleton, who hit more wrong notes than the correct ones.

Mr Poppleton breezed through the steps and stood aside, ordering the girls to repeat what they had just seen. He was not pleased and his stick worked over-time as he used it to underline his angry words.

'No, no, no. You are clumsy clodhoppers. You would make Terpsichore, the muse of dance, weep to see you ruining an elegant formation.' He staggered towards the chairs that lined the walls and sank down on one. 'I am exhausted already. Do it again, only get it right this time.' He turned to his wife, who was cringing on the piano stool. 'You play so badly you give me a headache, you stupid woman.'

Nancy waved her hand to attract his attention. 'Sir, might I be of assistance? Your wife is clearly distressed and I play the pianoforte reasonably well. Might I relieve her for a while?'

'You are here to learn, not to teach.'

'Of course, and I meant no insult to Mrs Poppleton's ability. It's just that she seems a little out of sorts. Maybe a short rest and a cup of tea would resuscitate her.'

Poppleton wiped his brow with a red silk handkerchief. 'All right. See what you can do, although this is very irregular.'

Nancy helped Mrs Poppleton to stand and she took her place at the piano. 'Right, ladies. Shall we try again?' She struck a chord and began to play a popular waltz. There was a murmur of appreciation and the young ladies partnered each other. At first they were stiff and stumbling over each other's feet, but as Nancy continued to play they moved in time to the music. Mr Poppleton tapped his toes and clapped his hands, leaving his stick propped up against the wall. It was only when Nancy stopped playing that he jumped to his feet and began to pace the floor.

'Without exception you all have two left feet, ladies. We will try a country dance.' Mr Poppleton turned to Nancy. 'We will try 'The Barley Mow', followed by a polka. I have to confess that I am quite exhausted by my attempts to make dancers out of clumsy schoolgirls.' He returned to his seat, mopping his brow with his handkerchief.

Nancy played 'The Barley Mow', but the girls were obviously not very well practised and they giggled, tripping over each other in their attempts to master the steps. Nancy could see that it was a lost cause and she launched into a lively polka, playing from memory as there did not seem to be any sheet music to hand. It was three years since she had accompanied Patricia Carey at the Goat and Compasses pub in Puddle Dock and at the ill-fated soirée in Paris, which ended in a jewel robbery. All that was in the past, but playing the piano brought back memories, some of them good and others bittersweet. She was lost in the pleasure of the music when she was aware of Mr Poppleton standing behind her. She lifted her hands from the piano keys.

'Is anything wrong, sir?'

'You play exceptionally well, Miss, er . . . I didn't catch your name.'

'Miss Sunday, sir.'

'Would you be interested in working for me, Miss Sunday? My wife has not an ounce of your talent.'

Miss Sharp stormed over to them. 'That would be most inappropriate, sir. Miss Sunday is a student at the Academy. She is not seeking employment.'

'A gentleman can only ask, Miss Sharp.' Mr Poppleton's ruddy complexion darkened to puce. 'I was simply enquiring.'

'Enquire elsewhere, sir. Your behaviour is unacceptable. I will tell Miss Maughfling.'

Mr Poppleton took a deep breath and exhaled in a loud snort, putting Nancy in mind of a steam engine arriving at a station. 'You insult me, Miss Sharp. I will report your behaviour to your employer.'

Nancy rose from the piano stool. 'It's three o'clock, Mr Poppleton. Isn't it time for us to finish our lesson?'

'Yes, yes. Clear the studio, young ladies. I have my next session booked and waiting. Where is Mrs P?' Mr Poppleton marched off, calling out for his wife.

'I'd hide, if I were her,' Tamara said in a low voice. 'What a dreadful man he is, and to think we have to come here at the same time next week.'

Miss Sharp bristled. 'Unfortunately he is the best we can afford, but I will be reporting his behaviour to Miss Maughfling.'

'I wasn't offended, Miss Sharp,' Nancy said firmly. 'He only offered me a position here at the dance studio. I don't think he meant to offend anyone.'

Miss Sharp glanced over Nancy's shoulder and her eyes narrowed. 'Miss Smythe, where do you think you are going?'

Eleanora blew her a kiss. 'I'll be back in time for dinner, or not, as the case may be.' She left the studio with her maid hurrying after her.

'Where is she going?' Miss Sharp demanded. 'Speak up, young ladies. Does anyone know where Miss Smythe is headed?'

Lady Jane peered out of the window. 'There's a good-looking gentleman in a Tilbury. I think he's waiting for Eleanora. I'm so jealous.'

'You won't be when Miss Maughfling hears of this latest escapade,' Miss Sharp said angrily. 'If Miss Smythe isn't expelled after this, I will be most surprised. Young ladies, go to the changing room and get ready to leave.' She stepped aside as the other girls rushed to the window to peek at Eleanora's gentleman friend. 'Ladies, please go to the changing room, now.'

Reluctantly they obeyed, but the chatter as Nancy followed them was of the handsome young man who had helped Eleanora into the carriage and driven off with her.

★   ★   ★

To Nancy's surprise, Eleanora was not expelled for her latest escapade. Tamara seemed to think that Lord Smythe had more influence with Miss Maughfling than anyone realised, and whispers rippled through the prim corridors of the Academy, although no one had the courage to ask Eleanora the truth. Careless of what others might think, she continued to see Sir Jack Marshall whenever the opportunity arose.

Nancy had no particular liking for Eleanora, but she found herself in the unlikely position of being

Eleanora's confidante. Not that she wanted to know the details of the trysts between the lovers, but Eleanora seemed desperate to talk about her affair with Sir Jack. Apart from that, life at the Academy fell into a routine broken only by weekly trips to Mr Poppleton's dance studio or walks in the park to admire the lake and the beauties of nature. There were lessons in etiquette as well as deportment, and the young ladies were encouraged to learn the pianoforte if they were not already accomplished performers. Singing tuition was optional, as was embroidery. Miss Maughfling had introduced a new series of lessons in managing a household, dealing with recalcitrant servants and the preparation of menus for special occasions, as well as feeding the family and the servants. Not that any of the students were expected to undertake such tasks, but Miss Maughfling insisted that an idle mistress makes idle servants, and the lady of the house, mansion or castle, must know at least as much as her housekeeper when it came to managing household affairs. Most of the young ladies yawned their way through these lessons, but Nancy found herself top of the class. Hester and Mrs Jackson's attempts to educate her in domestic subjects seemed to have been very successful.

Talking to Molly was the only way to overcome the creeping feeling of homesickness that sometimes almost overwhelmed Nancy. She had no interest in studying to become a debutante and no likelihood of being presented at Court anyway. Molly was a breath of fresh air from home, and surprisingly she seemed to have adapted well to city life. Perhaps it was due to the fact that the greengrocer, who delivered the vegetables and fruit to the kitchens several times a week, happened to be a handsome young man whose father owned a market garden in Highgate. On Sunday afternoons Reuben James arrived at the servants' entrance in a gig painted a bright yellow, which, according to Molly, aroused both amusement and jealousy amongst the other lady's maids, none of whom had managed to attract a gentleman friend. Molly went off eagerly and returned in time for supper, filled with enthusiasm for the market garden and Reuben's welcoming parents. It was, she said, like being back on the farm. They even kept a cow for milk, and several goats, plus a few chickens. It was home from home for Molly. Nancy could see romance blooming and she was pleased for Molly's sake, but she knew she would lose a good friend as well as a maid.

The summer drifted into autumn and the leaves began to fall from the trees in the park. The days were getting shorter and the nights colder. Nancy had grown accustomed to life in the Academy, although that did not stop her from thinking about home and missing her surrogate family. Then, one day in early October, an announcement by Mr Poppleton threw the students into a frenzy of excitement. He declared that they had made such good progress in their dancing lessons that they were invited to attend a ball at the studio. They were allowed to bring a gentleman to partner them, otherwise they would have to dance together as they had been doing since the beginning of term.

Eleanora shrugged and said she doubted if Sir Jack would be willing to attend such an event, but a swift dig in the ribs from Tamara made her add that she would try to persuade him. During their walk back to the Academy the conversation was all about who the girls would ask to accompany them. The students who had brothers were instantly besieged by requests to be introduced to their male siblings, while others boasted that they had several gentlemen who would be only too happy to stand up with them at Mr Poppleton's ball.

'I hope Sir Jack deigns to partner you, Eleanora,' Tamara said eagerly. 'I'm longing to meet him.'

'I can't promise anything.' Eleanora tossed her head. 'He's visiting a friend in the country at the moment, which is the only reason I came with you today. Jack has many wealthy and influential friends.'

'Maybe he can spare a couple to partner us young ladies who have no one to dance with us,' Nancy said, laughing.

Eleanora cast her a sideways glance. 'I dare say he would oblige, if you are unable to find your own partner.'

'I am not desperate.' Nancy wrapped her shawl tightly around her as an east wind whipped more leaves off the trees and they floated to the damp grass.

'My cousin Baldwin is in town, I believe,' Tamara said cautiously. 'He's very nice and kind, Nancy, but he's rather short in stature and his hair is receding although he's only twenty-three.'

Eleanora snorted. 'He sounds exactly right for you, Nancy. Or perhaps you'll be playing the pianoforte because old Poppleton is too mean to hire an orchestra.'

'I'm sure Baldwin is delightful,' Nancy said quickly. 'But I'm happy to sit and watch the others dance. I'm sure it will be great fun after so many evenings doing nothing apart from reading or embroidery.'

'Will William be able to come, Tamara?' Nancy asked in a low voice when Eleanora was out of earshot.

'I'm sure he will. I haven't seen him for weeks but he writes to me almost every day. Annie smuggles our letters in and out of the building and her brother Benny acts as postman.'

'I can't wait to meet William.'

'Perhaps he could find you a better partner than Baldwin. I realise he doesn't sound much of a catch.'

'Nonsense, Tamara, I'm not so shallow that I think looks are everything. I'm quite happy to go to the ball on my own. I will enjoy watching everyone twirling round the floor to the beat of Mr Poppleton's silver-headed cane.'

Eleanora puffed on her cigarillo. 'I dare say Jack could find you a suitable beau, Nancy. He has many friends.'

'Really, I will be fine on my own,' Nancy said firmly. 'But thank you all the same.'

* * *

The excitement in the Academy grew to fever pitch as the day of the ball drew nearer, and everything was forgotten apart from exchanging details of the gowns the young ladies would wear, and how they would style their hair. Some kept their partners a secret, while others boasted about the gentlemen who were queuing up to escort them to the ball at Poppleton's dance studio.

Molly helped Nancy to dress in the cream satin evening gown that Hester had considered unsuitable. Nancy also had her doubts, wondering if it was indeed too elegant for such an occasion. Mr Poppleton's studio was not the most fashionable address in London. However, the dinner gown she had brought with her was not designed for dancing, and she had no choice but to opt for Meggie Brewer's creation. The décolletage was daring and Molly had drawn the strings of Nancy's stays so tight that she was having difficulty in breathing, and the full skirts over a crinoline cage whittled her waist down to a handspan. Nancy had visions of being toppled over by a stiff gust of wind and rolling down the hill like a giant puffball.

'I wish I was going,' Molly said dreamily as she pinned a rosebud into the elaborate coils of the coiffure she had just created. 'I'd like to dance with Reuben. It would be so romantic.'

'I doubt if I will do anything but sit out like a wallflower,' Nancy said, laughing. 'I might even be asked to play the piano if poor Mrs Poppleton is indisposed.'

Molly stood back to admire her handiwork. 'There you are, miss. You look like a princess.'

'I do look different,' Nancy said, gazing at her reflection in the fly-spotted mirror. 'I don't often have the chance to dress up.'

'If there are any unattached young men, they will be queuing up to write on your dance card. You will be the belle of the ball, and Miss Eleanora will be mad with jealousy.'

Nancy smiled and shook her head. 'Eleanora has Sir Jack to partner her, and I dare say Tamara has persuaded William to attend the ball. Being unattached has its advantages, Molly. I can sit back and enjoy the spectacle.'

'You'd better put your woollen mantle on, miss. It's getting cold at night. Winter will be here soon.'

Nancy was about to agree when Eleanora burst into the room. Her cheeks were flushed and she looked stunning in a cerise silk gown lavishly trimmed with black lace and bugle beads. Nancy could only imagine Hester's face if she saw a young lady dressed in such a way. She would not approve.

'Did you want something, Eleanora?'

'Jack is here, Nancy. We have a spare seat in the barouche, otherwise you will have to walk and risk soaking the hem on your gown on the grass.'

'What about Tamara? Doesn't she want to go with you?'

Eleanora laughed. 'Don't worry about that little minx. Her beau picked her up in a hackney carriage. Her papa will be livid if he finds out.'

Molly took a blue velvet mantle from the clothes press, but Eleanora shook her head. 'You won't need that, Nancy. A shawl will do. That's all I'm taking. Hurry up because Jack is waiting.'

Molly exchanged meaningful glances with Molly. When Eleanora had her mind set on something it was easier not to argue. She slipped a shawl around her shoulders and followed Eleanora out of the room.

Sir Jack Marshall was waiting in the barouche and he climbed down to hold the door open for them. He kissed Eleanora on the cheek, despite the fact that a small crowd of students was preparing to leave for the walk to the dance studio.

'Jack, this is Nancy. I told you about her.'

He smiled and nodded. 'How do you do, Miss Sunday?'

'How do you do, sir?' Nancy bobbed a curtsey.

He handed Eleanora into the carriage and when she was seated he proffered his hand to Nancy. She climbed in and was instantly aware that she and Eleanora were not the only occupants of the barouche. It was dark in the interior and she could not make out his face, but the gentleman sitting in the far corner was stylishly dressed and there was something familiar about him.

Jack closed the door and sat down. 'I took the liberty of inviting a friend to accompany us, Nancy. I hope you don't object, but I believe you are already acquainted.'

5

'It's a pleasure to make your acquaintance again, Miss Sunday.'

In a shaft of flickering gaslight from a street lamp, Nancy recognised him. 'Mr North! I don't understand . . .'

He leaned forward and took her hand, raising it to his lips. 'Gervase North, at your service, Miss Sunday.'

Nancy snatched her hand away. 'No, really. I didn't agree to going anywhere with this person.'

'Too late,' Eleanora said casually. 'We're on the move so you can't get out. Don't be a bore, Nancy. Gervase is harmless, so there's no need to make a fuss. We're going to have a ridiculously silly evening at old Poppleton's. Honestly, my dear, we will need two strong men to help us escape when the evening becomes too dull for words.'

Nancy sat back in her seat. She could hardly fling herself out of a moving carriage, but she stared doggedly out of the window. It was an unfortunate coincidence that Jack's friend happened to be the man who had upset everyone at Rockwood Castle with his outrageous slur against the late Lady Carey. However, having to face an evening with him was quite another matter. There might be nothing she could do at the moment, but she would make her feelings very clear when they arrived at the dance studio.

Seemingly oblivious to Nancy's distress, Eleanora

chattered on, receiving monosyllabic responses from Sir Jack. However, Gervase was more forthcoming and the pair of them talked incessantly during the carriage ride to Poppleton's studio. When they arrived they were greeted by Mr Poppleton himself. He looked like a pantomime version of an Eastern potentate in a weird creation consisting of a silk turban and a flowing satin robe decorated with glass beads. He welcomed them with a theatrical flourish and invited them into his studio as if it were the smartest venue in London.

Nancy glanced anxiously at Gervase, willing him to keep his sarcastic comments to himself. The memory of the embarrassing scene in the drawing room at Rockwood Castle was still fresh in her mind. She hated to admit it but, for all that, she found Gervase dangerously attractive. Even worse, she could tell by the way he treated her that he was well aware of his fatal charm where women were concerned. He tucked her hand in the crook of his arm.

'Shall we go in and see what the strange fellow has to offer?'

Nancy would have liked to refuse, but she could hardly do so without causing a scene. Eleanora and Sir Jack had gone on ahead and Miss Sharp was standing in the doorway, giving them suspicious glances.

'Yes, we might as well,' Nancy said reluctantly. 'But this is just a school. Don't expect too much.'

He patted her hand as it lay on the sleeve of his expensive and extremely well-cut tail coat. 'My dear Nancy, nothing could be dull when I am in such charming company.' It was said with a smile that would have warmed the hardest heart, and Nancy felt the blood rushing to her cheeks in a rosy blush.

They entered the studio to find a small group of musicians playing a lively polka. The students who had arrived early were the girls without partners. They whirled around the floor with more enthusiasm than grace.

'There are refreshments in the anteroom,' Mr Poppleton said grandly. 'Fruit punch, cider and ale for the gentlemen. Never let it be said that Hartley Poppleton does not know how to entertain the gentry. Enjoy your evening, ladies and gentlemen.'

'I suggest we do a turn of the floor to satisfy the Gorgon at the door,' Sir Jack said, glancing in Miss Sharp's direction, 'and then we leave quietly and take these beautiful young ladies somewhere they will truly be appreciated.'

'I couldn't agree more.' Gervase smiled down at Nancy. 'Does that suggestion appeal to you, Miss Sunday?'

'I don't know,' Nancy said warily. 'Where are you thinking of taking us?'

'Don't be such a baby.' Eleanora shot a warning look in Nancy's direction. 'Jack and Gervase will take care of us. I, for one, am not prepared to stay here all evening.'

'Miss Sharp is watching,' Nancy said in a low voice. 'I think she might have overheard.'

'I'm prepared to charm the old harridan.' Gervase turned to give Miss Sharp a disarming smile, which she ignored with a toss of her head. 'Strange,' Gervase added. 'It usually works.'

'Never mind her.' Jack proffered his arm to Eleanora. 'Shall we show them how it's done, my dear?'

'Someone needs to take control.' Eleanora laid her hand in his. 'Poppleton could not train a seal, let alone a herd of unruly girls.'

At a signal from Jack, the group of musicians launched into a waltz and Jack led Eleanora onto the floor.

'Shall we?' Gervase asked, smiling.

'I think we should.' Nancy allowed him to take her hand and they merged with the other dancers. She had never been held in such close proximity to any man, let alone moving in time to the strains of a waltz. Even through the gloves they both wore she was very conscious of the warmth of his grasp, and the scent of his pomade and expensive cologne was more intoxicating than wine. It was almost impossible to believe that this handsome, charming man with his devastating smile was the same person who had caused such a stir at Rockwood. Nancy was in a dream as they whirled together in perfect unison, and she barely noticed Jack leading Eleanora towards the door at the back of the studio. The rest of the girls and their partners had arrived and Miss Sharp was hidden from view.

'Are you sure you want to go with me?' Gervase said in a low, caressing voice.

'Yes, please.' At this moment Nancy did not care about anything. She had experienced all manner of emotions during her time in London with Patricia when she was attempting to pursue her operatic career, but this was something new and completely different. She did not protest when Gervase manoeuvred them around the other couples and they followed Jack and Eleanora as they left the studio.

It was very cold outside but the carriage was waiting and, once seated, with Gervase's arm around her shoulders in a very familiar, exciting and totally improper manner, Nancy began to relax and enjoy the experience.

'Where are you taking us, Jack?' Eleanora demanded lazily. 'I fancy a nice meal and some dancing afterwards.'

'I know the very place,' Jack said, smiling. 'In fact, we're already on our way to the Strand. I know you so well, my love.'

Eleanora yawned. 'It's a pity you're just a baronet with limited means, Jack. Papa would have a fit if he knew we were consorting.'

'Consorting sounds very risqué, Eleanora.' Gervase squeezed Nancy's shoulders. 'Don't you think so, my dear?'

A sudden twinge of conscience made Nancy edge away. 'I don't know why I agreed to come with you this evening. My family would certainly disapprove.'

Gervase laughed and drew her back to the shelter of his arm. 'But that's what makes it so exciting, Nancy. Admit it, you find it quite exhilarating.'

'I do, but that doesn't make it right. You caused a scene and upset my family. I shouldn't even be speaking to you.'

Eleanora leaned forward. 'Heavens! Do tell, Nancy. What did this rogue do?'

'I simply told the truth, Eleanora,' Gervase said casually. 'Some people find it hard to take, that's all. The Careys and the Greystones are two very old families with plenty of skeletons in their cupboards. They don't appreciate having them brought back to life.'

'I don't want to hear it, Gervase,' Nancy said angrily. 'If you insult the Carey family you insult me and I want nothing to do with you.'

Jack laughed. 'There, Gervase, you've been put in your place. I think you should apologise to Nancy.'

Gervase took her hand and held it in a firm grasp. 'I apologise humbly, Nancy. I won't say another word about your family. Am I forgiven?'

Even in the dim light Nancy could see the self-mocking expression on his handsome features and she relented. 'All right. Just so that we understand each other.'

'That's settled then,' Eleanora said with a weary sigh. 'I'm famished, Jack. Where are we dining tonight?'

'You'll see, my love.' Jack wrapped his arms around Eleanora and kissed her soundly on the lips.

Nancy instinctively moved as far away from Gervase as she could in the confines of the carriage. She was surprised by Eleanora's forward behaviour and shocked by Sir Jack's lack of restraint. She closed her eyes, forcing the image of Hester's disapproving face from her mind, but an irrepressible giggle overcame her reservations and she covered her mouth with her hand.

Eleanora broke free from Jack's arms. 'What are you laughing at, Nancy?'

'I'm sorry. I was imagining Lady Carey's expression if she could see us now. She would be shocked to the core.'

Gervase laid his hand on her arm, his fingers stroking the tiny area of exposed skin between her gloves and her shawl. 'But she is not here now, Nancy.'

Nancy slapped his hand. 'No, Gervase, but that's not the way to behave and you know it. I'm not a naïve country girl, as you might think, so don't treat me like a simpleton.'

He withdrew his hand. 'I'm sorry, Nancy. I will try

to resist your charms. No doubt you will put me in my place if I forget myself.'

She nodded. 'Yes, Gervase. You may count on that.'

★   ★   ★

They dined at The George on the Strand but the company grew rowdy as the evening progressed. Gervase and Jack had been drinking heavily and Eleanora was quite tipsy, but Nancy had only sipped her wine. She was growing anxious and beginning to regret her rash decision to accompany them. An evening at Poppleton's ball was not the most exciting prospect but at least she would have been chaperoned and seen back to the Academy at a reasonable hour. The clock on the wall showed that it was nearly midnight but Gervase ignored her repeated pleas to be taken back to Miss Maughfling's.

'If you want to stay here, will you at least get a cab to take us to Regent's Park?' Nancy demanded, in a last attempt to get some sense from either Gervase or Jack.

'Don't be a spoilsport,' Eleanora said, giggling. 'You are beginning to sound like old Sharp.'

Gervase slipped his arm around Nancy's waist and drew her to him. She struggled but he tightened his grasp and his lips claimed hers in a drunken kiss. She twisted free and leaped to her feet. 'Take me home now, Gervase.'

He looked up at her, grinning foolishly. 'You can't walk that far, sweetheart. You wouldn't get two steps along the Strand without someone snatching you up for their pleasure.'

She raised her hand and slapped his face. He rose

72

to his feet, his face contorted with anger.

'That was a foolish thing to do, my love.' He seized her in his arms but she struggled to free herself.

'Let me go!'

'Here, mister, do as the young lady says.' A large hand clamped on Gervase's shoulder. 'Are you listening to me, cully?'

Gervase released her so suddenly that Nancy staggered backwards, saving herself from falling by clutching at a table. 'Jedidiah?'

The burly butcher gazed at her in surprise. 'Miss Nancy?'

'You remember me?'

A wry smile curved his lips. 'I never forget a face, nor a voice. Your lady had a fine voice, as I recall, and you was with her in Clare Market.'

'Yes, I was, and you saved us from being pelted with rotten fruit and tomatoes.'

Gervase shook himself and squared up to Jedidiah. 'What business is this of yours, my man? This is between the lady and myself.'

'She don't seem that enamoured of you, cully.' Jedidiah placed Nancy behind him. 'You ain't no gent if you try to force yourself on a young girl.'

'You should try minding your own damn business.'

'I'm making it my business.' Jedidiah fisted his large hands. 'Want to come outside?'

Jack released Eleanora from a passionate embrace. 'What's going on here, Gervase? Is this fellow causing trouble?'

'Mr Wilkins, I think you'd better leave us,' Nancy said in a low voice. 'I don't want any unnecessary fuss.'

Jedidiah shook his head. 'Looks like you got it anyway, Miss Nancy. I got me cart out the back. It ain't no fancy wagon but my old horse will get you home, wherever that is now.'

'I'm at Miss Maughfling's Academy in the Outer Circle of Regent's Park, Jedidiah. It's a long way from Clare Market.'

'I'll see you safely there, and the other young lady, too. If she's a mind to sit in the back of a butcher's cart.'

Eleanora waved him away. 'I'd sooner walk. Jack will take care of me, won't you, my love?'

Jack kissed her on the cheek. 'Of course I will. My rooms are not far from here. You'll be safe with me.'

Gervase squared his shoulders. 'You're not going anywhere with this uncouth fellow, Nancy. I don't know how you come to be friendly with a butcher from Clare Market, but you are with me.'

'No, Gervase. I asked you half a dozen times to take me back to the Academy and you refused. Mr Wilkins might be a butcher but he's twice the gentleman you are.' She turned to Jedidiah. 'I would be most grateful for a lift in your cart, Mr Wilkins.'

Jedidiah led her through the long narrow bar to a door at the back of the building. Outside there were a number of carriages and horses being held by tired, ragged boys, who would be lucky to get a farthing for their trouble.

'Well, miss, how come you were with such a raffish fellow? I'm sure Miss Patricia wouldn't approve.' Jedidiah helped her onto the driver's seat and climbed up beside her, taking the reins from a small child. He tossed a coin to the boy. 'Don't give it to your old man, Sidney. He'll spend it on liquor.'

The boy caught the penny deftly and pocketed it with a grin. 'Ta, Jed.'

'Mr Wilkins to you, you cheeky guttersnipe.' Jedidiah laughed as he flicked the reins and the horse ambled forward.

'You're right, Jedidiah,' Nancy said, shivering. 'Patricia would be horrified. It was a mistake, that's all I can say.'

'You're cold, miss. I'll never know why you young ladies don't wrap up warm.' He reached for an old horse blanket and wrapped it around Nancy's shoulders. 'It's a bit smelly but it will keep out the cold.'

Nancy nodded, trying not to wrinkle her nose. No doubt the coarse wool was full of fleas but she could feel the warmth seeping through her bones and she did not complain.

'Well, you're safe now, miss,' Jedidiah said as he guided the horse through the narrow alley towards the Strand. 'I've often wondered what happened to you two young ladies.'

'Patricia married Leo Wilder, and I've gone back to school, in a manner of speaking.'

'Nice chap — Leo. I got a great deal of respect for him. They was well suited, in my humble opinion. So the little nightingale ain't singing no more?'

'No, Patricia is a happily married lady and she's back with the family in Rockwood. We had an adventure in Paris and nearly got arrested in a jewel robbery, but Leo saved us. It all seems so long ago now.'

'And now they sent you back to school. Ain't you a bit old for lessons, girl?'

Nancy laughed. 'You could say that, but it's not that sort of school. I'm learning to be a young lady.'

Jedidiah sniffed. 'You are a lady already. You don't need no schooling in it.'

'Thank you, but my guardians think I do, and I

could hardly refuse to do as they ask. They've been very good to me over the years.'

Jedidiah grunted and concentrated on the road ahead. Nancy huddled in the warm, if scratchy, folds of the blanket and closed her eyes.

★　★　★

When they arrived at the Academy, Jedidiah drove the cart round to the servants' entrance in the mews and, as luck would have it, Watkins had waited up for Eleanora and, although she was half asleep, she unlocked the door to admit Nancy.

'Go to bed now, Watkins,' Nancy said gently. 'Miss Eleanora won't be coming back tonight.'

'She made me promise, miss.'

'She's staying with friends in town. She asked me to send you to bed and to thank you for waiting up for so long.'

Watkins eyed her suspiciously. 'Miss Eleanora never says thank you, no matter what I does for her.'

'Well, there's always a first time, Watkins. Go to bed and get some sleep.'

Watkins nodded and ambled off towards the back stairs, leaving Nancy to make her way through the silent building to her own room. She managed to undress and get into bed without waking Tamara, but although she was exhausted she found that sleep evaded her. It was hard to believe that she had allowed Gervase to charm her into doing something that she would normally have rejected out of hand. Eleanora might find it exciting to break all the rules but Nancy had been raised strictly, first by the women in the orphanage and then by Mrs Shaw. Even when

Rosalind took her to Rockwood Castle, there had been Hester to contend with, followed by the rigours of the expensive boarding school. But Nancy was no rebel, and she longed to be back in her old room at the castle with its faded grandeur and ill-fitting windows. She fell asleep as the first grey light of dawn filtered through the window.

★ ★ ★

Eleanora returned halfway through the deportment lesson next morning. Miss Sharp sent her straight to the principal's office, and everyone waited expectantly for the outcome of the interview. Nancy was still tired after their escapade last evening and she was surprised that no one had noticed her absence. While Miss Sharp was busy berating Eleanora, Tamara explained in whispers that a fight had broken out at the ball last night between two young gentlemen who had added a flask of brandy to the fruit punch. They had drunk deeply and then fallen out over who would ask Lady Jane for the next waltz. Lady Jane had refused them both, but they had blamed each other and punches had been exchanged. Mr Poppleton sent for a constable and the ball had come to an abrupt end.

'William brought me back here,' Tamara added, smiling. 'Everyone else had to make their own way, and it was utter confusion.'

'So no one noticed that I wasn't there?' Nancy glanced round the room at the young ladies who were practising rising gracefully from a chair while balancing a book on their heads.

'No, you got away with it, and so did Eleanora until she chose to walk in this morning as if nothing was amiss.'

'I think she wants to be expelled,' Nancy said softly. 'I almost wish they had found me out. I would love to go home to Devonshire.'

'Don't be sad. We have a treat tonight.'

'Not another ball at the dance studio?'

Tamara giggled. 'No, on the contrary. Miss Maughfling loves opera and she has been given tickets for the performance at the opera house this evening.'

'I used to help the wardrobe mistress to mend costumes when I was living in London,' Nancy mused. 'Being backstage was very exciting. I was reminded of that time with Patricia when Jedidiah brought me home on his butcher's cart last evening.'

'No talking, young ladies.' Miss Sharp pointed a baton at them. 'You should be practising with the rest of the class. Never mind what happens to Miss Smythe. She has gone too far this time.'

Nancy and Tamara exchanged glances but they did not argue. It was not until they were released from class at midday, that Nancy went to their room and found Eleanora sitting on her bed, pale-faced but defiant, while her maid, Jessie, worked feverishly packing Eleanora's belongings.

'I'm being sent home, Nancy.'

'I'm sorry, Eleanora, but what did you expect? You spent the night with Jack at his lodgings. I don't think anyone could get away with that.'

'He wants to marry me.'

'That's good, isn't it?'

'Not really. Papa wants me to marry the Earl of Woodley.'

'But you are in love with Jack.'

'Jack is a baronet with a relatively small income. If I

marry Woodley I will be a countess and live in a huge country mansion with servants and a carriage of my own. I'll live a life of luxury.'

'Is that so bad?'

'Not in itself, but Woodley is old. He must be nearly sixty, which is older than my papa.'

'Is he a widower?'

'Yes, and he only has daughters. If I can produce a son the boy will inherit the estate and the family fortune. If I marry Jack we will be poor by comparison.'

'I'm sorry, Eleanora. It must be a hard choice, but if it were me I'd choose love over money and title.'

'Well, you are not me. In any case, you made a fool of Gervase last evening. I doubt if he will ever speak to you again.'

'That suits me very well. I was mad to agree to accompany you all. Gervase is good-looking and charming, but he is not a nice man.'

Eleanora threw back her head and laughed. 'That's what makes him so attractive, my dear. You need to be careful because I saw how you looked at him. He only has to crook his finger and you will go running to him. Mark my words.'

'Never!' Nancy said firmly. 'I've learned my lesson.'

'Be careful, that's all I can say. I know Gervase well, and you are too good for him, Nancy. Remember that.'

'If that's what you think, why did you allow Jack to invite him to the ball last evening?'

Eleanora shrugged. 'Gervase heard me mention your name in passing, and he said he knew you. Jack thought that the ball at the dance studio would be amusing.'

'Did Gervase know that he was to be my partner?'

'Of course he did. He said he was looking forward

to seeing you again. What is the matter, Nancy?'

'I don't understand why Gervase wanted to see me. He upset everyone at Rockwood with unrepeatable accusations against members of the family who were not there to defend themselves.'

'Gervase loves to shock. It's his most amusing trait, providing one is not the victim. Anyway, I'm ready to go, Nancy. It's been nice knowing you and I don't say that of anyone else here — apart from Tamara, of course. Look after her, Nancy. She's a fragile flower.'

'I will, Eleanora. I'm sorry you're leaving. I hope everything turns out as you would wish.'

Eleanora rose from her bed. 'Take the portmanteaus downstairs, Jessie. Send Little up to fetch the trunk.'

Jessie bobbed a curtsey and staggered from the room carrying a heavy case in each hand.

'This is goodbye, then, Nancy. We haven't known each other long, but I'm sure we'll meet again.'

Eleanora swept from the room as if she were going on an outing instead of leaving the Academy in disgrace. Nancy could only admire Eleanora's audacity. She sighed and slumped down on her own bed. Eleanora had been caught because she did not care to obey the rules, but the matter might have been reversed and it might have been she, Nancy Sunday, who had been caught when she crept in after lights out and was facing expulsion.

Nancy felt unsettled for the rest of the day. Even the prospect of a visit to the opera that evening did not raise her spirits. However, Tamara's excitement was infectious and, after an early supper, the young ladies lined up in the hallway, waiting to be summoned to climb into the horse-drawn omnibus that

Miss Maughfling had hired for the occasion. Nancy pushed all thoughts of Gervase North to the back of her mind. If she let him upset her then he had won whatever strange game he was playing with her and her family. She waited her turn and walked down the path with Tamara, who was so excited that she could hardly contain her delight.

'I used to ride in omnibuses quite regularly when we lived in Spitalfields, but Papa considers it beneath us now. However, I don't think he'd object to our travelling privately in such a vehicle.'

'Your papa sounds like a bit of a snob, if you don't mind me saying so, Tamara.'

'You're right. But he doesn't realise it.' Tamara climbed onto the omnibus first and went to find a seat.

Nancy sat down beside her. 'What is it, Tamara? You've been all of a twitter all day. Has something happened?'

Tamara glanced over her shoulder but the two girls in the seat behind them were chattering and oblivious to anything other than the gossip they were sharing. 'William proposed to me again last evening, Nancy. It was so romantic. He took me back to the Academy in a hansom cab. When we alighted he went down on one knee and held one hand to his heart, holding the other out to me. He looked so handsome in the moonlight that it made me cry.'

'But you said yes?'

'Of course I did. Now all I have to do is tell Papa. I'm dreading it, Nancy. Will you stand by me when he visits me on Sunday?'

'Yes, if you think that will help.'

'It will. I need you to hold my hand because William won't be there. He is going to speak to Papa, but

I know what the answer will be. I need to persuade my father to allow us to marry.'

'I'll be happy to help, if I can.'

'Thank you, Nancy. You are such a good friend.'

Nancy settled down to enjoy the rest of the ride to Covent Garden. She had her doubts when it came to Tamara being able to change her father's mind about marriage to his head clerk, but she would do her very best to be supportive.

They arrived outside the opera house in good time and Miss Sharp marshalled everyone into the foyer. While they waited to be led into the auditorium Nancy studied the programme and the name that jumped out at her was that of Felicia de Marney, the famous opera singer.

'You've gone quite pale,' Tamara said anxiously. 'Are you all right, Nancy?'

'I know this lady.' Nancy's voice shook with emotion. 'She was a Carey of Rockwood Castle before she married Claude. Isn't that an amazing coincidence?'

'It most certainly is. Will you go backstage after the performance to see her?'

Nancy bit her lip. 'I don't know if I dare. She is such a famous person now. She might not want to see me.'

Miss Sharp leaned towards them. 'Do you really know the diva herself, Miss Sunday?'

'Yes, Miss Sharp.'

'How delightful. You must introduce us to her after the performance. I won't accept any excuses, Miss Sunday.'

6

The stage doorkeeper was sceptical at first, but as it happened Mrs Lake, the wardrobe mistress, was about to leave the building. She stared hard at Nancy.

'I know you, don't I?'

'Yes, Mrs Lake. I'm Nancy Sunday. I used to help you with the costume alterations three years ago when Patricia Carey had a part in Mr Thorne's production.'

'I never forget a face. I was sorry to lose you, Nancy. But I can see you've grown up to be a young lady.'

'I don't know about that, Mrs Lake. But I am here with Miss Maughfling's Academy and the girls would love to meet Mrs de Marney.'

'She is related to Patricia, I believe.' Mrs Lake's eyes shone with interest.

'Yes, ma'am. Mrs de Marney is Patricia's mother.'

'Ah, yes! I recall the story now.' Mrs Lake turned to the doorkeeper. 'Allow the young lady in. She is related to Mrs de Marney.'

'Thank you, Mrs Lake,' Nancy said, smiling. 'It's good to see you again.'

Mrs Lake beamed at her. 'If you need to find work I will always have a place for you in my sewing room, Nancy.'

The doorkeeper allowed them to enter, although he did so with obvious reluctance.

'I know the way to the dressing rooms,' Nancy said hastily.

'All right, miss. But if anybody says anything I'll

blame Mrs Lake.'

Nancy ignored this remark. 'Come on, Tamara. This way.' She walked purposefully through the maze of narrow corridors to the dressing room reserved for the star of the show. She knocked on the door and waited for an answer.

'Enter.' Claude's deep tones echoed off the high ceiling.

Nancy opened the door and stepped inside, followed by Tamara. It was a small, windowless room, lit by gaslight, which made popping sounds and sent flickering shadows off the walls. Felicia was seated at the dressing table taking off her stage makeup. She glanced at Nancy.

'Nancy? Is it you?'

'Yes, Mrs de Marney. We've just seen your performance. It was magical.'

Felicia's frown was wiped away by a smile. 'You've seen the opera?'

'We came with Miss Maughfling's Academy for Young Ladies. I don't suppose you know that the family sent me there?'

'We've rather lost touch recently.' Claude pulled up two stools. 'It's delightful to see you both. Won't you introduce your friend, Nancy?'

'I'm sorry, yes. This is Tamara Fitzallen. Tamara, may I introduce you to Mr and Mrs de Marney?'

Claude laughed. 'I'm generally known as Mrs de Marney's manager. I definitely come second these days. But it's delightful to meet you, Miss Fitzallen.'

'So you enjoyed my performance?' Felicia said eagerly. 'Did the other young ladies appreciate my vocal range?'

'I'm sure they did,' Nancy said earnestly. 'They

84

asked me if they could meet you. Just for a couple of minutes. We know your time is very precious.'

'It is indeed, but I can't refuse to see my admiring audience. I will come to the foyer when I am ready. Give me ten minutes and I'll be with you.'

'Better make that twenty,' Claude said, smiling.

Nancy backed towards the doorway. 'We'll wait for you, Mrs de Marney.'

Claude moved past her and opened the door. 'It's good to see you again, Nancy. You've grown into a beautiful young lady. I'm sure Rosie is very proud of you.'

'Thank you.' Nancy knew she was blushing but she never felt shy with Claude. 'You're very kind.'

'Nonsense, my dear. I only speak the truth. I was a little worried by the way you were treated by some people when we last visited Rockwood, but it seems that's all settled now or they wouldn't have sent you to the Academy.'

'Maybe they wanted to get rid of me,' Nancy said, laughing. 'Hester has always been uncertain as to my position in the house, but Rosie stands up for me. She makes me feel like one of the family.'

'I'm sure you are most valued. Hester is a dry old stick, but her heart is in the right place.'

'Claude, do come in and shut the door. There's a terrible draught.' Felicia's peevish tones made Claude back away with a rueful grin.

'We'll see you in the foyer, Nancy. You and I can have a long talk then.' He retreated into the dressing room and closed the door.

'What a lovely kind man,' Tamara said wistfully. 'I wish my papa would speak to me like that. He barks orders as if I were one of his underlings.'

'Claude is a really nice person. Felicia is lucky to have him. She can be a bit dramatic, as I recall, but he knows exactly how to handle her. Come on, let's go and tell Miss Sharp. I'll be in her good books forever.'

Miss Sharp was suitably impressed, and when Felicia breezed into the foyer dressed magnificently in a purple silk gown beneath a matching satin cape trimmed with swansdown, there was a sharp intake of breath from students and teachers alike.

'My dear ma'am, how kind of you to spare us a few minutes.' Miss Sharp smiled ingratiatingly.

'It's a pleasure to meet an appreciate audience,' Felicia said sweetly.

'We're honoured, ma'am,' Miss Franklin added shyly.

Claude stepped in, bowing to Miss Sharp and Miss Franklin in turn. 'I hope you will forgive us, ladies, but Mrs de Marney needs her rest. The part she plays in the production is very demanding.'

'Of course,' Miss Sharp said hastily. 'We are honoured that you have given us this much of your time, Mrs de Marney.'

Felicia leaned against her husband, waving graciously to the girls as he led her out of the theatre to a waiting hansom cab. Nancy followed them out onto the pavement.

'I really did enjoy the opera, Mrs de Marney. Will you be visiting the family at Rockwood soon?'

Felicia hesitated. 'I don't know. Is it in our itinerary, Claude?'

'No, my love, but we can always make a detour. We're staying in rooms in John Adam Street. It's not far from here. Why don't you come and see us tomorrow morning? Not too early, mind you.'

'I will,' Nancy said eagerly. 'I'm sure Miss Sharp will give me permission to miss the deportment class just this once.'

Claude pulled a face. 'It sounds a bit like prison to me, Nancy. Anyway, do come — and bring your friend, if she's a mind to join you.' He handed his wife into the cab and climbed in after her.

'Do you think Miss Sharp will allow it?' Tamara asked anxiously.

'Maybe a couple of tickets to see the next production might persuade her.' Nancy smiled mischievously. 'I'm sure that could be arranged.'

'A morning off would be so exciting.' Tamara's eyes shone with excitement. 'Maybe we could get a cab to the City and I could see William in the shipping office.'

Nancy was feeling reckless. 'Why not? We might as well take advantage of an hour or two of freedom.'

At first it seemed that Miss Sharp was about to refuse but, fortunately for Nancy, Miss Maughfling happened to overhear the conversation, and she gave her permission on the understanding that she would be the first to receive complimentary tickets for the next performance. Nancy agreed somewhat recklessly, taking it upon herself to speak for Claude, but she was certain he would agree to help. Claude could be relied on, whereas Felicia was as changeable as the weather.

With Miss Maughfling's blessing, a cab was summoned. Nancy and Tamara were on their way to John Adam Street and both were in high spirits.

'It feels like a holiday,' Nancy said as they alighted outside the terrace of eighteenth-century houses.

'I am so excited.' Tamara clasped her hands, her

eyes shining. 'I'll see William before we return to the Academy.'

Nancy knocked on the door. 'Yes, we will go to the office, I promise. But I think it's time you and William told your papa that you want to marry.'

'I know, but I'm so scared he will refuse and he might sack William. Without a job we can't even think of getting married.'

'Then your papa must be persuaded.'

'Could you do it for me?'

Nancy shook her head. 'No. I'm not the right person. I don't know your papa, for one thing.'

The door opened before Tamara had a chance to argue and a maidservant showed them upstairs to a sitting room on the first floor, where Claude greeted them with a warm smile.

'So the Gorgon let you off this morning?'

Nancy giggled. 'Don't let Miss Sharp hear you call her that.'

'Even if it is very appropriate,' Tamara said, smiling.

'What is so amusing?' Felicia swept into the room looking glamorous in a diaphanous silk dressing robe, tied at the waist with a pink satin sash. Her blond hair was loose around her shoulders and, devoid of face paint, she looked younger than her age, even though she was four years short of sixty. Claude, on the other hand, had always looked more mature than his years, and now his hair, although abundant, was silver, as was his moustache.

'I was being rude about the girls' teacher,' he confessed with a guilty smile.

'Dreadful woman,' Felicia said bluntly. 'Anyway, it's nice to see you again, Nancy. How is everyone at Rockwood? I didn't have the time to enquire last evening.'

'Very well, as far as I know, ma'am. I've been in London for the past four months and the end of the course is still four or five weeks away.'

Felicia shrugged and sat down in a comfortable chair by the window. 'I doubt if they can teach you much in that time. What you need is some town polish. Don't you agree, Claude?'

He gave her a searching look. 'What have you in mind, my love? I know that tone of voice and you're plotting something.'

'How well you know me, my darling.' Felicia raised her hand to her brow and sighed. 'You know how busy I've been this season.'

'I do, of course. Where is this leading, Felicia?'

She fluttered her long eyelashes. 'As you are aware, I've been looking for an accompanist for some time, and I really need someone trustworthy to act as my personal assistant.'

'You have Violet. I thought you were satisfied with her.'

'Violet does my hair and looks after my clothes, Claude. I'm not talking about another lady's maid. As I said, I need an accompanist for rehearsals, and that person could handle my appointments, taking some of the work from you, my love.'

'Have I ever complained, Felicia?' Claude's extravagant moustache quivered and Nancy thought for a moment he was going to cry.

'No, my love. But I need someone young, who will run errands for me. In short I want Nancy to come and work for us.'

Nancy stifled a gasp of surprise. 'You want me to leave the Academy, ma'am?'

'You can hardly do what I need if you're wasting your time at that school for silly debutantes.'

'But Rosie and Patricia wanted me to undertake the full course, ma'am.'

'You will learn a lot more from me. I don't know why I didn't think of it before. You are ideal, Nancy. I've heard you play the pianoforte and I know you accompanied Patricia during her attempt to conquer the operatic world. You will come with Claude and me when we attend parties and other functions, and you will fend off would-be admirers, using your youth and charm to persuade them to leave me alone.'

'That sounds very exciting,' Tamara said in a low voice. 'I'd rather do that than attend stuffy deportment classes and listen to lectures on etiquette.'

'Your friend is right.' Felicia bestowed a smile on Tamara. 'You will be out in society, Nancy, but with none of the fuss and bother of becoming a debutante.'

'Or the expense,' Claude said drily. 'I don't imagine that Rosalind or Patricia intended you to do the season.'

'No, of course not.' Nancy looked from one to the other. 'But perhaps I should ask for their permission before I do anything.'

'Nonsense,' Felicia said sharply. 'I am the head of the family. I am the matriarch and they will do as I bid. What do you say, Nancy?'

'I suggest you think about it, Nancy.' Claude sent a warning glance in his wife's direction. 'No need for you to decide today.'

'What will I do without you?' Tamara's pretty lips drooped and her eyes filled with tears.

'Don't be such a baby.' Felicia threw up her hands. 'I'm sure you don't need Nancy to hold your hand.'

Tamara sank down on the nearest chair and bowed her head. 'Of course not, ma'am.'

'Don't worry, Tamara,' Nancy said hastily. 'I haven't decided yet.'

'But you should accept the offer.' Tamara managed a tearful smile. 'Don't give up such an opportunity because of me or anyone.'

'We'll go and speak to William this morning. He'll look after you.' Eleanora's last words came back to Nancy and she knew she could not rest until Tamara had her father's permission to marry the man she loved.

'Well, it's lovely to see you young ladies, but my modiste will be here at any minute.' Felicia glanced at the brass clock on the mantelshelf. 'It's my final fitting. You would deal with this sort of arrangement in future, Nancy. And,' Felicia added, with a knowing smile, 'you would need a whole new wardrobe as well. I can't have people around me who look as if they've just come up from the country.'

'I will think about your kind offer, but I have a favour to ask?'

'Anything within reason,' Claude said cheerfully.

'Miss Maughfling, the principal at the Academy, loves opera, as does Miss Sharp. Would it be possible to have some tickets for Mrs de Marney's next performance?'

'Yes, of course. I'll arrange that and I'll send them round to the Academy.' Claude patted Nancy on the shoulder. 'Do think seriously about my wife's proposition, my dear. I think you might enjoy working for us.'

'Thank you. I promise I will let you know tomorrow.' Nancy left the room, followed by Tamara.

'Why did you hesitate?' Tamara demanded as they

stepped outside onto the pavement. 'It's a wonderful chance for you to see more of the world. You might even travel abroad.'

'I owe everything to Rosie and Patricia. I don't want to do anything that will upset them.'

'But Mrs de Marney is their mother. Surely they would want to do what she wishes?'

'They aren't like an ordinary family, Tamara. Mrs de Marney is not like a normal mother. As I understand it, she was rarely at home when her children were growing up, and that's how she continues now. I remember her infrequent visits to the castle and then she would go off for months or even years.'

'But the family still love her?'

Nancy shrugged. 'Yes, I suppose so.'

'My mother died soon after I was born. I wish that I could see her, just once.'

Nancy raised her hand to hail a hansom cab. 'Come on, Tamara. We'll take a cab to the City and you can see William. But we mustn't stop long or we'll be in trouble with Miss Sharp.'

Tamara's sad expression was replaced by a bright smile. 'Oh, yes. He will have such a surprise when I walk into the office.'

★ ★ ★

William was at his desk in the shipping office but, unfortunately for Tamara, her papa was also there, pacing the floor with an angry frown. He came to a halt when he saw his daughter.

'Tamara! What are you doing here? And who is this with you?'

The colour fled from Tamara's cheeks but she

managed a hint of a smile. 'Good morning, Papa. This is my friend Nancy Sunday.'

'How do you do, Miss Sunday,' Hubert Fitzallen said gruffly. 'But why are you here, Tamara? You should be studying whatever it is they teach at the Academy. I pay good money to have you turned into a young lady.'

Nancy stepped forward. 'How do you do, Mr Fitzallen? It's a pleasure to meet you, sir.'

His expression softened. 'At least you've learned something at that expensive school. Perhaps you can explain the reason for this unexpected visit.'

Tamara sent a pleading glance to William, who had risen to his feet and was gazing at her with undisguised admiration.

'Tell him, William,' Tamara said in a low voice.

'You have something to say, Russell?' Mr Fitzallen's tone was not encouraging.

William ran his finger round the inside of his starched white collar. 'This isn't the right time or place, sir.'

'Nonsense. Say what you have to say. I'm a busy man, Russell.'

'Papa.' Tamara laid a small hand on her father's sleeve. 'Please let William speak.'

'Out with it, man. And the rest of you get on with your work. This is none of your business.' Mr Fitzallen turned back to William, glowering. 'Speak up. I haven't got all day.'

Nancy could see that both Tamara and William were pale with fright and trembling visibly.

'Maybe we should leave now, Tamara.'

Tamara shook her head. 'William, please tell Papa what we spoke about at the ball.'

'The ball? What is this? Have you been gallivanting about town without my permission, Tamara?' Mr Fitzallen strode across the floor to fling a door open. 'Come into my office, the pair of you. And you, Miss Sunday. You seem to be involved in my daughter's sudden attack of disobedience.'

Nancy sighed. She had a feeling this had been a terrible mistake. Glancing at the expression on Tamara's face, it was obvious that both she and William were terrified of Mr Fitzallen. Somewhat unwillingly, Nancy followed them into the oak-panelled office. Ledgers were lined up on the shelves, all labelled in bold black letters. Wicker filing baskets were spilling over with documents, and stacks of *Lloyd's List* newspapers were piled against the walls. But what fascinated Nancy most was a row of impressive brass wall clocks showing the corresponding time in different parts of the world.

'Shut the door,' Mr Fitzallen said irritably. 'I don't want everyone to know our business.'

'Yes, sir.' Nancy closed it quietly. She could see the curious faces of the clerks through the glass panes, but they turned away when they realised she was looking at them.

'Papa, please listen to what William has to say.' Tamara's voice shook with emotion.

'I'm listening,' Mr Fitzallen said grimly.

William cleared his throat nervously. 'I love your daughter, sir.'

'Bah! Nonsense. Puppy love.'

'I am twenty-two, sir. I have worked my way up to the position I hold at present. I believe I am an asset to your company, and I will do everything in my power to make a good husband for Tamara.'

Mr Fitzallen's florid complexion deepened to a shade of puce. 'Over my dead body, sir. Tamara will marry a man who can keep her in a similar manner to the way she has been raised. I know what your wages are and you cannot afford to wed anyone, let alone a young lady of quality.'

'Papa, I am a merchant's daughter. I am not a lady of quality, no matter how much you pay for my education.'

'Did you put her up to this, Miss Sunday?' Mr Fitzallen demanded angrily. 'Tamara has never had the courage to challenge my authority in the past, so I can only think it is you who have persuaded her to do so now.'

'If I did I would not think I had done wrong, sir.' Nancy held her head high. 'Anyone can see that your daughter and Mr Russell are very much in love.'

'Thank you, Nancy,' William said firmly. 'I can speak for myself, but what you just said is true, Mr Fitzallen. I love Tamara with all my heart.'

'In that case you will leave her alone, Russell. I will find a suitable husband for my daughter and that does not involve a near penniless clerk.' Mr Fitzallen turned to Tamara. 'I'll send for my carriage and you will return to the Academy, both of you. I'll deal with you later, Russell.'

Mr Fitzallen marched out of the office. He grabbed the office boy by the ear and shouted instructions to him. The boy clutched his hand to his head and rushed out into the street.

'I won't leave you, William,' Tamara sobbed. 'I love you, too.'

'You'd better do as your papa says for now.' William held her briefly but released her as Mr Fitzallen stormed back into the office.

'Tamara, you will have nothing more to do with Mr Russell. Do you understand what I'm saying?'

'It's not fair, Papa. William and I have done nothing wrong.'

'You went behind my back, miss. Now, listen carefully. I will keep him on because he is a good worker, but if you try to meet in secret, William Russell will lose his job and be sacked without a character. Do you understand, both of you?'

Tamara nodded tearfully and William stood to attention, biting his lip.

'You, sir, are a mean man,' Nancy said angrily. 'I'm sorry, Tamara, but your papa is a bully. If you were half a man, William, you would stand up to him.'

'What right have you got to come into my office and interfere with my family?' Mr Fitzallen took a menacing step towards Nancy. 'You will leave my daughter alone in future, Miss Sunday. You are a bad influence. You can find your own way back to the Academy.'

Nancy tossed her head. 'I wouldn't ride in your carriage if you paid me, Mr Fitzallen. I'll see you back in class, Tamara.' Nancy strode out of the office, allowing the door to swing shut behind her. She had just reached the pavement when Tamara caught up with her.

'I'm coming with you, Nancy.'

'Don't be silly, Tamara. You've angered your father enough. Don't make things worse.'

'It's time I stood up for myself. I am coming with you. Papa can make of it what he likes.'

Nancy glanced over her shoulder to see Mr Fitzallen standing at the office window, glowering at them. 'All right, if you insist.' She stood back as a cab drew up at the kerb.

'Miss Maughfling's Academy, Regent's Park, please, cabby.'

★ ★ ★

Miss Maughfling was delighted with the complimentary tickets, but she was not pleased by Nancy's decision to leave the Academy. Tamara was tearful, but resigned to the fact that her friend would no longer be sharing their room. However, when Molly returned from taking a message to Felicia from Nancy, accepting the position, Molly confessed to having problems with the other maidservants. They were all hoity-toity and stuck-up because their mistresses were going to be presented at Court. The maids had laughed at her Devonshire accent and made fun of her farming background.

'I had to bite my tongue, Miss Nancy, or I'd have given them what for.'

'I'm sorry, Molly. They should know better, but we're leaving today. You may come with me or you can go home to Rockwood, whichever you choose.'

'You'll need someone to look after all those lovely clothes that Mrs de Marney has promised you,' Molly said, grinning. 'I can still see Reuben and visit his market garden on a Sunday, if that's all right with you.'

'Of course it is. I wouldn't want to break up a budding romance.'

Molly's round cheeks flushed and she smiled shyly. 'I do like him, miss.'

'We'll be in London for the rest of the season. I don't know where we'll go after that.'

'That'll be long enough.' Molly laughed softly as

she packed the rest of Nancy's clothes in a valise. 'I think he'll propose any day now.'

'Well, I wouldn't want to stand in the way of true love,' Nancy said, smiling. 'If only things were as easy for poor Tamara. Her romance looks doomed.'

'Then she'll have to run away with her man.'

'It's not as simple as that, Molly. William will lose his job at the shipping office if he doesn't do as Mr Fitzallen says. He can't support a wife without a steady income.'

'That's sad for them.' Molly fastened the leather strap. 'There we are. All done and ready to leave. Shall I go and find a cab, miss?'

'Yes, Molly. I'm ready. The address is John Adam Street. This could be the start of something really exciting.'

7

Nancy and Molly arrived at John Adam Street to find that Mrs de Marney and her husband had left for the theatre. A new production was in rehearsal and they would not be back until mid-afternoon. However, Mrs de Marney had left instructions for Nancy to be shown her room and offered all the comforts of home. Nancy suspected that the thought for her wellbeing had been Claude's suggestion, as Felicia was not known for considering the comfort of anyone other than herself. However, according to Violet, Felicia's personal maid, an appointment had been arranged with the seamstress, who would come later that day and measure Nancy for new garments.

Felicia and Claude arrived home just as the seamstress was about to leave. Felicia strolled into the morning parlour, eyeing the pile of magazines left open at the fashion plates. Swatches of material covered the tea table in the window and pins were scattered on the floor.

'Miss Bannister, I see you've been busy.' Felicia took off her gloves and bonnet, handing them to her maid who was hovering in the doorway. 'That will be all, Violet. Tell Rawlings to take tea and cake to the drawing room. I'm famished. We didn't have time for luncheon.'

Miss Bannister brushed a stray strand of hair back from her brow. 'I've taken Miss Sunday's measurements, ma'am. I have a list of the garments she would like.'

Felicia snatched the notebook from Miss Bannister's hand. 'Let me see.'

'I only chose what I thought I might need,' Nancy said apologetically. 'If it's too much I can manage with less.'

Felicia frowned as she studied the list and the dress patterns. 'These are not what I had in mind. Miss Bannister, pay attention, if you please.' Felicia leafed through the pages of the magazines, pointing out creations that Nancy would never have dreamed of ordering. 'You are my assistant, Nancy. We mix with the *crème de la crème* in society, and I cannot have you looking like a poor relation. You are my representative and I am always dressed in the height of fashion.'

'Yes, you are, Mrs de Marney.' Miss Bannister nodded so vigorously that Nancy was afraid she would do herself a mischief.

'Very well then.' Felicia sat down at the table and tore pages out of the journals, passing them to the bemused seamstress. 'I think that will do for a start. Now let me see the materials you've chosen, Nancy.'

'I didn't pick anything too garish, ma'am.'

'In other words you wish to look like a country mouse. Well, my dear, that won't do. You are not living in Rockwood now. You are in fashionable London. Miss Bannister, pay attention and make notes.' Felicia thumbed through the swatches, firing instructions at the seamstress until Nancy felt sorry for the woman.

At last Felicia was satisfied with her choices. Miss Bannister looked as if a puff of wind would blow her over and Nancy was left totally confused. The only person who seemed satisfied was Felicia. She beamed at Nancy. 'We are invited to a ball at Dorrington

House next week. Lord Dorrington is a well-respected patron of the arts, and his wife is particularly fond of opera. You will have the blue watered-silk gown ready by then, Miss Bannister.'

It was an order rather than a question and Miss Bannister paled visibly, but she nodded again, whispering something unintelligible. However, Felicia did not seem to notice.

'Splendid, Miss Bannister. You are a pearl amongst seamstresses. I always recommend you to my friends. We will leave you to collect your things together. Come, Nancy, we will partake of refreshment in the drawing room.'

Nancy cast a pitying glance at Miss Bannister, who was struggling to sort out the chaos of crumpled swatches, magazines and fashion plates that Felicia had left in her wake, not to mention the pins scattered about the floor.

'Do hurry, Nancy,' Felicia stood by the door waiting for Nancy to open it for her. 'I will expect you to be by my side at all times, unless, of course I say otherwise.'

'Yes, Mrs de Marney.' Nancy followed Felicia across the entrance hall, where a young housemaid was almost buried beneath a huge bouquet of flowers that had just been delivered.

'How lovely,' Nancy said, inhaling the heady scent of hothouse lilies.

'Another gift from one of my admirers,' Felicia said casually.

'Don't you want to read the card, ma'am?' Nancy accepted the folded sheet of card from the maid.

'No, that's for you to deal with. You will be expected to write letters of acceptance for all the gifts I receive, and answer my correspondence. It's all part of your day-to-day duties.' Felicia mounted the stairs, leaving Nancy no option other than to follow her to the first-floor drawing room, where a tray of tea and dainty cakes awaited them.

'You may pour, Nancy.' Felicia arranged herself on the sofa. She selected several cakes, considering each one as if it were the most important decision of the day. 'One has to be careful of one's figure. I try to eat in moderation or I fear I might become corpulent, like some of the Continental divas. My downfall, unfortunately, is cake. However, I ate very sparingly at breakfast.'

Nancy poured the tea into delicate bone-china cups, passing one on its matching saucer to Felicia, who drank thirstily.

'Am I to attend rehearsals with you, ma'am?'

'Of course you are. You will also make sure that my costumes are in perfect order. I understand that you used to help Mrs Lake in the wardrobe when you were with Patricia.'

'Yes, I did. I am quite good with my needle.'

'Excellent. I'm afraid Violet is not so talented. You and I will get along splendidly, Nancy. Just do as I tell you and everything will be perfect.'

★ ★ ★

Nancy's return to the theatre was like coming home. Garson Thorne not only remembered her but he welcomed her with open arms, planting a whiskery kiss on her cheek. Mrs Lake was equally pleased to see her and Nancy promised to help out in the sewing room when Mrs de Marney had no need for her services.

However, Felicia was a demanding mistress. They arrived early each morning and Nancy sat down at the piano to accompany Felicia when she rehearsed her arias before the rest of the cast began to wander into the auditorium. Nancy enjoyed playing the piano again and sometimes they had an audience of cast members or the people who worked backstage. In between running errands and keeping a diary of events for Felicia, Nancy had very little free time. Even that was curtailed by visits from Miss Bannister, who was desperate to finish the elegant ice-blue ball gown that Nancy was to wear to the Dorringtons' grand mansion in Piccadilly. Nancy gave her all the encouragement she could, even volunteering to sew a few seams herself so that Mrs de Marney could find no fault with Miss Bannister's work. Nancy discovered that Bertha Bannister was the sole support of her aged invalid mother. They lived in a room above a butcher's shop in Clare Market and it was no surprise to discover that the butcher was Jedidiah Wilkins. Apparently he had a soft spot for Miss Bannister and had been courting her for years, but seemingly had never had the courage to propose. Nancy made up her mind to have a word with Jedidiah when she could get away from John Adam Street.

As with everything, Felicia wanted to have her own way, and she was adamant that Nancy's dinner dress made by Meggie Brewer in Exeter was outdated and unsuitable for such a grand event. Nancy took some of the sewing up to her room in the evenings, keeping it away from prying eyes. She did not trust Violet, who told her mistress everything. Molly was a source of information as to events below stairs and she did not like Violet. The feeling apparently was mutual.

Eventually, having sewn until her eyes were sore into the early hours of Saturday morning, Nancy finished her part of the gown. When Bertha arrived mid-afternoon, they were able to use the final fitting to make a few adjustments and the shimmering creation was finished and ready to wear. Molly helped Nancy to dress and she took extra care when arranging Nancy's hair in a coronet of curls studded with rosebuds from Reuben's father's garden.

Molly had used the excuse to visit the Academy at a time when she knew that Reuben would call with the cart laden with fruit, vegetables and flowers. She had returned with a big smile on her face and a posy of white rosebuds. Nancy had a feeling that Molly had ordered these a few days ago on her evening off when Reuben had called to take her out. Their romance was blossoming and Molly had never looked happier. Nancy was delighted for her, but she knew she would soon lose her maid and old friend. Reuben was a nice young man and Molly deserved someone who would love and take care of her. That led to thoughts of Tamara, and Nancy decided that she would visit the Academy herself at the first opportunity. She missed Tamara and she worried about how she was coping without someone to encourage and comfort her.

A knock on the door startled Nancy out of her reverie and she jumped to her feet. 'Who is it?'

Molly opened the door. 'What is it, Violet?'

'Mrs de Marney is ready to leave. She don't like to be kept waiting.'

Nancy grabbed her velvet mantle, gloves and fan. 'I'm coming.' She slipped past Violet and hurried downstairs to the entrance hall where Felicia was standing by the door with Claude.

'I shouldn't have to send for you, Nancy. You ought to be ready before me in case I need something at the last minute.'

'I'm sorry, ma'am. I wanted to look my best. It won't happen again.'

'I'm sure it won't,' Claude said, smiling. 'You've settled in very well, Nancy.'

'Thank you, sir.' Nancy stood aside as Claude opened the door and proffered his arm to his wife. He handed her into the waiting cab. 'After you, Nancy, my dear.'

It was a short cab ride to Piccadilly, but Claude kept them entertained with stories about Lord Dorrington's escapades as a young man that made Nancy laugh outright. She wondered how she would keep a straight face when she met the gentleman.

When the cab drew to a halt, the street was lit by flambeaux on the pavement outside the mansion and lights spilled from the open door and the tall windows. As they stepped inside, the heat from hundreds of wax candles made it feel like a summer day instead of a cold early November evening. Servants rallied to take their outer garments and they joined the crowd of guests milling around as they waited to mount the stairs to the grand ballroom where Lord and Lady Dorrington were receiving their guests.

When it came to their turn, Lord Dorrington made a fuss of Felicia, who was clearly delighted. She blushed and simpered like a young girl, totally ignoring Nancy, who stood beside Claude, hoping that she could get into the ballroom without being noticed. Felicia acknowledged Lady Dorrington, who did not seem impressed with the diva, and Claude shook hands with Lord Dorrington. Nancy found herself largely ignored, which gave her time to observe their host, who was short, rather stout and with a dangerously florid complexion. It was hard to equate the middle-aged nobleman with the young roué that Claude had described. They should have moved on but Claude gave Nancy a gentle nudge forward.

'My lord, may I introduce a member of the Devonshire Carey family, Miss Nancy Sunday, who has been good enough to act as my wife's accompanist and social secretary.'

Lord Dorrington's brown eyes were almost lost beneath heavy lids and his fat cheeks, but he smiled benignly at Nancy. 'How do you do, Miss Sunday? I hope perhaps we will hear you play the pianoforte. I love a good tune.' He turned away to greet the next in line.

Lady Dorrington gave Nancy a cursory glance. 'I hope you enjoy the evening.'

Nancy curtsied. 'Thank you, my lady. I'm sure I shall.'

'Come along, Nancy.' Felicia beckoned to her, frowning. 'You keep yourself to yourself, my girl. Remember your place.'

'Don't be hard on her, my love,' Claude said gently. 'Nancy isn't used to such gatherings.'

'She has to learn, Claude. Why do you always take her side?' Felicia unfurled her fan and waved it vigorously as if to underline her words. 'Come with me. Nancy, follow on and speak only when you're spoken to.'

Nancy sighed. Life with Felicia was not easy, but she could see that Felicia had already forgotten her as she was claimed by someone who was clearly an old acquaintance.

'Enjoy yourself, Nancy.' Claude winked and walked away, following his wife and the gentleman who had claimed her attention.

'That man has the patience of a saint.'

Nancy spun round to see none other than Gervase North standing behind her. He was so close that she could smell his expensive cologne and a slight hint of Havana cigar smoke.

'What are you doing here?' she demanded crossly. 'Why do you always turn up wherever I happen to be?'

'That's the trouble with London society, my dear Nancy. It's a small world.'

'I don't want anything to do with you, Gervase. Go away and leave me alone.'

He pulled a face. 'Now, Nancy, that wasn't very nice. I don't see anyone rushing up to ask you to dance, or even to pay their respects. It's not easy for a newcomer to break into society.'

Nancy stood her ground. 'Then how did you accomplish it, Gervase? As I understand it, you have run through your inheritance at the gaming tables and you are not welcomed by your family in Devonshire.'

'That's rather harsh. In fact, hardly anyone is welcomed by my cousin Christina, and poor Sylvia is a chronic invalid. My mama was a Greystone and, as the only male heir, I should have inherited Greystone Park. That is why I return to Devonshire and my ancestral home.'

'I know nothing about that, nor do I want to. Now, please go away and leave me alone.'

'Don't be unsociable, Nancy. I was going to ask you to join me in the next waltz.'

'I would rather be a wallflower and sit with the

matrons and plain girls than dance with you.'

He proffered his arm. 'You don't mean that, my dear. I know you took a fancy to me when we were partners at the quaint entertainment laid on at your dancing school. And to tell the truth I find you very attractive.'

Nancy could see Felicia glaring at her from a distance and she knew she was beaten, albeit temporarily. She laid her hand on his sleeve. 'One waltz, if you promise to leave me alone afterwards.'

'On my honour as a gentleman.' Gervase smiled down at her in a way that made Nancy's heart beat just a little faster. She was making every effort to dislike him but she was aware of the envious glances of several young ladies, and she had to admit that Gervase was a fine figure of a man, and undeniably handsome. But as he led her onto the dance floor and slipped his arm around her waist, she remembered how he had behaved on the night of Poppleton's ill-fated ball, and she stiffened.

'Try to relax, Nancy. This is a waltz, not a walk to the guillotine.'

'You have such a way with words, Gervase.'

'And you are determined to place me in the wrong, no matter what I say or do. But I will convince you that you are mistaken. By the end of the evening you will be eating out of my hand.'

'I certainly hope not,' Nancy said drily, but she was prevented from saying anything more as he whirled her round the floor with such grace and ease that the other couples moved out of their way and people stopped to watch. Unfortunately, Felicia happened to be watching and her expression was anything but encouraging. The dance ended and Gervase led

Nancy from the floor.

'Leave me now,' Nancy said in a low voice.

'But, my dear, I was going to offer you some refreshment. A glass of champagne, perhaps?'

Nancy could see Felicia steaming towards them. 'Gervase, please move away. Mrs de Marney is coming and she doesn't look happy. I am supposed to keep in the background.'

Felicia caught up with them, holding her hand to her breast. 'Are you trying to bring on my palpitations, Nancy? What did I tell you about making a spectacle of yourself?'

Gervase stepped forward and seized Felicia's free hand. He raised it to his lips. 'My dear Mrs de Marney. Please forgive me. It was all my fault.' He flashed a smile at Felicia that would have ignited a bonfire.

'Who are you, sir? Do I know you?'

'You know my family, ma'am. My mother was Elizabeth Greystone. I am her son, Gervase North.'

Felicia's angry expression was wiped away by one of astonishment. 'Gervase? The last time I saw you was when you were a mere child.'

'But I remember you, ma'am. How could one forget a beautiful creature like yourself? I have become your devoted admirer over the years.'

'Gervase, I don't know what to say. Of course you must come and sit at our table and take some refreshment. Nancy, why didn't you tell me that you knew Elizabeth's son?'

'I — I didn't know you two were acquainted. I only met Mr North a short while ago.'

'Call me Gervase, please.' He raised Nancy's hand to his lips, but there was a mocking smile in his eyes.

Felicia left them and made her way to a table at the

side of the dance floor.

'What are you up to, Gervase?' Nancy snatched her hand away. 'You may think I am a naïve schoolgirl, but this is not my first time in London. When I came here with Patricia I was only fifteen, but I discovered then that people should be judged by their actions, not by their pedigree.'

'I assume that the burly butcher friend of yours was one of those people.'

'Don't look down at Jedidiah Wilkins, he's a good man. He has not had your advantages in life but he's honest and trustworthy. Can you say the same for yourself?'

Gervase pulled a face. 'There you have me, my dear. I admit that I am somewhat fickle in my relations with others, but there are exceptions, and I would like you to be one of them.'

'I still get the feeling that you are playing some deep game, and somehow I am part of it, which I don't understand.'

Gervase raised her hand to his lips and brushed it with a kiss. 'Then it will prove very interesting to discover the truth, won't it?'

Nancy withdrew her hand. His touch still had the power to send thrills through her body even though she knew he was teasing. 'What are you after, Gervase? If you think Felicia will give you money, you are completely mistaken.'

'You insult me, Nancy.' Gervase laid her hand on his sleeve as he led her through the scented crowd to join Felicia and Claude at their table.

'Do sit down, Gervase,' Felicia said, smiling. 'Claude, darling, will you catch the eye of the waiter? I think champagne is called for. Gervase is a Greystone on his mother's side, my dear. We are virtually neighbours.'

Claude shook Gervase's hand. 'Delighted to meet you, old chap. I've only come to know Rockwood fairly recently, but if there's anywhere I would like to spend my declining years, it would be in that area. I say that even though I'm a Londoner born and bred.'

Gervase smiled and nodded. 'When I was a callow youth I couldn't wait to escape from the country, but now I'm a man of the world I find myself drawn to a much quieter way of life.'

'The countryside is all right in very small doses,' Felicia said dismissively. 'I belong to the world of opera. Isn't that so, Claude?' She glanced at her husband, who had just managed to attract the attention of a waiter bearing a tray of champagne.

'Absolutely, my love. A talent like yours needs to be shared.'

'I am a fanatic when it comes to opera, Mrs de Marney, but I confess I haven't seen your latest triumph on stage.'

'Oh, but that's terrible, Gervase.' Felicia turned to Nancy. 'You must make sure that Gervase receives tickets for the best seats whenever convenient.'

'But surely there is a show tonight,' Gervase said innocently. 'How can they go on without you?'

'My understudy is taking my part. A young woman called Carlotta Corvi. She has a decent voice, but she has much to learn before she gets to my standard.' Felicia lowered her voice. 'I am supposed to be at home resting from nervous exhaustion. However, you will be able to see my performance next week, whenever it suits you.'

Nancy met Claude's amused look with a wry smile.

Felicia made up her own rules and everyone else had to abide by them.

'Are you listening to me, Nancy?' Felicia demanded impatiently.

'Yes, ma'am. I'll make sure that Gervase has a really good seat.'

'I need two tickets, if that isn't being greedy, Mrs de Marney.'

'Gervase, I insist that you call me Felicia, and of course you may have as many tickets as you wish. I hope you are bringing someone who appreciates opera.'

He smiled. 'It would be an insult to your talent to do anything less.'

Claude picked up his glass of champagne and raised it in a toast. 'To my beautiful and talented wife.'

Gervase saluted Felicia and Nancy joined in dutifully. She could not help thinking that Claude and the rest of the opera company were partly to blame for Felicia taking advantage of her prima donna status. Felicia de Marney was spoiled and probably had been since birth. Nancy sighed, but her attention was diverted by the appearance of a young man who stood to attention at her side.

'G-Gervase, w-will you be good enough to introduce me to your partner? I w-would really like to ask her for the next dance.'

He spoke with a slight stammer, which Nancy found oddly endearing. Despite the fact that his evening clothes were well cut and obviously expensive, she could imagine him looking more at ease in tweeds and riding breeches. His fair skin was tanned by the sun, making his blue eyes look even more arresting. He was a complete contrast to Gervase, who was every inch the man about town, polished, handsome and dressed in the latest fashion.

'I didn't know you were here, Freddie,' Gervase slapped him on the back. 'Of course, I'll do the honours. Miss Nancy Sunday, may I introduce my good friend, Viscount Ashton, or Freddie, as those of us who know him call him?'

Felicia eyed the young man over the rim of her champagne flute. 'Are you Lord Dorrington's son?'

Freddie inclined his head in a bow. 'Yes, ma'am. I — I know wh-who you are, of course.'

'Everyone knows Mrs de Marney,' Nancy said hastily. 'How do you do, sir?'

'You call him 'my lord',' Felicia said hastily.

Freddie laughed and his shyness seemed to vanish. 'No, really. Call me Freddie, everyone else does. May I have this dance, Miss Sunday?'

Nancy liked him instantly. He was above average in height, and he held himself as if he were on the parade ground. She smiled inwardly, wondering if the sons of the nobility had to undergo deportment tuition as she had at the Academy. However, his blue eyes were clear and honest as the Devonshire summer skies and although he might not be described as classically handsome, he had good features and a charming smile.

'I'd be delighted, Freddie.'

'No good will come of it, Claude,' Felicia said just loud enough for Nancy to hear. 'She's a foundling and he's the son of an earl. You must put a stop to it immediately.'

8

Freddie led Nancy into an energetic polka, followed by a quadrille and then a waltz. Freddie was not a particularly good dancer, but Nancy found this oddly comforting and they giggled like schoolchildren when they forgot the steps of a country dance.

'I think it's time we made room for the good dancers,' Nancy said, laughing.

'Maybe we should get some refreshment, but I have to t-tell you, N-Nancy, that I haven't enjoyed a b-ball so much ever.' Freddie's smile was so genuine that Nancy wanted to give him a hug, but that would never do and she simply nodded.

'Actually, Freddie, this is my first grand ball. I've attended smaller functions in the country, but never one in London.'

'I usually avoid them,' Freddie confessed, 'but tonight I c-couldn't think of an excuse and now I'm glad. L-let's get some supper and a glass of champagne.'

Nancy craned her neck to get a glimpse of Felicia, who was surrounded by admirers. 'I'm not supposed to leave Mrs de Marney's side in case she needs anything.'

'She's busy at the moment. You need some time off, Nancy. We'll sneak into the refreshment room together.'

Nancy smiled. It was the first whole sentence that Freddie had managed without stuttering and she did not want to spoil the moment.

'On your head be it, Lord Ashton.'

He grinned. 'Just Freddie, please.'

'All right, Freddie. I'm feeling quite reckless, but if Felicia grumbles I will blame you.'

'Precisely.' Freddie linked arms and they made their way to the refreshment room, where they were amongst the first to take their seats. They ate the delicious food and drank champagne, chatting as if they were old friends. Freddie, as Nancy had guessed, was a countryman at heart and he spoke lovingly of the family country seat on the Devonshire and Dorset border.

'W-we're almost neighbours,' Freddie said eagerly. 'It's less than a day's ride to Exeter. I b-believe Rockwood is not far from there.'

'Not too far.' Nancy sipped her glass of punch. 'I really miss home, Freddie. I know working for Felicia is a wonderful opportunity to see a bit of the world but I love Rockwood Castle, even though I'm not really part of the family.'

Freddie's blue eyes were alight with sympathy and he laid his hand on hers as it rested on the table. 'Why do you say that, Nancy?'

'I'm not a Carey. I was a foundling, left on the steps of the orphanage when I was a few days old. I don't know who I really am, Freddie.'

'I'd say that was a bit of an advantage, Nancy. You can make up your family history to be whoever you w-w-wish. You don't have to put up with tiresome aunts and uncles.'

Nancy smiled. 'I suppose you're right, and I really shouldn't complain. Rosie and Patsy have been like sisters to me and the rest of the family have been very kind.' Nancy looked up at the sound of Felicia's angry voice.

'Nancy, what are you doing in here? You should have waited for me —' Felicia broke off, having just noticed Freddie, who was partially hidden by the bulk of a woman wearing a diaphanous Tyrian purple gown with a headdress decorated with ostrich feathers.

Freddie rose to his feet before Felicia had time to say anything further. 'I do apologise, M-Mrs d-de Marney. It's my f-fault entirely.'

Felicia's angry frown was wiped away by a smile. 'That's quite all right, my lord. I was worried when I couldn't find Nancy, that's all.'

'I hope you will join us, ma'am. I can recommend the dressed lobster or —'

Felicia held up her hand. 'Too kind, my lord, but I will eat later. Your papa has asked me to sing and I need Nancy to accompany me.'

'We have a full orchestra, Mrs de Marney. I am sure th-they w-would be honoured to accompany you.'

'No, my lord, I need Nancy. We have rehearsed together and she knows exactly what I like.'

'Of course, ma'am.' Nancy rose to her feet. 'I'll come immediately. You will excuse me, Freddie?'

He jumped to his feet. 'Of course I w-will.'

Gervase emerged from the shadow of the purple lady. 'Ashton, why are you skulking in here? Some of us have been doing our duty on the dance floor, old man.'

Nancy did not wait to hear Freddie's reply as she hurried after Felicia.

'You need to be careful, my girl,' Felicia said angrily. 'Viscount Ashton is so far above you that you would be reaching for the moon if you think you have a conquest there.'

'I don't, ma'am. I was simply enjoying his company. I doubt if I will ever see him again after tonight.'

'And another thing, Gervase North is amusing but he's penniless. You would do better to avoid him also. Don't forget you are working for me now, Nancy. I will sing 'Sempre libera' from La Traviata. We've practised that often enough.'

'Very well, ma'am.'

'Are you sure you can accompany without the sheet music?'

'I know it off by heart, Mrs de Marney. It's one of my favourites.'

'It's a little different from the drinking songs you used to play at Leo Wilder's public house, but you are talented, Nancy. I grant you that. Come now. Let's make ourselves ready to perform.'

Nancy followed Felicia to an anteroom where Lady Dorrington's maid was ready with a hare's foot and powder, at Felicia's request, and a small pot of rouge to tint her cheeks and lips. Nancy stood by waiting for Felicia to make her way onto the middle of the dance floor, having been announced by Lord Dorrington himself. A grand piano had been manoeuvred into position and Nancy sat down on the stool, flexing her fingers as she waited for Felicia to make a short speech announcing her choice of aria. A ripple of appreciation echoed round the huge ballroom and Felicia signalled to Nancy to play the introduction. Out of the corner of her eye, Nancy could see Freddie standing next to Gervase. She resisted the temptation to smile at Freddie and concentrated all her attention on the music.

Felicia was undoubtedly a brilliant performer. Her voice was true and clear with a wide range and a depth of emotion that could make her audience laugh or cry as she chose. Nancy knew the aria well and she played faultlessly. When the final note died away there was a moment of silence and then a burst of applause and shouts of 'Brava, brava.'

Lord Dorrington strolled up to Felicia, arms outstretched. He kissed her on both cheeks and thanked her lavishly. The guests milled onto the dance floor, clamouring to give the diva their thanks and best wishes. Nancy went to join Gervase, who was standing with Claude. There was no sign of Freddie.

'Freddie's mama spirited him away,' Gervase said, grinning. 'I don't think she approved of him paying too much attention to you, Nancy.'

'I'm sure that wasn't the case.' Claude slipped his arm around Nancy's shoulders. 'Any young man would be lucky to have such a lovely partner for the evening. You played magnificently, Nancy. Of course, my darling Felicia will get all the plaudits, but you deserve a vote of thanks too.'

Nancy managed a smile. Suddenly she felt exhausted. The events of the evening had moved so fast that she was feeling quite disorientated.

'They're striking up a waltz,' Gervase said lazily. 'I claim you for this dance, Miss Sunday. After all, you have rather neglected me all evening.'

'That's right. You two young people enjoy the rest of the evening. I'm going to join the gentlemen in the smoking room. Lord Dorrington was generous enough to hand me a very fine cigar.' Claude wandered off, leaving Nancy little alternative but to allow Gervase to lead her back onto the dance floor.

'Freddie's a nice chap, but he's not exactly sparkling company, Nancy. You can do much better for yourself than a viscount whose ambition is to be a country squire, even if he is disgustingly rich.'

'You don't know what you're talking about, Gervase. I am not looking for a wealthy husband.'

'Come now, my love. All young women are on the lookout for a moneyed suitor. But I'm afraid Freddie is already spoken for, in case you're interested. His mama has arranged a match for him with the Duke of Brocklebourne's daughter, Lady Letitia. She looks a bit like a horse and all she's interested in is hunting and shooting, but she's the ideal partner for our Freddie with his st-st-stammer. What normal heiress would want to be tied to such a boring fellow?'

'Why do you have to spoil everything by saying horrid things, Gervase? It was a pleasant evening until now.'

Gervase proffered his hand. 'I'm sorry, I didn't mean to offend you. Of course Freddie is a fine fellow. I was just teasing you.'

Nancy had no answer to this but she allowed him to lead her onto the dance floor. As they whirled around to the strains of a waltz she caught sight of Freddie standing with his mother. Tiny Lady Dorrington seemed to grow in size as she shook her finger at him, and he bowed his head like a naughty schoolboy. Once again Nancy's heart went out to him. He was too nice and too well brought up to argue with his mama, but perhaps it was time that someone stood up to the small termagant. Nancy had seen this sort of behaviour at first-hand when she was just a child and taken into service by the vicar of Rockwood and his wife. Mr Shaw was too wrapped up in godly matters to pay attention to what was going on in his household, and Mrs Shaw, while paying lip service to her husband, was a tyrant when it came to those who served her. Nancy winced at the memory of the cane that Tabitha Shaw had used with grim satisfaction when a servant displeased her in any way.

'I have upset you,' Gervase said apologetically. 'I am a brute. I apologise humbly, Nancy.'

His comical guilty expression made her laugh in spite of everything. 'You flatter yourself, Gervase. I wasn't even thinking of you.'

'Now I am hurt.'

'No, you are not,' Nancy said, laughing. 'I think it would take a lot more than that to upset you. I remember how you behaved at Rockwood Castle. That's something I will never forget.'

'I allowed frustration with my family to get the better of me, Nancy. I bear no grudges against the Careys or anyone at Rockwood.' Gervase glanced over her shoulder. 'I think Claude is signalling to us. It looks as if the diva is planning to leave, no doubt exhausted after her performance this evening. You are being summoned, my dear.'

'Then I'll say goodbye, Gervase. I doubt if we will be seeing much of each other from now on anyway.'

'I wouldn't bet on that,' Gervase said as she walked away.

Nancy chose to ignore him, but as she joined Felicia and Claude in the splendid entrance hall, she saw Freddie hurrying towards them.

'I-I just wanted to th-thank you for your performance, Mrs d-de Marney. It was an unexpected treat.'

Felicia moved towards him, smiling and proffering her hand. 'It was my pleasure, my lord.'

'J-just Freddie, please, ma'am.' He bowed over Felicia's hand, but his gaze travelled to Nancy and his smile was for her alone.

'It was a wonderful evening, Freddie,' Felicia said graciously. 'We would stay but I have to get plenty of rest. I have a performance on Monday evening, I am sure you understand.'

'Of course, ma'am. Perhaps I m-might be permitted to call upon Miss Sunday one afternoon?'

Claude opened his mouth as if to answer, but Felicia shook her head. 'Out of the question, I'm afraid. Nancy has work that keeps her busy most of the time.'

'My love, surely . . .' Claude began, but was silenced by a meaningful look from Felicia.

'The cab seems to have arrived, Claude.' Felicia picked up her skirts and headed for the entrance where a footman stood to attention by the open door. 'Come along, Nancy. Don't dawdle or the cabby might decide to drive on.'

Nancy gave Freddie an apologetic smile as she hurried after Felicia and Claude. 'It was a lovely evening, Freddie.'

He followed her to the doorway. 'I would like to s-see you again, N-Nancy.'

She hesitated. Out of the corner of her eye she could see Gervase hovering in the background. 'I'm taking a cab to Miss Maughfling's Academy in Regent's Park tomorrow morning at ten o'clock. Felicia rarely rises before eleven, unless there is a special rehearsal.'

'I might just be passing your house in John Adam Street at that time.'

'How did you know where we live?'

He tapped the side of his nose and smiled. 'I h-have my s-spies.'

'Nancy, come along.' Felicia's irate voice made Nancy turn with a start and she hurried to join

Claude and Felicia as they climbed into the hackney carriage.

★ ★ ★

Next morning Felicia and Claude left for the theatre without Nancy. They had a meeting with Garson Thorne to discuss a new contract, although Nancy knew that Felicia had been receiving offers from other opera companies. It was likely to be a protracted discussion that did not include Nancy, and at precisely ten o'clock she left the house in John Adam Street with Molly in attendance. Nancy had wanted to visit the Academy to see Tamara on her own, but she knew that she would be in trouble if Felicia discovered that she had been out and about unaccompanied by her maid. Molly hailed a cab and it stopped at the kerb, but a brougham drew to a halt behind it and Freddie leaped out onto the pavement.

'Nancy, come with me.' He held the carriage door open.

'Shall I send the cabby away, miss?' Molly asked anxiously.

Nancy was feeling reckless. She had not taken Freddie seriously when he promised to pick her up that morning, but now he was here she was ridiculously pleased to see him and the brougham would be cramped with three passengers. She opened her reticule and took out a silk purse. She pressed some coins into Molly's hand. 'Take the cab and visit Reuben at Highgate, but be back before I have to go to the theatre with Mrs de Marney this evening.'

'You'll get us both into trouble doing this,' Molly whispered. 'What if she finds out?'

122

'Don't worry. I'll take the blame, now hurry. Tell the cabby where you want to go and enjoy your time with Reuben.'

Nancy went to join Freddie. 'I wasn't sure you'd come,' she said as he helped her into the carriage.

He climbed in and sat beside her. 'I always keep my word. I was afraid you might have left already.'

'You're not stammering, Freddie.'

He grasped her hand. 'I know. It's amazing, but I feel different with you, Nancy. I can't explain it.'

The carriage moved forward and Nancy began to relax. 'I'm glad you came, Freddie.'

'I didn't want you to think that I was ruled by my mother,' he said simply. 'I do respect both my parents, but I am my own man, and I'm over twenty-one.' He glanced at her anxiously. 'I hope you don't think I would take advantage of you, Nancy?'

She smiled and squeezed his fingers. 'That would be the last thing on my mind. Although I don't want you to fall out with your family because of me. I am a nobody, as I told you last evening.'

'You are somebody special in my eyes. I knew that the first moment I saw you.'

'You are so kind, Freddie. But this is a really mad thing to do. I shouldn't have agreed to come with you, and I most certainly should not have sent Molly to Highgate to visit her sweetheart.'

Freddie laughed. 'But you did both those things. I think you are a rebel, Nancy. I'm afraid I've always done exactly what was expected of me. I'm quite a boring fellow.'

'Never. I won't allow you to say that. Look at us now, we've broken all the rules, and if we're discovered we will be in trouble. I will probably be sent home to

Rockwood in disgrace.'

'I didn't consider such an outcome when I came to collect you. I just wanted to get to know you better.'

Nancy smiled and moved a little closer. 'Then let's forget everything else and enjoy our day out.'

'Everyone thinks because I stammer and I love the countryside that I am a dunderhead.'

'I don't believe that for a moment, but if that's what they say they are all stupid.'

Freddie turned to look at her and his smile melted her heart. 'Thank you, Nancy,' he said simply.

She realised that she was still holding his hand, but it felt right somehow and she raised it briefly to her cheek. 'We are both outsiders it seems, Freddie. But that's all right — we can be different together.'

He laughed. 'I like the sound of that.'

'But I have to visit the Academy. I need to see my friend Tamara to make sure that she is all right. You don't mind, do you?'

'Absolutely not. Of course you must visit her. I expect she misses you.'

Nancy explained Tamara's situation while the carriage tooled through the London streets, heading for the Outer Circle of Regent's Park. When it drew up outside the Academy Freddie climbed down first and held out his hand.

'I can't ask you in, Freddie,' Nancy said apologetically. 'It's not allowed, even for you.'

'Being the son of an earl doesn't open as many doors as people might think. I'm happy to wait for you. Take as long as you like.'

'Thank you, Freddie.' Nancy opened the gate and walked up the path.

Watkins opened the door. 'Yes, miss.'

'I want to see Miss Fitzallen, Watkins. Do you know if she's available?'

'Such a to-do, miss. You only just missed her. There was shouting and crying, and Miss Tamara walks out of the door without stopping to put on her cape and bonnet. She was off running as if the devil was after her.'

The sound of footsteps clattering on the tiled floor made Watkins glance over her shoulder.

Miss Franklin pushed past the curious housemaid. 'Oh, it's you, Miss Sunday. I was hoping it was Miss Fitzallen.'

'Watkins says she's run away,' Nancy said anxiously. 'What happened?'

Miss Franklin's grey eyes filled with tears. 'Such a scene, Miss Sunday. Apparently Miss Fitzallen has been having a clandestine relationship with a young man. Her papa arrived less than half an hour ago and he was furious.'

'He was really angry,' Watkins added gloomily.

'Go about your business, Watkins,' Miss Franklin said firmly. 'We don't want the whole of London to know our problems.'

Watkins slouched off, head bent and shoulders hunched.

'What happened, Miss Franklin?' Nancy demanded. 'Why was Tamara so upset?'

'Her papa said he was about to announce her engagement to another gentleman in *The Times*, but she was having none of it, Miss Sunday. I've never seen her so angry or so bold. She faced her papa and told him outright that she was in love with someone called William, and she would never marry anyone else.'

'Oh dear.' Nancy turned to gaze at the expanse of parkland, trees and the shimmer of the lake. 'You don't think she would have done something stupid, do you?'

'Mr Fitzallen has sent his man to search for her and Miss Maughfling has ordered Little to go out and see if he can find her. We're in uproar, Miss Sunday. I've never known anything like it, not even when Miss Smythe was doing her best to break all the rules.'

'I'll see if I can find her first, Miss Franklin. Try not to worry.' Nancy turned on her heel and ran down the path to where Freddie was waiting for her.

'What's wrong, Nancy?' Freddie's brow creased in a frown.

'Tamara has run away. I must find her.'

'I'll help you.' Freddie walked to the front of the vehicle. 'Wait here for us, Mason. W-walk the horse if he gets restive.'

'I understand, my lord.'

Freddie took Nancy by the hand. 'Where do you think she will have gone?'

'She will try to get to Spitalfields, where William works for her father, but she's on foot so we might be able to catch up with her.'

'She has a head start,' Freddie said calmly. 'Do you think she will go through the park, or the side roads?'

'Let's try the park. I think her papa has taken his carriage so he'll go by road.' Nancy grabbed Freddie's hand. 'We'd better hurry.'

They raced through the park, attracting curious stares from passers-by, but Nancy did not care. She was desperate to find Tamara before her father laid hands on her. Having met the gentleman, Nancy did not think he would change his mind easily. Tamara would be forced into a marriage of convenience and her spirit would be broken. If Eleanora had still been sharing a room with Tamara she would have encouraged her to stand up for herself, but Eleanora and Sir Jack Marshall were now officially engaged. Nancy had seen the announcement in a copy of *The Times* that Claude had left on the table in the drawing room.

Nancy and Freddie skirted the boating lake and headed towards a stand of trees in the Inner Circle.

'Just a moment.' Freddie came to a sudden halt. 'Why would she go this way? If she wanted to get to the City she needs to head east.'

Nancy clasped her side as a painful stitch momentarily robbed her of speech. She took a deep breath. 'She isn't thinking straight, Freddie. She's terrified of her papa. I saw that when they were together. All she's thinking about is getting away from him.'

Freddie held up his hand. 'Can you hear that?'

Nancy put her head on one side, trying to catch her breath so that she could listen. She nodded. 'Someone is crying. It could be her.' She broke away from Freddie and ran towards the trees. Curled up on the grass beneath a London plane tree, Tamara looked like a broken flower. Nancy rushed up to her and went down on her knees, wrapping her arms around her sobbing friend.

'It's all right, Tamara. I'm here to help you.'

Tamara looked up and trembled at the sight of Freddie. 'Who's that?'

'Freddie is a friend. We've been searching for you.'

'I'm not going back to the Academy, and I'm not going home either.'

Freddie produced a clean white cotton handkerchief and passed it to Nancy.

'Don't cry, Tamara,' Nancy said, mopping away her friend's tears. 'We're not going to make you do anything you don't wish to do. Just tell us exactly what your papa said.'

'He's arranged it all. He's announced my engagement to Sir Dudley Cholmondeley and the first of the banns will be called next week.'

Nancy exchanged worried glances with Freddie. 'What can we do for her? How can we help?'

Freddie kneeled on the ground beside Tamara. 'Is there anywhere you could go where you would feel safe?'

'My cousin Baldwin lives in Doughty Street. He might help.'

'Wait here and I'll fetch my carriage. We'll take you to your cousin. That's a start.' Freddie stood up. 'Will you be all right here, Nancy?'

She smiled. 'Of course, we will. You go, Freddie, and please hurry.'

'I'll be back before you know it.' Freddie rushed off, leaving Nancy to comfort Tamara, who was clearly terrified of her father, and worried about what he might do to William. Nancy did her best to soothe Tamara's fears, but it took some time, and Nancy breathed a sigh of relief when she saw the carriage, only this time Freddie was on the driver's seat. He drew the horse to a halt and leaped to the ground. 'Let's get you inside, Tamara, and you, Nancy.'

She waited until Tamara was seated. 'Where's the coachman?'

'I sent him home in a cab. The fewer people who know about this the better. But don't worry,' Freddie added, grinning, 'I'm used to handling the reins.'

'But you'll be seen driving your own vehicle,

128

Freddie. Won't tongues wag?'

'Everyone thinks I'm a bit eccentric because I'm a countryman at heart and I don't conform to their idea of what an earl's son should be. They won't think it strange at all.'

Nancy climbed into the brougham and sat down beside Tamara. 'Don't be afraid. I'm sure we can work things out between us. You told me before that Baldwin is a nice man.'

'Yes, I had hopes that you and he might make a match. I'm very fond of Baldwin, but I think you've already found your heart's desire.'

'Do you mean Freddie?' Nancy turned away as she felt a blush flooding her cheeks. 'I've only just met him. I like him, of course, who would not? But we hardly know each other.'

'I knew at once when I first met William,' Tamara said dreamily. 'If I can't marry him, I won't marry anyone, least of all Sir Dudley.'

'Don't upset yourself again. I'm sure we can make your papa understand, given time.'

'I hope Baldwin is at home. I don't know what I'll do if he is out or, worse still, away on a visit.'

★ ★ ★

The maid who opened the door in Doughty Street told them that Mr Fitzallen was at home, although he was about to leave for an appointment. Tamara insisted that she wanted to see him and, somewhat reluctantly, the maid showed Nancy and Tamara into the parlour, leaving Freddie to wait outside with the brougham. Baldwin stood in front of a wall mirror, admiring his reflection as he set his top hat on at a rakish angle. However, the moment he saw Tamara's distress he abandoned his hat and rushed to her side.

'You'd better sit down and tell me what's wrong,' he said anxiously. 'Please take a seat also, Miss . . . ?'

'This is my good friend Nancy Sunday, Baldwin.' Tamara sank down on the crimson-velvet upholstered sofa. 'I don't know what I would have done if she hadn't found me in the park.' She buried her face in Freddie's already sodden hanky.

'What is she talking about, Miss Sunday?' Baldwin's brown eyes were wide with concern.

'You'd better explain, Tamara,' Nancy said firmly. 'Tell your cousin about William and the man your papa wants you to marry.'

Baldwin looked from one to the other. 'Are you talking about William Russell, my uncle's head clerk? I've met him once or twice. He seems like a decent enough fellow.'

'He is a fine man, Baldwin. I love him, but Papa insists that I must marry an old man. A rich old man. I'd rather jump off London Bridge and drown in the Thames.'

'Steady on, old girl. There's no need to be so dramatic.'

'I can't go home, Baldwin. May I stay here with you and Aunt Flora?'

'You'll have to ask Mama, but you're very welcome as far as I'm concerned.'

Tamara's hand flew to cover her mouth. 'Oh, Nancy. I've forgotten poor Annie. I left her at the Academy with all my things.'

'Don't worry. If your aunt says you may stay here, Freddie and I will go to the Academy and collect Annie and your baggage. Perhaps you'd better ask

Mrs Fitzallen first.'

'Mama will probably agree,' Baldwin said confidently. 'She loves to spike Uncle Hubert's guns whenever she gets the opportunity. Anyway, if you'll excuse me, ladies, I'm already late for my appointment. I'll send the maid to fetch Mama if you would like to wait here.' He picked up his top hat and gloves. 'I'll see you later, Tamara.' He left the room, closing the door behind him.

'Do you get on well with your aunt?' Nancy asked anxiously.

'Yes, I think so. We've never had cross words if that's what you mean. I don't know whether she would approve of me marrying William. She might feel the same as Papa.'

They lapsed into silence, apart from the occasional sniff from Tamara and the incessant ticking of the brass clock on the mantelshelf. Minutes later the door opened and a woman dressed in deep mourning glided into the room. She took one look at Tamara and pulled up a chair.

'Tell me all about it, my dear. I can see that you're upset, but first you must introduce me to your friend.'

Nancy could see that Tamara was struggling with a fresh bout of tears and she bobbed a curtsey. 'How do you do, ma'am. I'm Nancy Sunday and I was at Miss Maughfling's Academy with Tamara.'

'I suppose this is all about that nice young man who works for my brother-in-law.' Mrs Fitzallen laid her hand on Tamara's shoulder. 'Tell me what's happened, my dear.'

Words tumbled from Tamara's lips, punctuated by sobs, and occasionally Mrs Fitzallen looked to Nancy for translation.

'Well, there's a pickle for you,' Mrs Fitzallen said slowly when Tamara finished speaking.

'Might she stay here for a while?' Nancy asked boldly. 'Just until the matter is settled.'

'Yes, of course she may. There's no question of that. I will give my brother-in-law a stern talking-to for handling the affair so badly.'

'I won't marry Sir Dudley,' Tamara cried passionately. 'I don't care what Papa says or does.'

'My husband died five years ago and I still wear full mourning,' Mrs Fitzallen said sadly. 'If you truly love this young man, I think every attempt should be made to make the match possible, but your papa is not an easy man to persuade.'

'But you will help me, Aunt Flora?'

'Indeed I will. But practical things first. We must send for your things.'

'My maid is still at the Academy, Aunt Flora.'

'She's welcome here, too. I've forgone the luxury of a lady's maid since my husband passed away, but it would be handy to have someone to care for me as well as you.'

'Freddie and I will go to the Academy now, Tamara,' Nancy said hastily. 'We'll bring Annie and your things, but if we should cross paths with your papa, what shall I say?'

Mrs Fitzallen rose to her feet. 'You may tell my brother-in-law that his daughter is safe with me in Doughty Street and I want a word with him.'

★ ★ ★

Freddie was waiting patiently with the horse and brougham. He climbed down from the box to help Nancy into the carriage.

'Tamara needs her things from the Academy and her maid, Annie. Would you mind, Freddie?'

'Of course not. I'm glad she has somewhere to stay.' Freddie held onto her hand rather longer than necessary. 'This isn't how I imagined our day out would be, Nancy.'

She laughed. 'Nor I. I'm sorry if I've ruined it for you, Freddie.'

'On the contrary — it's been an adventure.'

'Unfortunately I'll have to return to John Adam Street when we've delivered Tamara's things to Doughty Street.'

'I'm not going to let you get away so easily.' He raised her hand to his lips, meeting her gaze with a genuine smile. 'There's always tomorrow, Nancy.'

9

Nancy was in the drawing room next day, seated by the window. Felicia and Claude had gone to the theatre after luncheon, but when Nancy offered to accompany them Felicia had been sharp in her refusal. Nancy had been puzzled, but she was used to Felicia's temperament and she forgot all about it, choosing to spend a few hours on her own. She needed to think of a way in which to help Tamara, but Freddie's parting words had left her hoping to see him again today. However, as time wore on, she was beginning to think he had either forgotten or that he had not meant his comment to be taken seriously. Perhaps that was the way society people behaved in London, although she had thought Freddie was different from the rest of his set.

When Felicia and Claude finally returned late that afternoon Nancy had been trying to take her mind off her problems by reading a book she had found on the shelf, but she had only managed three pages so far, and already she had forgotten the title.

Felicia's expression was ominous. She tossed her reticule on the sofa. 'Garson will regret his decision when he's had time to consider it, Claude.'

'I still think you should have allowed me to speak to him, man to man, my love.'

Nancy put the book on the table beside her. 'What's happened, ma'am?'

Felicia threw up her hands and sank down on the

sofa. 'I don't want to talk about it, but put it this way, Nancy: we won't be staying in London for Christmas. In fact, I've a good mind to spend the festive season at Rockwood, and that is saying something about the way I feel right now.'

'The terms offered by Mr Thorne were not acceptable, Nancy,' Claude said simply.

'He forgets that I am an international star. I refuse to be upstaged by a nobody. Who is this Carlotta Corvi anyway? The girl is my understudy, totally inexperienced in handling a major role.' Felicia pointed to the bell pull. 'Ring for the maid, Claude. I need a glass of sherry wine to calm my nerves. I shouldn't be put through this sort of ordeal when I have a performance to give this evening.'

'Of course, my love.' Claude reached for the bell pull and tugged it twice. 'You were magnificent, you put your point of view succinctly.'

'We've already started rehearsals for the next production and I am the leading lady.'

'I don't think Garson was left with any doubts as to your feelings. But you will finish the season, won't you?'

'Of course I will. I won't disappoint the people who pay good money to see me and hear me sing. I have a duty to my public.'

Nancy rose to her feet. 'Perhaps a rest on your bed might help, ma'am.'

'I will lie there going over and over it in my mind. A glass of sherry will be more efficacious.'

'If we return to Rockwood, does that mean we'll be leaving London for good?' Nancy asked anxiously.

'That's really none of your concern, Nancy.' Felicia lay back on the cushions and closed her eyes. 'My head is throbbing. Send for Violet. I need a cold compress.'

Rawlings, the housemaid they had inherited with the rented accommodation, entered the parlour without waiting for an answer to her sharp rap on the door.

'You rang, miss?'

'Mrs de Marney would like sherry wine. Please find Miss Tinker and ask her to bring a cold compress.'

Rawlings' already thin lips tightened to a straight line, but she acknowledged the instructions with a nod and walked off with a measured tread. Nancy had never liked Rawlings and she knew that the feeling was mutual. However, she was too anxious to worry about whether or not she was popular below stairs. It seemed as though their tenure in John Adam Street was coming to an end, but if they were to leave London she might never see Freddie again and that would be very sad.

'Nancy, what are you doing?' Felicia's plaintive voice brought Nancy back to the present with a jolt.

'I've just instructed Rawlings to bring you some sherry, ma'am. And I told her to send Violet with a cold compress.'

'What would I do without you, Nancy?' Felicia held up a shaking hand. 'Come and sit by me and tell me what you've been doing today.'

Nancy pulled up a stool and sat down. 'Nothing much, ma'am. But it sounds as if you have had a very testing time.'

'That man Thorne has given himself airs above his station. He more or less told me that I am too old to play the leading role, and I should step down and play the matriarch to Carlotta Corvi as the heroine. It is I who draws in the crowds that pay his salary. I have offers from far and wide, isn't that so, Claude?'

'Well, my love, not at the moment. Although La Scala, Milan, is a possibility for next season.'

'They love me in New York,' Felicia said dreamily. 'I triumphed there, didn't I, Claude?'

'You are a brilliant success wherever you perform, my love.'

'Well, I am not taking second place to Carlotta. Garson will come begging me to return when she fails to draw the crowds.'

Nancy sighed. 'I am so sorry, Mrs de Marney.'

'We will have to return to Rockwood for Christmas,' Felicia said tearfully. 'But I forbid you to tell anyone the real reason. We will say that the doctor has ordered me to rest.'

'Everyone will understand.' Claude eyed her warily. 'Don't upset yourself, my dear.'

'I want you to check with New York, Claude. We could sail for America as soon as possible in the New Year if you succeed in getting a booking.'

'Milan is a possibility, Felicia. New York have not made any definite offers.'

'Then make sure they do, Claude. You are my manager as well as my husband. Do I have to do everything myself?'

Nancy could see a full-scale row brewing, but fortunately Rawlings arrived with a decanter of sherry and three glasses, followed by Violet with the cold compress and a bottle of sal volatile.

Nancy chose the interruption to make her escape and she went to her room. It was a few short weeks until the end of the season, and then a pantomime would take the stage at the opera house. She had been looking forward to a brief visit to Rockwood, but now with the sudden change in Felicia's fortunes, it looked as if their return home might be permanent. The upheaval could not have come at a worse time. Nancy was beginning to enjoy being in London and getting to know Freddie, not that there could ever be anything romantic between them. Nancy was well aware of her own unsuitability to marry into the aristocracy. She did not need Gervase to keep reminding her of her uncertain origins and probable illegitimacy. She changed out of her day clothes into something more suitable to wear to the theatre. Although there was little she could do, Felicia expected her to be there, ready to run errands or to fetch coffee in between acts. As she dressed, Nancy thought of Tamara, whose future was even more uncertain than her own. If Mr Fitzallen could not be persuaded to accept the fact that his daughter was in love with William Russell, there was little anyone could do to help the star-crossed lovers.

★   ★   ★

An hour later, with Felicia fortified by several glasses of sherry and the application of the cold compress, Nancy accompanied them to the opera house. Claude stayed in the dressing room with his wife while she applied her stage makeup and her costume, and Nancy kept Felicia supplied with cups of coffee and a glass of seltzer for the headache brought on by drinking sherry on an empty stomach. Then there were messages that Felicia liked to send to her leading man and anyone else who came to mind, including Mrs Lake, the wardrobe mistress. During the interval Nancy had just collected a garment from Wardrobe that had been mended after it had split at the seams, when she almost collided with someone in the dimly lit, narrow passageway.

'Nancy, is that you?'

'Freddie. What are you doing backstage?'

'Looking for you, of course. I had to bribe the doorkeeper to let me in.'

'I'm not surprised. Is anything wrong?'

'On the contrary, I just wanted to see you.'

Nancy laughed. 'We saw each other yesterday.'

'I know, and I intended to visit you this morning, but I had arrangements to make.'

'Arrangements? That sounds exciting.'

'I had to make sure that Mama hadn't invited all and sundry to our country estate for the festive season.' Freddie produced a sealed letter from his pocket. 'It's addressed to Mr and Mrs de Marney and Miss Nancy Sunday. My father was so impressed with Mrs de Marney's singing that he's written personally to invite you all to spend Christmas at Dorrington Place. We always have a huge house party, which I generally detest, but if you come it will be different.'

'Really? That's wonderful, but I think Felicia wishes to go to Rockwood Castle.'

'Do you think you could persuade her to change her mind? We're less than a day's ride to Rockwood.'

'I think you should give her the invitation in person, Freddie. She's a bit down at the moment because she's had a difference of opinion with the theatre manager, and she has no further engagements booked.'

'Excellent,' Freddie pulled a face. 'I didn't mean that to sound unfeeling, Nancy. But Papa would be prepared to offer a fee if she were to give a single performance for the guests.'

'Come and see her for yourself, Freddie. It will

sound much better coming from you.'

'Of course. I'll use my ch-charm.'

'Don't be nervous. Mrs de Marney won't eat you. Anyway, I must get this costume to her. She needs it for the next act.' Nancy led the way through the maze of corridors to Felicia's dressing room.

'Where have you been?' Felicia demanded crossly. 'You could have walked to John Adam Street and back in the time you've taken.' Her glance fell on Freddie and she managed a smile. 'My lord, how nice of you to seek me out.'

Freddie acknowledged her with a polite bow. 'I hope I-I'm not d-disturbing you, ma'am.'

'Not at all, do come in. Nancy, pull up a chair for Lord Ashton.'

'F-Freddie, please.' He produced the sealed letter and handed it to her. 'F-from my papa, Mrs d-de Marney. I h-hope you w-will accept the invitation.'

Felicia tore it open and scanned the contents. When she looked up her face was wreathed in a wide smile. 'How perfectly lovely. What a charming note. Of course we will be delighted to accept.' She handed the paper to Claude. 'Won't we, my darling?'

Claude studied it for a moment. 'You will be expected to perform, my love.'

'Of course I will.' Felicia stepped behind the screen. 'Help me to change, Nancy. I don't know where my dresser has gone.'

Nancy did as she was asked and fastened Felicia into the tight-fitting costume.

'Ouch,' Felicia said crossly. 'You're worse than that woman. She always manages to pinch my flesh. Lake must have taken this garment in at the seams, it's too tight.'

'I'll loosen it a little.' Nancy began to untie the laces but Felicia pushed her away. 'I need to look young and slender, but if I faint from being constricted so tightly I will have Lake sacked. You may tell Garson that from me, Claude.'

'I should go,' Freddie said hastily. 'I need to t-take my seat for the s-second act.'

Felicia emerged from behind the screen. 'Do thank the earl for his kind invitation. I will, of course, reply in writing when I get a moment.' She spun round to face Nancy. 'You may take the rest of the evening off, my dear. I'm sure that Lord Ashton would enjoy your company.'

'He might have come with others, ma'am.'

'N-no,' Freddie said hastily. 'I c-came on my own. M-my family have reserved a box for the season.'

Felicia treated him to the full beam of her most engaging smile. 'Then you may take Nancy to enjoy the rest of the performance.'

Nancy murmured her thanks as she left the dressing room accompanied by Freddie. 'I'm sorry about that, Freddie.'

He took her by the hand. 'Why? I'm delighted to have your company for the next hour or two.'

There was no time to reply as they hurried through the passageways and up the stairs to the main part of the theatre. Freddie led the way to the family box and opened the door.

'I have a surprise for you, Nancy.'

She stepped into the luxurious box with a commanding view of the stage, and to her surprise she saw Tamara seated next to Mrs Fitzallen. Nancy turned to Freddie with a delighted smile.

'You arranged this, Freddie?'

He nodded. 'I did.'

Tamara rose to her feet. 'Lord Ashton has been so kind, hasn't he, Aunt Flora?'

'He has indeed, and there's more to come, Tamara. I didn't tell you earlier but Freddie has another surprise for you.'

'Yes, I had to work quickly, but there's someone you may wish to see, Tamara.' Freddie stepped outside for a moment. 'Come in, sir.'

Nancy stood aside. She knew instinctively what Freddie had done and it was all she could do to refrain from hugging him. She watched Tamara's expression change when she realised that it was her beloved William who was the unexpected guest.

'William.' Tamara glanced nervously over her shoulder as if expecting her father to materialise from nowhere. 'I don't know what to say, but thank you, Freddie.'

William clutched both her hands and raised them to his lips. 'Your papa has forbidden me to see you again, Tamara, but I couldn't keep away.'

Nancy drew them aside. 'I happen to know that the box next door is free this evening. I know the attendant so if you would like to be private for a while, I'll make sure you are not disturbed.'

William turned to her with a grateful smile. 'Thank you, Nancy. And thank you, my lord, for making this possible. Heaven alone knows when I'll be able to see Tamara again.'

'Quite so,' Mrs Fitzallen said impatiently. 'You're wasting time. Do as Nancy suggests, both of you. I shouldn't condone such behaviour, but on this occasion I agree with Nancy and Freddie. My brother-in-law is being unreasonable.'

'Thank you, ma'am.' William bowed to her before ushering Tamara from the box.

'I'll make sure they have some privacy.' Nancy stepped outside and went in search of the attendant. By this time she knew most of the permanent staff, both backstage and front of house, and she had often exchanged pleasantries with the man on duty that evening, who had a daughter of a similar age to Tamara. He was unsure at first, but Nancy was persuasive and in the end he agreed to turn a blind eye. Nancy returned to Freddie's box with an easy mind.

'You've both been so kind to Tamara,' Mrs Fitzallen said earnestly. 'She is lucky to have such good friends.'

Nancy sat down next to Freddie. 'Do you think your brother-in-law will relent, Mrs Fitzallen?'

'I doubt it. I don't want to sound pessimistic, but I know Hubert of old and he is not the sort of man who gives in easily. He wants his daughter to marry well, and who can blame him? But to force her to wed a man so much older than herself is harsh, to say the least.'

At that moment the conductor tapped his baton on the music stand and the orchestra began to play. The lights were dimmed and the buzz of conversation from the auditorium died away as the curtains were drawn back to reveal the stage illuminated by gaslight. Freddie reached out to hold Nancy's hand and she glanced nervously at Mrs Fitzallen, but she was enthralled by the action on the stage, and seemingly oblivious to anything going on around her. Nancy knew that Felicia would not approve of such forward conduct but she did not care. She curled her fingers around Freddie's hand and settled down to enjoy the rest of the performance.

When the final curtain went down Nancy sighed. It had been a delightful interlude but now she must interrupt the tryst in the next box. She went to knock on the door and when there was no answer she opened it and looked inside. She rushed back to Freddie and Mrs Fitzallen.

'They've gone. There's no one in the box.'

Mrs Fitzallen threw up her hands. 'Oh, no. Hubert will be furious if they've run away together.'

Nancy turned to Freddie. 'Did you know what William planned? Were you party to this, Freddie?'

He shook his head. 'No, on my honour, I only arranged for William to be present. I didn't know that he had other ideas.'

'I assisted them by suggesting that they have some time alone together,' Nancy said sadly. 'I'm sorry, Mrs Fitzallen.'

'What's the matter?' Tamara's voice from the doorway made them all turn with a start. 'Why are you looking so worried?'

'Where have you been?' Nancy demanded. 'We thought you and William had eloped.'

'It was tempting,' Tamara said with a smile. 'But William came to tell me that he has found another position in the City with better pay and prospects. I went to the foyer with him, but I said goodbye and came back straight away.'

Mrs Fitzallen clutched her hands to her bosom, closing her eyes. 'Please don't give me a fright like that again, Tamara. Your papa would never speak to me again if I allowed you to do anything rash.'

Nancy glanced at Freddie. There was something about his innocent look that made her suspicious.

144

'Do you know anything about that, Freddie?'

'Me? Of course not. I dare say William had his eye set on a better position all along. We should give the man credit for trying.'

Mrs Fitzallen reached for her cape. 'I think it's time we went home, Tamara. Perhaps your papa will change his mind about William in the light of recent events.'

'I won't marry the man Papa has chosen for me. I will elope with William if there is no choice, although I would far rather marry him with the approval of my family.'

'I believe the company that William will be working for is very reputable,' Freddie said innocently.

'I don't think anyone mentioned where he will be employed,' Nancy said in a low voice as Tamara and Mrs Fitzallen left the box. 'You had something to do with this, didn't you, Freddie?'

'Of course not. I never interfere in other people's lives.'

Nancy tucked her hand in the crook of his arm. 'Why don't I believe you?'

'I have no idea. I think we should all go out to supper to celebrate. What do you think, Nancy?'

'In my opinion you are very clever, Lord Ashton. Forgive me if I don't believe a word of what you just said, but I would love to go out to supper. I really don't want to go back to John Adam Street just yet.'

'Don't worry about Mrs de Marney. She'll be the toast of the house party at Christmas. My father will make sure that she is kept very busy entertaining the guests.'

★　★　★

The prospect of being entertained at one of the grandest houses in England overcame Felicia's anger and distress at being side-lined by a younger up-and-coming star of the opera world. Bertha Bannister was called upon to complete the garments already ordered and to make several more outfits for Felicia. The poor seamstress was in tears at the end of her visit to John Adam Street.

'What's the matter, Miss Bannister?' Nancy asked gently. 'I thought you would be happy to have more business put your way.'

Miss Bannister mopped her eyes with a scrap of material. 'Of course, miss, but I have only one pair of hands and even if I work all night every night I will never get the gowns finished in time.'

'You had this problem before. I thought you would take on another seamstress to help you.'

'I let you think that, miss, but the truth is I can't afford to pay anyone. Mrs de Marney is like a lot of my clients — she doesn't settle her account for a few weeks, and in that time I could be evicted from my lodgings for not paying the rent.'

'But I thought you were living above Mr Wilkins's shop. Surely he wouldn't turn you out?'

'My dear mother passed away and Jedidiah thought it unseemly for me to stay on. He found me the new lodgings, which are nice, but when my clients don't pay on time I find myself in difficulties.'

'That's very serious. If I had any money I would pay you myself.'

'I shouldn't have said anything, miss. It's not fair to burden you with my troubles.'

'You know that I'm good with my needle, Miss Bannister. I helped you before and I can do so again.

After all, it will be to my advantage.'

'I couldn't do that, miss. What would Mrs de Marney say if she found out?'

'What she doesn't know won't hurt her, as Hester used to keep telling me.'

'Hester?'

'It doesn't matter. She's someone back at home in Devonshire. Now I want you to bring any unfinished garments to me. I will take some of the sewing to the theatre with me.' Nancy held up her hand as she saw Miss Bannister was about to protest. 'I've done it before and they were used to seeing me sewing when I helped Mrs Lake, so please don't worry.'

'I don't know, miss. It doesn't seem fair. I will be paid for something I haven't done.'

'Nonsense. You will have completed the most difficult part in the cutting and tacking. I will simply sew seams. I find it quite restful, as it happens.'

'It would help, but only if you're sure . . .'

'I am absolutely certain, and I'll do my best to see that your bill is paid on time. Mr de Marney is very good that way. I know he settles the household accounts on a regular basis.'

Miss Bannister clasped Nancy's hands in hers. 'Thank you, miss. I don't know what I would have done had you not offered to help.'

'There you are then. It will give me something to do instead of sitting idly while I wait for Mrs de Marney to call upon my services.'

Miss Bannister left for her rented room in Wych Street, returning an hour later with a carefully wrapped bundle, which she placed into Nancy's hands. She gave detailed instructions as to what needed doing and Nancy took the garment to her room where she unwrapped and examined it. The shimmering silk in a rich peacock blue ran through her fingers like water and the basic shape of the gown was tacked ready for stitching. Nancy packed it up again and took it with her to the theatre that evening. She found a quiet spot in Wardrobe and worked on it until Felicia sent the call boy to fetch her. When they left the theatre after the performance Nancy hid the bundle beneath her cape and took it back to John Adam Street, where she sewed fine seams until late into the night.

Next morning, her work finished, Nancy decided to take the garment to Miss Bannister's lodgings. She had considered sending Molly, but Wych Street was not far from the notorious Clare Market and Nancy had first-hand experience of that area. It did not seem fair to send Molly, a country girl born and bred, into such a potentially dangerous situation. Nancy decided it would be quicker and safer if she went alone. But when she was only halfway along the narrow street lined with overhanging Elizabethan houses squashed between pubs and brothels, she was beginning to regret her decision. However, it was fairly easy to find Miss Bannister's lodging house and Nancy handed over the finished garment. Miss Bannister begged her to stay until she was ready to go out, so that she could make sure Nancy reached home safely, but Nancy had to be at the theatre and she insisted that she was perfectly capable of getting there without mishap.

Nancy noticed a group of young street urchins loitering in a nearby doorway but she walked past them with a confident step. However, she had not gone far when she realised that she was being followed and she quickened her pace. The footsteps behind her were getting closer and Nancy changed direction, hoping

to throw them off. Instead of heading towards the theatre, she chose to lose them in the busy streets around
Clare Market, but her plan failed and she could hear
them baying like hounds in pursuit of a fox. She was
alone in alien territory and they were closing in on
her.

10

Nancy forced herself to keep calm. She was about to turn on her pursuers and demand that they leave her alone when to her intense relief she spotted Jedidiah Wilkins's cart. The smell of rancid meat would have led her straight to it anyway, and she began to run. She almost bumped into Jedidiah as he emerged from a tavern, his leather apron bloodstained and his hands red with blood and grease.

He took in the situation with a single glance and raised his fist, shaking it at the boys, who turned tail and ran.

'What are you doing round here, Miss Nancy? I thought you'd learned your lesson.'

'I am so glad to see you, Jedidiah. I was trying to get to the theatre and I took a wrong turn because I knew I was being followed.'

'I've delivered my last order this morning. I'll see you safe to the theatre.' Jedidiah handed her onto the driver's seat and climbed up to sit beside her. He took the reins and flicked the whip over the horse's ears. 'What was you doing in this area anyway, miss?'

'I was taking some work to Miss Bannister. She has several creations to complete for Mrs de Marney and I was helping out.'

'You was?' Jedidiah turned his head to gaze at Nancy in surprise. 'That was good of you, miss.'

'She works so hard, and gets very little in return when you think of the long hours she spends sewing.

She often works all night, most probably by the light of a single candle. She's such a nice lady.'

'She is indeed.'

'It's a hard life for a single lady with limited means.' Nancy shot him a sideway glance. 'I'm surprised that no one has snapped her up and married her.'

'Do you mean me, miss?'

'I think you like her a lot, Jedidiah.'

'Which is true, but a lady like Miss Bannister wouldn't want anything to do with a rough fellow like me.'

'You don't know that for certain. I think she likes you, too.'

'Even if that was true, what could I offer her but rooms above the shop, and smells and grease what goes with my trade.'

'But I understand she rented a room from you until recently, so she can't mind too much.'

'That was when her old ma was still alive, miss. When the old woman passed away recently I didn't think it was proper for a lady like Miss Bannister to stay on.'

'There was a simple remedy, Jedidiah. You could have proposed marriage.'

Jedidiah snorted with laughter. 'And what d'you think she would have said to such a proposition?'

'There's only one way to find out,' Nancy said, smiling. 'And I can't help you with that.'

He reined in his old horse outside the theatre. 'I got no prospects other than my business in Clare Market. That ain't no life for a lady like Bertha.'

Nancy was about to climb down from the cart but she hesitated. 'Would you consider moving to the country, Jedidiah?'

'If the opportunity arose I'd be there like an arrow from a bow, but that ain't likely to happen.'

'You never know what's coming next. Maybe your luck will change. Anyway, thank you for saving me yet again, Jedidiah. I am very much in your debt.'

'Stay away from the backstreets, miss. Give my respects to Miss Bannister when you see her next.' Jedidiah flicked the reins. 'Walk on.'

Nancy watched him drive away. An idea occurred to her, but there was nothing she could do about it until she returned to Rockwood Castle. The draw of home was strong these days and she longed to have Rosie to confide in, or even Patsy, although the latter was not always the most sympathetic person in the world. Nancy walked round to the stage door and entered the theatre, wondering what upsets the day would provide.

She could hear Felicia's raised voice even before she reached the dressing room. Garson Thorne emerged scowling ominously. He brushed past Nancy without saying a word and stomped off towards the auditorium. Nancy opened the door and narrowly missed being hit by one of Felicia's shoes, which she had hurled with some force. Nancy bent down and retrieved it.

'What's going on?'

'That man is impossible. Well, I told him I won't be treated like this. I'm the prima donna, not that upstart of a girl. We're leaving, Claude. I refuse to sing another note for that man.'

'But, my love, don't be too hasty,' Claude said softly. 'We've been through this before. You will harm your career if you walk out now.'

'I don't care,' Felicia sobbed. 'As if it weren't bad enough to be upstaged by that — that Corvi woman — I've just seen the playbills and her name is in letters so much larger than mine have ever been. I'm doubly insulted.'

'Rise above such trivialities, my pet. When Garson's protégée proves to be a mere shadow of you, he will learn to regret his decision. Until then you are the prima donna, as you quite rightly said. You must not disappoint your public, my love. Finish the season as we agreed — after all, it's only another week or so — and then we are invited to Dorrington Place. Forget Garson Thorne and his opera company — the world awaits you, my love.'

Felicia shrugged and slumped down on the stool in front of her dressing table. 'I suppose you're right. I must rise above such pettiness, but he will live to regret treating me as if I were a member of the chorus. Nancy, fetch me a cup of coffee.' Felicia opened a drawer and took out a silver flask. 'A tot of brandy will help to calm my nerves.'

Nancy made her escape. There was a coffee stall in the street near to the theatre, patronised by the backstage staff and performers alike. Nancy bought two mugs of coffee and took them to Claude and Felicia, who was holding the flask to her lips and sipping brandy with obvious enjoyment.

'I won't need you until this evening, Nancy,' Felicia said, smiling tipsily. 'You may take the rest of the day to do whatever you wish. I will drink my coffee and then you may take me back to John Adam Street, Claude. I will rest until this evening's performance. They don't need me at rehearsals now.'

'I'll take you home as soon as you feel well enough, my love.'

'I am still the star of the show, Claude. I won't be

treated in such a cavalier fashion.'

Nancy left the dressing room, not wishing to be drawn into the argument. She knew that Claude was right, but she sympathised with Felicia. It was a humiliating situation for anyone to be in.

Nancy collected her outdoor things and was about to leave the theatre when she saw Gervase strolling towards her. She hoped he had not spotted her, but he stopped and tipped his top hat.

'My dear Nancy, I was hoping to see you.'

'I'm in a hurry, Gervase. I have an appointment.'

He leaned on his silver-headed cane. 'Now let me see. Would that be Ashton, by any chance?'

'As a matter of fact I am going to spend the afternoon with Freddie. He's taking me to the zoological gardens.' It was not strictly true, although Freddie had mentioned that it would be a pleasant way to spend an afternoon if Nancy had any free time. She eyed him curiously. 'Did you come to see Felicia? If you did, it's probably not the best time.'

'Really? That sounds interesting. Tell me more.'

'It's Felicia's business. You must ask her if you wish to know, although I wouldn't advise it.'

'That makes me even more curious. I was hoping to find out when you were planning on returning to Rockwood. I assume you will all be going there for Christmas.'

'Even if we were, I doubt if you would be invited, especially after your outburst when we were last there.'

'I was thinking of spending Christmas at Greystone Park.'

'But it's been closed up since Sylvia left for Switzerland. Has she come home?'

'Not to my knowledge, but I am challenging my

cousins' right to the estate.' Gervase fell into step beside her as Nancy walked off in the direction of John Adam Street. She had hoped he might stay behind and take his chances with Felicia, but he seemed determined to follow her.

'How are you doing that, Gervase? I believe Sir Michael left it to his daughters in his will. Your mama was his younger sister, was she not?'

'That is correct.'

'So you are not in line for the inheritance.'

'But I am the only surviving male Greystone. I intend to challenge my uncle's will, even if I have to spend the next few years doing so.'

Nancy walked a little faster. 'I wish you good luck with that, but I think Christina will fight you through the courts if you try to take Greystone Park away from her and her sister.'

'I look forward to a battle royal. I will have Greystone Park for myself. I want you to know that, Nancy.'

They reached the Strand and Nancy came to a halt. 'As I said, I wish you well, but it really has nothing to do with me. I don't want to hold you up, Gervase. I'm sure you have better things to do than stand here chatting to me.'

'Not at all. I think I'll accompany you and Ashton to the zoological gardens. It will make a change from the dreary round of gentlemen's clubs and luncheons in expensive restaurants.'

There seemed to be nothing that Nancy could say to deter Gervase from his purpose. He insisted on accompanying her and Freddie, despite her lack of enthusiasm. Now she would have to think of a valid reason for Freddie's failure to turn up. However, she was saved from embarrassment when they arrived at John Adam Street to find Freddie standing at the front door.

Nancy thought quickly. 'Freddie, you're early. I was just telling Gervase that we had arranged to visit the zoological gardens this afternoon.'

Freddie met her anxious gaze with his slightly lopsided smile. 'Th-then it's fortunate I w-was early. I th-thought we might take a picnic.'

Gervase stared at him in amazement. 'Ashton, old chap, it's December. It's cold and it might even snow. Are you quite mad?'

Freddie indicated a wicker hamper at his feet. 'F-Fortnum and Mason's best, Gervase. S-Scotch eggs and g-game pie. H-hothouse peaches. What more could you ask for?'

'I think it's a lovely idea, Freddie,' Nancy said enthusiastically. 'I'm sure we can find shelter somewhere, even if the weather turns nasty. What a pity you don't like the outdoors, Gervase. Of course you won't want to join us.'

For once Gervase seemed to be lost for words. He took a step backwards, glaring at Freddie. 'It's a stupid idea. Typical of you, Ashton. You have no thought for a lady's comfort.'

Nancy rapped on the door knocker. 'That's not true. Freddie is one of the nicest, kindest people I have ever met. If you think differently I suggest you go away and leave us alone. We are going to have a picnic at the zoo. I don't care what the weather has in store for us.'

Freddie picked up the hamper. 'Sorry, old chap. It looks as if we're going on our own. Maybe another time.'

Rawlings opened the door and Freddie followed

156

Nancy into the house, leaving Gervase standing on the pavement outside.

Nancy rushed into the parlour and peered out of the window. 'He looks furious, Freddie. Thank you so much for being here. I wasn't expecting you but I said the first thing that came into my head when Gervase insisted on following me.'

'I came on the off chance that Mrs de Marney might spare you for an hour or two.'

'Thank goodness you did. Felicia has given me the rest of the day off.'

'That doesn't sound like her.'

'She's still furious because a younger woman has been given the part she coveted, and then she discovered that the playbills had been printed with Carlotta Corvi's name in larger print than her own. I left Claude trying to placate her, but Felicia can be very difficult.'

'It's given us time together, Nancy. We're free from Gervase for now, so let's forget everyone else and enjoy ourselves.'

'I don't know what Gervase thinks he's doing, but he keeps popping up like a jack-in-the-box. I wish he would go away.'

'I'll have words with him if you like, Nancy. I don't want him to pester you. He keeps company with the sort of people you wouldn't wish to know.'

'He's a bit of a mystery, Freddie. I can't make head or tail of him.' Nancy glanced out of the window and sighed with relief. 'He's hailed a cab. Thank goodness for that. He's gone to bother someone else.'

'Excellent.' Freddie placed the hamper on the floor. 'I suggest you go and find something warmer to wear. It's going to be cold at the zoological gardens.'

'Perhaps we could call in at Doughty Street on the

way home,' Nancy said eagerly. 'I want to find out how Tamara is getting on. I keep wondering if her papa has changed his mind now that William has a better-paid position.'

'We can do that.' Freddie followed her to the door and opened it. 'I told Mason to walk the horse while we waited for you. I'll catch his eye as he drives past.'

'How long were you waiting for me, Freddie?'

'Long enough, but it was worth the wait.'

★ ★ ★

They spent the afternoon in the zoological gardens, having eaten their picnic on a wooden seat beneath the trees on the Terrace Walk. It was cold and the pot-bellied clouds threatened rain or even a sprinkling of snow, but Nancy was enjoying herself too much to bother with such details. The food was delicious, and when they had eaten they moved on to view the seals and the camels. Then they visited the monkey house and the hippopotamus enclosure, as well as the giraffes. In fact, they walked until Nancy's feet were sore, but she was oblivious to anything but the excitement of seeing exotic creatures and birds. In particular she enjoyed Freddie's company. They were as light-hearted as two children freed from parental supervision, and she discovered that they shared a similar sense of humour. Freddie was knowledgeable and entertaining at the same time. Gervase and some of his cronies might sneer at Freddie because of his shyness, his slight speech impediment and his preference for country life, but Nancy found his idiosyncrasies endearing. She could only imagine that the people who chose to demean Viscount Ashton were simply jealous of his wealth and position. Nancy had never laughed so much as she had that cold wintry afternoon, and by the time they climbed into the waiting carriage she felt as if she had drunk several glasses of champagne.

They were still laughing over the silly jokes they had shared as the carriage drew up outside the house in Doughty Street. However, Nancy's smiles faded when she was shown into the parlour to find Flora Fitzallen seated on the sofa, sobbing as if her heart would break.

Nancy sank down beside her and instinctively placed her arm around Flora's shoulders.

'What has happened, Mrs Fitzallen?' Nancy glanced up at Freddie, who was standing by the fire, gazing at them helplessly.

'C-can we d-d anything f-for you, ma'am? Do you n-need a d-doctor?'

Flora wiped her eyes on her already sodden hanky. 'It's Tamara. The ungrateful child has run off with that young man.'

'With William?' Nancy took her own hanky from her reticule and pressed it into Flora's hand. 'Where have they gone?'

'Eloped. My brother-in-law refused once again to consider William as a suitable husband for Tamara.'

'I thought it would be different now that William has a better-paid position,' Nancy said anxiously. 'Are you sure they've eloped?'

'When d-did they leave, ma'am?' Freddie asked gently. 'How long ago?'

'I don't know, maybe an hour, perhaps two hours. I've sent a message to Hubert and I'm expecting him to arrive at any moment. He'll blame me but it was that Eleanora woman who persuaded Tamara that elopement was the only answer.'

Nancy stroked Flora's hand. 'Perhaps she was right, Mrs Fitzallen. If Tamara's papa won't sanction the match, what else could they do?'

Flora ignored this remark. She clutched the two hankies in her hand, gazing hopefully at Freddie. 'You have influence, my lord. Can you do something to prevent them from going to Scotland, which is where I'm afraid they are heading. I don't know what Baldwin will say when he returns from his club. I sent one of the servants to fetch him and he should be here very soon.'

'Mrs Fitzallen, Flora, please don't distress yourself.' Nancy spoke firmly and calmly. 'Surely it is better to allow them to do as they wish? I mean, would you really want Tamara to marry an old man, just for his money?'

'N-no, I suppose not. Although Hubert was set upon it. He won't change his mind. I know my brother-in-law only too well. Lord Ashton, you have fast horses. Could you go after them and bring Tamara home before her reputation is ruined forever?'

'It's getting dark,' Nancy said thoughtfully. 'Do you think they will stop at a roadside inn, Freddie?'

'Possibly, but it would be a wild-goose chase to go after them now.' Freddie glanced out of the window. 'A cab has just pulled up. I think that might be your son, Mrs Fitzallen, or maybe it's Tamara's father.'

Flora jumped to her feet, clasping and unclasping her hands. 'Please, I'm begging you. Go now and see if you can find them and bring Tamara home before it's too late. A night in William's company will ruin her.'

'I have an idea, Freddie.' Nancy stood and picked up her reticule. 'I think we should leave now. This is a family matter.'

'Please do what you can,' Flora said tearfully. 'I will try to placate Hubert, but I'm afraid he will be absolutely furious.'

Her prediction seemed to be accurate, judging by the expression on Hubert Fitzallen's face as he stormed into the room, passing Freddie and Nancy in the doorway without even glancing at them.

Freddie closed the door. 'Let's get out of here before Baldwin arrives. You can tell me your plan when we get into the carriage.'

'It's not really a definite plan of action,' Nancy said, as she allowed Freddie to hand her into the brougham. 'Do you know where Sir Jack Marshall lives?'

'I believe he has rooms in Duke Street but his country house is a mile or so from Highgate.'

'Can we go there now, Freddie? If Mrs Fitzallen thinks that Eleanora is involved in Tamara's decision, I wonder if that's where we will find the runaways. After all, you said yourself it's almost dark and they have probably taken shelter for the night.'

'It's worth a try, but we will be out late. Are you sure you won't get into trouble from Mrs de Marney?' Freddie climbed into the carriage and sat down beside her.

'She'll be on stage in a couple of hours. She won't even notice that I'm missing.'

'All right, if you think it's possible, we'll try there. But what then? Do you intend to take Tamara back to her father? Even if she would agree to go, which I doubt.'

'No, I just want to know that she's safe and that

161

William Russell is going to take care of her. I won't sleep a wink tonight unless I see her and speak to her. You do understand, don't you, Freddie?'

He smiled. 'I know you follow your heart, Nancy. Of course we'll do our best to find your friend and make sure she's all right.'

★ ★ ★

Sir Jack Marshall's home was a mansion by any standards, built in the style of Robert Adam. The portico gleamed white in the moonlight and frost sparkled on the carriage sweep as Mason drew the horse to a halt outside. Freddie leaped to the ground.

'Wait here in the warm, Nancy. I'll find out if Jack is at home.' He moved swiftly to the front door.

Nancy sat very still, hoping against hope that Tamara and William had chosen to come here instead of heading for the open road. Her patience was rewarded when Freddie returned moments later, holding out his hand.

'Jack is at home. I didn't ask about the others.'

Nancy accepted his help to alight from the carriage and they entered the hall, which was dimly lit and it was obvious that Sir Jack had not been expecting company. The butler led them to the drawing room and ushered them inside.

The spacious room was lit by dozens of candles in silver candelabra and crystal chandeliers. A fire roared up the chimney, casting its light on the people grouped around it. Nancy breathed a sigh of relief when she saw Tamara seated with Eleanora on a damask-covered sofa. Jack and William stood with their backs to the fire, but Jack stepped forward holding out his hand.

'Ashton, welcome. I haven't seen you for a while.'

Freddie shook his hand. 'Y-you know m-me, Jack. I d-don't come up to town very often.'

'I see you have good reason for your visit now.' Jack smiled at Nancy, inclining his head. 'It's good to see you, too, Nancy. You know William, of course.'

'We have met,' Nancy said warily.

'If you're here to persuade me to return to Doughty Street, you're wasting your time,' Tamara said defiantly.

'We came to tell you that your aunt is distraught and your papa is very angry, which of course you will know.'

'You won't make us change our minds,' William said grimly. 'I've done everything required of me and yet I'm still not good enough for Tamara. I acknowledge that, but I love her more than life itself and all I want to do is to make her happy.'

Eleanora rose from her seat. 'You must be cold and in need of some refreshment. We were about to dine. Won't you join us?'

'Yes, please do. We can discuss what is best for everyone over a civilised meal.'

'My c-coachman is outside with the horse and carriage,' Freddie said cautiously. 'We don't want t-to intrude.'

'Yes,' Nancy added hastily. 'We just need to have something to tell Mrs Fitzallen and your papa, Tamara. We didn't come to try to dissuade you from eloping. I think your aunt Flora is more concerned about your reputation and your wellbeing than anything else.'

'Baldwin won't approve,' Tamara said with a wry smile. 'But I don't care. I love William and we are going to be married no matter what anyone says. I don't care if we have to walk to Gretna Green, we will do it one way or another.'

'Fortunately, I have an uncle in the clergy,' Jack said seriously. 'And we obtained a special licence from the powers that be, so no elopement is necessary.'

William nodded. 'You see, we have gone into this with thought for everyone. Tomorrow morning Jack's uncle is going to marry us quietly in the local church. There will be no cause for scandal.'

'You must admit it's a good plan,' Eleanora said, laughing. 'Jack and I used the same strategy and we're now a respectable married couple. We even attend morning service every Sunday. What would Miss Maughfling say if she knew that?'

'I think she would be amazed.' Nancy took a seat next to Tamara. 'If you are happy with this arrangement then we are, too.'

'Ring for Poole, Jack.' Eleanora resumed her seat. 'You will stay for dinner, I insist. Your coachman will be looked after.'

Nancy glanced at Freddie. 'It will be too late to return to Doughty Street if we dine here.'

'We could be on the road chasing after the runaways as far as they know,' Freddie said, laughing. 'I'm starving and I expect you are, too, Nancy. It's a long time since our picnic at the zoo.'

'What's this?' Eleanora demanded. 'Who on earth picnics at this time of the year, especially in a park filled with beasts of all kinds?'

'You'd be surprised,' Nancy said, smiling up at Freddie. 'It was absolutely lovely.'

Jack tugged at the bell pull. 'You can tell us all about it at dinner. It seems that we have been ousted from our place as the young rebels, Eleanora, my love. We are a respectable married couple, giving shelter to runaway lovers, and now Ashton and Nancy are the unconventional pair.'

Nancy joined in the laughter but she could not help wondering what Felicia would say if she discovered her absence.

11

When Nancy returned to the house in John Adam Street, she was relieved to discover that Felicia and Claude had returned from the theatre earlier and had gone straight to their room. This was according to Molly, who was the only one in the house who seemed to have worried about Nancy's prolonged absence. She listened eagerly to Nancy's account of the evening's happenings while she helped her to undress.

'My goodness, miss. Did you know that Reuben's dad rents his land from Sir Jack? Isn't that a coincidence?'

Nancy reached for the silver-backed hairbrush. 'It is indeed. Are you serious about Reuben, Molly?'

Molly's cheeks reddened. 'Yes, I suppose I am.'

'We will be going to Devonshire for Christmas. You'll miss him.'

'Yes, I will. I keep hoping he'll ask me to marry him, but he's a bit shy.'

'Maybe he needs a little nudge.'

'In what way, miss?'

'If you tell him that we're returning to Devonshire in a week or so and you might not be able to come back to London, that should do the trick. If he's in love with you, as I suspect he is, he won't want you to leave.'

'But if he doesn't say anything, what will I do?'

'Trust your heart, Molly. If you think he loves you and you love him, he won't want to lose you. From what I've learned of him, he works hard and he'll provide well for you.'

Molly laughed. 'You sound like my ma. Begging your pardon, miss.'

'Not at all. Those who love you want only the best for you, Molly. I plan to take a cab to Highgate early tomorrow morning. Tamara and William are to be married in the local church and I want to wish them well. You may come with me and perhaps you'll see Reuben. The wedding might give him ideas.'

★ ★ ★

A small crowd had gathered outside the church. Nancy and Molly were the last to arrive and they slipped into a pew unnoticed. William stood in front of the altar with Jack as his best man, while Eleanora and Flora sat together at the front of the congregation. A slight disturbance outside marked the bride's arrival and Tamara entered on her cousin Baldwin's arm. She was simply dressed in her best gown with a fur-lined cape and a matching bonnet, which Nancy suspected had been borrowed from Eleanora. There was no sign of Tamara's father and Nancy wondered if anyone had told him about the wedding, but Tamara gave her a radiant smile as she walked past and Nancy was happy for her. The ceremony was simple and short, and after the signing of the register the bride and groom processed down the aisle rather more quickly than was usual. Nancy followed the party outside, where it had started to rain mixed with sleet. However, the happiness on Tamara's face banished any greyness in the weather, and William looked very inch the proud husband.

167

'Thank you for coming, Nancy.' Tamara handed her the posy of hothouse roses. 'None of this would have been possible without your help in the first instance.'

'True love always wins,' Nancy said, smiling. 'Congratulations, to you both.'

'We're leaving straight away.' William slipped his arm around his bride's waist.

'I don't want to risk a scene with Papa,' Tamara added wistfully. 'I hope by the time we return from our honeymoon he will have come to accept the situation.'

'I wouldn't count on it.' Baldwin puffed out his chest. 'But I will have a few words to say to him, Tamara. Don't worry about a thing.'

'We're going to have the wedding breakfast without the happy couple.' Eleanora smiled happily. 'You are welcome to join us, Nancy.'

'I would love to but I have to get back to John Adam Street. Felicia is a late riser, but she'll be furious if she finds out I came here without asking her.'

'The woman is a tyrant.' Jack placed his arm around his wife's shoulders. 'You missed our wedding, Nancy. You could at least come and help us celebrate Tamara and William's nuptials.'

Nancy laughed. 'I don't think you need me, Jack. And as I recall, you and Eleanora married in secret.'

'We did. It was so exciting.' Eleanora smiled up at her husband. 'We were married in London and went back to Jack's rooms in Duke Street. No one would believe we were a respectable married couple. It was so amusing. We kept up the fiction for a week or two and then someone found out and told Papa. Of course, he was furious and now he's not speaking to me, even though Jack and I are boringly respectable.'

'You're happy,' Nancy said, sighing. 'That's all that matters.'

Molly cleared her throat. 'Might I go and speak to Reuben, miss? He's standing by the lich-gate.'

'Of course. Have a word with him and perhaps he could find me a cab to take me back to John Adam Street.'

'I have my carriage waiting,' Flora Fitzallen said hastily. 'You may travel with me if you wish, Nancy.'

'Won't you stay awhile?' Eleanora turned to Nancy with a persuasive look. 'Surely an hour or two won't make much difference? Stand up to that prima donna. She doesn't own you, Nancy.'

'I agree, but I should get back, in any case. I just wanted to share Tamara's big day.' Nancy's gaze strayed to where Molly and Reuben were talking animatedly.

'Why isn't Freddie with you?' Eleanora lowered her voice. 'You seem to be on very good terms with Ashton.'

'I like Freddie. We get on well, it's true, but don't make something of it that doesn't exist, Eleanora. I know you. You're a born matchmaker and a terrible gossip.'

Eleanora laughed. 'Those are my good qualities, Nancy dear.'

'Come along, Nancy. I'm leaving now.' Flora headed towards the gate, leaving Nancy little option but to follow her. Nancy said goodbye hastily and hurried after Mrs Fitzallen.

Molly was about to part from Reuben when Nancy waylaid her. 'Take the rest of the day off, Molly. There's no need for you to hurry back to John Adam Street. Spend some more time with Reuben.'

'He almost did it, miss,' Molly whispered. 'He started on about weddings, and then he got all tongue-tied and shy.'

'Humour him, Molly. Put him at his ease and enjoy your time together. I'll see you this evening after the performance. I'm sure Reuben will bring you home.' Nancy smiled at him over Molly's shoulder and he managed a bashful grin. 'Be patient, Molly.'

'Do hurry, Miss Sunday,' Flora called from the door of her carriage. 'I want to get away before Hubert arrives. I'm sure he'll have got wind of the wedding somehow or other and I don't want to be here when he discovers that his daughter is a married woman.'

Nancy was about to obey when she heard the sound of horses' hoofs. A familiar brougham came into view and she recognised Mason, Freddie's coachman.

'It's all right, Mrs Fitzallen. Thank you, but I think Freddie has come for me.'

Flora acknowledged her with a brief wave before climbing into her vehicle.

'Why didn't you tell me what you planned?' Freddie demanded as he leaped to the ground. 'I would have brought you here this morning. Have I missed the wedding?'

'Yes. I am so sorry, Freddie. I only decided to attend after we parted yesterday, and there was no time to get a message to you this morning.'

He smiled. 'Don't look so worried. I had a prior appointment anyway. I thought I passed the happy couple in their carriage, but I am in time to take you home.'

'Thank you, Freddie. But you could stay and enjoy the wedding breakfast with Jack, Eleanora and Baldwin.'

'I'd rather be with you anyway.' Freddie handed her into the carriage. 'John Adam Street, Mason.' He climbed in after her and sat down. 'Tell me all about it.'

★ ★ ★

Nancy had hoped to find Felicia and Claude in the morning parlour with their newspapers and coffee, but the house in John Adam Street appeared to be in a serious state of disorder. Rawlings was visibly upset when she opened the door to let them in, and the entrance hall was piled high with trunks, and travelling cases of all types. Servants were running up and down the stairs carrying bundles of clothing, bedding and a variety of household goods and the ornaments that Felicia insisted on taking from one set of rented rooms to another.

'What's going on, Rawlings?' Nancy asked anxiously.

'You'd better ask the mistress.' Tight-lipped as ever, Rawlings stalked off in the direction of the back stairs.

'It looks as if you're leaving,' Freddie said slowly. 'I thought Mrs de Marney had accepted Papa's invitation to Dorrington Place. We'll be going there next week anyway.'

'I don't know, Freddie. None of this had happened when I left this morning.'

Nancy headed for the morning parlour, where Claude was pacing the floor, smoking a fat cigar. This was something that Felicia would never normally have allowed. She appeared to be oblivious to everything going on around her as she sat drinking coffee. The strong smell of brandy and the silver flask on the table went some way to explain her behaviour.

'What's happened?' Nancy looked from one to the other. 'Are we leaving?'

Felicia drained her cup and set it back on its saucer with a clatter. 'Tell her, Claude. I can't bear to speak of it.'

'Felicia has decided that she cannot accept —'

'Oh, Claude. Don't mince words. I had a terrible row with Carlotta, and Garson Thorne took her side. I walked out for good this time.'

'But the luggage in the entrance hall — are we leaving today?'

Felicia reached for the coffee pot and refilled her cup, adding a generous tot of brandy from the flask. 'I told Garson Thorne exactly what I thought of him.'

'We have no choice other than to visit Rockwood,' Claude said carefully. 'I will put it about that it is long overdue and family matters call us home.'

'No one will believe that.' Felicia swallowed a mouthful of coffee. 'Everyone knows that I would never abandon a role, unless of course there was a very good reason.'

Freddie cleared his throat. 'I-if I might s-suggest s-something?'

'Go ahead, my lord.' Claude tossed the butt of his cigar into the fire. 'Any suggestions would be welcome.'

'Dorrington will be ready and waiting for the guests to arrive next week. There may be a few rooms that are not aired, but I'm sure we can accommodate you comfortably. My business in London is done, so I am free to travel home at any time. I know my parents would welcome you warmly if you choose to accompany me.'

Nancy clasped Freddie's arm, smiling. He had uttered a whole sentence without stammering and she felt a surge of pride. 'Well said, thank you, Freddie.'

'Do you mean it?' Felicia asked slowly. 'What will your papa say?'

'H-he invited you i-in the f-f-first place.'

Claude stepped forward to shake Freddie's hand. 'I say that's a generous offer we can't afford to refuse.' He turned to his wife. 'What do you say, my dear? After all, an invitation from the Earl of Dorrington cannot be refused without causing offence. It gives us a good excuse to walk away from the theatre before the end of your contract.'

'Garson will sue me,' Felicia said grimly. 'He's never recovered from the rebuff I gave him years ago when he tried to seduce me.'

'What are you saying?' Claude demanded angrily.

Felicia blinked nervously. 'Don't lose your temper, Claude. It was a long time ago, as I said. But Garson isn't a man to forgive or forget. I think that is why he has taken on the Corvi woman for his next production.'

'Then I have no qualms about you leaving before the end of the season, my dear. I would have called him out had I known about his behaviour.'

'That's settled then,' Nancy said hastily. 'It looks as if we are leaving for Devonshire.'

'If you will permit me, I will organise the t-travel arrangements. I w-w-will send a t-telegram to Dorrington t-to tell them of our arrival.' Freddie left the parlour with Nancy following him.

'Thank you so much, Freddie.' Nancy grasped his hand. 'I know that Felicia can be difficult, but this business with Carlotta Corvi has really upset her.'

Freddie squeezed her fingers. 'I know. I could tell, which is why I suggested we leave for Dorrington today. I'll send Mason to get the tickets and arrange for a carrier to take the luggage to the station.'

'I've just remembered that I left Molly with Reuben in Highgate. I can't leave without telling her.'

'Mason can fetch her when he's been to the station. Maybe Reuben will be moved to propose.'

Nancy laughed. 'I believe you are a true romantic, Freddie.'

'I surprise myself sometimes, Nancy.' Freddie edged his way past the piles of baggage and let himself out into the street, closing the door behind him.

★ ★ ★

The journey to Devonshire had been tedious, with the train stopping at almost every station, but the first-class compartment was warm and comfortable. Felicia slept for most of the way and Claude read his newspaper. He used each stop to get out onto the station platform and stretch his legs or to smoke a cigarillo, only returning to the carriage when the guard blew his whistle. Freddie and Nancy played cards and chatted or lapsed into amicable silences to gaze out at the countryside flashing past the windows. Molly and Violet Tinker travelled third class.

When they stepped off the train at the railway station, Mason appeared with a couple of footmen from Dorrington Place. They unloaded the luggage and strapped it onto the roofs of the two carriages that they had brought to pick up the guests, and everyone travelled on in style.

It had been dark for some time when they finally

arrived at their destination, and it was impossible to see the splendour of the parkland surrounding the great house. The carriages were driven through an avenue of tall trees, which opened out into a wide sweep of gravel in front of the house. Dorrington Place was illuminated by flambeaux, the dancing flames reflecting on the white stucco. Nancy caught her breath at the sight of Freddie's imposing home. Elegant in its symmetry, it was even grander than the Nash terraces in Regent's Park. A columned portico sheltered the front entrance and liveried footmen awaited their arrival, standing stiffly to attention on either side of the open door.

Nancy had been used to visiting Greystone Park, which she thought was the grandest house she had ever seen, but it was eclipsed by the splendour of Dorrington Place. The interior was even more spacious and impressive. The marble-tiled hall was furnished with stylish simplicity and made welcoming by fires blazing in ornate fireplaces facing each other on opposite sides of the room. Urns filled with hothouse roses, orchids and carnations made splashes of vibrant colour against the silvery white walls, while crystal chandeliers and wall sconces filled with wax candles gave the impression of daylight. Servants appeared as if from nowhere to divest the arrivals of their outdoor clothes.

'I'm s-sorry for the short n-notice, Pickering. I hope it hasn't caused t-too much b-bother.' Freddie addressed the stony-faced butler, who stood waiting for instructions.

Pickering's lined face creased into a semblance of a smile. 'Of course not, my lord. We are always prepared to welcome you and your guests.'

Freddie turned to Felicia and Claude. 'I'm sure you would like to see your room. We're rather late for dinner but I expect Mrs Maple will have something set by for us.'

'I believe she has your favourite, my lord.'

'Game pie, Pickering?'

'Made just for you, my lord.'

'I'll visit the kitchens and thank her personally.' Freddie turned to Nancy with a wide smile. 'Mrs Maple spoils me, Nancy. She used to make my favourite jam tarts when I came back from boarding school.'

Felicia yawned. 'I'm sure we're delighted to hear it, my lord, but may we go to our room? I need to change out of my travelling costume and wash some of the railway dirt off my hands and face.'

Pickering beckoned to a young maidservant. 'The cherry blossom room for Mr and Mrs de Marney, Iris. And the waterlily room for Miss Sunday.'

The chambermaid curtsied to Felicia and Claude. 'This way, if you please.' She led them across the hall to the staircase at the far end.

'Thank you for everything, Freddie,' Nancy said, smiling. 'You have a wonderful home. I understand completely why you prefer living here to London.'

'Tomorrow I'll show you around the estate. We'll choose a Christmas tree and have it brought into the house.'

'That's what we used to do at home in Rockwood Castle. I love Christmas.'

'Better follow Iris. You'll get lost if you try to find your own way, and I don't think Pickering will approve if I take you upstairs.' Freddie shot a mischievous smile in Pickering's direction, which the butler acknowledged with a raised eyebrow and a hint

176

of a smile.

Nancy hurried after Iris, who took Felicia and Claude to their room, and a few doors along a wide landing they came to a stop outside the waterlily room. Nancy entered to find Molly sitting on a pile of cases by the fire, sobbing as if her heart would break.

'Whatever is the matter?' Nancy rushed over to her and went down on her knees. 'Why are you crying? Are you ill?'

Molly wiped her eyes on her sleeve and sniffed. 'I'm sorry, miss. I thought he would ask me to stay in Highgate but he just said goodbye like it was an ordinary day.'

'You mean Reuben, of course.'

'Yes, miss. He seemed shocked that we was leaving so suddenly, but he didn't pop the question.'

'I'm so sorry, Molly. I don't know what to say.'

Molly scrambled to her feet. 'I shouldn't bring my troubles to you, miss.'

'It's all right. We're friends, Molly. Just help me to unpack what I need and then I want you to go down to the servants' hall and get some food. Violet Tinker is here with you, and Mason seems quite a nice person. They'll look after you, and we're very near home. Perhaps you'd like to go there for a few days. I could manage on my own.'

'I'll be all right, thank you, miss.' Molly undid the leather straps on one of the valises. 'I brought some hot water up for you to have a wash.'

'Unpack a gown for me and then go and get your own meal. I'll change my clothes and find my own way to the dining room. I expect someone will come and rescue me if I get lost.'

This drew a reluctant smile from Molly, but she

busied herself sorting out clean garments for Nancy to wear that evening. In the end Nancy had to almost throw Molly out of the room in order to make her go to the servants' hall for some food. She hoped that her maid would feel better when she had eaten and had enjoyed a good night's sleep. If Reuben had been living close by, Nancy would have marched up to his door and demanded to know why he had led Molly on, but he was safe in Highgate, for the time being at least. Nancy was not about to let him get away with such behaviour. She made up her mind to visit him when she returned to London, although when that would be was uncertain. It all depended upon Felicia obtaining a part in another production. Nancy decided to put everything out of her mind other than finding the dining room and enjoying her first meal at Dorrington Place.

She dressed, brushed her hair and tied it back in a simple style with a piece of ribbon. It was getting late and she was hungry. It could not be so difficult to find the dining room, even in a mansion the size of Dorrington Place. However, when she reached the ground floor she was suddenly unsure of herself. There was nobody to ask and she had a choice of going left or right. She found herself in a wide corridor, lit by candles in sconces, which reflected off the glass panes of the windows that stood floor to ceiling along one side. Every few yards another corridor branched off, equally well lit with closed doors hiding rooms as yet unexplored. Nancy walked slowly, hoping to hear the sound of voices or the clatter of cutlery, but when she saw a green baize door, which she suspected led to the servants' quarters and kitchens below stairs, she knew she had come too far.

She came to a halt as it opened and Freddie almost barged into her.

'Nancy, are you lost?'

'I am, of course. It's such a big house.'

'I've just been to the kitchen to thank Mrs Maple for holding dinner for us. She's a real treasure, a bit like your Hester, from what you've told me.'

Nancy laughed. 'I'm not sure anyone at home would call Hester a treasure, but she does keep everyone on their toes, and you can always rely on her for good advice, whether you want it or not.'

Freddie placed his arm around her shoulders. 'Dinner is about to be served. I'll make sure you get to the dining room.'

★ ★ ★

That night Nancy slept from sheer exhaustion, but she awoke next morning to the sound of someone stoking the fire in her bedroom. For a moment she thought she was back in John Adam Street, but this was not the small rather shabby bedroom she had grown used to — even in the half-light of the flames licking over the coals she could see the difference.

A young housemaid rose shyly to her feet. 'I'm sorry I disturbed you, miss.'

'I was waking up anyway. What time is it?'

'About half past six, I think, miss.'

'Thank you for lighting the fire. What's your name?'

'It's Lizzie, miss. Please don't tell on me. I wasn't supposed to disturb you.'

'Of course not.'

'I'll bring you some hot chocolate, miss. If you'd like some.'

'That would be lovely.' Nancy watched as Lizzie gathered up the dustpan and brush. 'Would you draw back the curtains, Lizzie? I like to watch the dawn come up.'

'Of course, miss.' Lizzie did as Nancy asked, although outside it was still dark.

'Have you met my maid, Molly?'

'Not really, miss. I did catch a glimpse of her last evening.'

'I hope you'll be friends with her, Lizzie.'

'I'm sure I shall, miss.'

Lizzie hurried from the room, returning minutes later with a steaming cup of hot chocolate and a ewer filled with hot water. She placed the cup on the table by the side of Nancy's four-poster bed and proceeded to fill the pitcher on the washstand. 'Will there be anything else, miss?'

'No, thank you, Lizzie.'

'Shall I send Molly to you, miss?'

'No, it's all right. Let her sleep on. I'm sure she's worn out with travelling and everything.'

Lizzie bobbed a curtsey and left Nancy to enjoy the luxury of sipping delicious hot chocolate while the fire blazed up the chimney, warming the room. She watched the first grey light of dawn edging the darkness from the sky and was about to rise from her bed when Molly hurried into the room.

'I'm sorry, miss. I overslept. I'd still be in my bed if that girl Lizzie hadn't brought me a cup of tea. It was so kind of her.'

'She seems nice enough, Molly. It sounds as if you've made a friend already.'

'Maybe it won't be as bad here as I thought.'

'If you want to spend Christmas with your family,

180

that would be all right with me. I would understand, Molly.'

'No, miss. My place is here with you. Maybe I can see them soon, but only if it suits you.'

'Of course. I want to see my family, too. We are only a day's ride away.' Nancy stretched and swung her legs over the side of the bed. 'I will get dressed now, Molly. Something warm and practical, I think.'

'I'll finish unpacking your clothes this morning, miss. Apparently there's a laundry room and a drying room, too. It will take me a while to work out where everything is.'

'At least I know where to find the dining room now. I suppose the family go down to breakfast when it suits them, as we did at Rockwood.'

'They were busy preparing food in the kitchen when I came up. You should just see the size of it, and there are different rooms for preparing meat and another for baking. I've never seen anything like it.'

Nancy smiled and reached for her wrap. She was just as impressed as Molly, but she was not about to admit it, not even to herself. The pale pink and white decorations of the waterlily room, with the flower theme on the wallpaper and the curtain material, as well as being woven into the soft Axminster carpet, was fresh and beautiful. If this elegant bedchamber was anything to go by, the rest of the house must be very sumptuous. Nancy washed, dressed and sat impatiently while Molly did her hair.

Downstairs in the dining room the servants were busy filling a battery of silver salvers and breakfast dishes with revolving lids where the bacon, devilled kidneys and sausages were kept warm. The rectangular mahogany table would have seated thirty in comfort, but it was set for a much smaller number. Silverware and crystal glasses gleamed in the firelight. Nancy hesitated, not knowing whether to take a seat or to wait for someone to join her, but then the door opened and Freddie strolled into the room. His face lit up when he saw her.

'Nancy, you look rested. Did you sleep well?'

'I did, thank you, Freddie. The bed was so soft and the room was warm. I slept like a baby.'

'I'm glad. I want you to enjoy your stay here. I thought we'd go for a ride in my gig. It's too cold for a walk around the grounds. But let's have breakfast first and we can decide what to do then.'

Nancy helped herself from the dishes on the groaning sideboard and took her plate to the table.

'Sit beside me, Nancy. I doubt if the others will rise early.' Freddie followed her to the table and pulled up a chair for her.

Nancy sat down and placed a starched linen table napkin on her lap. A maid appeared with a coffee pot and filled her cup. 'How many house guests will there be, Freddie?' Nancy asked when the maid returned to her place standing well back from the table.

'I don't know exactly. Most of them will arrive next week, just before Christmas. Judging by the number of places set there must be half a dozen here already, not counting those who prefer to take breakfast in their rooms, which is what most of the ladies do.'

'Should I stay in my room tomorrow, Freddie? I don't want to upset the order of things here.'

'No, of course not. You must do whatever you want, and I like having breakfast in your company. It's a good start to the day.'

'So it is.' Nancy sliced the bacon on her plate and

ate a mouthful. 'Perhaps I could have a conducted tour of the house before we go out? I don't want to get lost again like I did last evening.'

'Of course. I'll show you round and introduce you to the servants. I know it's not the done thing, but I like to treat everyone equally. They look after us, so we should take care of them.'

Nancy smiled. 'I agree entirely, Freddie. We've always behaved that way at home, except when Lady Pentelow comes to stay, which isn't too often these days.'

Freddie swallowed a mouthful of toast. 'Lady Pentelow?'

'She's Alexander's great-aunt, although he thought she was his grandmother until a few years ago. She lives in Trevenor, on the Cornish coast, and the family own a clay mine. It's all very complicated, and really nothing to do with you and me.'

'I'd like to meet your family, Nancy. They sound interesting.'

'They are, and to be honest I don't know why Mrs de Marney doesn't want to return home for Christmas. I know she loves to sing and to be the centre of attention, but to me family are very important, even though they are not my blood relations.'

Freddie laid his hand on hers as it rested on the table. 'They brought you up, Nancy. I'm sure they regard you as one of them. You should try not to think about it too deeply.'

'I know, and you're right. I promise I won't mention it again.'

'You should feel free to tell me anything that's on your mind, Nancy. I want us to be good friends.'

Before Nancy had a chance to respond the door

opened and Lady Dorrington walked into the room. Freddie leaped to his feet and Nancy stood up.

'M-Mama, you don't usually grace the breakfast t-table,' Freddie said nervously.

'I was told that we have new arrivals,' Lady Dorrington said coldly. 'Have we met, young lady?'

Nancy curtsied. 'Yes, my lady. We were introduced at the ball you gave at your home in London.'

'M-Mama, this is Nancy Sunday. She is a ward of Sir Bertram Carey of Rockwood Castle.'

Lady Dorrington raised her lorgnette, eyeing Nancy curiously. 'You're related to that singing woman. Personally, I loathe opera, but Dorrington loves it. I believe she's here, too. Am I correct?'

'Yes, my lady. We arrived quite late last evening.'

'May I pull up a chair for y-you, M-Mama?' Freddie moved towards the foot of the table, but his mother shook her head.

'I've breakfasted, thank you, Freddie. You'd better introduce the new guests to me when they choose to make an appearance. I'll be in the library if anyone wants me.' Lady Dorrington swept out of the room.

Nancy sank back onto her seat. 'Your mama doesn't approve of me, Freddie. She doesn't seem to think much of Mrs de Marney, either. I do hope our being here isn't going to prove awkward.'

'Mama is like that with most people.' Freddie refilled his coffee cup. 'She has to do what my father says when he is here, but when he's away she decides to take charge. Anyway, when we've finished our breakfast, let's escape before the other guests descend upon us.'

12

Freddie's gig was ready and waiting for them when they walked to the stable block, which incorporated a large coach house complete with living accommodation. Freddie handed Nancy onto the driver's seat and climbed up to take the reins from the stable boy.

'Are you comfortable?' Freddie asked as he guided the horse skilfully out of the stable yard. 'There's a blanket under the seat if you're cold.'

'I'm fine, thank you. Although I'm sure we could have walked around your estate. The exercise would be welcome.'

Freddie laughed. 'You would regret that if I agreed. It's a long way if we do a tour of the farms and the village. Beside which, just look at that sky. I wouldn't be surprised if we had some snow.'

Nancy huddled in her warm cloak. 'Now you come to mention it, the clouds do look a bit threatening.' Even so, she sat back and enjoyed the view of the extensive deer park, and the surrounding woodland.

There seemed to be a folly built on the top of a steep rise, which Freddie explained had been erected by the fourth Earl of Dorrington so that his young wife could entertain her friends without getting wet in bad weather. 'The view from up there is lovely,' Freddie added. 'You can see the lake and the surrounding countryside for miles around. We'll have to make a special trip to see it, but you'll need a stout pair of boots.'

'That's one item of clothing I do have,' Nancy said, smiling. 'I had to do a lot of walking at Rockwood, even if it was just to visit Patricia in her home next to the sawmill.'

'I'd love to see Rockwood Castle. It sounds very romantic.'

It was Nancy's turn to laugh. 'It's more like something from a gothic novel when compared to Dorrington Place, but I do love it, even if the windows don't fit properly, the damp creeps in through the stone walls, and there are parts of the castle still in need of repair.'

'Will you return there, do you think? Or will Mrs de Marney take you on her next tour, wherever that might be?'

'I don't know, Freddie. That's the honest truth. Felicia walked out on Garson Thorne, and I don't know how that will go down in the operatic world. She hasn't any other bookings, as far as I know, but they don't discuss business with me.'

'You could go home to Rockwood.'

'Yes, but the older I get the more aware I become of my position in the household. Can you understand that?'

'I'm not sure I do. From what you've told me, they treat you like one of the family.'

'Perhaps that's the trouble. If Hester had had her way I would have been brought up in the servants' quarters and trained to be a housemaid or a cook. I would know my place.'

'But you said that Rosalind treats you like a sister.'

'That's true, but Rosalind is lovely to everyone. I would give anything to know where I came from, but that isn't going to happen. I just have to live with the knowledge that I was abandoned when I was a tiny baby. Nobody wanted me.'

Freddie reached out to clasp her hand. 'There must have been extenuating circumstances. If you think about it, Rosalind saw that you were a special person. She chose to save you from a life of drudgery when she could have simply walked away.'

'You're right, of course, and I'm being maudlin. I'm sorry, Freddie. Let's enjoy the drive. I do love what I've seen of your home and the estate.'

'There's the pleasure garden and the lake still to see. We'll walk there tomorrow, if the weather permits. What I had in mind now was to choose a Christmas tree. I've arranged for some of the groundsmen to meet us in Foxhole Woods. I'll leave the ultimate choice to you.'

'How exciting. We do this at home every year. I love decorating the tree.'

When they reached the wood, which to Nancy's eyes looked more like a forest, Freddie left the horse in the care of one of the under gardeners and they went on foot into the cool darkness of the ancient woodland. Gnarled oaks and stately beeches raised their bare branches to the sky, together with ash and coniferous trees, a group of which was being cleared of undergrowth to enable Freddie and Nancy access.

After much deliberation they chose a huge fir tree for the grand entrance hall, and a slightly smaller one for the drawing room. Freddie instructed the men to cut another tree for the servants' hall.

'We have a servants' ball a few days before Christmas,' he explained as they walked away. 'The family join in the dancing, although the meal is for the servants only. The rest of us make do with a cold collation above stairs. It's an old custom and one we are keen to keep up.'

'We do something similar at Rockwood, but not on such a grand scale. I think it's a splendid idea.'

'There's a clump of holly bushes close by,' Freddie said, taking Nancy by the hand. 'I've told the men to choose the best branches with as many berries as possible.'

'And some mistletoe?' Nancy added with a mischievous smile.

'Of course. Christmas wouldn't be Christmas without mistletoe. I just hope the Brocklebournes haven't accepted the invitation. I can't stand Lady Letitia. She makes me feel like an idiot, and my stammer comes back at the thought of her.'

'Just try to avoid her, Freddie. You said there would be many house guests.'

'Don't worry, I'll try, but Mama will make it impossible. She has a way of organising people without them realising what's happening. If she'd been born a man she would have made a great general. The enemy would not have known what hit them.'

'Consider me your reinforcements. I'll stand between you and the heiress.'

'Let's forget Letitia Barclay and concentrate on enjoying ourselves.' Freddie handed Nancy into the gig. 'We haven't finished the tour yet and the weather is just about holding, so we'll take advantage of that.' He took the reins from the gardener with a smile. 'Thank you, Brewster. How are the family?'

'Right as a trivet, my lord. Thank you for asking.'

'My regards to your father, Brewster. He used to allow me to push the wheelbarrow when I was a small boy. I thought I was very honoured.'

188

Brewster laughed. 'I'll remind him, my lord.'

Freddie climbed onto the driver's seat. 'Walk on.'

'Do you know all your servants by name, Freddie?' Nancy asked as the horse moved on eagerly, breaking into a brisk trot.

'Of course. We all pull together to make Dorrington a good place to live.'

Nancy smiled. If only those who criticised Freddie in London could see him here, in his element, they would revise their opinion of Viscount Ashton. It was obvious that this was where Freddie belonged and was truly happy. Nancy settled down to enjoy the tour of what proved to be an enormous estate.

They stopped at the village inn at midday and Freddie received a genuinely warm greeting from both the landlord and the men who clustered around the bar. The landlord's wife ushered them into a private parlour where a welcoming log fire blazed up the chimney. She brought them steaming bowls of mutton stew and a platter of freshly baked bread, with a generous helping of butter.

When they finished their meal the landlord saw them out, glancing up at the louring sky. 'The weather is going to turn soon, my lord. I wouldn't go too far if I were you.'

'You're right, Reynolds. I can feel snow in the air. We'll be heading home.'

'What a shame,' Nancy said as she took her seat. 'It's been a lovely day, Freddie.'

'What do you think of the estate, Nancy?' Freddie joined her and took up the reins.

'I think you have a wonderful home and I don't wonder that you hate leaving here to go to London. If I were you I would never want to live anywhere else.'

'I knew you'd understand, Nancy.' Freddie urged the horse to walk on. 'I'm sorry to curtail the expedition, but I think we'd better return to the house before it starts to snow.'

'Maybe we could decorate the trees, or at least one of them. That is my favourite thing to do before Christmas.'

'Of course. That's a good idea, and don't forget the servants' ball is tomorrow evening. We like to get that done before the rest of the guests arrive, otherwise the staff are too exhausted to enjoy themselves properly.'

'You really care about people, don't you, Freddie?'

He gave her a lopsided smile. 'Of course I do. What else is there in life if you can't make people happy?'

A sudden vision of Gervase North clouded Nancy's mind and she shuddered. At least they had left him in London to cast his gloomy spell over some unfortunate person or persons at Christmas.

'Are you cold, Nancy?' Freddie asked anxiously.

'No, but, as Hester would say, someone walked over my grave. I'm fine, thank you, Freddie.'

They lapsed into companionable silence until they reached the carriage sweep at Dorrington Place. Freddie sighed heavily.

'That's the Brocklebournes' carriage. I know the coat of arms only too well. They've arrived before the snow. Just my luck!'

'They can't make you marry the heiress, Freddie. Surely you have some say in the matter.'

'You don't know my mama when she has her mind set on something. I might have to retire to the folly on the hill and spend Christmas on my own.'

Nancy laughed. 'Then I'll come with you. We can

pretend we are on a desert island like Robinson Crusoe.'

'If only it were that simple.' Freddie leaped to the ground and handed the reins to one of the stable boys, who had rushed to assist him.

Nancy waited for Freddie to help her down from the high seat. At home she would have risked snagging her skirts on the projecting foot rest, or landing in a way that Hester would call inelegant, but with the eyes of the Dorrington servants upon her she decided she had better act like a lady.

They entered the house to find the Brocklebourne family being greeted by Lady Dorrington, who spotted Freddie and summoned him to her side with a single glance. Nancy stood back, not wishing to intrude, and it gave her time to observe the newcomers. Lord Brocklebourne was an imposing figure with a fine head of silver hair and a booming voice. He was in deep conversation with his host. Lady Brocklebourne was also tall but she was thin and angular, with a permanent frown etched on her face. She might have the advantage of height over Lady Dorrington, but the latter was on home ground and, away from the glare of her husband, she bristled with determination.

'Freddie, come and greet Lady Brocklebourne and Letitia.'

He stepped forward, acknowledging Lady Brocklebourne before turning to Letitia with a shy grin.

'I h-hope y-you had a p-p-pleasant journey.'

Nancy had to stifle the urge to rush to his side and hold his hand. It was obvious that the two mothers had decided between them that Freddie would be the ideal husband for Letitia and, despite her reservations, Nancy felt sorry for the plain young woman.

She looked as though she would be more comfortable riding to hounds than standing in the great hall at Dorrington Place, being sized up as a good marriageable prospect for Freddie.

Letitia made a movement that was a casual attempt at a curtsey. 'Yes, thank you, my lord.'

'F-Freddie, p-please.'

Letitia shrugged. 'May we go to our rooms, Mama?'

Lady Dorrington beckoned to Lizzie, who was hovering in the background. 'Show Lady Brocklebourne and Lady Letitia to their rooms. Pickering will see that your luggage is brought up directly.'

Lizzie led the way, with Letitia and her mother following.

'Come to my study, Brocklebourne,' Lord Dorrington said jovially. 'We'll join the ladies later.'

Lady Dorrington watched her husband and their guest as they strolled off together. She turned to Freddie with an ominous frown.

'That wasn't much of a greeting, Freddie. How many times have I told you to remember what your tutor told you about stuttering like a fool? Stop and think about what you are going to say.'

'I-I'm s-sorry, Mama.'

'Sorry doesn't help, Freddie. You must show Letitia that you are a gentleman and a good prospect. She will inherit a fortune from her papa and from her maternal grandfather.'

'P-please, Mama, I am not interested in her f-fortune. She d-doesn't even l-like me.'

'Are you surprised about that, Freddie? A codfish would have shown more enthusiasm than you did when you greeted her. I don't want to see that behaviour repeated. Do you understand me?'

'Y-yes, Mama.'

'You will be a fool and a disgrace to the family if you allow this opportunity to slip through your fingers.' Lady Dorrington flounced off in the direction of the morning parlour.

Nancy moved swiftly to Freddie's side and laid her hand on his sleeve. 'I'm sorry, Freddie.'

He managed a smile. 'I don't care what anyone says, Nancy. I am not going to propose to Letitia.'

'She seems nice enough,' Nancy said cautiously.

'I'm sure she is, but I will marry for love.' Freddie glanced over his shoulder. 'That sounds as if we have another arrival. I'm going to see what's happened to the Christmas trees. Are you coming with me?'

He looked so much like a naughty schoolboy that Nancy wanted to laugh. 'Run away and hide, Freddie. I think I'd better change into something more appropriate, and I really should find out if Mrs de Marney needs anything. I am supposed to be working for her and her husband.'

Freddie hesitated. 'Do they pay you a wage?'

'No, not as such. I get free board and lodging and Felicia pays for my clothes. Money was never mentioned.'

'Then it's slave labour and slavery was abolished years ago. Let her come looking for you if she needs anything.'

'I doubt if she'll see it your way, Freddie, but I will go and change.'

'Meet me here in half an hour and we'll decorate the tree, if you've still a mind to help me.'

'Of course. There's nothing I'd like better.'

★ ★ ★

It took Nancy less than half an hour to change into an afternoon gown. It was a simple, grey woollen dress with little embellishment apart from mother-of-pearl buttons on the bodice and a modest trim of braid around the cuffs. It was a style that Felicia had decided was suitable for someone in Nancy's lowly position, but it was well cut and the style flattered Nancy's slender figure and small waist. Molly was still red-eyed, as if she had cried herself to sleep the previous evening, but she said little as she fashioned Nancy's hair into a neat chignon.

Nancy studied Molly's sad face reflected in the dressing-table mirror. 'Does Reuben know where you are spending Christmas?'

'Yes, I told him we would be at Dorrington Place. I don't suppose he knows where it is.'

'I'm sure he could find out if he tried.'

Molly's eyes filled with tears. 'That's the trouble, miss. I don't think he wants to marry me. We talked about it, but he never proposed.'

'I'm so sorry, but there will be others, Molly. You are a lovely girl. You need someone who really appreciates you.'

'Yes, miss.' Molly stood back, admiring her handiwork. 'Your hair looks nice, if I say so myself.'

'I'm going to help decorate the Christmas trees. Why don't you come with me?'

'They wouldn't approve of that below stairs, miss. They are very particular here, not like at Rockwood.'

'If you are unhappy here I could still send you home to Rockwood Castle, Molly. Would you like me to do that?'

Molly sniffed. 'I am your maid, miss. I'll stay with you.'

'Well, if you change your mind you must let me know.' Nancy rose from the stool. 'Don't suffer on my account, Molly.'

Nancy left Molly to tidy up and she was about to descend the wide staircase when she saw Letitia hurrying towards her.

'Miss — I'm sorry, I don't know your name. We weren't introduced.'

'I'm Nancy Sunday, my lady.'

'I could see that you and Freddie are friends. Please call me Letitia. I don't get on very well in company.'

'But you must know most of the other guests, surely?'

'It doesn't make them my friends. I am not a sociable sort of person. To be honest I prefer horses and dogs to people.'

Nancy laughed. 'I can understand that, to a point.'

'I've only visited Dorrington Place once before. I know I will get confused by the maze of corridors downstairs.'

'I'm not expert myself. I was completely lost last evening when I tried to find the dining room. If Freddie hadn't come to find me, I might still be wandering. Come with me — we'll find the way together.'

They made their way downstairs to the great hall, where the Christmas tree had been set up. It was a truly magnificent specimen and it towered above everything, almost reaching the ceiling. The scent of pine filled the air, reminding Nancy of past Christmases at Rockwood Castle. A wave of homesickness made her want to cry, but the sight of Freddie garlanded with tinsel drove away the sad thoughts and she smiled.

He unhooked a glass bauble from one ear. 'I think

I would make a good pirate, don't you?'

'You might have to take off the tinsel,' Nancy said, laughing.

'I'll go and look for Mama.' Letitia's lips trembled.

Not for the first time, Nancy felt sorry for her. She realised that Letitia was not a mere replica of her mother, she was a young woman with feelings akin to her own, who was being pushed into a marriage of convenience in order to please his family. Letitia and Freddie had that in common.

'Why don't you stay and help us with the tree?' Nancy raised her voice, hoping that Freddie could hear and would take the hint. 'It's a huge fir and there's another in the drawing room.'

Freddie stepped forward, smiling. 'Yes, come and help us, Letitia. We'll get it done much faster if there are three of us.'

'Do you really want me to decorate the tree with you?'

'Of course,' Freddie said casually. 'Or you could just stand back and tell us where to hang the ornaments and tinsel.'

'No, I would love to help. I haven't done anything like this since I was a child.' Letitia turned to Nancy as they sorted through the box of decorations. 'Thank you for suggesting this. I can see that you and Freddie get along well. I am not a rival, I promise you,' she added in a low voice.

'Freddie and I are just friends, as I said before. That's all.'

'I don't want to marry him. Not that I've been consulted in the matter, but the truth is I am happy with my life as it is. I like being single. I have no desire to be a wife and mother. Does that seem odd to you?'

'To be honest I've never given the matter much thought. Anyway, you must do what is best for you, Letitia. Never mind what other people say.'

'Thank you, Nancy. I knew you'd understand.'

Nancy smiled. 'Let's get on with the tree. It's going to look beautiful.'

Nancy eyed Freddie warily, but he seemed to relax when he realised that Letitia was genuine in her desire to assist them decorating the huge tree. Nancy was surprised to find Letitia joining in enthusiastically at first, although it was obvious that she was unused to doing anything so time-consuming and she soon tired. Nancy and Freddie managed to dress the tree with only minimal help from Letitia, and when it was done they all stood back to admire their work. More guests had arrived while they were occupied and they had been greeted by their host and hostess before being shown to their respective rooms.

Nancy eyed the mountain of holly and ivy left by the front entrance, but Freddie instructed the two footmen to make the greenery into swags and drape them around the banisters and over the many oil paintings. Nancy was secretly relieved that the prickly task had been allocated to others, and she was more than happy to follow Freddie and Letitia to the drawing room to decorate the second tree.

It was dark outside by the time they finished and were satisfied with their efforts, and Freddie had sent for a tray of tea and cake to keep them going until dinner. The guests had started to trickle into the drawing room, which to Nancy's eyes was large enough to hold a grand ball. Couples sat at small tables or crowded on the two sofas set on either side of the ornate marble fireplaces. Scantily clad caryatids supported the marble mantelshelf where silver candelabra gleamed in the firelight. The servants had lit dozens of candles so that the room was filled with light, warmth and the comforting aroma of beeswax, burning apple logs and pine needles.

Nancy was seated beside Freddie on a window seat with Letitia comfortably ensconced in a wing-back chair, while they drank tea and ate small iced cakes. But the harmony was broken by the sudden appearance of Felicia, who marched over to Nancy and stood glaring at her with arms akimbo.

'I haven't seen you all day, Nancy. Where have you been?'

Freddie rose to his feet. 'Mrs de Marney, I am t-to b-blame. I'm s-sorry, but I t-took Nancy on a t-tour of the estate.'

'And we've been decorating the Christmas trees for Lord and Lady Dorrington,' Letitia said brightly. 'You must agree they look splendid.' She stood up, smiling at Felicia. 'How do you do, ma'am? I am Letitia Barclay. I expect you've met my papa, Lord Brocklebourne.'

'How do you do, Lady Letitia?' Felicia's high colour deepened and she bobbed a curtsey. 'The trees look magnificent,' she added weakly.

'I've heard that you are a famous opera singer,' Letitia continued airily. 'It's not something I am interested in myself, but we are honoured by your presence. I hope you will treat us to an aria or two.'

'Why, yes, thank you,' Felicia said uncertainly. She glanced over her shoulder and beckoned to Claude, who had just entered the room. 'Lady Letitia, may I introduce you to my husband, Claude de Marney?'

Lady Letitia extended her hand graciously. 'How

do you do, Mr de Marney? It's a pleasure to meet you and your wife.' She turned to Nancy. 'You will excuse me, Nancy. I think I should change for dinner. My clothes are prickly with pine needles.'

Nancy thought for a moment that staid Letitia actually winked at her, but she managed a casual smile. 'That's an excellent idea. I really should do so myself.'

Letitia strolled out of the room and Nancy made to follow her but Felicia caught her by the wrist. 'No you don't,' she said, lowering her voice. 'I've been looking for you all day. You are supposed to be working for me, not gadding around with people above your station in life.'

'I'm sorry, Mrs de Marney. It won't happen again.'

'Is anything wrong?' Freddie moved swiftly to Nancy's side. 'D-don't be angry with Nancy, Mrs d-de Marney. I persuaded her to accompany me on a t-tour of the estate.'

Felicia drew herself up to her full height, although she only came up to Freddie's shoulder. 'Nancy knows better than that, my lord. She should have asked my permission first.'

'I think Nancy deserves a day off, my dear,' Claude said gently. 'It is the season of goodwill, after all.'

'You are always on her side, Claude. I'll thank you not to interfere. Nancy is little more than a servant when it comes down to the truth of the matter. I don't think your mama would approve of you consorting with someone of such lowly birth, my lord.'

Freddie's blue eyes hardened to the colour of steel. 'I will ignore that remark, Mrs de Marney. Perhaps I should remind you that you were invited here to entertain my father's guests.'

Felicia paled alarmingly and Claude slipped his

arm around her shoulders. 'Nancy, smelling salts.'

Nancy snatched Felicia's reticule and took out the small bottle, which she uncorked and wafted beneath Felicia's nose.

Coughing and gasping for breath, Felicia allowed her husband to guide her to the nearest chair. She sank down onto the cushions, fanning herself vigorously. 'I am the toast of Milan and New York,' she said faintly.

'Precisely. We all have our place in the universe, Mrs de Marney. We n-need t-to respect each other for what w-we are.' He proffered his arm to Nancy. 'Shall we take a walk?'

Nancy allowed him to lead her from the room, not daring to look back to see how Felicia was taking their departure. Once outside in the wide corridor Nancy came to a halt, peering out of the window.

'It's dark and it's snowing. We can't go out in this, Freddie.'

He laughed. 'I know that, but it made a dramatic exit. I couldn't think of anything else to say. But, seriously, Nancy, you ought not to allow her to speak to you like that. You are twice the lady she is, no matter who your parents were.'

Nancy laid her hand on his arm. 'Thank you, Freddie, but I have to survive in a difficult world. You are so safe and secure here at Dorrington that you couldn't begin to know what it's like to be in my position.'

'I can't, it's true, but while you are here you are an honoured guest, just the same as anyone else. I won't have it any other way. Now, shall we go outside and play snowballs like errant schoolchildren?'

'I would love to, but I think I'd better go and change for dinner or I will be in even more trouble with Mrs de Marney.'

Freddie acknowledged her decision with a nod and a smile. 'I'll make sure you are seated next to me at dinner, even if I have to alter the place cards.'

'Mrs de Marney is going to give a performance later this evening. I will accompany her at the pianoforte. I should have been here to go through the arias with her, Freddie.'

'I've heard you play. You'll be fine. Stop worrying, Nancy.'

★ ★ ★

Whether it was Freddie's stern rebuke or the amount of brandy that Felicia had consumed both before and after dinner, her performance in the ballroom rivalled any she had given at the opera houses of Europe. Nancy accompanied her flawlessly and the applause at the end of the recital was enthusiastic with cries of 'Brava' and 'Encore'. Felicia bowed graciously, smiled and blew kisses to her admirers as she left the dais.

'Don't think I've forgotten what you did today,' Felicia said in an undertone when Nancy followed her to their table. 'That young man might be a viscount but he has no manners. I will deal with you in the morning, Nancy.'

Nancy managed to avoid Freddie, who had been waylaid by Lady Brocklebourne with Letitia standing at her side. It was obvious that neither Freddie nor Letitia wanted to be part of the conversation, but they were trapped. Nancy left the ballroom and was making her way to the grand staircase when she heard a commotion outside. She came to a halt as a gust of cold air brought a flurry of snowflakes into the entrance hall when Pickering opened the door. Two men stumbled in, their greatcoats and hats powdered with snow.

'Might I ask your name, sir? Are you on the guest list?'

'No, my man. We were caught in the storm and only just managed to get this far.'

Nancy shrank into the shadows as she recognised the voice. She held her breath as he turned his head to glance in her direction.

13

There was no escape. Gervase had seen her.

'Miss Sunday will vouch for me,' Gervase said loudly. 'We are old friends, are we not, Nancy?'

She walked slowly towards him. 'I wouldn't say that exactly, Gervase.'

'But this person is known to you, miss?' Pickering gave her a searching look.

'Yes, I know him. He is Gervase North.'

'Here is my card. I am Gervase North of Greystone Park, Rockwood, in the county of Devonshire. Please tell Lord Dorrington that I am here. He does know me.'

Pickering remained stony-faced. 'If you will kindly wait here, sir, I will inform his lordship.' He placed the visiting card on a silver salver and strode off with a measured step in the direction of the ballroom.

'What are you doing here, Gervase?' Nancy demanded angrily. 'Who is this you've brought with you?'

Gervase tapped the man on the shoulder. 'I believe you know this fellow, Nancy? I found him loitering on the front step in John Adam Street.'

'Reuben.' Nancy stared at him in surprise.

He snatched off his cap, sprinkling lumps of melting snow onto the floor. 'I'm sorry to intrude, miss. Mr North brought me here, but I thought we was going to your castle. I want to find Molly.'

'She thinks you don't care for her, Reuben.'

'That I do, miss. I loves her with all me heart, but I didn't think she would want to be tied to a poor man like me.'

'I think you should allow her to make that decision,' Nancy said firmly. 'But that doesn't explain why you're here, Gervase. You haven't given me an answer.'

'I came to find you, Nancy.'

Pickering returned before Nancy had a chance to question Gervase further.

'His lordship is unable to see you now, sir. But if you would like to follow me, both of you gentlemen, you will be given a meal while rooms are being prepared for you. It's obvious you cannot travel on tonight.'

'I was hoping to speak to the earl or his son personally.'

'Maybe tomorrow, sir. They are otherwise engaged at present.'

'Don't argue, Gervase,' Nancy said firmly. 'His lordship is entertaining his guests, but he could have had you thrown out or you might have been sent to the stables to sleep. I would count myself lucky, if I were you.' She went to mount the stairs but Gervase called out to her.

'Wait, you could come and sit with us.'

'I'll bid you good night, Gervase, but I will send Molly to speak to you, Reuben. After all, you came a long way to see her, so you must have something important to say.'

Nancy did not wait for his response. She went straight to her room.

Molly was turning down the bed. The fire had been banked up with coal and the curtains drawn. The room was warm and inviting, but Nancy was too excited to notice.

'Molly, I have some wonderful news for you.'

'Yes, miss.'

'No, it really is what you've been waiting for. Guess who has just arrived?'

Molly's rosy cheeks paled. 'Not Reuben? He wouldn't know how to get to a place like this.'

'Well, he has, Nancy. He's come all this way to find you. Leave what you're doing. I can put myself to bed. Go downstairs and ask Pickering where Mr North and the other gentleman are having their meal.'

'Mr North, miss?'

'Yes, I'm not too pleased about that, but he'll be on his way in the morning. Now brush your hair and pinch your cheeks to put some colour back in them. Go downstairs and put him out of his misery. Remember that Reuben is shy, and he must have been desperate to make the journey here.'

'I will, miss.' Molly patted her hair in place, and pinched her cheeks to bring a little colour into her pale face.

'Go on, now. Don't worry about anything other than making things right with Reuben.'

Nancy slumped down on her bed as the door closed behind Molly. She was happy for Molly and Reuben, but her own future looked bleak. She had thoroughly enjoyed her time with Freddie, but she knew it could not last. No matter what she or Freddie felt, they were up against a solid wall of prejudice and greed. The Dorringtons had no need of more land or money, as far as Nancy could see, and yet Lady Dorrington wanted her son to marry an heiress. Letitia was adamant that marriage was not one of her priorities, and maybe she would be happier on her own anyway. There seemed to be too many people wanting to interfere in the lives of others, but Nancy knew that invisible boundaries would prevent her from getting too close to someone like Freddie. Pressure would be brought to bear on him and eventually they would have to part. Moreover, Nancy had the feeling that Felicia would have more than a few words to say to her next morning, and it was not going to be pleasant.

* * *

Having awakened early, Nancy had just finished dressing when she received a summons from Felicia. Nancy knew better than to keep Felicia waiting and she hurried to her room. There was no sign of Claude, and Felicia was still wearing her wrap over a diaphanous nightgown. Her hair was confined to a nightcap and her face was pale with fatigue.

'You are an ingrate, Nancy. After everything I have done for you, and all the money I have spent on clothing you like a lady, this is how you repay me.'

'I'm sorry, Mrs de Marney. I don't know what you mean.'

'Don't pretend to be so innocent, miss. You have been making eyes at Freddie Ashton ever since you met him. It's clear to me that you think you can make him fall in love with you — well, I'm telling you that his parents will never allow him to make such a misalliance.'

'I haven't been flirting with Freddie. We get on well together, but I know he's not for me.'

'You are right there, but I don't think you really believe that. If you continue to act as you have done, we will be asked to leave before Christmas. I will have to suffer because of you.'

'That is very unfair, Mrs de Marney.' Nancy stood her ground, glaring at Felicia. 'You were invited here to entertain the guests and I am just your accompanist. Everyone knows that.'

'Claude and I are honoured guests, just the same as everyone else. It's you who are dragging us down to the level of the servants' hall by your lewd behaviour.'

Nancy took a step backwards. 'I have done nothing wrong. I am not staying here a moment longer. You can find someone else to accompany you on the pianoforte.'

'You can't walk out on me. You work for me, Nancy Sunday.'

'I've been your slave for the past few weeks, Mrs de Marney. You haven't paid me a penny piece for my labours. I am leaving and you can't stop me.'

Felicia threw herself down on the nearest chair and began to sob hysterically. 'Send for Violet. I need brandy.'

'You drink too much brandy. A seltzer would do you more good,' Nancy said angrily. 'I'm done. Ring the bell yourself.' She stormed out of the room, almost knocking Violet over as she went. 'I suppose you heard all that, Violet Tinker. You'd best fetch the sal volatile.' Nancy marched off in the direction of her own room. She rang for Molly and began throwing her clothes into a large valise.

Molly appeared in the doorway, wide-eyed and flushed. 'What's happened, miss? Why are you packing?'

'We're leaving, Molly. I've told Mrs de Marney what I think of her and I'm going home to Rockwood. You and Reuben had better come with me, because I doubt if you'll be welcome here.'

'But, miss, the snow is thick on the roads. Reuben said it was really difficult travelling last night, and we haven't got any transport.'

Nancy hesitated. 'You're right. It's too far to walk, especially in bad weather. I'll see what I can do. Finish packing my things, please, but leave the new gowns that were made in London. I don't want to be accused of stealing.'

'Oh, miss. What a to-do.'

Nancy shrugged and left the room. There was only one person who could help. She would have to try to make Freddie understand her predicament, but that might not be easy. She hoped to catch him in the dining room, having a late breakfast, but when she was waylaid in the entrance hall by Lady Dorrington herself.

'I want a few words with you, Miss Sunday.'

'Yes, my lady.'

'I won't dissemble. I'll tell you to your face that I want you to leave Dorrington Place immediately.'

'I've done nothing wrong, my lady.'

'Not yet, but you have only to cast those big brown eyes in my son's direction and I can see the way the wind is blowing. You, as I've been told, are a foundling, raised to be a servant but educated above your station in life. I don't want you associating with my son. Do you understand what I'm saying?'

'As a matter of fact, I do, Lady Dorrington, and I agree with you entirely.'

Lady Dorrington opened her mouth as if to argue and shut it again with a snap. She took a deep breath. 'Are you being impertinent, miss?'

'No, my lady. I am very fond of Freddie and I believe

he likes me, but I know it must end there. I refuse to work for Mrs de Marney any longer. In fact, I intend to leave right away. The only problem is the weather and lack of transport.'

'I'm astonished that you are being so sensible about things, Miss Sunday. However, I can help you there. I will send for a carriage to take you and your maid-servant to Rockwood Castle, which is where I assume you wish to be.'

'Indeed I do, my lady.'

'Consider it done, but I forbid you to see my son before you leave. I will advise Freddie of your decision when I know you are well on your way.'

'Thank you, my lady. Please tell him not to follow me. I think too much of Freddie to do anything that would hurt him.'

A slow smile lifted the frown from Lady Dorrington's features. 'It seems we are on the same side, Miss Sunday. Now hurry. The carriage will be at the side of the building to keep your departure as secret as possible.'

* * *

As Lady Dorrington had promised, Mason was waiting with the carriage at the side of the house, out of sight of the main windows. Nancy and Molly sat inside, but Reuben opted to sit with Mason on the driver's seat. They had just started slowly down the tree-lined avenue when the door was wrenched opened and Gervase threw himself into the carriage, clutching his portmanteau.

'What are you doing?' Nancy demanded angrily. 'Get out, Gervase.'

He hauled himself onto the seat opposite them. 'I can't, Nancy. I'm not welcome at Dorrington Place and I want to get to Greystone Park. This is the only way I can get there until the weather breaks.'

A quick glance out of the window at the leaden sky seemed to confirm his suspicions.

'How did you know we were leaving?' Nancy demanded angrily. 'It was a sudden decision.'

'I spent a sleepless night in the servants' quarters trying to get comfortable on a straw palliasse placed in the hall. The boot boy snored and so did your maid's gentleman friend. He seemed to take it all in his stride. I suppose that's how he sleeps anyway.'

Nancy felt Molly squirming with indignation at her side and she gave her a comforting pat on the hand. 'That's unkind, Gervase. Reuben is a good man.'

'And I'm not, I suppose. Well, you're probably right, but I know where I'm not wanted so I followed Reuben and I waited until the carriage had left before throwing myself on your mercy.'

'I could ask Mason to stop and put you out at the gate, but I suppose you would find some way of getting to Rockwood on your own.'

'I told you, I want to go to Greystone Park.'

'Then why did you go out of your way to find me? From the little I know of you, Gervase, you never do anything unless it's going to benefit you in some way.'

He laughed. 'How astute you are, Nancy.'

'Well then, Gervase, we have a long journey ahead. I suggest you tell me exactly what you are planning.'

He sat back in his seat, eyeing her with an inscrutable expression. 'I intend to claim my rights.'

'And what are they exactly?'

'I should have inherited Greystone Park, as I've

said before. I intend to take up residence and claim my rightful place in society.'

'And I've told you that Christina won't allow it.'

'What is she going to do? Her pious husband won't declare war on me, that's for certain. She can nag and bully all she likes but I am going to stand up to her.'

'What about poor Sylvia? What will you do when she returns from Switzerland?'

'If she returns.'

'Don't say things like that, Gervase. Of course she will get better. Mr and Mrs Pennington will make sure she has the finest treatment that money can buy.'

'She can have her old room, if she wishes. I've nothing against Sylvia, it's Christina I cannot abide.'

'We've had this discussion before. You won't win, Gervase.'

He tapped the side of his nose. 'I have plans, my dear. You'll see.'

'If we are to travel together I suggest you keep your thoughts to yourself. I don't mean to be rude, but I have problems of my own.'

'Ah, yes, the titled buffoon. I could see that you and he were getting a bit too close.'

Nancy leaned forward, eyeing him coldly. 'Freddie is not a buffoon. He is the kindest, nicest person I have ever met, but it's better for everyone if I leave before things get too complicated. In that, I actually agree with his mother, which is why we have the luxury of the Dorringtons' carriage to take us home.'

Gervase smiled. 'You know best, my dear.' He closed his eyes and slept.

The roads were hazardous and the carriage wheels slipped on the icy surface, but Mason was an experienced coachman and by midday they were halfway to

Rockwood. They stopped at a village inn to rest the horses and they ate in the landlord's parlour before travelling on. Nancy tried to put Freddie out of her mind. She knew she was doing the right thing by removing herself from a deepening relationship, but it troubled her that she had not been able to say good-bye to him. Molly was quietly sympathetic, perhaps because she had found happiness with Reuben. They sat together in the parlour, talking in whispers, which obviously irritated Gervase, who kept giving them warning looks. Nancy ignored him.

When they were refreshed and the horses back in harness, they set off again heading south towards the Devonshire coast. The snow was not so deep here and as they neared the sea the roads became more passable. As the sky darkened Nancy could not help thinking about the servants' ball at Dorrington Place. She had promised Freddie that she would attend, but by now he would know that she had abandoned him, and the thought of his distress brought tears to her eyes. She knew she was doing the right thing, but that would not cure the ache in her heart for the loss of a dear friend.

It was a relief when she began to recognise familiar landmarks in the gathering gloom, although by the time they reached the outskirts of Rockwood village the only lights came from candles in cottage windows reflecting on the soft white snow. She had given Mason instructions to stop outside the gates of Greystone Park, having no intention of burdening her family with Gervase's presence, even for one night. He wanted to claim what he considered to be his birthright, so he could start there and then.

'Why are we stopping here?' Gervase demanded,

peering out of the carriage window.

'This is where you wished to be,' Nancy said firmly. 'Out you get, Gervase. This is your home, or so you say.'

'Yes, but I don't intend to arrive on foot. That wouldn't impress the servants. There might not be anyone at home.'

'As far as I remember, Foster and Mrs Simpson are still there, and Mrs Banks, the cook. You will be quite comfortable.'

'Nancy, I really would prefer to spend the night at Rockwood.'

'Do you want me to ask Reuben and Mason to drag you from the carriage, Gervase? You imposed yourself upon us, so now it's your turn to do the gentlemanly thing and leave us in peace.'

'You are a hard woman, Nancy Sunday. I used to think you were young and sweet.'

'Maybe I was, once. But now I am gaining knowledge of how the world outside Rockwood works. So are you going to get out, or do I have to call for assistance?'

Gervase hooked his portmanteau onto his arm as he opened the door. 'One day you will be sorry that you treated me so unkindly.'

'Goodbye, Gervase.'

He slammed the door and stomped off towards the tall gates.

'If he hadn't gone then I would have pushed him out myself,' Molly said with a grim smile. 'He's trouble, that one, miss. I wouldn't trust him an inch.'

'I think you're right.' Nancy tapped on the roof as a signal for Mason to drive on. 'We'll be home soon. I wish I could have let them know we were coming.'

213

'We'll be in time for Christmas. I haven't seen Mother and Father for ages.'

'We're nearly there, Molly. You have Reuben now.'

'Yes, he proposed last evening, miss. I didn't like to tell you before.'

Nancy gave her a hug. 'I'm delighted for you, Molly. You deserve to be happy and Reuben is a good man. Now you can introduce him to your family.'

'But I'll have to leave you, miss. We'll be living in Highgate.'

'Then I will have to come and visit you there. Or maybe Reuben will want to come and live in Rockwood. You never know what might happen.'

Nancy settled back against the squabs to enjoy the last lap of the journey home. In the distance, silhouetted against a dark sky, she could see the square towers of her old home, and her pulse quickened. She might not be related to the family by blood, but she loved them all, even Hester. She could hardly contain her excitement as the carriage rumbled over the bridge and entered the castle grounds. As they entered the bailey Nancy was amazed to see that the flambeaux had been lit and Jarvis was standing in the open doorway with James at his side. Pip Hudson appeared as if from nowhere to hold the horses while Mason and Reuben climbed down from the box.

James stepped forward to open the carriage door and he proffered his arm to help Nancy alight.

'Welcome home, Miss Nancy.'

'Thank you, James. But how did you know we were coming?'

He grinned. 'News travels fast in Rockwood, miss. The carriage was seen stopping outside Greystone Park. Young Pip had been visiting his granny in the village and he saw you through the window. That boy runs like the wind.'

'James.' Jarvis's stentorian voice rang out across the cobbled yard and James snapped to attention. 'See to the luggage and keep your comments to yourself.'

'Don't scold him, Jarvis,' Nancy said, smiling. 'It's good to be home. I've missed you all.'

'Thank you, Miss Nancy.' Jarvis inclined his head, keeping a straight face, but Nancy had seen the twinkle in his eyes.

She entered the castle, breathing in the familiar smell of home. The slightly musty odour of an ancient building was almost obliterated by the scent of pine needles from the massive Christmas tree, with a hint of the outdoors emanating from the boughs of holly interwoven around the banisters. Swags of ivy festooned the sombre portraits that gazed down at her from their lofty position on the wall. Nancy patted Sir Denys's visor as she walked past the rusty suit of armour, keeping up the family tradition. Sir Denys Carey had died in battle several centuries earlier and his spirit was supposed to haunt the castle. Nancy did not believe in ghosts, but she was not taking any chances. It would be a mistake to anger Sir Denys, especially just before Christmas, which was when he was said to have breathed his last. Before she had time to move on she was enveloped in a double hug from Rosalind and eight-year-old Dolly.

'You've come home, Nancy,' Dolly cried enthusiastically. 'Mama said I had to go to bed but she allowed me to stay up to see you.'

Rosalind kissed Nancy on the cheek. 'Welcome home. You can tell me all about it when you've had time to catch your breath.'

Nancy was about to speak when Hester bustled up to them. 'This is a surprise, Nancy. Have you fallen out with Felicia?'

'She doesn't need me anymore,' Nancy said evasively.

'But you're home in time for Christmas,' Dolly added gleefully. 'If I go to bed now will you come up to the nursery and tuck me in?'

Nancy met Rosalind's amused glance and she smiled. 'Of course I will. Just give me time to take off my outdoor things and I'll come up and tell you a story.'

'And me.' Six-year-old Rory reached out to clasp Nancy's hand. 'Phoebe is only little so she's asleep in bed.'

'But we're allowed to stay up later,' Dolly added proudly. 'You will come to the nursery, promise?'

'Of course,' Nancy said, giving them both a hug. 'Now off you go and do what your mama says.'

'I don't want to go to bed,' Rory protested.

Hester seized him by the hand. 'Less of that, young Rory. I've dealt with bigger boys than you. Come along now. No nonsense.' She led him protesting up the stairs with Dolly dancing on ahead.

'Don't let my children bully you, Nancy.' Rosalind took Nancy by the hand. 'They'll get away with as much as they dare, except when Hester is in charge. Then they behave like little angels.'

'That doesn't surprise me,' Nancy said, smiling.

'What happened between you and Mama? I know she can be difficult at times.'

'It's a long story, Rosie.'

'And you're tired, of course, after travelling from London.'

'No, actually we came from Dorrington Place, on the Somerset border. I'll tell you all about it.'

'Come to the drawing room where it's warmer.' Rosalind led the way and took up her usual seat by the fire. 'Sit down and tell me what happened.'

Nancy glanced round the room with its slightly shabby but comfortable furniture and faded curtains. Deep shadows pooled in the corners where the candles had not been lit, but it was cosy rather than eerie, and the apple logs on the fire crackled, exuding their distinctive scent. It might not be as luxurious as the rooms in Dorrington Place, but it felt like home.

'Where is everyone? It's almost Christmas; I thought the whole family would be here.'

Rosalind's smile faded. 'A lot has happened since you were last here, Nancy.'

'What's wrong? Where is Alex? He's never far from your side.'

'That's just it. I don't know exactly.'

'What do you mean, you don't know? What is it you aren't telling me, Rosie?'

14

Rosalind folded her hands in her lap, avoiding Nancy's anxious gaze. 'It all started with a visit from Lady Pentelow.'

'I thought she never left Trevenor these days.'

'She doesn't usually, which made her sudden appearance quite disturbing. It's all down to Piers, as usual.'

'What has he done now? Didn't he receive a pardon?'

'Yes, he was pardoned when Ewart Blaise was tried and found guilty, but Piers could never resist a challenge. Lady Pentelow had word that he had joined a group of mercenaries. He's involved in blockade running between the armies of the North and the Confederates in the South.'

'He's in America?'

'No, apparently he's in Barbados. I don't know anything more but his grandmother was distraught. Piers is her only grandson, Alex is her great-nephew. It's not quite the same, in her mind.'

Nancy stared into the flames, frowning. 'But Piers can take care of himself, surely? Why would she be so upset?'

'The mine hasn't done well, even with Martin Gibbs running it. Aurelia has left him and has moved back to Trevenor.'

'I'm confused. What does it matter whether Piers is in Australia or Barbados?'

'Lady Pentelow wants him to come home. She begged Alex to go to Barbados and persuade Piers to give up what he's doing and return to Trevenor. If the clay mining business fails, she would be in danger of losing everything. Piers is the only person who can save it, but I was married to him for two years. I know how stubborn he can be.'

'So Alex has gone to Cornwall. Is that correct?'

'Yes, and Leo went with him. I am trying to run the house and help Bertie to manage the estate. Frank Bayliss is good man but he isn't in a position to make decisions when it comes to business matters. We have to make a profit in order to keep going.'

'I'm so sorry you've had this thrust on you, Rosie. But why did Leo go as well as Alex?'

'The miners threatened to strike. I think Alex thought it best to have someone like Leo to back him up. Bertie couldn't cope without Wolfe, so Leo went instead.'

'Doesn't Walter help you?'

'Of course he does, to the best of his ability, but he is in the middle of writing his next novel and he's not very practical. We're managing, but I worry about Alex and Leo. I keep promising the children that Papa will be home in time for Christmas, although I'm beginning to doubt it.'

Nancy rose to her feet and went to kneel by Rosalind's side. She grasped her hands and gave them a squeeze. 'Alex and Leo can look after themselves. I'm certain they'll see sense and return to Rockwood in time for the festivities.'

'I hope you're right. I'm sorry, Nancy. This isn't much of a homecoming for you. Now, tell me what's been happening. Did you fall out with my mother? I know how difficult she can be at times.'

Nancy was about to explain when Hester entered the room. She slumped down on the sofa.

'Well, young lady. Why are you here without the prima donna and her husband?'

'They are spending Christmas with the Dorringtons,' Nancy said carefully.

'But you were supposed to be at her beck and call.' Hester fixed Nancy with a hard stare. 'There's more to it than that, isn't there?'

Nancy could tell by Hester's expression that she would only be satisfied when she knew everything. She launched into an account of her time in London, ending with the visit to Dorrington Place, but she was careful to omit mentioning Freddie's name.

'I can't say I'm surprised,' Hester said, pursing her lips. 'Although I don't know why the Countess of Dorrington would be so generous as to send you home in her private carriage.'

'Thank goodness she did. This weather makes travelling hazardous. The coachman should stay tonight.' Rosalind stood up and rang the bell. 'I'm sure they can find him a bed in the stable block.'

'Molly came with me, and her fiancé.' Nancy smiled. 'That's something I forgot to tell you.'

'I wonder what else you've omitted.' Hester eyed her curiously. 'No doubt it will all come out in time. You always kept things close to you, Nancy.'

'Then that means there will be two more for Mrs Jackson to feed.' Rosalind rang the bell for the second time.

Nancy rose to her feet. 'I promised to read the children a story. I can't let them down.'

'Of course not,' Rosalind said, smiling. 'Go to the

nursery and I'll send Tilly to light the fire in your room and put clean sheets on the bed. We'll dine in an hour.'

Nancy made her way to the nursery where she found Dolly and Rory waiting eagerly for their story. By the time she had finished they were both curled up in their respective beds, rosy-cheeked and their eyelids drooping sleepily. Nancy kissed them both and crept out of the room. It was good to be home, but the news was disturbing. She remembered liking Piers, but even as a child she had known he spelled trouble, and that had been the case. His short marriage to Rosalind had not been an entirely happy one, despite their obvious love for each other. But Piers was a rover and he had scant respect for the law, which had landed him in the penal colony in Australia. It was clear that he was still an adventurer at heart, but even in his absence he continued to hold sway over the family, and as Dolly's father he was someone to be reckoned with. Nancy went downstairs to the drawing room. It was not going to be the wonderful family Christmas she had hoped for.

★　★　★

Next morning Nancy was just finishing her breakfast when Patricia burst into the dining room.

'Nancy, I heard that you had arrived home.'

'Won't you join us for breakfast?' Rosalind rose from her seat. 'I've just finished but I have a meeting with Frank Bayliss in ten minutes. Bertie is seeing the bank manager in Exeter and I can't always rely on Walter for help.'

Patricia laughed. 'You can't rely on dear Walter any

221

of the time, Rosie. You are too kind and patient. He's useless.'

'He's a talented author, Patsy. Give him his due.'

'That's as may be, but he's not much use at anything else.' Patricia went to the sideboard and helped herself to a generous portion of bacon and buttered eggs.

'Why are you here so early, Patsy? You don't normally rise until nearly midday.'

'That's not true.' Patricia took a seat at the table. 'I am going to Cornwall today.' She shot a sideways glance at Nancy. 'I'd like you to accompany me.'

'But I've only just arrived home.'

'Then you won't need to unpack.'

Rosalind stared at her sister in disbelief. 'It's only a few days until Christmas. You can't go away and leave us. The children will be heartbroken.'

'They won't even notice.' Patricia reached for the coffee pot and filled a cup. 'I am not spending Christmas without Leo. I don't know what he's doing at Trevenor, but I'm going to bring him home in time for the festivities.'

'Is that wise, Patsy? Surely you should give him the chance to make his own decisions?'

'Nonsense. When did a man ever know what was best for him? The sawmill doesn't run itself and Robbins is only fit to look after the horses. I'm closing the mill down for a few days.'

'But, Patsy, travelling in this weather is best avoided.'

'Nancy got here safely, and I gather she's deposited Gervase at Greystone Park. That will be interesting when Christina finds out that he's stormed the battlements, so to speak.'

'That doesn't concern us, nor should it bother you,

Patsy. You lost control of Greystone Park when Sir Michael willed it to his daughters.'

'You don't have to remind me of that.'

'I think I do. Just forget Gervase. He is the least of our worries.'

'I intend to bring Alex back to you, Rosie.'

'Alex will come when he's satisfied that Lady Pentelow is safe.'

Nancy buttered a slice of toast. 'Gervase says he intends to challenge Sir Michael's will. He thinks he is the rightful heir to Greystone.'

Patricia tossed her head. 'That man is mad. Let him try. I don't care.' She turned to Nancy. 'Are you willing to come with me to Cornwall?'

Nancy eyed Rosalind warily. She did not want to offend either of her surrogate sisters.

'Go with her if that's what you want,' Rosalind said slowly. 'Perhaps Patsy is right. Maybe we should make a stand. Lady Pentelow only shows an interest in Alex when she wants something.'

Nancy nodded. 'I'll come with you, Patsy. I've never seen Trevenor, so it will be interesting.' She did not add that doing something active would help to heal the pain in her heart from abandoning Freddie without a word of explanation. She knew she had done the right thing, but that did not make it any easier.

Patricia took her place at the table. 'I haven't had any breakfast. Who knows when we'll get a chance to eat again? Get your things, Nancy. We'll leave as soon as I've eaten.'

★ ★ ★

They travelled by carriage and then train with an overnight stay in Plymouth, continuing next day by train to St Austell and then by hired carriage. It was late afternoon when they finally arrived at Trevenor, having driven past the mine entrance. All seemed to be quiet there and in the village. The gates to the estate were locked but a groundsman appeared eventually in response to the coachman tugging on the bell pull.

He seemed reluctant to let them in but Patricia insisted that they were guests of Lady Pentelow, and eventually he opened the gates and they alighted outside the main entrance. Patricia paid the coachman, leaving Nancy to gaze in wonder at the snow-covered parterre garden leading to a sweep of lawn, which seemed to disappear into nothingness. It was dark, but the moonlight illuminated the white stucco frontage of the house, and the rhythmic pounding of the waves crashing on the rocks below the cliffs was quite magical. Nancy realised then how much she had missed the sound of the sea and the tang of salt in the air.

Patricia rapped on the knocker and they waited for a minute or two until the door creaked open.

'May I help you, ma'am?' The butler blinked at them in the light of a lantern he held high above their heads.

'Patterson, you might remember me as Patricia Carey. I am now Mrs Leo Wilder. I believe my husband is Lady Pentelow's guest.'

'He's not here, madam.'

'Patterson,' Patricia said grimly, 'we have travelled all the way from Rockwood in Devonshire, and we are cold, tired and hungry. Kindly tell your mistress that we are here.'

'What's going on, Patterson?' A shabbily dressed

young woman came hurrying towards them, clutching a silver candlestick. The candle flame guttered in a gust of wind but recovered to give a flickering light.

'Aurelia?' Patricia pushed past the startled butler to hug her. 'What have you done to yourself?'

Aurelia's hand flew to pat her dishevelled hair into place. 'Patsy, what are you doing here?'

Nancy took advantage of the butler's momentary lack of concentration and slipped past him.

'Wait, please, miss. I have to find out if Lady Pentelow is at home to you.'

'Don't be ridiculous, Patterson,' Aurelia said crossly. 'Of course she is. Come this way, Patsy, and you, too. It's Nancy, isn't it? I remember you as being much younger.'

'Yes, ma'am. I'm Nancy.'

'Of course she's older, Aurelia. It must be a few years since we last met.' Patricia slipped her arm around Aurelia's shoulders. 'What has happened to you?'

'Come to the drawing room. There's a good fire going there. We've had rather a hard time of things recently, Patsy.'

Nancy followed as Aurelia led Patricia into the depths of the house, leaving Patterson to deal with their luggage.

The narrow corridors were dark and twisting, lit only by Aurelia's single candle. Nancy noticed that the wall sconces were empty and a cold draught whistled round her ears. Seated in a wing-back chair by the log fire, Lady Pentelow peered at them in amazement as they entered the poorly lit drawing room.

'Grandmama, look who's come to visit us?' Aurelia gave Patricia a gentle shove.

'Patricia? Why are you here?' Lady Pentelow's voice was querulous and her hand shook as she fumbled beneath the thick woollen blanket wrapped around her and drew out a silver lorgnette. She held it to her eyes. 'Who is that with you? Servants belong below stairs.'

'This is Nancy, Lady Pentelow,' Patricia said hastily. 'She is my sister's ward, in case you've forgotten.'

'There's nothing wrong with my memory, young woman. As I said, why are you here?'

Aurelia gave Patricia a warning glance. 'Grandmama, Patricia is Leo's wife. I dare say she wonders why he has not returned to Rockwood.'

'Don't talk to me as if I were a simpleton, Aurelia. I am well aware who Patricia is. I recall the wedding that never took place when she was supposed to marry Alexander, and her mama decided to use her daughter's misfortune for her own advantage. Felicia married that manager of hers, I don't recall his name.'

'That all happened years ago, Lady Pentelow. Where is Leo?' Patricia demanded angrily. 'And why are you living like this? I remember Trevenor in the old days.' She turned to Aurelia. 'You look terrible, if you don't mind me saying so. Why have you allowed yourself to get in such a state?'

Aurelia's hazel eyes filled with tears. Nancy had to resist the temptation to reprimand Patricia for her cruel taunt. She remembered seeing Aurelia at Rockwood Castle before she married the manager of the clay mine, but Aurelia showed little sign now of the beauty she had once been. Her face was too thin and pale and her once luxuriant dark hair hung in lank strands where it escaped from the net at the nape of her neck. Her gown was faded and stained and her hands looked grimy, her fingernails bitten to the quick.

'I didn't marry a wealthy politician, as you did, Patsy,' Aurelia said bitterly. 'Martin was a bad manager and an equally bad husband after he took to drink.'

'And he beat her when things went wrong,' Lady Pentelow added. 'He almost ruined us and allowed the mine to sink into debt. The men are on strike as we speak.'

'If we don't pay their wages soon there'll be a riot,' Aurelia said anxiously.

'I am sorry to hear that, but it doesn't answer my question. Where are Leo and Alex?'

'The mine has stopped producing clay. Our two ships were laid up for months until we started shipping supplies to Barbados.'

'You mean you're helping to break the blockade to the Southern states?' Nancy looked from one to the other.

'What do you know about such things, miss?' Lady Pentelow glared at her. 'You speak when you're spoken to.'

'Lady Pentelow, I understand that you are having a difficult time, but you do not treat Nancy like a servant. She is part of our family and my particular friend.' Patricia pulled up a chair and sat down. 'You'd better tell me exactly what's been going on, Aurelia. I'm fast losing patience.'

'Piers is in Barbados assisting the blockade runners.' Aurelia sank down on a chair close to the fire. 'He didn't want to return to Cornwall after his years in New South Wales, but what he's doing now is fraught with danger. We need him here or we might lose Trevenor forever. Leo and Alex have gone to bring him home, it's as simple as that.'

'They must be mad to undertake such a journey,' Patricia said angrily. 'When did they leave?'

'About four weeks ago. They should be on the way home by now. We're expecting the *Corinthian* to arrive tomorrow. She is the sister ship to the *Cyrene*, which is the one that took Leo and Alex to Barbados. She should bring news, and hopefully the captain will have brought enough money for us to pay the miners and prevent a full-scale riot.'

'My husband is risking his life to save Piers Blanchard, who is interfering in another country's politics! I've no doubt Piers will make a fortune out of it.' Patricia threw up her hands. 'I've heard everything now.'

'My grandson is doing what he believes is right,' Lady Pentelow said haughtily. 'I don't expect you to understand.'

'We have to survive. It's as simple as that.' Aurelia mopped her streaming eyes with a scrap of cotton hanky. 'Look at us, Patricia. We're in desperate straits financially.'

'Then why isn't Piers here to help you instead of playing the hero in another country? I seem to recall he did much the same thing to us at Rockwood.'

'I don't know what you're talking about,' Lady Pentelow said crossly. 'Have you come here simply to insult my grandson?'

'You obviously don't know what Piers is really like, my lady. He insinuated himself into our family years ago, pretending to be the rightful heir to the estate, and when that was proved to be untrue he managed to make my sister fall in love with him. Piers thinks only of himself. Why should Rosie and I allow our husbands to risk their necks to save someone as worthless as Piers Blanchard?'

'My grandson has paid handsomely for his mistakes,' Lady Pentelow said sharply. 'Piers has served his time in the penal colony. He might be misguided in what he's doing now, but I want him brought home.'

'Please can we stop arguing about the rights and wrongs of Piers' actions?' Aurelia shook her head vehemently. 'Why are you being so difficult, Patsy?'

'We've come a long way,' Nancy said quickly. 'But if it's inconvenient for us to stay here, there was a hostelry in the village. Perhaps we ought to go there.'

'No, of course not.' Aurelia rose to her feet. 'We can't offer luxury but I'll send Ada to make up a fire in your room. You don't mind sharing, do you?'

'Of course not.' Nancy could see that the slightest thing would send Patricia off on another rant against Piers and the Blanchard family, which would only make matters worse.

Aurelia stood up, clutching her shawl tightly around her. 'I'll let Mrs Witham know you're here. We have very few servants left but the older ones have stayed on. I don't know what we'd do without them.'

Patricia watched Aurelia as she pulled the tasselled cord to summon a servant. 'How is it that your affairs have altered so quickly? Why wasn't Alex told? I believe he has shares in the mine.'

'Trade has been bad for several years.' Aurelia sat down again, sighing. 'Things would have been different had Piers chosen to come home as soon as he was set free.'

'Just as I said. He's irresponsible and selfish, but I dare say he's making money out of his exploits in Barbados.'

'If Aurelia had done what I ordered and married a man of means, none of this would have happened, but she insisted on marrying Martin Gibbs, a jumped-up miner.' Lady Pentelow leaned back in her chair. 'All this is too much for me. Leave me in peace until supper is ready. We no longer dine like civilised people, Patricia. You will have to live like peasants, as we do.'

'Enter,' Aurelia said in answer to a timid knock on the door.

'You rang, ma'am?' Ada edged into the room, glancing nervously at Lady Pentelow.

'We have guests,' Aurelia said simply. 'Light a fire in the Chinoiserie bedchamber and make up the bed, please, Ada.'

'Yes, ma'am.'

'And tell Cook there will be two more for supper tonight.'

'Yes, ma'am.' Ada curtsied, giving Patricia and Nancy a curious glance before hurrying from the room.

Aurelia turned to Nancy and Patricia with a hint of a smile. 'We dine at six o'clock these days and retire to bed early in the winter to save money on coal and candles. I'm sure that Alex and Leo are much more comfortable on board ship than they were here, although neither of them complained.'

Patricia smiled. 'Alex was a soldier and Leo spent time at sea, amongst other things, so they have both known discomfort. It's you I'm worried about, Aurelia. You look —'

Aurelia held up her hand. 'Don't say it again, please. I know I've let myself turn into a slattern. It's been a question of surviving, and I've had to turn my hand to all manner of things because so many of the

230

servants have left.'

Patricia glanced at Lady Pentelow, who had nodded off to sleep and was snoring gently.

'What happened to Martin? Is he still living in your old house?'

'Yes, and he works at the mine. It was he who called the strike. He has nothing but spite for us now. I think he's intent on ruining us, even if it means losing his job and his home. It was my fault, Patsy. I fell in love and I was blinded by my feelings for him.' She gave Nancy a wry smile. 'You might fall into the same trap one day, Nancy. Please be wary and listen to the advice of others.'

'Nonsense,' Patricia said sharply. 'Nancy is far too sensible to allow her heart to overrule her head. She's just escaped from my mother's clutches, haven't you, Nancy?'

'I wouldn't put it quite like that, but Mrs de Marney doesn't need me now. Maybe I can help out here. I'm quite good at household matters.'

Patricia shook her head. 'I'm afraid we won't be here long enough to be much use. When I find out what has happened to Leo and Alex, we'll be on our way home, Nancy. It's Christmas next week and we don't want to disappoint Dolly and Rory. Rosie is suffering because of Alexander's idiotic quest to save his cousin. It's not just about me, Aurelia.'

'I understand. But there's nothing we can do about it, so shall we forget Piers and the trouble he's caused for an hour or two? There's a decanter filled with blackberry wine — I made it myself and it's quite potent. We haven't been able to afford any luxuries, but I've become quite good at simple things like working in the still room.' She sighed and then laughed. 'I've become a good housewife even if I've lost my home and my husband.'

Nancy reached out to pat Aurelia on the shoulder. 'I admire what you've done. I don't know if I would be so brave in your circumstances.'

'Just remember my example if you think you've fallen in love.' Aurelia gave her a searching look. 'I know that expression, Nancy. You have met someone, haven't you?'

'Of course not,' Patricia said scornfully. 'She would have confided in me, wouldn't you, Nancy?'

Nancy glanced from one inquisitive face to the other and she knew she had been found out. There was no evading the truth now. Neither Patricia nor Aurelia would take no for an answer.

'Well, there is someone,' Nancy said slowly. 'But he's not for me. I know that and I'm not going to see him again.'

'Who is it, Nancy? Has someone been toying with your emotions?' Patricia glared at her. 'I'll have words to say to that gentleman. It isn't Gervase, is it?'

Nancy laughed, shaking her head. 'No, he's the last man on earth I would want to marry.'

'You can tell us.' Aurelia caught hold of Nancy's hand. 'We might be able to help.'

'No, you can't. No one can. He's too far above me in every way.'

'Nonsense.' Patricia leaned forward. 'Tell us who it is. We are more experienced in such matters.'

Nancy could see that she was not going to get away without telling them the truth, but if she did it might rebound on her in a catastrophic way. She had no intention of placing Freddie in an awkward situation. 'I'm sorry, I can't tell you. Please forget about it.'

'You cannot leave it there, Nancy. Who is this fellow who has been tugging at your heartstrings? You're very young. Is it someone in the opera company? If so, Mama should have been taking better care of you.'

Aurelia shrugged. 'Your mama is only interested in one thing, Patsy. Herself.'

'That is true.' Patricia acknowledged her words with a sigh. 'Who is he, Nancy? Don't suffer heartbreak on your own. Please, tell us who he is.'

15

'Freddie Ashton!' Patricia stared at Nancy in amazement.

'Who is Freddie Ashton?' Aurelia frowned. 'I don't think I know him.'

'Viscount Ashton,' Patricia said flatly. 'Only the second wealthiest bachelor in England. He's the heir to Dorrington Place and a mansion in London, not to mention a huge estate.'

Aurelia shook her head. 'We are so out of touch these days. I vaguely recall the name.'

'Please don't make a fuss,' Nancy pleaded. 'I wouldn't have told you if you hadn't insisted. Freddie is a wonderful person but he's not for the likes of me.'

'Shame on you, Nancy,' Patricia said passionately. 'You are good enough for any man alive. I won't allow you to belittle yourself.'

'I know you think so, but Lady Dorrington made it perfectly clear that Freddie could not marry a nobody, and I have to agree with her.'

Patricia rolled her eyes. 'You don't have to listen to his mama, Nancy. No one will be good enough for her son. You'll learn that as you get older.'

'I can think for myself, and I know she's right. Anyway, we were only just getting to know each other. I had to get away before it became serious, but I really don't want to talk about it now, and you have more pressing problems at the moment.'

'That's true,' Aurelia said sadly. She walked over

to a side table half hidden in the gloom and returned moments later with a tray and three glasses of wine. 'My best homemade blackberry. As I said, it's quite potent, so sip it slowly.'

Lady Pentelow's eyes opened wide. 'Thank you, Aurelia. I'll have a small glass — for medicinal purposes, of course.'

Aurelia and Patricia exchanged amused glances and Nancy turned away to stifle a giggle.

★ ★ ★

Later that evening, they ate in the grand dining room, although Nancy could see blank spaces on the walls where paintings had once hung, and gaps on the huge sideboard where silver and china had been sent to the sale rooms. Two candles on the vast table were the only source of light in the huge room, but Lady Pentelow took her place at the head as if nothing had changed. Ada placed a tureen of vegetable soup on the table in front of Aurelia, who served it into the second-best china.

'Peasant food.' Lady Pentelow broke off a chunk of freshly baked bread and dropped small pieces into her bowl. 'We used to dine in style. Now look at us.'

'It's delicious,' Nancy said hastily. 'Really tasty.'

'You won't say that when you've had the same meal day in and day out for a month or more.' Aurelia sighed heavily. 'The captain had better bring good news tomorrow. I don't know what we'll do if there isn't enough money to pay the miners' wages, let alone to buy supplies.'

'I just hope that Leo and Alex are on board,' Patricia said grimly.

'I'm thinking about the poor miners' families.' Aurelia stared down at her plate. 'This is luxury compared to what some of them have been having. I've sent bread to those who are near destitute, but we're running low on flour and soon there will be none left for us.'

Patricia raised her glass of blackberry wine. 'Here's a toast to the return of the *Corinthian*. May she arrive safely and bring an end to all our troubles.'

Nancy and Aurelia joined in the toast, but Lady Pentelow was too busy spooning soup into her mouth to bother. 'What will be, will be,' she muttered, breaking off another chunk of bread. 'Is there no butter, Aurelia?'

'No, Grandmama. We haven't been able to pay the farmer or the village shop. We owe money to everyone.'

'That's how we've always done business. They trust us because they know that we are good for our word.'

'I don't think that applies now, Grandmama. The whole village knows our business. If Piers hasn't sent money tomorrow, we face bankruptcy.'

★ ★ ★

Next morning, at first light, Nancy and Aurelia stood on the cliff top, gazing out across the bay.

'What will you do if the Corinthian doesn't arrive?' Nancy shivered as a bitter wind spiked with sleet tugged at her skirts and the thick wool of her cape.

'We've tried to sell off the mine, but no one in their right mind would buy a business that is making a steady loss. Especially with miners who are on strike and threatening violence. We can't sell Trevenor without Piers' permission, and if we cannot contact him we are helpless.'

'Couldn't Alex do anything to help? After all, he was supposed to have an interest in the mine, or so Patricia said.'

'He did, but Martin was quite clever at making out everything was running smoothly. He made all sorts of excuses for the shares doing badly and Alex believed him.' Aurelia turned away from the view. 'We could be here all day, Nancy. I think we'd better go indoors and have breakfast. I'll walk down to the village later and see if there's any news.'

Nancy glanced over Aurelia's shoulder. 'Someone is coming up the cliff path. Do you recognise him?'

'It's Daniel Comer. He's the mine manager now.' Aurelia set off at a run with Nancy hot on her heels. They arrived at the locked gates to find Daniel leaning against them gasping for breath.

'What's wrong, Daniel?' Aurelia cried anxiously. 'What's happened? There's blood on your clothes. Are you hurt?'

He shook his head. 'Not mine.' He struggled to control his breathing. 'Bad news, ma'am.'

'What is it?' Aurelia tried to open the gates but he held up his hand.

'Keep 'em locked, ma'am. News has just come in that the *Corinthian* has gone down off the Azores. No survivors, as far as we know.'

Aurelia sank to her knees, clutching the intricate wrought iron. 'None?'

'No, ma'am. All hands lost, so they say.'

Nancy helped Aurelia to her feet. 'What haven't you told us, Mr Comer?'

'News has got round, miss. The men knew there

237

was money for their pay on the ship and now it's at the bottom of the Atlantic Ocean. There was a riot.'

Aurelia leaned against the gate. 'This is so dreadful. Was anyone badly hurt?'

'A few, miss, and one fatality. I don't like to say more.'

'Who was it, Daniel? I need to know.'

Daniel glanced at Nancy, his dark eyebrows lowered. 'You should take the missis into the house. There's going to be more trouble.'

'Who was killed, Daniel?' Aurelia insisted desperately. 'I should see his family and give them my sympathy.'

Daniel shook his head. 'No need, ma'am. You knew him well enough. I'm sorry.'

'Martin?' Aurelia's voice cracked and she began to tremble.

Nancy put an arm around her waist and held her. 'I'm so sorry, Aurelia.'

'Are you sure, Daniel?' Aurelia leaned heavily on Nancy. 'Could there be a mistake?'

'No, ma'am. Again, I'm sorry to be the bearer of bad news.' Daniel hesitated, glancing over his shoulder. 'If I was you I'd keep away from the village. When the news gets round that there is no money, there will be more trouble.' He backed away. 'I have to go, ma'am.'

Nancy had to drag Aurelia away from the gate. 'It's too cold to stand about here, Aurelia. Come indoors.'

'What will we do? We're ruined and Martin is dead. If I hadn't left him, maybe I could have stopped this before things got out of hand. I loved him once.'

'It's no use thinking about what might have been. We have got to do something now.'

Aurelia nodded mutely and allowed Nancy to help

her back to the house.

Nancy took her to the dining room where she knew a fire would have been lit. Patricia was already there, seated at the table with a slice of toast in her hand.

'Where have you been?' Patricia dropped the toast onto her plate and rose to her feet. 'What's happened? What the matter, Aurelia?'

'The *Corinthian* is lost at sea,' Nancy said briefly. 'Daniel Comer came to tell us, and there's been a disturbance at the mine.'

'Martin is dead.' Aurelia collapsed onto the nearest chair. 'He's dead. Killed in a brawl and it's all my fault.' She began to sob convulsively.

'Nonsense.' Patricia took her by the shoulders and shook her. 'Stop that, Aurelia. All your tears won't bring him or the crew of the *Corinthian* back.'

'That's harsh, Patsy,' Nancy said sharply. 'She's upset. All the money went down with the ship.' She lowered her voice. 'We don't know for certain if Alex and Leo were on board.'

'Don't say that,' Patricia sank back onto her seat. 'Nothing bad has happened to Leo. I'd know it in my heart if he was in danger.'

'We don't know any details.' Nancy eyed Patricia warily. 'The ship foundered off the Azores. There might have been survivors.'

'This happened before.' Patricia sighed heavily. 'Only last time it was Alex and Piers who were almost drowned. I was at home waiting for Alex to return for our wedding, and I thought he was dead. The irony of it was that he was secretly in love with my sister.'

'That's all in the past, Patsy. We have to hope that they weren't on board, but it's a tragedy for the families of the crew.' Nancy filled a cup with coffee and handed it to Aurelia. 'Sip this and you'll feel better.'

'You don't understand,' Aurelia said tearfully. 'If I hadn't left Martin I could probably have prevented this. He might have managed the business better.'

'I doubt it.' Patricia shook her head. 'From what I've heard it was the drink that made him incapable of running the mine.'

'I don't know what to do.' Aurelia hiccupped on a sob. 'If the *Corinthian* is lost we won't be able to pay the miners, and the whole village will suffer.'

'I think you need to worry more about yourself and Lady Pentelow. Things are likely to turn nasty.' Patricia bit into her piece of toast, frowning. 'We need to decide what to do next.'

'We should return to Rockwood,' Nancy said firmly. 'Aurelia and Lady Pentelow must come with us for their own safety.'

Aurelia lifted her head, raising a tear-stained face to stare at Nancy in astonishment. 'We can't abandon Trevenor.'

'You heard what Daniel Comer said about the miners, Aurelia. They are desperate men and the mine still belongs to Trevenor. What do you think they will do?'

'They will try to take the house and everything in it,' Patricia said grimly. 'Nancy is right, you and your grandmama must come to Rockwood with us. We should leave immediately, before anyone gets wind of what's happening.'

'But the house . . . Grandmama loves this place.'

'Then let her stay and defend it from the mob,' Patricia said icily. 'You are coming with us, Aurelia. You can start by going to your grandmama and explaining the situation. I will explain the situation to

Mrs Witham and Cook. They can decide whether or not to stay.'

'I'll send to the stables for your coachman to make the carriage ready,' Nancy added hastily. 'With luck we will get away before anyone in the village realises what's happening.'

Patricia rose from the table. 'Pack only what you need, Aurelia, but bring all your jewellery and any small valuables.'

Aurelia staggered to her feet, mopping her eyes with a crumpled hanky. 'I'll speak to Grandmama, but I can't believe this is happening.'

Nancy watched her walk slowly from the room. 'This is terrible, Patsy. You don't think that Alex and Leo were on that ship, do you?'

'I refuse to believe it, Nancy. Someone brought the news of the *Corinthian*. Perhaps they would have more information.'

'But how will we find out?'

'I'm trying to think, but my mind is in a fog. I don't want to be widowed for a second time.'

Nancy reached out to lay a sympathetic hand on Patricia's arm. 'We have to hope for the best.'

'We need to get Aurelia and Lady Pentelow to safety, but there must be someone who can tell us more.'

'No one in the village knows me. I could go to the inn we saw when we first arrived. I might be able to find someone who can give me more .information.'

'Would you really do that, Nancy? I'd come with you, but that might look suspicious.'

'I'm not afraid to go on my own. Everyone blames the family because Piers still owns the mine, even if he wasn't responsible for its failure. The loss of the *Corinthian* is only going to make matters worse.'

'You're right, Nancy. If you go down to the village I'll take care of things here, but be careful. An angry mob isn't going to make exceptions. If they know you have come from Trevenor you will be in danger, too.'

'I'll be discreet. It's important that we get as much information as possible. Send Aurelia and Lady Pentelow to safety, if necessary. You and I can follow later. It's a bit like the old times, Patsy.'

Patricia answered with a sad smile, 'Not quite. My heart wasn't breaking then, Nancy.'

★ ★ ★

With Ada's borrowed shawl wrapped around her head and shoulders, Nancy braved the bitter wind and sleet to walk to the village pub. The high street was all but deserted, although there had been a hive of activity at the mine when she hurried past. The Anchor Inn was busy, but no one took any notice of a poor girl making her way through the crowd of drinkers. She wanted to avoid the bar as being too public, but she spotted a young potman collecting empty tankards and she stepped inside.

'I heard that the *Corinthian* went down with all hands,' Nancy said in a low voice. 'My pa was one of the crew. Do you know who brought the news?'

The young man barely looked at her. 'He come off the ship moored in the bay.' He jerked his head in the direction of a man seated in the inglenook, surrounded by eager listeners. 'He done nothing but spout off for the price of a pint of ale.'

'Thank you.' Nancy glanced round nervously. She was the only female in the bar and she knew that the landlord would turn her out the instant she was spotted. There were so many people milling around, all eager to hear the details of the wreck, that she decided to wait outside in the hope of catching the seaman when he staggered out of the pub. It was even colder now that sleet had turned to spiteful hailstones, and she sheltered in the doorway, moving aside as men pushed past her. Some of them eyed her speculatively and one or two made lewd suggestions, but she ignored them.

Shielding her eyes with her hand, Nancy spotted a longboat being rowed ashore. When it drew nearer she could see a man seated in the stern, who appeared to be the ship's captain. If anyone could give her a true account of what happened it must be he. She tightened her clasp on the flimsy shawl and ran down to the jetty to wait for the boat to pull alongside. When the man climbed ashore she moved closer.

'Please, Captain, might I have a word with you?'

His bushy eyebrows drew together in a frown. 'Who are you, girl?'

'I won't keep you a minute, sir. I have relations who were on board the *Corinthian*. We've been told that she went down with all hands. Is that true?'

He glared at her for a moment and then his expression softened. 'She went down off the Azores, but there were survivors, despite what people have been saying. They managed to get ashore at Graciosa, and we picked them up in Porto where they had been taken by a whaling vessel.'

'Are they on board now, Captain?'

He jerked his head in the direction of the longboat. 'These are the men. Do you recognise any of them?'

Nancy leaned over the side of the jetty, but despite the rain and sleet blowing in her face she knew the

243

answer already. 'No, sir.'

'Well, speak to them, miss. Maybe they can give you more information.' The captain strode off in the direction of the Anchor Inn, leaving Nancy to wait until the men had disembarked. She stopped the first of them to step ashore.

'Excuse me. Do you remember if Mr Alexander Blanchard or Mr Leo Wilder were on board the *Corinthian*?'

The man shook his head. 'No, miss. I never saw they folk. Never heard of them neither.' He strode off without looking back.

Nancy questioned each man as they passed her, but the answer was the same, and she made her way back to the house relieved, but she wished she had better news to give Patricia. As she hurried past the entrance to the mine offices the sound of raised voices made her quicken her pace. She caught glimpses of the men gesticulating wildly and she knew that trouble was coming. She broke into a run.

★ ★ ★

Corbin, Lady Pentelow's coachman, was seated on the box of the barouche while the stable boy held the horses' reins. The luggage was piled into a dog cart with Ada perched next to the groom on the driver's seat. Patterson helped Lady Pentelow into the barouche, followed by Aurelia. Patricia was standing in the doorway. Her expression lightened when she saw Nancy.

'You've been gone for ages. I was about to send them off without us.'

'They weren't on board,' Nancy said breathlessly.

'I spoke to several of the survivors as they landed on the quay. There were no passengers on the *Corinthian*, only the crew.'

'We'll have to go now.' Patricia turned to the butler. 'Are you sure you wish to remain here, Patterson? We could take you, Cook and Mrs Witham to somewhere safer.'

'Trevenor is our home, ma'am. We will stay and do our best to keep the house in order until Lady Pentelow returns. I will hide what's left of the silver and porcelain in the cellar.'

'Won't you be in danger from the mob?' Nancy asked anxiously.

'They have no complaints against us, miss. We are employees, just as they are. I suggest you leave immediately. The gates are locked but Corbin will take you along the back road. By the time the mob realises you've left, it will be too late for them to catch up with you.'

He handed Patricia into the carriage, followed by Nancy.

'I'm not happy about abandoning my home,' Lady Pentelow complained as the carriage door was slammed shut and the horses moved forward. 'If any harm comes to Trevenor I will blame you, Patricia. This was your idea.'

Nancy and Patricia exchanged weary glances. Nancy could see that it was going to be a long journey home and they had not accomplished what they had set out to do. It was nearly Christmas and they would be spending it without Leo and Alex. It was going to be difficult to explain to the children why their papa had not come home, let alone Rosalind.

They spent the night at a hotel close to the railway station in Plymouth and travelled on the next day, arriving at Newton Abbot late in the afternoon. Nancy was sent to organise two carriages to take them to Rockwood, and it was early evening when they reached home. Nancy had never been so glad to see the comfortingly square and solid outline of Rockwood Castle against a lowering sky.

Lady Pentelow marched into the grand entrance hall as if she owned the castle, but was met by Hester.

'We've come to stay for a while. Kindly have rooms made ready for myself and Aurelia.'

Hester folded her arms across her chest and met her ladyship's demands with an icy stare. 'I don't recall anyone inviting you for the festive season.'

'Remember your place. You might have married your employer but you will always be the housekeeper in my eyes, Hester Carey.'

'What's going on, Patricia?' Hester demanded angrily.

Patricia hastened to explain why they had fled from Trevenor, and the danger that Lady Pentelow and Aurelia had so narrowly escaped.

'We will make you as comfortable as possible,' Hester said grimly. 'But I don't want to hear a barrage of complaints from you in the morning, Clarissa Pentelow. You and I are equals now, whether you like it or not.'

Lady Pentelow's cheeks puffed out and her breath exploded in a gasp of annoyance. 'How dare you speak to me in that tone, Hester? I demand respect from persons of lower standing.'

'Demand all you like.' Hester turned away. 'You are not in a position to make demands upon us. As I see it, we are saving you from being torn apart by a mob. The trouble is of your own making.'

'Hester, please.' Patricia laid a hand on her shoulder. 'We are all tired, cold and hungry. Is my sister around?'

'She's saying good night to the children. Come into the drawing room and get warm. I'll order rooms to be made up for Lady Pentelow and Mrs Gibbs.'

Aurelia shuddered. 'I've gone back to using my maiden name, Hester. My late husband and I were separated by mutual consent.'

Hester eyed her speculatively. 'Dead, is he? Did you poison his rum?'

'I'll send word to Cook that there will be four extra at the table for dinner,' Patricia said hastily. 'I take it you haven't dined yet, Hester?'

'No, we haven't. But there might not be enough to go round.'

Nancy managed to keep a straight face. 'Come with me, Aurelia. We'll wait for your rooms to be ready in the drawing room.' She turned to Lady Pentelow. 'Would you like to come and get warm by the fire, my lady?'

'I know my way around this old ruin better than you, my girl.' Lady Pentelow sailed on ahead, leaving Nancy and Aurelia to follow her.

Nancy could see that this was not going to be an easy time at Rockwood. 'Perhaps I'd better go and explain matters to Rosalind. I'll be down directly.'

'You are getting away easily,' Patricia whispered as Nancy walked past her, heading for the staircase.

'I don't want Rosie to walk into a difficult situation,' Nancy said softly. 'I'll leave it to you to keep

Hester and Lady Pentelow from tearing each other's hair out.' She shivered as a cold wind gusted through the open front door as James brought in the last of the luggage. Ada was standing by the oak coffer, looking uncomfortable.

'James, will you take Ada to the servants' hall, and show her round? She'll be staying with us while Lady Pentelow and Miss Aurelia are here.'

James nodded and gave Ada a friendly smile. 'Come this way, Ada. I dare say you'd like a nice hot cup of tea and a slice of Mrs Jackson's fruit cake.'

Ada blushed and nodded. 'Thank you kindly, sir.'

James grinned. 'It's just James, Ada. You'll soon get used to our ways here at Rockwood.'

Nancy went upstairs, confident that at least one member of the Trevenor household would be looked after and made welcome.

She met Rosalind on the landing outside the nursery. 'Am I too late to say good night to the children?'

Rosalind wrapped her in a warm embrace. 'They're fast asleep. I was reading to them for ages until they finally dropped off. But this is a lovely surprise. We weren't expecting you. Did you bring Alex and Leo home?'

'I'm sorry, Rosie. They weren't at Trevenor. It's a long story.'

16

The warm aroma of steaming Christmas pudding and the scent of cinnamon, ginger and nutmeg wafted from below stairs in the castle. The sharp tang of oranges spiked with cloves that Dolly and Rory had hung on the boughs of the tree in the entrance hall added to the festive atmosphere. But Nancy knew that the adults were putting on a display of harmony and goodwill for the sake of the children. It was Sunday, just three days before Christmas, and there was still no word from Alex or Leo. It was obvious that Rosie and Patsy were desperate for news, even though they took care not to voice their fears.

Lady Pentelow and Hester had declared a truce for the festive season, but it seemed as though there were times when both of them were biting their tongues. Silence was not one of Hester's attributes, and speaking her mind was as necessary to her as breathing. Lady Pentelow was much the same, although she would not admit such a failing. Nancy sensed that trouble was bubbling beneath the tense surface, but there was nothing she could do to prevent the inevitable outpouring of emotions due to the absence of Alex and Leo.

Bertie had greeted Lady Pentelow and Aurelia with his usual good humour, and Tommy was polite but kept his distance. Wolfe stuck by Bertie's side, glowering at anyone who dared to say a word out of place in his master's presence. However, Walter and Louise brought their young daughter, Charlotte, to visit, which seemed to please Aurelia. She was more at home with Dolly, Rory and Phoebe than she appeared to be with the adults. Barely four years old, Charlotte was still small in stature, having survived a difficult premature birth. According to Dr Bulmer, Louise was unable to bear another child without risking her life, and that made Charlotte even more precious to her doting parents, and to Cora Fletcher, who was now Charlotte's devoted slave. The only person tougher than Cora was Wolfe, and no one argued with either one of them.

Christmas was just two days away now and the snow had melted in all but the most sheltered north-facing spots on the estate. Nancy was kept busy helping Mrs Jackson in the kitchen, which was her own choice. Rosalind had said it was quite unnecessary and no one expected Nancy to do menial work, but to tell the truth Nancy enjoyed cooking, especially when it came to making fancies. She spent hours in the pantry making marzipan fruits and figures to decorate the Christmas cake and treats for the children.

She had just enjoyed a pleasant two hours in the relative peace and quiet, and had gone outside to the pump to wash the sticky sweet sugar and almond mixture from her hands, when she heard the sound of horses' hoofs and the rumble of carriage wheels in the bailey. She hurried through the archway that led to the front of the castle, and her heart missed a beat when she recognised the coat of arms on the carriage door. She hesitated, waiting to see who stepped out of the vehicle, but she could not contain her excitement when she realised it was Freddie, and he was on his own. He had spotted her almost before she saw him and he came striding across the cobblestones to lift her off her feet and spin her round.

'Put me down, Freddie.' Torn between laughter and tears of joy, Nancy struggled to free herself from his grasp. The familiar scent of him made her even dizzier than the relief and pleasure of seeing him again, but reality was never far away and she faced him uncertainly. 'What are you doing here?'

'That's a nice greeting. I thought you were pleased to see me.' Freddie's blue eyes twinkled mischievously. 'I've come all this way to find you, Nancy.'

She shivered as a cold wind whipped her hair from the mobcap she wore and tugged at her apron. 'How did you know where to come?'

'It was obvious that you would return to your old home eventually. Anyway, I think we'd better go inside. You'll catch your death of cold out here.' He eyed her curiously. 'You're dressed like a servant. Surely Rosalind hasn't sent you below stairs, has she?'

Nancy smiled and tucked her sticky hand into the crook of his arm. 'No, of course not. As a matter of fact, I like cooking, especially baking and making fancy cakes. I was making marzipan.'

'I need to talk to you, Nancy. I couldn't believe it when Mama said you had left of your own free will.'

She extricated herself from his grasp. 'It's true, Freddie. I wanted to do the right thing.'

'Didn't I have a choice in the matter? Let's go indoors, Nancy. It's freezing out here.'

'I can't allow Viscount Ashton to walk into the castle through the servants' entrance.' Nancy started walking towards the main entrance where Jarvis was standing stiffly to attention.

Freddie laughed. 'I suppose it would look a bit

furtive, and that's not what I want. I care deeply about you, Nancy.'

'Do you, Freddie? That's not what your mama said. In fact, she pointed out, quite rightly, that there is no future for us together.'

He came to a halt, twisting her round so that they faced each other. 'I won't allow that, Nancy. I am of age and free to choose the people I want close to me.'

Nancy walked on, stopping only when she reached the doorway. 'Will you see that Lord Ashton's coachman is taken care of, please, Jarvis?'

She entered the great hall and waited until Jarvis was out of earshot. 'I don't know what my family will make of this, Freddie. How do we explain your visit?'

'A courtesy call, of course. I've come to wish you all the compliments of the season.'

'They won't believe that. You must have driven for hours to get here so early.'

'What does it matter? I'm here now and I want to make things right between us, Nancy.'

'You can't achieve the impossible. Some things are not meant to be, Freddie.' Nancy led the way to the morning room and opened the door. She peeked inside to make sure that there was no one present. 'Come in, Freddie. We can have a few words in private before anyone interrupts us.'

Freddie strode into the room and stood with his back to the fire. 'I would have been here sooner, but I was sent on a wild-goose chase.'

Nancy realised that her legs were trembling and she sank down on a chair, making an effort to look unconcerned, which was difficult when her pulse was racing. 'How was that?'

'I followed you to Rockwood the moment I

discovered you had left Dorrington Place. It was late when I arrived and I booked a room at the Black Dog. Who should I meet in the taproom but our old friend Gervase North?'

Nancy pulled a face. 'He's not my friend. He insisted on travelling with me when I left Dorrington Place.'

'He told me that. He also said that you and Patricia had gone to Cornwall, chasing after Captain Blanchard and Patricia's husband. He gave me a long and garbled explanation as to why you would travel so far just before Christmas, so I left for Cornwall.'

'You went to Trevenor?'

'I did, and I was told at The Anchor that Lady Pentelow and Mrs Gibbs had fled because the ship carrying gold from Barbados had gone down in the Atlantic Ocean. No one in the village knew their whereabouts.'

'Leo and Alex had sailed to Barbados weeks earlier, intending to bring Piers home.'

'Why would they do that? I thought you said that Piers was in Australia.'

'When he was pardoned he went to Barbados to help the blockade runners taking arms and supplies to the Southern states.'

Freddie pulled a face. 'He can't seem to keep out of trouble.'

'That's true, but Lady Pentelow wanted him to take over running the mine. I'm not sure about gold, but the money Piers sent home was certainly lost at sea when the *Corinthian* sank off the Azores. Lady Pentelow couldn't pay the miners and there was a riot.'

'That's more or less what I was told in Cornwall so I came here hoping to find you.'

'Where else would I be?'

'I don't know. I had a feeling you and Patricia might have done something rash like chasing off to Barbados.'

'If it were possible that's exactly what we would have done, but we had to bring Lady Pentelow and Aurelia to safety. They were in genuine danger. Aurelia's husband died in the riot.'

'I'm sorry.'

'She isn't heartbroken, Freddie. It wasn't a happy marriage and they had separated some time ago. Lady Pentelow can't run the mine and neither can Aurelia. They need Piers to come home now he's a free man.'

Freddie stared into the flames. 'I might be able to help.'

'Really? I don't see how, unless you have a ship ready to sail for Barbados.'

'I haven't, but I know who's in a position to be of assistance.'

'Who is that?'

'William Russell. He knows the shipping business inside out. He has a position with one of the biggest ship owners in England.'

'Of course. Why didn't I think of that?'

'If I leave now, I could be in London by this evening. I think William owes us a favour or two.'

'I'm coming with you,' Nancy said firmly.

'But tomorrow is Christmas Eve. You'll want to be with your family.'

'Yes, but if we can get news of Leo and Alex it will mean so much to Patsy and Rosie and the children. Maybe William will know if the *Cyrene* has left Barbados and is on the way home.'

'That's what I was hoping, but it would be better if you remained here. I promise I'll return as soon as I have news.'

'You're not leaving me behind, Freddie. I'll speak to Rosie. She will understand.'

'I can do this on my own. Stay here with your family, Nancy.'

'No, Freddie. This is my family business. I intend to come with you, but first I'll send Flossie with coffee and something to eat. You must be hungry after your journey.'

'I can see that nothing I say will change your mind.'

'Yes, Freddie. My mind is made up.' Nancy left the room and went in search of Rosalind. She found her in the still room below stairs.

'What's wrong, Nancy? You look flushed. Are you ill?'

'No, really I am quite well.' Nancy took a deep breath. 'Freddie has arrived.'

'How delightful. Is he going to stay for Christmas?'

'He followed me and Patsy to Cornwall, Rosie. He knows all about Trevenor and that Alex and Leo are in Barbados. He suggested that we speak to William Russell, the man who married my friend Tamara. William works for one of the largest ship owners in the country.'

Rosalind put a bottle of rose-water back on the counter. 'I don't understand. What has that got to do with us?'

'William might be able to give us news of the *Cyrene*. At least we will know if she has set sail from Barbados. He might even have a ship about to leave for the island.'

'What are you thinking, Nancy? Surely you're not suggesting that we go in search of them?'

'Somebody has to do something. I can't bear to see

you and Patsy so worried all the time.'

'If it makes you feel better, let Freddie go to London and speak to your friend. I would certainly welcome any news about Alex and Leo. I wish they hadn't gone on such a wild-goose chase. Piers always manages to cause trouble.'

'I want to go to London with Freddie.'

Rosalind stared at her, eyes widened. 'But, Nancy, you can't do that. You'll ruin your reputation if you travel alone with Freddie, and anyway it's almost Christmas. You should be here with us.'

'No one will know, and I really don't care what people think. I'm going anyway, but I didn't want to do it without warning you. Please don't try to stop me.'

'I can see how much it means to you, but I want to speak to Freddie, on my own, before I agree.'

Nancy nodded. 'He's in the morning parlour.'

★ ★ ★

Nancy and Freddie arrived in Doughty Street late that evening. It had been a tiring journey by train and a cab from the station. The somewhat reluctant maid-servant showed them into Mrs Fitzallen's parlour.

'Nancy! Freddie! I wasn't expecting you.'

'Mrs Fitzallen, we need to know where Tamara and William are living now.'

'Good heavens, why? And why are you calling at this time of the evening?'

Freddie placed Nancy's valise on the floor by the sofa. 'I think N-Nancy had b-better explain, ma'am.'

Nancy did her best to outline the situation as simply as possible, but Mrs Fitzallen continued to look bemused.

'I don't really understand what you think William could tell you, but one thing is clear to me. You cannot go gallivanting around town at night without a chaperone, Nancy.'

'I can stay tonight at Dorrington House,' Nancy said casually. 'There are dozens of servants so it must be quite proper.'

'Nonsense. I understand that the Dorringtons are still in the country. Your good name will be compromised beyond redemption. You must stay here with me. Tomorrow you may visit my niece.'

'That's extremely k-kind of you, ma'am,' Freddie said hastily. 'I'll call for you early tomorrow morning, Nancy, and when we have the information from William I'll take you home to Rockwood.'

Nancy was about to protest but she could tell by Freddie's set expression that it would be useless. This was a side of him she had not previously seen, although she knew in her heart that he was right. It would be both rude and foolish to refuse Mrs Fitzallen's generous offer of accommodation. She was suddenly overcome by a feeling of exhaustion and the thought of a warm, comfortable bed was too tempting to refuse.

'Thank you, ma'am.'

'Tamara and William have a pretty little house in Chelsea. They seem very happy.' Mrs Fitzallen turned to Freddie. 'It's getting late, my lord. Perhaps you had better be on your way.'

★ ★ ★

Freddie called for Nancy early next morning. When they arrived at the house in Chelsea Tamara threw her

257

arms around Nancy in a welcoming hug. 'How wonderful to see you again. Will you come for Christmas dinner tomorrow? We have a huge goose and all the trimmings. Papa is coming, too. He's come round to our marriage, especially now he's going to be a grandpapa.'

'That's wonderful news.' Nancy returned the embrace. 'I'm delighted for you.'

William cleared his throat. 'It's very nice to see you, but there is obviously a reason for your visit.'

'William!' Tamara stared at him in amazement. 'That's not very polite. Nancy is my best friend.'

'N-no, y-you're right.' Freddie acknowledged William's comment with a wry smile. 'Of course Nancy wanted to see you again, Tamara, but the reason we've come all the way from Devonshire is we need your help.'

William nodded. 'Take a seat, please. Tell me what I can do for you. I'll do anything in my power to help.'

Nancy explained the situation. '. . . So you see we need to find out what's happened to Alex and Leo. If we could persuade Piers to return to Cornwall it would solve the problems at Trevenor.'

'Oh, William. Do say you can help,' Tamara said eagerly. 'You know everything that's going on in the shipping business.'

He smiled indulgently. 'Not quite everything, my love. But I have the latest *Lloyd's List*, and that should give us some information about the *Cyrene*. I know you don't like me bringing my work home with me, but I have a copy in my study.' He stood up and left the room, returning moments later with a newspaper, which he placed on the table and spread the pages. 'Come and see for yourself, Ashton.'

Nancy sat with Tamara while Freddie and William pored over the small print.

Freddie looked up. 'It says that the Cyrene is in dock for repairs. So it doesn't look as if it would have been ready to sail for a while.'

'Which means that Alex, Leo and Piers are still in Barbados,' Nancy said excitedly.

'It takes some time for news to reach London.' William frowned. 'It's possible the repairs were minor and the ship has sailed for home.'

'Is there a ship leaving port for Barbados any day soon?' Nancy tried to sound casual, but her nerves were on edge. The fate of Trevenor depended upon Piers' speedy return to Cornwall.

'One of our vessels left for Barbados yesterday, but I don't know of any other merchantman taking that route for a while.'

Nancy bit back tears of frustration. 'How disappointing. We've travelled all this way for nothing. I mean, other than the pleasure of seeing you both so content in your lovely home.'

'I am so sorry, Nancy.' Tamara rose to her feet and tugged at the bell pull. 'You must have some refreshment. Perhaps you could stay for luncheon?'

'Just a minute.' William held up his hand. 'The *Bonaventure* sailed from Portsmouth, but it is due to put in at Exmouth to pick up a cargo. If you wished to send someone as a paying passenger it should be possible to make arrangements at the port office.'

Nancy leaped to her feet. 'We must leave immediately, Freddie. If we can get home to Rockwood tonight we will be able to make arrangements to travel to Barbados.'

'I hope you aren't thinking of going there on your

own,' Freddie said warily.

'Of course not,' Nancy said, smiling sweetly. 'I have it all planned. You'll see, Freddie.' She gave Tamara a hug. 'I will come and see you again and stay longer next time.'

'Let me know how it all works out. Don't lose touch, Nancy.'

'Never. We will always be friends. Thank you, William. You'll never know how much you've helped us.'

Freddie shook William's hand. 'I'm in y-your d-debt.'

'Nonsense, Ashton. You and Nancy helped us when we were in need. I hope I've been able to do something in return, however small. I'll see you out.'

Freddie handed Nancy into the waiting carriage. 'Are you sure about this, Nancy? Wouldn't it be enough to tell Lady Pentelow that as far as we know the *Cyrene* is safe?'

'No, not at all. That would make it worse. She stands to lose her home and most of her income if the mine goes bankrupt. Aurelia deserves more in life than dwindling into a sad, penniless widow. I remember how she used to be.'

'Then we'll do all we can to help them.' Freddie gave instructions to the coachman and climbed in to sit beside Nancy. 'This is getting to be a habit.'

★　★　★

They arrived back at Rockwood Castle in the early evening to find that Bertie, as head of the family, had called a meeting and all the adults were assembled around the dining table.

Bertie waited until Nancy and Freddie were seated

before he tapped his wineglass to call for silence.

'I don't approve of what you did, Nancy. But Rosie tells me that you asked her permission before you set off for London with Ashton.' Bertie turned to Freddie, frowning. 'You should have asked my permission first. Nancy is only eighteen and I am her unofficial guardian.'

Freddie rose to his feet. 'I apologise, sir. It was a s-sudden decision, but I should h-have spoken to you in person.'

Bertie grinned. 'Well, we cleared that up. So what did you discover in London?'

Lady Pentelow glared at him. 'Is that all you have to say, Bertram? I would put it in much stronger terms if it were my ward.'

'I trust my sister's judgement, Lady Pentelow. If Rosie did not raise any objections she must have thought the journey necessary. Anyway, they are back now and I can tell by Nancy's expression that she has something to tell us.'

Nancy rose to her feet. 'We went to see a friend who is in the shipping business. He checked with *Lloyd's List* and discovered that the *Cyrene* is in dock for repairs, so it doesn't look as if Leo and Alex have set off for home.'

'That's nonsense,' Lady Pentelow said crossly. 'By the time the news reached London the ship could have been back at sea.'

'That's true, but we had to start somewhere.'

'What are you thinking, Nancy?' Rosalind demanded eagerly. 'What else did you learn in London?'

'The *Bonaventure* has set sail for Barbados and will be calling in at Exmouth to pick up a cargo. William thought they might take paying passengers. I would

261

like to volunteer and Freddie has agreed to accompany me.'

'The devil he has,' Bertie said angrily. 'I say no.'

'I echo that,' Walter added hastily. 'You don't know that they are still on the island. It could be a wild-goose chase.'

Lady Pentelow held up her hand. 'I say let her go. I stand to lose everything if my grandson is not brought back to Trevenor very soon.'

'I'll go with you,' Aurelia volunteered. 'Piers is my brother and Alex is my cousin. I want to see them safely home.'

'I'd go myself,' Bertie said thoughtfully. 'But a cripple in a Bath chair is no use to anyone.'

'Don't say that, Bertie.' Patricia shook her head vehemently. 'If anyone should go with Nancy it is I. Leo is my husband.'

'I would go too, but I can't leave the children,' Rosie said wearily. 'I think we all agree that something should be done.'

'If anyone is going to that foreign island, it should be me.' Lady Pentelow stood up, resting both hands on the table. She looked round the astonished faces, glaring at each one in turn as if daring anyone to argue with her. 'I have the most to lose.'

'My husband has risked everything to go in search of Piers,' Patricia said angrily.

'As has mine.' Rosalind also rose to her feet. 'The father of my children is also risking his life to search for his errant cousin.'

Patricia laid her hand on her heart. 'The father of my unborn child is also in danger, Rosie.'

There was a moment of silence and then everyone rose to their feet, with the exception of Bertie.

'Patsy, that's wonderful news,' Rosalind cried, rushing round the table to hug her sister.

'Why didn't you tell us before?' Bertie demanded. 'Why do women make such a big secret of a perfectly natural occurrence?'

Hester shook her fist at him. 'You be quiet, Bertie. You aren't too old to be scolded by me. I gave birth many years ago and I can tell you it isn't an easy procedure. You would know if your late wife, Tommy's mother, had not kept silent, God rest her soul.'

Nancy turned to Bertie. 'I know it's not my place to say anything, but there isn't much time to decide. I have no ties and I owe this family so much. Let me do this one thing for you all.'

17

The captain of the *Bonaventure* stared at Lady Pentelow in undisguised contempt.

'Madam, this is not a passenger ship. There are no facilities for ladies on board.'

'My husband, Sir Edmund Pentelow, ran a fleet of merchantmen. I need to get to Barbados. I do not ask for special treatment, other than a cabin to myself, of course.'

'Grandmama, can't you see that this is impossible?' Aurelia tugged at the sleeve of her grandmother's fur mantle.

'If anyone is to go to Barbados to persuade Piers to return home, it should be me,' Lady Pentelow said flatly. 'I am the head of the family.'

Bertie signalled to Wolfe, who manoeuvred the Bath chair so that Bertie was facing Lady Pentelow. 'I am the head of this family, ma'am. Your home is Trevenor, which is in danger of being taken from you in your absence.'

'Sir, I am a busy man. When the cargo is loaded we will set sail. I haven't time for this.' The captain was about to turn away but Nancy slipped in between him and Lady Pentelow.

'Captain, please. I agree that Lady Pentelow might find the conditions trying, but I am prepared to go in her place.'

'As am I.' Patricia stepped forward. 'My husband is one of those who appear to be stranded on the island.

My understanding is that you do take fare-paying passengers occasionally.'

'Yes, sometimes in extreme circumstances, ma'am. But there is one available cabin with two bunk beds. As I said, the accommodation is very basic to say the least.'

'We've been on such voyages before.' Nancy nodded earnestly. 'Mrs Wilder and I will be happy to share a cabin.'

'Just a minute, Nancy.' Freddie moved swiftly to her side. 'Are you sure about this? I don't like the idea of you venturing so far without someone to protect you.'

'You heard the captain, Freddie. There's only one cabin.'

'I don't want you to go, Nancy. Heaven knows what dangers you might face.'

Nancy clasped his hand. 'Don't worry, Freddie. I can take care of myself. You should return to your life at Dorrington Place.'

'Did my mama say anything to make you walk away from me, Nancy?'

'Please, Freddie, not now. I have to do this on my own.'

'Is that your final word?'

'It is, Freddie. I'm sorry.'

Freddie backed away, shaking his head. 'I'm not going to allow it to end like this, Nancy.'

Hester marched to the front. 'Captain, we haven't been introduced. I am the Dowager Lady Carey from Rockwood Castle.'

'Captain Wilson Mockridge, ma'am.'

'I'm telling you now, Captain, Mrs Wilder cannot go — not in her delicate condition — and Lady

Pentelow would never survive the journey.' Hester turned to Nancy. 'I will come with you to Barbados. Piers Blanchard will listen to what I have to say and we'll bring him home. I've had years of dealing with difficult men and boys.'

Rosalind laid her hand on Hester's arm. 'Are you sure about this, Hester? It's not going to be a comfortable voyage.'

'You cannot overrule what I say.' Lady Pentelow's cheeks reddened. 'You are a housekeeper, who has risen above her station in life. If anyone travels on this vessel, it should be me.'

Bertie held up his hand. 'Captain Mockridge, are you willing to take Lady Carey and Miss Sunday as passengers?'

Captain Mockridge glanced over his shoulder as the crane pulled back, having loaded the cargo into the hold. 'We are about to sail. I can take two passengers. It matters little to me who chooses to take up my offer, but I'm not delaying any longer. You'd best get aboard before the gangplank is raised.'

Bertie caught Nancy by the hand. 'You don't have to do this. I'm not sure it is the best solution after all.'

'I want to go with you,' Patricia said angrily. 'I need to see Leo and give him the good news.'

'All the more reason for remaining safely at home.' Rosalind placed her arm around Patricia's shoulders. 'You have a baby to think of now, Patsy. You don't want to risk losing it, do you?'

'I never wanted children,' Patricia said sulkily.

'You'll feel differently when he or she is born. Believe me, you will.' Rosalind led her sister away, still protesting.

'That's settled then. I'm going to Barbados with

you, Nancy.' Hester beckoned to Fletcher, who was standing quietly behind Walter and Louise. 'I'll take my valise, thank you, Fletcher.'

'You intended to come all along.' Nancy picked up her bag.

'You didn't think I'd let you go on your own, did you? Sir Lucius would never forgive me if I allowed any of the family to undertake such a risky venture without someone to protect them.'

'You think I'm one of the family?'

'Of course I do. We'd better hurry or we'll miss our chance.' Hester charged forward, ignoring Lady Pentelow's shrill protests.

'Good luck,' Aurelia cried excitedly. 'Tell Piers he's needed desperately. Make him come home.'

Nancy was left with little alternative but to follow Hester, who was already halfway up the gangplank. She snatched up her bag and quickened her pace.

'Well then, Captain Mockridge. Your man had better show us to our cabin.' Hester placed her valise at the captain's feet. 'I don't know how much Sir Bertram has agreed to pay for our passage, but I'm sure it's a considerable sum, and we expect to be treated accordingly.'

Captain Mockridge eyed her coldly. 'I trust you will remember that this is not a passenger vessel, my lady. We will do our best to accommodate you comfortably, but we are likely to meet adverse weather conditions. Mr Harding, the first mate, will show you to your cabin. If you have any requests you will speak to him.'

Nancy turned to see a tall, well-built man with light brown hair and a neatly trimmed beard and moustache. He was, she guessed, probably in his forties.

His skin was tanned and his blue eyes narrowed as if he spent most of his time gazing out at the distant horizon.

'If you would come this way, please, ladies.' He picked up their luggage and walked on ahead, leading them down a companionway to the deck below, where their cabin was just behind the captain's day room, as he explained.

'If you need anything let me know, ma'am.' He set their cases on the deck, giving Hester a charming smile as he prepared to leave the cabin. Hester stared at him, seeming to be at a loss for words.

'Thank you, Mr Harding,' Nancy said hastily. She waited until the door closed on him. 'Why didn't you say anything?'

Hester shook her head. 'I don't know. For a moment I thought I knew him, but it's obvious that I was mistaken.'

Nancy was intrigued. 'You must have met a great many people. Perhaps you have seen him somewhere.'

'It was a fleeting likeness. An inflection in the voice or a trick of the light.' Hester took her valise and placed it on the bottom bunk. 'You will have to take the top one, I would never get up there.'

The deck moved beneath their feet and Hester staggered against the bulkhead. 'What's happening?'

Nancy giggled. 'We've cast off, that's all. I hope you're a good sailor, Hester.'

'I'm afraid I'm not,' Hester said gloomily.

Nancy rushed to the porthole to watch the coast slipping away with surprising speed. The ship was steaming along at an impressive rate of knots and, if the weather held, she hoped they would reach Barbados

in record time. She had not expected to be trav
with Hester and the thought of sharing a cabin w
her was daunting, but the sooner they reached the
destination, the sooner they could get home. Piers
would be restored to his family and he would take his
grandmother and Aurelia back to Cornwall. Alex and
Leo would resume their normal lives, and everything
would go back to normal.

There was only one thing that she could not mend
and that was a broken heart. The look on Freddie's
face when she had chosen to leave him behind was
still fresh in her memory, but she knew she had done
the right thing. He would have to return to Dorrington Place and then his old life would claim him. It
would be hard, but perhaps one day he would meet
someone worthy of him. She knew she had hurt him,
but her own pain was just as deep and would probably last her until the end of her days.

A sharp rap on the door made her turn with a start.

'See who's there,' Hester said feebly. 'I don't feel
too well.'

Nancy went to open the cabin door.

'I'm sorry to disturb you, miss.' Harding smiled and
handed her a pitcher. 'I've brought you fresh water.
We have to use it sparingly.'

'I understand,' Nancy said nodding.

'Captain Mockridge has asked me to invite you
and her ladyship to dine with us in the saloon at six
o'clock.'

A groan from the bottom bunk made Nancy turn
to look at Hester. 'Are you unwell, Hester?'

'I don't think I'll be eating anything for the rest of
the voyage.'

'The feeling should pass in a day or two, my lady,'

with a sympathetic smile.

...nk the captain. I will be delighted to join ...r. Fortunately for me I am a good sailor.'

...indeed, miss.' Harding backed away and ...the door.

...he's right, Hester. You will feel better soon.' Nancy spoke with more conviction than she was feeling, but it was important to keep their spirits up.

Unfortunately for Hester, the weather deteriorated as the afternoon wore on. There was little Nancy could do other than to empty the slop basin when Hester was overtaken by seasickness.

At six o'clock Harding came to take Nancy to the saloon, where she dined with the captain, Harding and the chief engineer, Thompson, a dour Yorkshireman with very little conversation. He obviously did not approve of having passengers on board, and he did not seem to like women. Harding, however, was quite charming and went out of his way to keep Nancy amused with accounts of their previous voyages. Captain Mockridge was civil but he obviously had much on his mind and he concentrated mainly on eating his meal.

Nancy thought longingly of Christmas dinner at Rockwood Castle with all the family seated around the table, but there was little festive spirit on board and she resigned herself to taking each day as it came. There would be plenty of time to celebrate when they returned home.

That night, despite groans from the bottom bunk, Nancy slept quite well, and she awakened in the morning to find Hester snoring loudly. Not wanting to disturb her, Nancy dressed quietly and made her way to the saloon, where she found the table laid with freshly baked bread rolls, butter and marmal... pot of coffee was still hot enough to drink and... helped herself. However, she gave a guilty start wh... the door opened and Harding entered.

'I hope I haven't taken your breakfast,' Nancy said hastily.

'No, please enjoy your food. I ate earlier. I've just come off watch, but I wanted to make sure you knew that you could have breakfast whenever you wanted it. How is Lady Carey? Is she any better?'

'I hope so. I left her sleeping soundly after a bad night.'

He nodded. 'Seasickness is very unpleasant. I'm lucky I never suffered from it, but I've seen grown men sobbing their hearts out because they felt so ill.'

'I don't think Hester is as bad as that, but thank you for asking.'

'She seems like a nice lady. Not grand at all, considering she has a title.'

'It wasn't always the case.' Nancy broke a warm roll into small pieces. 'I believe she had a hard life at the beginning, before she came to Rockwood Castle, that is.'

'We've all had crosses to bear, Miss Sunday. I dare say you have also.'

Nancy swallowed a mouthful of bread. 'Why do you say that?'

'I don't mean to offend you, but I noted a certain sadness in your expression when you boarded the ship yesterday. I apologise if I am wrong.'

'No, you are right. I left behind someone I care about deeply, but it wasn't to be.'

'I'm sorry.'

'We parted as friends. It was for the best. Are you

271

Harding?'

...is head. 'I never seem to be ashore long
...ablish a relationship with a woman, Miss
...s one of the penalties of a life at sea.'

★ ★ ★

The weather was bad enough in the English Channel,
but even worse when the *Bonaventure* tackled the great
Atlantic waves. Captain Mockridge seemed intent on
getting to their destination as fast as possible, and he
kept the ship on course no matter how much discomfort his passengers were suffering. Hester remained
in the cabin, lying prone on her bunk, unable to take
anything other than sips of water. Nancy, on the other
hand, was enjoying the voyage. She had found her 'sea
legs', as Harding called them, and when the weather
eased a little she spent as much time on deck as possible. She loved the wildness of the ocean and took
great pleasure in watching the changing moods and
colours of the sky and the ever-moving water. The
whole ship shuddered as it crested each wave and
dropped into the trough, only to rise again to tackle
the next wall of water. When it was too rough to venture on deck Nancy spent most of her time in the
saloon, where Captain Mockridge had a small supply
of reading material.

The crew were polite but too busy to do more than
pass the time of day, and if it had not been for her
conversations with Harding, Nancy would have found
herself very much alone. She discovered that they
had much in common. Harding had been abandoned
by his mother shortly after his birth and had been
adopted by a childless couple, who were wonderful

parents, but he was always left wondering about his birth mother. Nancy was able to relate strongly to this, and she told him her own story. The relief of speaking openly to someone with similar problems was intense and she looked forward to the time of day when Harding came off watch and could sit and chat to her.

After a gruelling week of almost continuous bad weather the *Bonaventure* steamed into calmer waters and sunnier climes. Hester recovered slowly and was able to take small amounts of food. She had been longing for a cup of tea, and the cook, who was similarly dependent upon a good brew, made sure she was kept supplied. They even had fresh milk from Llewellyn, the ship's goat and Cook's special pet. After a few days of reasonably good weather, Hester was able to walk to the saloon for her meals. She still picked at her food but Nancy was satisfied that Hester was growing stronger every day. Nancy noticed that Hester made the effort to get to the saloon when she knew that Harding would be there. Even stranger was the fact that Hester watched him covertly, but with an intensity that was puzzling.

They were two days out of Bridgetown and had just enjoyed a meal of salt beef stew. Nancy and Harding were playing a game of backgammon and Hester was seated at the table with a mug of tea.

'How old are you, Mr Harding?' Hester leaned forward, fixing him with an intense gaze.

He looked up, smiling. 'I'm forty-three, my lady.'

'Nancy tells me that you were adopted by a tailor in Teignmouth.'

'That's true. I never knew who my birth parents were.' Harding conceded the game to Nancy. 'But I had a good upbringing by my adoptive parents.'

273

'What is your first name, Mr Harding?'

Nancy stared at Hester in surprise. She could not imagine what had prompted this cross-examination.

'It's Tobias, my lady. I believe that my mother was most particular that I kept the name she had given me.'

Hester moved so quickly that she knocked her mug over, spilling tea on the table top, which she ignored as she leaned closer. 'So you do know something about her?'

'Is this necessary?' Nancy asked anxiously. 'It's very personal.'

'It's all right, Nancy.' Harding met Hester's questioning look with a serious face. 'I know that my mother was very young, possibly a housemaid. It happens sometimes that girls in service are taken advantage of by someone of a higher rank in the household.'

'Yes,' Hester said softly. 'It does. If you'll excuse me, I feel rather tired. I'm not as strong as I thought I was.' She rose somewhat unsteadily to her feet and lurched out of the saloon.

'I'd better go with her,' Nancy said, rising to her feet.

Harding reached out to catch her by the hand. 'No, let her go, Nancy. She needs time on her own.'

'How can you say that?' Nancy asked angrily. 'I've known Hester for most of my life. She's upset.'

Harding released her as he stood up. 'I'll go, Nancy. I think I know the truth now. I suspected it the first time I spoke to Hester, but it was just a feeling. Now I'm sure, and I need to speak to my mother.'

Nancy stared after him. Of course, it should have been obvious to her from Hester's first meeting with Tobias Harding that there was something between them. It had never occurred to her that the first mate on the *Bonaventure* was Hester's long-lost son, but it seemed as though a miracle had happened and now, however strange the circumstances, they were reunited. She could only imagine the touching scene but she knew better than to interrupt them as they came to terms with their newfound relationship.

The rest of the voyage passed without incident. The sea was calm and each day was warmer than the last. By the time they docked in Bridgetown everyone on board knew that Hester was Harding's mother. Captain Mockridge gave Tobias permission to see Hester and Nancy safely ashore with orders to find them suitable accommodation. The fierce heat of the sun was made worse by their winter clothing, tight stays and flannel petticoats. Nancy could see that Hester was suffering even more than herself as they walked beside Tobias to a small hotel not far from the waterfront. They shared a room from choice this time, as both of them were slightly nervous of being in a strange land so far from home. Tobias left them with instructions to remain in their room until he returned with news of Alex and Leo. He said he would check first on the Cyrene, and if it was still being repaired he would seek out the captain or the mate and ask them where he might find Captain Blanchard and Mr Wilder.

Hester took off her woollen gown and unlaced her stays as she lay on the bed, fanning herself vigorously.

'I wouldn't have been so keen to come with you had I known how blooming hot this island was.'

'But if you'd stayed behind you would never have found your son. It was fate, Hester.'

'I still can't believe it. Tobias is a fine man, and he

doesn't seem to blame me for giving him up.'

'He understands how it must have been for you in those days. He's a man of the world, Hester, and he's a very nice person. I like his sense of humour and his kindness.'

'But he's a seafarer, Nancy. When the *Bonaventure* sails, that might be the last I ever see of my son.'

Nancy went to sit by the open window, although there was very little breeze to relieve the relentless heat.

'I don't believe that for one moment. Tobias will visit you whenever he comes home on leave. His adoptive parents are both dead. He told me that, and he has no other relations. Of course he will come and see you.'

'I hope so, but I gave him away, Nancy. I can't forgive myself for that.'

'How would a fifteen-year-old maidservant have raised a child?'

'That's true. My ma was too ashamed of me to do anything other than find a home for my baby. They all told me it was for the best. I had no say in the matter.'

'There you are then. Stop feeling guilty and be glad you've found each other.'

'You're right. We have to concentrate on finding Alexander and Leo. They will know where Piers is and when we've convinced him to return to Cornwall, we can all go home.'

Nancy sighed. It sounded so easy when Hester said it, but she had a feeling that it was going to be more difficult than they imagined. Hester fell asleep, giving herself away by snoring gently, and Nancy gazed out at the view, hoping to catch sight of Tobias on his return.

During the long wait her imagination ran riot. Alex and Leo might not have found Piers, or perhaps he refused point-blank to return to Cornwall. The difficulties that this would raise were unimaginable. Without his guidance Lady Pentelow would be unable to save Trevenor or the clay mine. Aurelia would stand little chance of meeting someone willing to marry a penniless widow, and the feud between Lady Pentelow and Hester would go on and on . . . ..

Nancy jumped at the sound of someone knocking on the door. She went to investigate and breathed a sigh of relief when she saw Tobias standing in the corridor.

'Did you have any luck?'

'The *Cyrene* is still in dry dock. The repairs have taken longer than expected, but I haven't managed to find Captain Blanchard or Mr Wilder. I did get word on Piers Blanchard's whereabouts.'

'Where is he, Tobias? I want to see him.'

'He's just arrived back from Bermuda where his ship delivered a supply of arms and munitions to be taken to Savannah.'

'He's a gun runner? That sounds terrible.'

'There's money to be made in other people's misery. It seems that Piers has decided to help the Confederate Army.'

'I don't know anything about the war between the North and South, but Piers is wrong to interfere. He's needed desperately at home. Do you know where I might find him?'

'Surely you aren't thinking of going on your own? If Captain Blanchard and Mr Wilder can't persuade him to return to Cornwall, what chance do you think you might have?'

'I only know that someone must try. If Piers is sailing on those ships, he's putting his life at risk. His grandmother needs him to come home.'

'How do you propose to get to him, Nancy? This is a dangerous place for a young woman. You should not go out unattended.'

'Just tell me where I might find Piers. I'll do the rest. I'm not afraid. This won't be the first time I've been in dangerous territory — you don't know Clare Market.'

'Leave it to me, Nancy. I'll find out where Piers is staying and I'll let you know, but we won't be in port for long. Once we've discharged our cargo and taken on a load of sugar cane and molasses we'll be sailing back to England.'

'I understand. Just find out where Piers lodges and I'll do the rest.' Nancy glanced over her shoulder at Hester's inert body. 'Please don't tell Hester. She's very protective but I don't want her stepping into danger and I'm sure you don't either.'

'If I find out where Piers is, I'll take you to him. You mustn't even think of going anywhere on your own.'

Nancy smiled sweetly. 'As if I would do anything so rash.'

18

Nancy opened the door just wide enough to see who was knocking so impatiently. 'Tobias, you're back. Have you found him?'

'Aye, I have. He's staying at a dockside inn where he has a room. They even keep it for him while he's away. The good news is that he's there now, drinking in the bar to celebrate a successful run.'

'Tell me how to find it. I'll go as soon as I've made myself tidy.'

'As I said before, you're not going alone. It's not safe. I'll wait and I'll take you there myself.'

Nancy did not argue. She closed the door and finished dressing. Minutes later she and Harding were walking along the waterfront. She was excited but nervous, and she was glad that Tobias Harding had refused to allow her to seek out Piers on her own. It was not the sort of area where any lone female would be safe. She realised that she was attracting a great deal of unwanted attention, but she held her head high and walked on purposefully.

The doors of the bar were flung open but, even so, the heat inside was stifling. The smell of tobacco smoke, sweating bodies and rum pervaded the atmosphere. The chorus of male voices shouting to make themselves heard was drowned out by bursts of raucous laughter. Nancy kept close to Harding's side as they made their way to the bar. A swarthy man reached out to catch her arm, but Harding was too quick for him and his fist shot out, hitting the fellow on the nose so that he backed away, swearing loudly.

'There he is,' Nancy whispered, pointing to Piers, who was standing with a group of men at the end of the bar. She ignored the salacious remarks of the drinkers and the groping hands that reached out to touch her as she pushed her way to where Piers was standing. He had his back to her and she tapped him on the shoulder.

'Piers Blanchard.'

He turned to stare at her in surprise. 'Who's asking?'

'It's me, Nancy Sunday. Don't you recognise me?'

He frowned. 'You've grown a bit since I last saw you.' He grabbed her by the arm and propelled her out of the building with Harding following them. Piers turned on him. 'Who are you?'

Nancy wriggled free from Piers's grasp. 'There was no need to do that. I've come a long way to find you, and I wouldn't have known where to start if Tobias hadn't helped me.'

'Much obliged to you, I'm sure, mister. You can go now. I'll see Miss Sunday back to where she's staying.'

'You don't understand,' Nancy said crossly. 'This is Tobias Harding. He's the first mate on the *Bonaventure*, the ship that brought me and Hester here. He's Hester's son.'

Piers gave Tobias a searching look. 'Well, I'll be damned. So Hester has a past — who would have thought it?'

'Don't you want to know why we've travelled all this way to find you?'

Piers shrugged. 'I've heard it all from Alex and Leo. They haven't made me change my mind. I'm not interested in home now. I'm doing what's right for me.'

Harding made a move towards Piers, but Nancy laid her hand on his arm. 'You are very selfish, Piers Blanchard. Your grandmama, who raised you from a child, is in danger of losing everything, including Trevenor. Aurelia is a penniless widow and you'd hardly recognise her now. If you have any feeling for them you must come home, even if it's only for a short time.'

'I'm sorry, but maybe it's too late to save the mine. Alex told me it wasn't doing well.'

'So you're going to turn your back on your family and play at being a gun runner. I used to look up to you when I was a child. I can see how mistaken I was.'

'Look here, mister. I know I'm not part of this, but it seems to me you could at least give what Nancy asks some thought. My ma isn't a young woman and she's come all this way to try to persuade you to go home. At least give her the courtesy of hearing what she has to say.'

'Hester never approved of me. She's not interested to know what I think or want. I'll tell you what I told Alex. I was sent to the penal colony on false charges, or at least they were exaggerated by Ewart. No one in the family spoke up for me.'

'But, Piers, you own Trevenor and the land surrounding it. Don't you have any feelings for your old home?'

'I might have died in Australia and no one at home would have been any the wiser. I doubt anyone really and truly missed me, so why should I put myself out now?'

'Don't you care at all about your grandmama, Piers?'

'You won't get to me by appealing to my better nature, Nancy. I lost that breaking up rocks in the penal colony.' Piers shook free from her restraining hand and turned away. 'If you want to find Alex and Leo, they are staying in style at the Charnley sugar plantation. Apparently, Alex was at school with their son, so he and Leo have been having the royal treatment, which of course was not extended to me.'

'I'm not surprised,' Nancy said angrily. 'Let's go, Tobias. We're obviously wasting our time here.' She marched off with Harding on her heels.

★ ★ ★

Hester was still prone on the bed when Nancy reached the hotel.

'I'm not asleep, just resting my eyes.' Hester raised herself on one elbow. 'I don't know how these people stand the heat. Did you find Piers?'

Nancy took off her straw bonnet and laid it on the ottoman at the foot of the bed. 'We did but he won't come home with us. He's a very bitter man and he doesn't seem to care what happens to his family.'

'I can't say I'm surprised. That man always had a hard streak. He used Rosie to better himself. All he cared about was making money and it seems he hasn't changed.'

'There is slightly better news, Hester. I know where Alex and Leo are staying.'

Hester reached for a cloth and wiped her brow. 'Where are they?'

'Piers told us that Alex knows the son of the owner of Charnley sugar plantation. They were at school together. Anyway, Tobias says it's the biggest

282

plantation on the island and the *Bonaventure* ships cargoes of their molasses and rum back to England. It seems as though Alex and Leo have landed on their feet.'

Hester scratched her shoulder. 'I think there are bedbugs in this mattress. I don't want to stay here any longer than necessary.'

'It's too late today, but I suggest we put on our best gowns and pay a visit to the plantation first thing tomorrow morning. We need to persuade Alex and Leo to come home. They won't change Piers' mind, so it's a waste of time them being here.'

'I agree. Anything to get out of this heat and this flea-ridden hotel. Maybe we can sail back on the *Bonaventure*. Where is Tobias, by the way?'

'He had to return to his duties on board.'

'I don't want to lose him again, Nancy. I never forgave myself for giving him up, even though it would have been impossible for me to raise him. I need to get to know my son.'

'Of course you do. I just wish I knew who my parents were. Not knowing is awful.'

'I never considered your feelings before, and I'm sorry,' Hester said softly. 'I could have been kinder to you when you were growing up.'

Nancy laughed. 'You took me in and you fed and clothed me. I had a good education so I am not complaining. I was very lucky that Rosie saw fit to rescue me from a life of servitude.'

Hester swung her legs over the side of the bed and it creaked ominously. 'Do they provide food in this establishment? I'm starving.'

★ ★ ★

That night neither Nancy nor Hester managed to get much sleep. The noise from the ground floor of the hotel kept them both awake into the small hours, and then they were plagued by bites from bedbugs. Mosquitoes were also a problem, despite the netting draped over the bed, and the heat was intense. When Hester did finally doze off she mumbled in her sleep and Nancy lay awake, longing for the coolness of her room at home.

Next morning, Nancy rose early and washed in tepid water from the ewer on the washstand. She dressed and went downstairs to order coffee, which she had to carry upstairs herself as the maids were busy elsewhere, although she suspected that most of them were still in their beds.

Hester was groggy from lack of sleep but a cup of strong black coffee revived her enough to get up and dress in the best clothes she had brought with her. Nancy found the sleepy-eyed concierge and persuaded him to find them transport to the plantation. He eyed her curiously and demanded payment for the room before he would do anything. She gave him the money and he sloped off to find someone who would take them to Charnley. Eventually a shifty-looking individual drew a sad-looking sway-back horse to a halt outside the hotel, and the concierge sent a boy to help Nancy and Hester with their luggage.

'What do we do if they don't invite us to stay?' Hester asked in a stage whisper.

'We find another hotel. I'm not spending another night in the one we've just left.'

'Very wise,' the driver said grimly. 'Check your purse, ladies. They is a lot of light-fingered peoples who run that place. Now I can show you a decent hotel where ladies are safe and no bedbugs.'

'Thank you,' Nancy said hastily. 'We'll bear that in mind.'

The sun beat down on them and Nancy could feel her clothes sticking to her body. She longed for a patch of shade and a cool drink, but there seemed to be no relief. Dust clouds blew up around them and they were plagued with sand flies. Their bites were painful and left red welts on their skin, adding to their intense discomfort. Hester was not happy, and by the time they reached the Charnley plantation she was downright miserable. However, when she viewed the elegant white stucco frontage of the plantation house she brightened considerably. Surrounded by exotic palms, jacaranda and mango trees, with bougainvillaea clambering over its walls, the house looked cool and welcoming amidst the dust and heat.

'I'll wait here then?' The driver took a pipe from his pocket and sucked on it. 'They're an uppity lot, these plantation owners. I'm warning you, ladies.'

'Thank you,' Nancy said politely. 'We'll leave our luggage here, but there's no need to wait.' She thrust some coins in his outstretched hand and heaved her case out of the cart. Hester followed suit and they walked slowly up the wide flight of steps to the arched veranda.

The door was opened by a black male servant who ushered them inside.

'We are looking for Captain Blanchard and Mr Wilder,' Nancy explained hurriedly. 'Are they staying here?'

'If you would kindly wait, I'll see if they are at home, miss.' The butler bowed and walked away, leaving them to gaze in awe at the splendid entrance hall in the colonial style. The white walls reflected the sunlight slanting through louvered doors and shutters, and lush green house plants created a touch of the exotic outdoors.

Nancy was busy admiring her surroundings when the butler returned and asked them to follow him.

The drawing room was equally bright and furnished with comfortable but elegant rattan sofas and easy chairs. A middle-aged gentleman wearing a cream linen suit with a matching waistcoat over a white shirt rose from his seat to greet them.

'Welcome to Charnley, ladies. Rudolph Charnley at your service. How may I help you?'

Hester acknowledged him with a nod. 'Lady Hester Carey of Rockwood Castle, and this is my ward, Nancy Sunday. I believe you have Captain Blanchard and Mr Wilder staying with you.'

Nancy said nothing. She did not challenge Hester's description of her as her ward. After all, their relationship was difficult to categorise. She watched Mr Charnley closely and she could tell by his expression that he had weighed Hester up and had her measure. If he was unimpressed by her title he was gentleman enough to conceal his feelings.

'How do you do, my lady? In answer to your question, they are both here. My son Rupert is showing them round the plantation as we speak.'

'We need to speak to them quite urgently, sir.'

'Nothing happens fast here at Charnley, my lady. Please be seated.' Mr Charnley tugged at a bell pull by the mantelshelf. 'I'll send for refreshments. I take it you have arrived on the island recently.'

'We came on the *Bonaventure*,' Nancy said quickly. 'We hope to return to England when she sets sail again.'

A servant entered the room and stood waiting for his master to speak.

'Bring refreshments for the ladies, James.' Mr Charnley turned to Hester and Nancy. 'Would you like iced lemonade or tea?'

'Tea for both of us, please,' Hester said firmly. She shot a sideways glance at Nancy. 'The water has been boiled,' she added in a whisper. 'You can't be too careful abroad.'

'Tea it is, then, James. And send a boy to find Mr Rupert and our guests. Tell them we have important visitors.'

James nodded and left the room as quietly as he had entered.

Mr Charnley turned to Hester with a smile. 'I can assure you that we purify our water, my lady. By the way, where are you staying while you are on the island?'

Hester opened her mouth to speak but Nancy answered first. 'We spent one night in a hotel on the waterfront, Mr Charnley. It was less than comfortable. Perhaps you could recommend somewhere more suitable.'

'You must stay here, of course. I cannot allow two ladies to expose themselves to the discomforts you might face otherwise. I know a little of the reason for your making such a long voyage. Captain Blanchard confided in me and I understand the situation.'

'That's very kind of you, sir,' Hester said hastily. 'We are much obliged to you. Our luggage is on the veranda.'

Nancy felt a blush of embarrassment rise to her cheeks and she looked away. She sensed that Mr Charnley was silently mocking Hester. It was as if he knew that she had worked hard to earn her right to the title and he was looking down on her. Difficult and prickly Hester might be, but she deserved respect as much as anyone, and probably more than some, including Mr Charnley. Nancy decided that she did not like him. For all his smooth and courteous manners, she suspected that he thought himself to be much more important than he really was.

It was a relief when James returned with a tray laden with freshly made lemonade, a pot of tea and a plate of small cakes.

'The ladies' luggage is on the veranda,' Mr Charnley said firmly. 'Have it taken to the Wedgewood suite, James. Lady Carey and Miss Sunday will be staying for a few days.'

'Yes, sir.' James backed out of the room, closing the door behind him.

Hester took charge of the teapot without being invited to do so and she filled two cups with tea. 'Will you join us, Mr Charnley?'

'No, thank you, Lady Carey. I prefer something a little stronger at this time of day. I'm afraid we are an all-male household, apart from the servants, of course. My wife passed away several years ago and neither of my sons has yet succumbed to the charms of any of the planters' daughters.'

Nancy sipped her tea, wondering whether Rupert was as snobbish as his father, but Hester was smiling and patently unaware of any undercurrents. She reached for a cake.

'You have an excellent cook, Mr Charnley. Are servants difficult to come by on the island?'

He laughed. 'If you are asking tactfully whether my servants are slaves, the answer is no, definitely not. My grandfather freed the slaves nearly sixty years ago.

Our workers are all paid for their labours and housed on the estate.' He moved closer to the French window. 'I see Rupert coming and he's bringing your friends with him.'

Nancy sat on the edge of her seat. She put her cup and saucer back on the low table, forcing herself to be patient. She could see Alex and Leo and the man who accompanied them, laughing and chatting as if they were old friends. As he entered the room she knew she liked him as much as she disliked his father. Rupert Charnley was probably in his early thirties. He was about the same height as Alex but of slighter build. He was not classically handsome but he had an open face with eyes the colour of molasses that crinkled at the corners when he laughed. His dark brown hair was streaked blond by exposure to the sun and his skin had a healthy tan as if he enjoyed the outdoor life.

Alex and Leo stopped in the doorway, staring in stunned silence. Nancy wanted to laugh at their startled expressions, but she managed to control herself. She sat very still, her hands folded demurely in her lap while she waited for them to realise that they were not seeing things.

'Rupert, these ladies have come all the way from England to find Captain Blanchard and Mr Wilder. They are to be our guests for the next few days.' Mr Charnley, seemingly oblivious to the astonishment of his other guests, turned to Hester. 'Lady Carey, may I introduce my son, Rupert?'

'How do you do?' Rupert said politely. 'It's a pleasure to meet you, ma'am.'

'And you, sir.' Hester glanced past him, frowning. 'Alexander Blanchard and you, Leo Wilder, your wives have been worrying themselves to death because you have been away for so long without sending a word home. What do you have to say for yourselves?'

She sounded more like an irate nanny than the widow of a baronet, and Nancy was embarrassed for Hester's sake. Nancy jumped to her feet and ran to hug Alex and then Leo. 'I'm so glad we found you.'

Leo held her at arm's length. 'How did you get here?'

'We shared a cabin on the *Bonaventure* — it's a long story, Leo, but we're here now.'

'Why did you travel all this way?' Alex demanded. 'You must have known we would return as soon as we had persuaded Piers to come with us.'

'That's not likely to happen, is it?' Nancy looked from one to the other. 'We found Piers in a dockside pub, drinking with the locals. He refused point-blank to come home.'

'Let me handle this, Nancy.' Hester stepped forward. 'We need to speak in private, but things are bad at Trevenor. Piers must be made to return. It's as simple as that.' She turned her head to give Mr Charnley an apologetic smile. 'I'm sorry, sir. This isn't the sort of thing you might want to hear.'

'Of course you need privacy to discuss family matters. Anyway, I have business in Bridgetown, so I must leave you now, but we'll meet again at dinner this evening. Rupert will look after you until then.' Charnley bowed politely and strolled out of the room, calling for his manservant.

Rupert sat down opposite Nancy and reached for a cake. 'You must have an interesting tale to tell of your journey from Devonshire. Alex and Leo have told me why they are so keen to persuade Piers to return home, but you know how bad men are at recounting the interesting details. I can't wait to hear it from your lips, Nancy.'

'Leave her alone, Rupert,' Alex said sternly. 'Nancy isn't a gossip, but I'm sure Leo and I both want to know why you brought her here, Hester?'

'I came of my own accord. Hester volunteered to come with me.' Nancy sighed. 'We wouldn't have had to make the journey had you returned in time for Christmas. There was a riot at the mine and Aurelia's husband was killed. Lady Pentelow stands to lose everything and heaven knows what will happen to Aurelia.'

Rupert frowned. 'That does sound serious, Alex. Isn't there anything you could do that would persuade your cousin to return to Cornwall?'

'No, I'm afraid not. Piers is a law unto himself. He's very bitter about the way the courts treated him, although as far as I can see he brought it on himself.'

'Nevertheless, we'd best get a passage home as soon as possible,' Leo said firmly. 'I've left my wife handling the business at the sawmill.'

'There's something you should know, Leo,' Nancy said in a low voice.

He turned to look at her. 'Is anything wrong?'

'On the contrary. It's wonderful news — you're going to be a father. I know Patsy would have wanted to tell you herself, but you should return home as soon as humanly possible.'

Leo paled beneath his weathered tan, and was silent for a few seconds, digesting the news. 'Are you — are you sure, Nancy?'

'She told me so herself. I wouldn't lie about anything so important.'

'Women are having babies all the time,' Hester said impatiently. 'The thing is that you two are needed back in England. I'm sorry if it brings the real world to you when you are obviously enjoying life here, but there it is. You have to come home with us.'

'Of course we'll return on the next ship bound for England.' Alex eyed Rupert expectantly. 'Didn't you say you have a vessel loading a cargo of rum and molasses, bound for Plymouth?'

'That's correct. The *Charnley Queen* is due to sail tomorrow morning, but there is only one cabin available for passengers.'

'We can't leave Hester and Nancy here,' Alex said regretfully. 'Otherwise I would have jumped at the chance to get home and see my family.'

'Hester's son is the mate on the *Bonaventure*,' Nancy said proudly. 'Wasn't that an amazing coincidence? He's helped us since we arrived on the island. We can have the same cabin for the return journey. I think they are also sailing tomorrow.'

Alex frowned, shaking his head. 'We ought to travel together.'

'Nonsense, Alexander. We made it here on our own, didn't we?' Hester gave him a stern look. 'You and Leo must take advantage of Rupert's offer and leave in the morning. The sooner you get back to Rockwood, the better.'

'That's if you don't mind us staying here tonight, Rupert?' Nancy turned to him. 'We can always find a hotel if it's going to inconvenience you.'

'I would be delighted if you were our guests tonight,' Rupert said with a charming smile. 'As to the sailing, Alex, I'll send a boy to the docks to tell my brother, Dolph, to make the necessary arrangements.'

'Does he help to run the plantation as well as you and your papa?' Nancy eyed him curiously. She could not quite get the measure of Charnley's second son.

'Dolph prefers the shipping side of things. It gives him a chance to spend time in town.' Rupert's smile faded. 'He hates the process of cutting and pressing the sugar canes in the mill, and all the processes afterwards, which is a pity as he'll inherit the plantation one day.'

'It seems to me that you do pretty well at running it on your own,' Leo said seriously.

'The business side appeals to me. In fact, I was supposed to be travelling to Plymouth tomorrow to do a deal with a new agent.'

'We don't want to take your cabin.' Alex sighed. 'You've been good to us, Rupert.'

'You saved me from the school bullies, Alex. I might not have survived if you hadn't stepped in and taken care of me when I was a skinny little eight-year-old. Anyway, don't worry about me. I'll have the captain's day cabin. He's a friend of mine, so he won't mind.'

'That's settled then,' Hester said triumphantly. 'We leave tomorrow for England. I couldn't be happier. Not that this isn't a beautiful island and you have a wonderful place here, Rupert, but I miss my home.'

He smiled. 'I understand. As a matter of fact I, too, love England. I even love the damp foggy weather and the howling gales. I used to spend some of my school holidays with the Knighton family at Knighton Hall in Cornwall. They own a plantation on the other side of the island.'

'I know that family,' Alex said, nodding. 'My cousin Aurelia was almost engaged to their son, Hugo, at one time.'

'Who would have thought it?' Hester shook her head. 'We've come all this way only to find you know people back in Cornwall.'

'I hope you can visit Rockwood Castle while you're in Devonshire, Rupert,' Nancy said eagerly. 'I know that Lady Pentelow and Aurelia would love to meet you.'

'If I conclude my business in Plymouth quickly I might even be able to visit you at your home,' Rupert said, smiling. 'It would do Dolph good to carry on without me for a while.'

'We could travel to Rockwood together.' Leo rose from his seat. 'Alex, what do you say to one last go at persuading Piers to return home?'

Alex nodded. 'Might we borrow a pair of horses from your stables, Rupert? I doubt if we'll change my cousin's mind, but if we try again we'll know we've done everything we can.'

'Of course.' Rupert rang for a servant. 'Perhaps Hester and Nancy would like to join me for luncheon and then I'll give them a tour of the plantation. Tomorrow we'll be on our way to England.'

19

The strong south-westerlies were behind them all the way, buffeting, pushing and driving the *Bonaventure* and the Charnleys' vessel towards home. Hester was ill for most of the voyage but she picked up a little when they reached the quieter waters of the English Channel. When it was time to disembark, Nancy stood back while Hester said her goodbyes to her son. Tobias was clearly moved and he promised to visit Rockwood Castle on his next shore leave. Nancy thought she saw a tear trickle down Hester's cheek as Tobias walked away, but, being Hester, she recovered quickly and told Nancy off for staring at her.

It was too late to travel on and they spent the night in a Plymouth hotel. Next morning, first thing, Rupert had a meeting with the agent who was to promote the Charnley plantation sugar, molasses and rum, and when it was over he was clearly delighted with the result. Rupert had intended to spend a couple of weeks visiting places he had known as a youth, but after only a little persuasion he agreed to accept Alexander's invitation to spend a few days at Rockwood Castle. They travelled by train to Newton Abbot, where they hired a carriage and a slightly ramshackle dog cart to take them on the rest of their journey.

After the comparative heat of Barbados, the cold January weather came as a shocking reminder of the English winter. Sleety rain poured from heavy cumulus clouds and the roads were muddy and treacherous, which slowed down their progress. It was late afternoon when they arrived at the castle and already dark. Alex had sent a telegram from Plymouth announcing their homecoming so it was not a complete surprise for the family, who were assembled in the drawing room, seated round a roaring fire. The children were first to leap to their feet and they rushed to Alex, throwing themselves into his arms. He kneeled down on the floor and allowed them to get over their excitement, promising to tell them stories of his travels when they were tucked up in bed.

Leo swept Patricia off her feet, hugging her and kissing her soundly until she protested and made him put her down, but she was laughing and they went to sit side by side on the sofa.

'I'm sorry I had to tell him about the baby, Patsy,' Nancy said apologetically. 'He and Alex were a little too comfortable at the Charnley plantation.'

Hester took off her bonnet and shook raindrops into the fire so that they sizzled. 'Where are your manners, Alex? You should introduce Rupert to the family first.'

Alex stood up, even though the children were still clinging to him. He slipped his arm around Rosalind and kissed her. 'I'm sorry, Rupert. You'll have to forgive me.'

Rupert smiled and nodded. 'Of course. You are a lucky man to have such a wonderful family.'

'I'd like to introduce you all to my old friend Rupert Charnley. We were at the same boarding school, although he is three years my junior.'

'I was being bullied mercilessly,' Rupert added with a rueful grin. 'Alex stepped in and reminded the bullies what it was like for someone bigger and stronger to frighten the wits out of them.'

'We've been friends ever since, even though we are separated by miles of ocean.' Alex slapped Rupert on the back. 'Leo and I have been guests at his family's plantation near Bridgetown. I should add we were treated royally.'

Hester pulled a face. 'Yes, you didn't have to stay in that awful hotel where the mattresses were heaving with bedbugs, as we did. You were living like kings while Nancy and I spent the most uncomfortable night of our lives.'

'Well, you are all home safe and sound. That's all that matters to me.' Rosalind moved from her husband's embrace to hold out her hand to Rupert with a welcoming smile. 'I'm Rosalind and the three little limpets attached to Alex are Dolly, Rory and Phoebe.'

Rupert bowed and smiled at the children. 'I am delighted to meet you all.'

'I expect you've guessed that I am Leo's wife,' Patricia said happily.

Wolfe cleared his throat and pushed the Bath chair closer to Rupert.

'Bertie Carey.' Bertie held out his hand. 'A war wound prevents me from rising to my feet, but it's good to meet you, Rupert. Wolfe is my right-hand man. He can help you if you need to find your way around the castle or the village.'

They shook hands, and then Walter stepped forward to introduce himself, Louise and their four-year-old daughter, Charlotte.

The only person not included was Fletcher, who stood aloof and glowering. Nancy was quick to see the look of chagrin on Fletcher's gaunt features. 'And this is Cora Fletcher,' Nancy said hastily. 'She is an invaluable part of our family here at Rockwood.'

Fletcher bobbed an ungainly curtsey and retreated into the shadows.

Alex glanced round the room. 'I think you've met us all, Rupert. It just remains for someone to ring for Tilly, who will show you to your room.'

'I'm delighted to meet you all,' Rupert said, gazing round at the smiling faces.

'I thought my great-aunt and Aurelia were here,' Alex said, frowning. 'Have they returned to Cornwall?'

'They are here.' Rosalind picked up Phoebe. 'Lady Pentelow went to lie down with a sick headache, and Aurelia went with her. She's very good to her grandmother.'

As if on cue the door opened and Aurelia walked into the room. She came to a sudden halt, gazing at the newcomers with a delighted smile. 'Alex, Leo, you've come home. Thank goodness.'

Alex moved to her side and gave her a hug. 'We came at once when Hester and Nancy explained what had happened. I am sorry for your loss.'

'Thank you, but we hadn't been living as husband and wife for a long time.' Aurelia's gaze strayed to Rupert and her pale cheeks flushed prettily. 'I suppose you didn't manage to persuade Piers to return home, but I see that you've brought a guest.'

'Yes, I'm sorry, Aurelia,' Alex said gently. 'Your brother refused point-blank to return to Cornwall. However, may I introduce my old friend Rupert Charnley? We've been staying at his family's plantation.'

Aurelia extended her hand. 'How do you do, Mr Charnley?'

He raised her hand to his lips. 'How do you do, ma'am? It's a pleasure to meet you.'

'What time is dinner, Rosie?' Hester demanded, sighing. 'We seem to have been travelling for weeks and I'm starving.'

Rosalind put Phoebe down on the sofa. 'What am I thinking of? Of course you'll want refreshments after such a long journey. Dinner is at seven, but I know that Cook has been baking ever since we had the telegram announcing your imminent arrival.' She gave the bell pull a sharp jerk. 'There is so much I want to hear about your travels.'

Aurelia gave Rupert a sideways glance. 'Do you plan on staying long, Mr Charnley?'

'I came to England on business, which I completed more speedily than I anticipated. Then Alex invited me to visit Rockwood and I couldn't refuse such a generous offer.'

She smiled. 'I hope you will stay long enough to get to know us all. Although now Alex is home I think Grandmama will want to return to Cornwall.'

'Alex has told me about Trevenor. It sounds beautiful.'

Nancy had been listening to their conversation and she sensed an instant attraction between the two of them. 'I'm sure you would love it, Rupert,' she said eagerly. 'You are a businessman — you might be able to suggest something that would revive fortunes of the clay mine.'

'Oh, could you?' Aurelia's hazel eyes brightened. 'We were putting all our faith in my brother, but it seems that Piers has little interest in what happens at home. It would be wonderful if you could suggest something that would make it possible for us to keep Trevenor.'

Alex slapped his friend on the back. 'Would you

come to Cornwall with us, Rupert? I saw how you handled matters at the plantation. Maybe you could offer some suggestions.'

'I would most certainly try.'

Rosalind sighed. 'Alex, you aren't thinking of leaving us again, are you?'

'You could come with me, my love. I don't want to go away again, but if we do nothing it's almost certain that Trevenor will have to be sold to pay off debts or face bankruptcy, and the mine will be closed.'

'I can't leave the children, Alex. Who would take care of them?'

'My love, we have servants who are devoted to them. Hester will make sure that the children are looked after properly.'

'I suppose I have this to come.' Patricia rose to her feet. 'It's lovely to meet you, Rupert, but I think it's time we went home. I find myself a little fatigued these days.'

'Are you all right, darling?' Leo stood up and put his arm around her. 'You should be resting.'

She laughed. 'I'm not ill, Leo. I've been taking care of everything while you were away, but I am a little tired, that's all.' Patricia beckoned to Fletcher. 'Cora, will you send a message to the stables for our chaise to be brought to the front entrance?'

'Yes, missis.' Fletcher ambled from the room, narrowly avoiding a collision with Tilly, who had brought a tray of tea and cakes.

'We should go home, too,' Louise said firmly. 'It's getting late, Walter, and Charlotte goes to bed early.'

Walter rose from his seat and went to shake Rupert's hand. 'We'll see you again soon.'

Rosalind poured tea and Tilly handed it round to

those remaining. Jennet came to take the children up to the nursery. They went reluctantly, and only after Alex had promised to tuck them in when they were ready for bed.

Nancy sat back and watched. The old feeling of being the odd one out had returned, leaving her sad and set apart from the family. She found herself wondering what Freddie was doing at that moment. Had he missed her? He had never been too far from her thoughts, especially during the sea voyage home. Perhaps his mother had managed to persuade him to propose to the heiress. That thought was even more depressing.

'You will come to Cornwall with us, won't you, Nancy?'

Nancy turned to Aurelia with a start. 'I'm sorry. I was miles away. Did you just ask me to accompany you to Trevenor?'

Aurelia gave her a hug. 'Please say yes. I need someone on my side. Grandmama has never forgiven me for marrying Martin.'

'Why me? I mean, Rosie will be going too.'

'I know, but she and Alex will be together all the time, and I'll have no one to talk to.'

'What about Rupert?' Nancy glanced at Rupert who had moved away and was talking to Rosalind and Hester.

'He's so nice, isn't he? But you know me, Nancy. My heart rules my head. I don't want to make a fool of myself over a man. Not again. Please say you'll come with us.'

Nancy nodded. 'Of course I will.'

★ ★ ★

301

Later that evening Nancy was getting ready for bed when someone tapped on her door. She went to open it and found Rosalind standing in the corridor, holding a chamber candlestick.

'May I come in for a moment, Nancy?'

'Of course. Is anything wrong?' Nancy stood aside to allow Rosalind to enter her room, closing the door after her. 'Are you all right?'

'I'm fine, but I wanted to talk to you.' Rosalind set the candlestick down on a side table. She perched on the edge of the bed. 'A couple of days after you left for Barbados, we had a visit from Lord Ashton.'

Nancy slumped down on the dressing-table stool. 'What did he want?'

'It was clear that you are still very much on his mind, Nancy. He was very sweet and totally honest about his feelings for you.'

'I thought we'd agreed not to see each other again.'

'That's not how he sees it. He told me that his mother is trying to make him propose to some heiress, whom he cannot abide. But he loves you, Nancy.'

'I can't say I like Lady Dorrington, but I have to agree with her, Rosie. Freddie will one day inherit the title and the estate, he can't marry a nobody like me.'

'Surely he is the best judge of who he wishes to be at his side for the rest of his life?'

'Perhaps it would work for a while, but sooner or later he might come to regret it, and I couldn't bear that.'

Rosalind gave her a searching look. 'But do you love him, Nancy? Surely that's what counts the most.'

'I love him too much to bring him down to my level. Freddie is worth more than that.'

'I think you are wrong, Nancy. I also think that you

should talk to Freddie. You can't run away to Cornwall and expect him to forget you. He's too nice a person to treat in that way.'

Nancy jumped to her feet and went to stare out of the window into the swirling darkness. 'I know he is, but I'm not running away. Aurelia asked me to accompany her.'

'I've known Aurelia for a long time. I can deal with her. Freddie intends to return here. I think the least you can do is to stay and tell him how you feel.'

Nancy turned her head to meet Rosalind's gaze. 'Yes, you're right, of course. If he comes here again I will be honest and straightforward with him. If he doesn't arrive, I'll know that he has changed his mind.'

'I knew you'd see sense, Nancy. I just want you to be happy. You are good enough for any man. It doesn't matter who your parents were — you are a wonderful person and we all love you. I'm sorry if anyone in the family made you feel differently.' Rosalind rose from the bed. She picked up her candle and opened the door. 'Sleep well tonight, and tomorrow I'm sure you will do the right thing.'

Nancy remained by the window, staring out into the dark night sky, until eventually the cold made her lose the feeling in her fingers and toes, and she was forced to take refuge in her bed. She huddled beneath the covers, trying to put Freddie from her mind, and eventually slipped into a fitful sleep.

★ ★ ★

Nancy was late down to breakfast next morning and found that everyone had eaten, except her. She had lost her appetite and, having drunk a cup of rapidly

303

cooling coffee, she went in search of Rosalind. She found her coming out of the nursery, wiping tears from her eyes.

'It's the first time I've ever left them,' she said sadly. 'I know I'll worry all the time we're in Cornwall.'

'They have Hester and me to help look after them,' Nancy said with more confidence than she was feeling. 'You mustn't worry about the children.'

'That's easy for you to say, but when you have a family you'll know what I mean.'

'My parents obviously didn't care about what happened to me,' Nancy said bitterly.

'That's something you have to forget if you are ever going to have a happy life, Nancy. You don't know the circumstances. It could have been something like Tommy's mama, who tried to bring him up on her own but she succumbed to an illness. Bertie knew nothing about his son or else Tommy would have been raised here, with the people who love him.'

'I know. I'm being selfish and maudlin,' Nancy said with a wry smile. 'But I'm going to do as you say, Rosie. I'll be here if Freddie comes looking for me, and I'll talk it over with him. Now go. Sort things out in Cornwall and then hurry home.'

An hour later Nancy was standing in the bailey, watching the second of the two carriages drive out through the gates. She went back into the entrance hall, which suddenly felt very empty. Hester emerged from her private parlour and came bustling towards her.

'Don't look so gloomy, Nancy. They'll be back before you know it. Rosie won't be parted from her babies for long.'

Nancy managed a smile. 'Yes, I know that. It just

feels very quiet without them.'

'Bertie is here, although he and Wolfe have gone out on their rounds of the estate. Patricia is not far away — you could visit her. I know she'd be delighted to have your company and you need to keep yourself occupied, young lady. There's always something to be done in the still room, if you have nothing else to do.'

'You're right, of course. Perhaps you could show me how to make that rose-scented cream for hands and face.'

'I've been making lavender oil recently from the dried flowers we picked last summer. I can help you to make some of that.'

'Yes, thank you.'

The sound of carriage wheels and horses' hoofs made them look out of the window onto the bailey and Jarvis moved as swiftly as he was able to stand by the door.

'I know that carriage,' Hester said grimly. 'I'm going to the still room. You can join me later when you've sent that madam packing.'

'Who is it?'

'It's Christina Cottingham. I preferred her when she was Christina Greystone. She's hoity-toity now that she lives in Cottingham Manor, even though that husband of hers is just a clergyman. She had her eye on Bertie years ago. He had a lucky escape, if you ask me.'

Jarvis opened the door and Hester fled in the direction of the back stairs, leaving Nancy to greet their visitor.

Nancy held back, watching out of the window as Christina Cottingham was assisted from her carriage by a uniformed footman. She was wrapped in a fur-trimmed mantle over a voluminous skirt, and a fur hat perched at a smart angle on top of her elaborate coiffure. She marched towards the main entrance, leaving Nancy little alternative other than to move forward to greet her.

'Where is everyone?' Christina demanded. 'We passed two carriages heading out of the village.'

'Come into the morning parlour. It's warmer in there.'

Christina shivered theatrically. 'Yes, I remember how cold and draughty this old place is. Cottingham Manor is bad enough, but this pile of old stones is ten times worse.'

Nancy ignored the criticism and led the way to the morning parlour.

'Has anything happened to Sylvia?' she asked anxiously.

Christina shook her head. 'Sylvia is making good progress, as far as I am aware. No, this is another matter entirely.'

'Would you like some tea or coffee, Mrs Cottingham? A glass of sherry wine, perhaps?'

'No, thank you. I don't intend to stay long. I have a meeting with the land agent at Cottingham Manor. I have had to take charge of everything since Papa-in-law passed away.'

Nancy sat down by the fire. 'What about your mother-in-law, Lady Cottingham? Doesn't she do anything to help?'

'Glorina isn't interested in the estate. She has her eye set on Sir Wilfred Madison, who owns a vast estate in Wiltshire. She's hardly ever at home these days, which is a blessing, because I cannot abide that woman.'

'How does your husband feel about the prospect of his mother remarrying?'

Christina tossed her head. 'Ossie is too busy with his parishioners to bother much about anything else. I never thought he would be such a conscientious clergyman. I might have changed my mind about marrying him had I known that he would suddenly become so sanctimonious.'

'But you have the children.'

'Oh, yes. Although Nanny looks after them. I am too busy with estate matters and showing my face at church and parish council meetings. It's not a glamorous life, Nancy.'

'Why did you come here today? I don't mean to be rude, but you have never bothered with me before, and you fell out with Patricia years ago.'

'That was different. Patricia married my father and she thought she was going to inherit the estate. We have barely spoken since.'

Nancy eyed her warily. 'What can I do for you, Mrs Cottingham?'

'Did you know that Gervase North has taken over Greystone Park?'

'Taken over? I'm not sure I understand your meaning. I knew he was visiting but that was some time ago. I've been out of the country.'

Christina's thin lips drew together in a tight line of disapproval. 'So I heard. News gets round very quickly. Mr North is a cousin of mine and Sylvia's, but he insists that he is the rightful owner of the estate.'

'I'm sorry, but it really has nothing to do with me.'

'I thought you were his friend. He boasts about his connection to the Carey family.'

'He is most definitely not my friend. I know him a

little, but that's as far as it goes.'

'That's a pity. I was counting on you to persuade him to leave.'

'I don't know why you think he would listen to anything I had to say.'

'You were good to my sister. I'll always be grateful for that. I had hoped that your affection for her might convince you to help me to oust the man from our property. I've tried to see him but he refuses to speak to me.'

Nancy could see that Christina Cottingham was not going to give up easily. 'I think you overestimate my powers of persuasion, but if it means so much to you and Sylvia, I am willing to try. Just once, you must understand.'

Christina stood up, smiling triumphantly. 'I knew you would agree to help, if only for my sister's sake. Aunt Pennington writes that Sylvia is in good spirits and the physicians are optimistic for her complete recovery. I don't want anything to get in the way of that.'

'Of course. I agree entirely.'

'So you will go to Greystone Park and speak to Gervase.'

'I will try. That's all I can say.'

'Excellent.' Christina made for the doorway. 'I'll leave now, but thank you, Nancy. I'll see myself out.' She left the room, allowing the door to swing shut behind her.

Nancy sat down suddenly. The last thing she wanted was to see Gervase North again, but she had promised to help, and the memory of Sylvia, who had looked so pale and thin when she left for Switzerland, made it impossible to go back on her word. After all, she would just pay a quick visit to Greystone Park and put the case to Gervase.

★ ★ ★

Next day, Nancy drove herself to Greystone Park in the dog cart. She had not told Hester the real reason for Christina's visit, nor had she told her that she intended to call on Gervase North. Patricia would be furious if she found out, and Bertie would certainly forbid her to get involved. Tommy was in his first year at university, and there was no one else in whom she could confide. It would be a very brief visit, she managed to convince herself, and she handed the reins over to a stable boy, telling him to walk the horse while she was inside the house.

Foster opened the door in answer to her knock and he ushered her into the entrance hall.

'Is Mr North in residence, Foster?'

'I'll go and enquire, miss.' Foster made his way slowly across the hall. He returned moments later followed by Gervase himself.

'Nancy, my dear. This is a pleasant surprise.'

'Good morning, Gervase.'

'As a matter of fact I planned to visit you at Rockwood this very day.'

'That is a coincidence.'

'Come to the drawing room where we can talk properly. Foster, we'll have coffee and biscuits or cake, if there is any.' Gervase dismissed Foster with a brief wave of his hand. 'Come with me, Nancy. The fire should have been lit hours ago. I'm having difficulty with the lack of proper servants at the moment.'

Nancy followed him to the drawing room. The last

time she had been here was when Sylvia had left for Switzerland where she hoped for a cure. It seemed a very long time ago and the house felt quite strange. The drawing room was not untidy, but there were hints of male occupancy everywhere. A pile of field sports magazine spilled over onto the floor; a pair of walking shoes complete with mud were abandoned by the French windows, and there was a distinct smell of stale cigar smoke in the room.

'Do take a seat, Nancy. Make yourself comfortable.' Gervase stood with his back to the fire. 'As you see, I am very much at home here. This is my family seat and I have taken ownership, as is my right.'

Nancy remained standing. 'But it isn't yours, Gervase. The estate belongs to Christina and Sylvia.'

'Sylvia is an invalid and Christina is married to that prosy bore, Oscar the clergyman. What use have they for Greystone Park?'

'Whatever you think, this is their home. You have no right to be here.'

'I have every right. As the only surviving male member of the Greystone family the estate should have come to me in the first place.'

'But as I understand it, your mama was a Greystone but your papa was a member of the North family. Surely you should have inherited something from your father's side of the family.'

'I might have exaggerated the extent of my fortune in the past. Papa gambled on the stock market and lost. The only relatives I have are all poor, begging for scraps from my table. I have nothing to do with them.' Gervase's brows drew together in an ominous frown. 'Anyway, why are you here? Who sent you?'

Nancy sat down on a high-back chair, folding her

hands in her lap. She did not like the way Gervase could suddenly change from being charming to being overtly threatening. 'Christina asked me to come. To put it bluntly, Gervase, she wants you to leave.'

'Why couldn't she come and tell me that to my face?'

'Apparently you won't talk to her.'

'I'm a reasonable man, as you know. I will soon have proof of my right to inherit the house and the estate. Until then she will have to be patient.'

'Come now, you don't expect her to believe that, do you? She could call in the bailiffs and they would oust you from the property.'

'She would need a court order. I know my rights, Nancy. Besides which, you are also involved.'

Nancy stared at him in disbelief. 'How so?'

'I'm not prepared to reveal that now, but soon you will know who you are and why you are important to me. But never mind that now. I need your help to prove my case one way or the other.'

'I don't understand.'

'I might know now who your birth parents were, Nancy.'

'Then you must tell me. Please, Gervase.'

'Come back tomorrow morning at the same time and I will reveal all.'

20

Nancy returned to Rockwood Castle still puzzled by Gervase's comments. He had refused to expand on his statement that he knew her true identity and nothing she had said would make him change his mind. She went straight to her room to take off her outer garments, but she needed to speak to someone and Rosie, her usual confidante, was far away. There was one person who would understand and that was Bertie. His doomed love affair when he was little more than a boy himself had resulted in Tommy's birth. Bertie might be able to give her some advice and at the very least he would listen to what she had to say.

She made her way downstairs to Bertie's study, where she could be reasonably sure of finding him at this time of day. Wolfe was just leaving.

'Is it convenient for me to interrupt, Sir Bertram?'

Wolfe nodded and grinned. 'He's always got time for you, miss. I'd say you was one of his favourites.'

Nancy was too taken aback to answer. Wolfe rarely gave an opinion on anything, let alone a compliment. 'Thank you,' she murmured as she entered the room.

Bertie was seated in a chair on the far side of his desk. He looked up and smiled. 'Nancy. This is nice. Have you come to keep me company? We seem to be the only members of the family left after the exodus to Cornwall.'

'I've come to ask your advice, Bertie. I hope you aren't too busy to talk.'

'No, of course not.' Bertie leaned his elbow on the desk, eyeing her intently. 'What is it?'

Nancy pulled up a chair and sat down. 'Christina asked me to visit Greystone Park. She wants Gervase North to move out, but he refuses.'

'I heard that he'd taken up residence. Some nonsense about him being the rightful heir to the estate. Christina needs to get legal advice. She shouldn't have involved you, Nancy.'

'Yes, I think so, too. She seems to be under the impression that I am friendly with Gervase, which isn't true. Far from it, I can't stand the man.'

'In that case you should keep out of it, Nancy. If Christina tries to involve you again just send her to me. I won't stand for any nonsense.'

'Thank you, Bertie.' Nancy was about to rise from her chair, but she sank down on it again. 'There's one other thing that's puzzling me.'

Bertie gave her a sympathetic smile. 'Tell me.'

'Gervase said he knows who my parents were, but he wouldn't tell me.' Nancy's voice caught on a sob and she reached into her pocket for a hanky. 'Do you think it could be true?'

Bertie frowned thoughtfully. 'I suppose it's possible, although I don't see how he could have such information. Do you believe him?'

'I don't know, but he wants me to go back tomorrow morning. He said I can help him with something, although he didn't say what.'

'I'm afraid there's only one way to find out. If you want to go there tomorrow I'll send Wolfe with you. It's a brave man who takes him on.'

Nancy shook her head. 'I'm not afraid of Gervase. I don't think he'd harm me.'

'Think about it, Nancy. The offer is there if you wish to take it up.'

She rose to her feet. 'Thank you, Bertie. I'll see how I feel tomorrow morning.'

Nancy left the study deep in thought. She had no intention of telling Patricia everything that Gervase had said, but if anyone knew more about the Greystone family it would be the woman who had been married to Sir Michael until his untimely death.

After luncheon with Hester, who talked so much that conversation was very one-sided, Nancy set off for the house next to the sawmill.

Patricia was seated by the fire in the drawing room. She looked up and smiled when Fletcher showed Nancy into the room.

'I'm so pleased to see you, Nancy. I've been forbidden to do anything other than rest. Fletcher watches me like a hawk and Leo is little better.'

'I'm sure they mean well.' Nancy took a seat, sitting on the edge of an upright chair.

'Is anything wrong? You seem very tense?' Patricia eyed her curiously.

'No, not exactly. I need some advice, that's all.'

Patricia laughed. 'I'm not sure I'm the best person to ask. What is it about?'

'You were married to Sir Michael for four years, Patsy. What do you know about the family?'

'What brought this about?'

'I had a visit from Christina. She wants me to make Gervase leave Greystone Park, which is ridiculous, of course. Why would he pay any attention to anything I said? I wanted to know if you think he has a justifiable claim to the estate.'

'Honestly, Nancy. I know very little about the

Greystones, apart from the fact that Michael had an older brother, Oliver, who disgraced the family and was never spoken about. They had a younger sister called Elizabeth who married Francis North and Gervase is their son. That really is all I know.'

'What happened to Oliver Greystone? Did he marry?'

'Yes, his wife was Helena Collins. Her younger sister, Mary, was Sir Michael's first wife. Helena died in tragic circumstances shortly after Sir Oliver left for Spain. Sir Oliver was killed in the duel.'

'Who did Sir Oliver fight?'

'I believe it was the cuckolded husband of Oliver's lover. The story is that Oliver fled to Spain about nineteen years ago and Sir Rutledge Cooper, the wronged husband, followed him, intent on revenge, leaving Lady Cooper, his pregnant wife, at home. Sir Rutledge later returned to the family estate and his wife.'

'And the baby?'

'He grew up to be the image of Sir Rutledge, who never recovered from the fact that he had killed a man, despite the provocation, and drank himself to death a few years later. It was all very sad and a huge scandal at the time, which is why Oliver Greystone is never mentioned by the family.'

Nancy was silent for a moment. 'Do you think that Gervase has a valid claim to the estate, Patsy?'

'Only a court of law could settle that. It's up to Gervase to decide whether or not he wishes to take them to court. I really have no interest in their squabbles, and you should keep out of it, too.'

'I agree. If Christina approaches me again, I will suggest that she should get herself a good lawyer.' Nancy smiled. 'But more importantly, how are you keeping?'

Patricia rolled her eyes. 'Everyone keeps asking the same question. I am perfectly fit and well. I don't know what the fuss is about. I will go quietly mad if I have to stay indoors any longer than necessary. Leo won't allow me to go to the mill, which is ridiculous. I keep the books and make sure that the bills are paid.'

'Perhaps you could have the ledgers brought to you here, and you could do them at home.'

'How dull. I miss talking to the customers and I hardly see Leo. He's so busy all the time.'

'I will come and see you every day, if that helps.'

'You are so sweet, Nancy. I love you like a sister.'

Nancy stood up and leaned over to kiss Patricia on the cheek. 'Thank you, Patsy. That means so much to me.'

'You aren't leaving, are you? Not so soon?'

'I have to go, but I promise to be back tomorrow and I'll stay longer.' Nancy left hurriedly before Patricia's disappointed look persuaded her to stay. She would go and see Gervase tomorrow as he demanded, and find out what information he thought he had as to her origins, but his relationship with his cousins was none of her business.

★ ★ ★

Next morning, Nancy went to Greystone Park, as arranged. Foster greeted her with his customary dour expression. 'Mr North is in the drawing room, miss.'

'Thank you, Foster. I know my way there.' Nancy was in a hurry. She wanted to get the meeting over quickly and leave without giving Gervase time to argue.

He looked up as she entered the room without

316

knocking. 'I thought you weren't coming. Didn't I tell you that I had important information for you?'

'I believe you did, but I'm under no obligation to you, Gervase.' Nancy stared at the pile of papers that he had spread across the floor. 'What are you doing?'

'Looking for documented proof.' He went down on his knees and began sifting through the documents.

'Proof of what?' Nancy was curious now. 'What exactly are you looking for?'

'Sir Oliver's will. I think he might have named me as his son and heir.'

'You think he was your father?'

'I am sure of it.'

'What makes you think that, Gervase?'

'My mother was sickly and Papa was often away from home. I spent most of my early years in the care of Aunt Helena. Uncle Oliver was often absent, but when he was at Greystone he was very good to me. He taught me to hunt and fish, and we had a small boat which we took out on the lake at every possible opportunity.'

'But if that's true, it would mean that your mother was really your aunt. I don't understand why they would want to deceive everyone in such a way.'

'This is why I've been going through all the papers in the study and this boxful was in the attic. It hadn't been opened for years. I want you to help me, otherwise it will take ages.'

'Why don't you put it all in the hands of your solicitor, Gervase? Anyway, I don't see how any of this concerns me. You said yesterday that you had an idea who my parents were.'

He gave her a sly look. 'Yes, I did, didn't I? Well, you help me with this and I'll tell you.'

Nancy picked up a bundle of yellowed documents, tied with red tape, and took them to a side table. She pulled up a chair and sat down, untying the dusty paper.

'Surely your parents loved you. Why do you doubt them?'

'Something happened when I was a young boy. I must have been six or seven. It was the middle of the night and I was awakened by a lot of noise. I got out of bed and went onto the landing to look over the banisters. Uncle Oliver was wearing a black cloak. There was rainwater dripping off his wide-brimmed hat as he handed a bundle to my father. Even from that distance I could see it was a small baby and it began to cry. Papa and Uncle Oliver argued and then my uncle left, slamming the door so hard that the windows rattled. I never saw him again.'

'What happened to the baby?'

'I don't know. Next morning it had gone and Mama spent the day lying on her bed, sobbing. She wouldn't speak to me and she didn't even get up to go to church. That was very unusual because Mama was a devout churchgoer. I was left to the mercies of my governess. How I hated that woman.'

'Did your parents ever tell you what had happened?'

'No, and when I asked Mama about the baby she told me I was a wicked boy to make up such a tale. I was telling lies.'

'Were you?'

Gervase shook his head. 'That baby was real and it was crying.'

'Did you ask your aunt Helena what had happened?'

'I wasn't allowed to see her. They told me she was very ill and she didn't recover. It was then that my uncle Michael inherited the land and the title. He and his wife moved into Greystones with Christina and Sylvia. I was only a child but I was angry. I should have lived there. Sir Oliver was my papa, I know it.'

'But the baby, Gervase. Did you find out what happened to it?'

He shrugged. 'It was the early hours of Sunday morning when Uncle Oliver came to our house. You are Nancy Sunday — you were found on the orphanage steps on that day of the week.'

'Yes, I was discovered on a Sunday, but the dates would have to match.' Nancy frowned. 'It could be a coincidence. Anyway, what are you saying? Whose child am I?'

'That's one reason for sifting through these papers. Sir Oliver must have made a will. If we can find that it might tell us both who we really are.'

'All right, I'll help you, Gervase. But I still don't know why you doubt your parentage.'

'It's a feeling, Nancy Sunday. Just as I have a feeling that you were the baby I saw that night.'

'I don't think feelings count for much in a court of law. Anyway, these are just household accounts,' Nancy said, sighing. 'I don't want to disappoint you, but from what I have heard your uncle was not a reliable person.'

'He was my hero. I would like to be just like him.'

Nancy could see she was not going to get anywhere with Gervase when he was in this mood. She was disturbed by his suggestion that she was the baby who had been brought to his parents' house and then abandoned. If that was so then it was a double betrayal, assuming that she was related to the Greystones in some way. Even that was too far-fetched for her to contemplate seriously.

She sat quietly for a while, going through sheaf after sheaf of what turned out to be documents concerning estate matters. Eventually, seeing that Gervase was so absorbed in his quest to prove that he was Sir Oliver's son, she rose from her seat. 'I'm leaving now, Gervase. I hope you find what you're looking for.'

He did not seem to hear her and she left the room to find Foster hovering outside the door. She hesitated, eyeing him curiously.

'You've served the Greystones for many years, Foster.'

'I have, Miss Nancy.'

'Did you know Sir Oliver Greystone?'

'I was the late Sir Michael's butler before he inherited Greystone Park. I did meet Sir Oliver occasionally.'

'His wife died quite young, I believe,' Nancy said tactfully.

'Lady Greystone was a lovely woman, if I might be allowed to say so. She took her husband's disgrace very much to heart.'

'Did she die in childbirth, Foster?'

His grey eyes widened in surprise. 'No, indeed. The poor lady was found early one morning, drowned in the lake. It's rarely mentioned, but it's true.'

'Thank you, Foster. Would you send for my carriage, please?'

* * *

Nancy returned to Rockwood Castle with more questions than answers. She was shocked by Foster's revelation as to the cause of Lady Greystone's death, but that put an end to Gervase's theory that the baby

320

left in his parents' care was Lady Greystone's child. The mystery remained as to what happened to that baby and if, in fact, she had been abandoned by both Sir Oliver and his brother, Michael. She left the dog cart at the stables and walked the rest of the way, still mulling over the information that Gervase had handed out so casually.

★ ★ ★

When she entered the bailey she was surprised to see an unfamiliar carriage, but a cry of delight escaped her lips when she recognised the tall young man who leaped to the ground.

'Tommy.' Nancy ran to greet him and he swung her off her feet in an affectionate hug.

'Where have you been, Nancy?' Tommy glanced up at the louring clouds. 'This isn't the sort of day to be out for a walk?'

'I am so glad to see you,' Nancy said breathlessly. 'Sometimes I think you are the only sane member of the Carey family.'

'You're shivering.' Tommy slipped his arm around her shoulders. 'Come inside and tell me everything.' He saluted Jarvis as they entered the hall. 'Good afternoon, Jarvis. It's good to see you again.'

'Good afternoon, sir. It's always a pleasure to welcome you home.' Jarvis signalled to James, who rushed out to bring in the luggage.

Nancy glanced over her shoulder. 'Have you come home for good, Tommy? That's a lot of baggage for a short stay.'

He laughed. 'Honestly, Nancy. I'm not the academic type, unlike Uncle Walter. I'm more like Papa.

I'm a practical fellow and I've had enough learning to last me a lifetime.'

'In other words, you've been sent down.' Nancy smiled up at him. 'I am so glad to see you.'

'You are a sight for sore eyes, even if you have a smut on the tip of your nose.' He brushed it off with the tip of his finger. 'I am starving. I haven't eaten since very early this morning, and travelling always makes me hungry.'

'We'll go to the dining room and I'll ring for Tilly.'

'No, don't do that.' Tommy shrugged off his great-coat and tossed it onto a carved oak coffer. 'Let's go to the kitchen and see what Cook has to offer, as we did when we were children.'

'You are trying to avoid your papa, aren't you?'

'He's not going to be best pleased that I've been sacked from university. But I don't care. I'm home now and I'm not going away again.'

'I'm hungry, too. You can work your charm on Cook. She was always susceptible to your big brown eyes.'

'I can't help it if women fall at my feet. At least, older ladies do. I haven't had much success with the younger ones, but that's because my heart belongs to you, Nancy. It always has.' He gave her a hug and brushed her cheek with a kiss.

Nancy laughed. 'It's so good to have you back where you belong, Tommy. Let's go down the servants' stairs. If we bump into Hester you'll be in for a grilling.'

'She's best avoided at all times. I could never work my magic on Hester.' Tommy looked round. 'Where is everybody, anyway? The old pile seems very quiet.'

'I'll tell you over luncheon. So much has happened

since you went back to university after Christmas that I don't know where to begin.'

Tommy closed the visor on Sir Denys's helmet. 'Still gaping at us, are you, Denys old fellow?' He laughed. 'I used to think that Sir Denys really was inside that suit of armour when I was a nipper.'

'So did I. Even now I sometimes think he's watching us at night, although if anything he's being protective. I was never frightened of old Sir Denys.'

Tommy grabbed her by the hand. 'I can hear foot-steps and it sounds like Hester. I'd know that tread anywhere. She marches like an army.'

Giggling like children, they raced to the back stairs and made their way to the kitchen.

Edna Jackson looked up from rolling out pastry and her smile was genuine. 'Lord, Master Tommy, you gave me a fright. What are you doing here?'

'I had to leave university because I missed your deli-cious meals, Cook. Look at me — I'm half-starved.'

Cook wagged a floury finger at him. 'You might be all grown up, Master Tommy, but you are still a cheeky boy at heart.'

'Ignore him, Cook,' Nancy said, smiling. 'We are really hungry. I know we're too late for luncheon, but could you find us something to eat, please?'

'You are as bad as he is, Miss Nancy. Go into the servants' hall and I'll see what I can do.' Cook beck-oned to Flossie, who had started as a scullery maid and was now Cook's assistant.

'There's some lamb stew left over from luncheon, Flossie. Heat it up and cut into the new loaf. Master Tommy needs feeding up.'

'Thank you, Cook. I love you,' Tommy said, blow-ing her a kiss as he led Nancy through the kitchen to the servants' hall. They sat at a long refectory table and Flossie darted in and out with cutlery, crockery, a plate of butter and a basket of freshly sliced bread.

Tommy leaned toward Nancy, his expression suddenly serious. 'So how are you? What's been happening? I know there's something wrong. You could never keep anything secret from me.'

Nancy filled a glass with water and took a sip. 'I suppose it all started with Lady Pentelow and Aurelia coming here because things were so bad at Trevenor.'

'Go on, tell me everything.'

Nancy took a deep breath and related everything that had happened since Tommy was last at home; however, she did not mention Freddie's name. She had hoped he would make a return visit, but she was beginning to wonder if his mother had managed to bully him into offering marriage to the heiress.

Flossie brought plates brimming with savoury-smelling lamb stew and they ate hungrily. Tommy did not ask questions until they had finished eating. He sat back on the bench, eyeing her curiously.

'What happened to that wealthy fellow you were so sweet on? The one with the stammer.'

'You mean Freddie Ashton. I haven't seen him for a while.'

'If he's been playing fast and loose with your affections, he will have me to deal with. I won't allow anyone to hurt you, Nancy.'

She smiled sadly. 'I know it, Tommy. I think you are the only person in the whole world who really understands me. I trust you absolutely and I can't say that of many people.'

He grasped her hand. 'Then marry me, Nancy. I've loved you since we were nine or ten years old.'

'You are so sweet, Tommy,' Nancy said gently. 'I love you too, but we're more like brother and sister, aren't we?'

He withdrew his hand. 'Yes, of course.' His expression changed and he looked up at the sound of heavy footsteps. 'Hester, you've found us.'

Hester came to a halt, standing arms akimbo. 'What do you think you two are doing down here in the servants' hall? And why are you home, Thomas Carey? Have you been sent down?'

Tommy rose to his feet and embraced Hester. 'Don't be cross, Hester. We were hungry so we threw ourselves on Mrs Jackson's mercy. Now do I have to make the same pleas to you? I mean, Papa will not be pleased when he sees me. You'll be the kind lady you are and you'll tell him for me, please?'

Hester took a deep breath. 'You always were an impossible boy. You haven't changed despite the fact that you are almost a man.'

'So you will tell him?'

'Certainly not. I don't know what you did to get sent down, but that is between you and your papa. He has the whole estate to run with only Wolfe to help him since Alex went to Cornwall and there's no word as to when we might expect them to return.'

'Then he will be pleased to see me. I intend to give up my studies in order to learn land management. One day I will inherit Rockwood Castle and the estate. Practical experience will be worth much more to me than anything I can learn from a fusty old book.'

'We'll see about that, shall we?' Hester's implacable expression was not encouraging.

'Yes, we will. I'll go now, Hester.' He sauntered off at a leisurely pace.

'That boy will be the death of me,' Hester said grimly. 'The future of Rockwood Castle will be in his hands — heaven help us!'

'Don't be too hard on him.' Nancy rose to her feet. 'Tommy will be a credit to the family.'

'You and he were always thick as thieves when you were growing up.'

Nancy smiled. 'Yes, we got into all sorts of scrapes, most of which we managed to keep from you and Rosie.'

'You thought I didn't know, but I know everything that goes on in the castle and the village.'

Nancy eyed her thoughtfully. 'Did you know Gervase North's parents?'

'I wouldn't say I knew them, but their mansion outside Exeter is where I first went into service with Gervase North's grandparents. His mother and father inherited the property when the old couple passed away.'

'So Gervase would have been born there?'

'Yes, I suppose so. I had left long before then.'

'Was that where you had the problem with the butler?'

Hester laughed. 'That's one way of putting it, but yes. Tobias was the result of that unfortunate incident, although now I know him I am glad it happened.'

'Will Tobias visit you here when his ship is in port?'

'He's promised that he will see me as often as possible. We have so many years to catch up on.'

'You must be so proud of him, Hester.'

'I am indeed. Anyway, I haven't got time to stand and chat. I hope Rosie comes home soon. I'm too old to keep an eye on the schoolroom and the nursery.'

'But Hester, Jennet looks after the children, and

Louise comes in every day to give them lessons.'

Hester rolled her eyes. 'But I am responsible for the running of the household. I want to hand everything back to Rosie in good order.'

'Let me do something to help.'

'No. I can manage on my own. I was brought up to work hard and nothing changes.' With a martyred sigh, Hester marched off in the direction of the kitchen.

Nancy stood for a moment, frowning. An idea had come to her. She might just be able to prove Gervase's real identity one way or the other, and in doing so she might also gain a clue as to her own. She went in search of Tommy.

21

'I thought the old man was going to have a fit when I told him I'd been sent down,' Tommy said, grinning. 'But he actually laughed and said he wasn't surprised. He'd been expecting it and it was only a matter of time. Anyway, he said I didn't need a degree to manage the estate. He is only too happy to have me at home and he wants to pass on all the knowledge he's learned since he left the army.'

Nancy clutched Tommy's arm as they walked slowly towards the village church. 'That's wonderful news. With Louise and Walter turning up unexpectedly yesterday, as well as Patsy, who somehow managed to escape from the house, I didn't have a chance to ask you what your papa said.'

'Poor Patsy. She isn't the sort of person to sit quietly at home.'

'Leo is being very strict with her until the baby is born, but she's going mad being shut up in the house. If we find out anything we could call on her at home and let her know. Although I haven't told her everything as yet.'

'We're here,' Tommy said, coming to a halt outside the lich-gate. 'Are you sure you want to do this?'

'Gervase was born at Heathleigh Hall in this village. His birth should be recorded in the parish records, and maybe mine, too, if what Gervase said was true. Although I'm not sure I believe him.'

'There's only one way to find out.' Tommy leaned

forward to unlatch the gate and ushered Nancy into the churchyard. They found the verger in the vestry and he was only too pleased to show off the meticulously kept parish register. Without much difficulty they found the entry for Gervase North's baptism, noting his date of birth and the names of both parents, Francis and Elizabeth North, with the address of Heathleigh Hall. However, when it came to finding anything concerning Nancy, there was nothing.

'There's no disputing Gervase's parentage. I'm not sure what to do next,' Nancy said as they walked back to where their horses were tethered. 'Gervase suggested that the baby he saw Sir Oliver hand over to his father was me, but why would a man give away his own child?'

'He was obviously planning to leave for Spain. Perhaps he wanted his sister to look after the baby until he returned.'

'Why take it from its mother? The Greystones had money and position with servants to care for the baby if Lady Greystone was unwell.'

'What do we know about Lady Greystone, apart from the fact that she drowned herself in the lake, if what Foster said was true?'

Nancy frowned. 'Maybe she killed herself because her husband had taken her baby from her?'

'Then we need to look elsewhere. The birth wasn't registered, as the baby disappeared, but maybe Gervase was telling the truth. Perhaps North did not want to be saddled with another man's child? Maybe it was he who took the infant and abandoned it on the orphanage steps?'

'Gervase said he remembered his mother lying on her bed, sobbing. Perhaps she wanted to look after the child. But if the baby was newborn there would be no record of it in the parish registers.'

Tommy lifted Nancy onto the saddle as if she weighed less than nothing. 'We need to find a servant who was employed at Greystone Park while Sir Oliver and his wife lived there.'

She looked down at him, a smile curving her lips. 'When did you get to be so grown-up, Tommy? I am very impressed.'

He vaulted onto his mount. 'You've just been so busy yourself that you didn't notice. I'm only a few months younger than you.'

'Not that it makes any difference now, although it did when you first came to Rockwood Castle. I remember how small and frightened you were and you had soot ingrained in your hands and feet. It took months for Rosie to clean you up.'

'And you were a bossy little madam,' Tommy said, smiling. 'We've both changed a lot, Nancy.'

'We virtually grew up together, Tommy. We'll always be the best of friends.'

They rode on, exchanging childhood reminiscences and laughing at their shared memories. Nancy knew she could be herself with Tommy. There was no shadow of her past to come between them, and even when the skies darkened and they were caught in a sudden shower of rain, nothing seemed to dim their enjoyment. They were both soaked to the skin by the time they reached home and they headed for their own rooms to change. Nancy happened to meet Hester on the stairs and she had a sudden thought.

'You're wet through,' Hester said suspiciously. 'Where have you been?'

'Tommy and I got caught in a shower.'

Hester grunted and was about to walk on when Nancy caught her by the sleeve. 'I believe you knew Greystone Park in the days when Sir Oliver and Lady Helena lived there.'

'Yes, I suppose so. Not that I ever went there in person, but I did meet their housekeeper sometimes in the village shop.'

'Does she still live in the village?'

'What is it to you?'

'I'm just curious. Something Gervase said made me wonder, that's all.'

'I wouldn't believe anything that man told you. He makes things up to suit himself.'

'Maybe, but I would like to speak to the house-keeper.'

'Biddy Corrigan lives with her daughter in the cottage next to the village shop. She's house-bound, so I believe. Why do you want to speak to her?'

'If I solve the mystery, you will be the first to know.' Nancy ran upstairs to her room where she changed into dry clothes. She could not wait to see Tommy and tell him about the Greystones' aged housekeeper, but she had to wait until after the family luncheon in the dining room. Despite the fact that Alex and Rosalind were still away, Hester insisted that mealtimes must be punctual and everyone was expected to attend. It kept the servants on their toes and those present had a chance to discuss matters relating to the estate or the household.

Tommy was as eager as Nancy to interview Mrs Corrigan, but they had to wait until Hester left the dining room before they made their escape. They slipped out of the house unnoticed.

Mrs Corrigan's daughter opened the door and her eyes widened with surprise. 'Miss Nancy, Master Thomas. What can I do for you?'

'Would it be possible to have a few words with your mother, Miss Corrigan? We won't keep her long.'

'Ma ain't too well, miss. She's got the rheumatics very bad, poor soul.'

Tommy produced a wicker basket laden with items they had purloined from the castle larder. 'Lady Carey sent these for your mother, Miss Corrigan,' he lied glibly. 'I would like to pass her best wishes on in person, if you have no objection.'

Miss Corrigan eyed the food, licking her lips. 'Well, now, sir. That's powerful good of Lady Carey. Won't you come in?' She stood aside and ushered them into the small front parlour.

Mrs Corrigan was propped up in a saggy old armchair by the fire with a knitted blanket wrapped around her legs. It seemed as if she was asleep, but her eyes opened at the sound of their footsteps.

'Who is it? I can't see too well these days.'

Nancy went down on her knees by the chair. 'Mrs Corrigan, it's Nancy Sunday and Master Thomas from the castle. We've brought you some calf's foot jelly, jam and cake, which Lady Carey thought you might enjoy.'

'Cake?' Mrs Corrigan's faded blue eyes brightened. 'I got hardly any teeth left so cake is what I likes best to eat.'

Tommy pulled up a chair and sat down. 'Lady Carey told us that you were housekeeper at Greystone Park for many years, ma'am. That must have

332

been very interesting.'

'I don't know about that, young man. It were hard work. No rest for any of us when Sir Oliver was present.'

'Of course not,' Nancy said hurriedly. 'Was Lady Greystone easier to deal with?'

'Poor soul, she had hardly a word to say for herself. Not that I speak ill of my employers, but she had a sad end.'

Nancy laid her hand on Mrs Corrigan's gnarled fingers as they plucked nervously at the blanket. 'We heard about that, ma'am. It's a pity she had no children to comfort her.'

Tommy winked and nodded. 'Nicely said,' he whispered.

'She suffered through all the disgrace her husband brought upon them. It's no wonder she miscarried so badly.'

'She bore a child?' Nancy held her breath.

'She went eight months but the shock of Sir Oliver being called out by a jealous husband sent her into labour.'

'What happened to the baby?' Tommy leaned forward to slip his arm around Nancy's shoulders.

'Stillborn. So people said.' Mrs Corrigan held out her hand. 'You said there was cake?'

'I'll cut you a slice, Ma.' Miss Corrigan placed the basket on the table. She put the cake on a chipped plate and cut a slice, which she handed to her mother. 'It's fruit cake, Ma. It's your favourite.'

Mrs Corrigan broke the slice into pieces and stuffed them into her mouth, rendering herself speechless. Nancy and Tommy rose to their feet at the same moment.

'Thank you, Mrs Corrigan,' Nancy said gently. 'You've been very helpful.'

'I'll show you out.' Miss Corrigan went to open the front door. 'Don't pay no mind to everything Ma says. Sometimes her memory wanders and she gets things in a bit of a muddle. I did hear that Lady Greystone gave birth to a child, but it was said she took it to a watery grave. However, I am not one to gossip.'

Nancy hesitated on the threshold. 'Is there anyone who would know for certain?'

'Mrs Betts, the midwife, might remember. How long ago was it, miss?'

'Almost nineteen years. If what your mother says is true, it was covered up very well.'

'Likely it would have been, miss.'

'Where can we find Mrs Betts?' Tommy asked eagerly.

'She lives two doors along, Master Thomas. I dare say she'll be at home now, providing there's no one gone into labour recently. I saw her go past an hour or so ago.'

'Thank you.' Nancy stepped out into the street. 'I'll make sure we bring a basket to you every week or so, Miss Corrigan. You've been most helpful.'

Tommy grabbed Nancy by the hand. 'Come on, let's see if we can get Mrs Betts to confirm or deny the story.'

'Even if it's true, it doesn't mean I was that baby. It was Gervase who put the idea into my head. Although he is convinced that he is Sir Oliver's son, so I don't think he's a reliable source.'

'He says what he wants to believe, Nancy. Let's speak to Mrs Betts, if she's still at home.'

The midwife's house was just two doors away and,

luckily for them, Mrs Betts herself answered the door.

'Miss Nancy, Master Thomas? What can I do for you? Is anyone ill at the castle?'

'Might we come in, Mrs Betts?' Nancy glanced over her shoulder to see if anyone was watching. The village gossips would have a wonderful time if they saw them visit the midwife.

'It's not what it seems, ma'am,' Tommy said hastily. 'I have accompanied Nancy purely out of interest. We believe you might be able to help us with some information.'

Mrs Betts pursed her lips. 'I don't discuss my patients with anyone other than close family and then only with the person's permission. Maybe you ought to see Dr Bulmer for whatever it is you want.'

Nancy shook her head. 'It's something that happened many years ago, Mrs Betts.'

'As I said, I don't talk about my patients.'

'We wouldn't dream of putting you in a difficult position, ma'am,' Tommy said, smiling. 'A simple answer will suffice with no details. Nancy has been told that Lady Helena Greystone gave birth to a stillborn child nineteen years ago. Is that true?'

Mrs Betts stiffened. 'No, it is not.'

'But Lady Greystone did give birth.' Nancy clasped her hands tightly together. 'We've been told that by a very reputable person.'

'Yes.' Mrs Betts nodded.

'The same person said the child was stillborn. Is that true?'

'No, and I'm not saying anything else. You haven't had any information from me and if it gets round that I've told you anything I will deny it strenuously.'

'Mrs Betts, this is very important to me. As you

335

probably know, I was a foundling left on the steps of the orphanage. It's been brought to my attention that the date of my birth and the date when Lady Greystone was delivered of a baby are roughly the same. You must have an idea of what happened to the infant.'

Mrs Betts gave her a searching look. 'What makes you think that you were that child?'

Tommy cleared his throat. 'Might we step inside, ma'am? We don't want the whole village to know our business.'

'Yes, come in.' Mrs Betts glanced up and down the road as she closed the door after them. 'Like I said, what makes you think you are related to the Greystones, Miss Nancy?'

'You must know that Mr Gervase North is living at Greystone Park.' Nancy could tell by Mrs Betts' expression that she was well aware of the fact. 'Well, it was he who suggested it. He is at present looking through the family papers trying to find Sir Oliver's will. He thinks he is Sir Oliver's son, but he remembers the night Sir Oliver left for Spain. Apparently Sir Oliver handed a newborn babe to his brother-in-law, Francis North, Gervase's father. The baby disappeared mysteriously.'

'And you think it was you?'

'I don't know, and that's the honest truth. This is what I'm trying to find out.'

'All I can tell you is that I delivered a healthy baby girl late on Saturday evening, the thirtieth of March. It was 1844 and I remember the date clearly because it was the next day that they found Lady Greystone's body floating in the lake. I was never so shocked. I think we all assumed that she had taken the baby with her, but its body was never found.'

Nancy dashed tears from her eyes. 'How tragic. Why would she do such a thing?'

'I'm breaking no confidences in telling you that the poor lady was very ill. She suffered from consumption and she knew she was dying. It seems like the curse of the Greystones, what with Miss Sylvia in a sanatorium in Switzerland.'

Tommy placed a protective arm around Nancy's shoulders. 'Thank you, Mrs Betts. I think perhaps we ought to leave you in peace now, but we're grateful for the information.'

'You won't tell anyone that I told you, will you?'

Nancy shook her head. 'No, of course not. Thank you, ma'am.' She allowed Tommy to lead her from the cottage. The cold air made her gasp and take a deep breath. 'What do you think, Tommy?'

'I think you now know who your parents were, although I don't see how it could be proved. All the people involved in the deception are dead and gone.'

'Except for Gervase. Although I don't know why he chose to tell me. If he hadn't mentioned the fact that Sir Oliver left a baby with Francis North, I would not have been any the wiser. Now I think I have more questions than answers.'

Tommy looked up as the first drops of rain fell from a pewter sky. 'Let's go home, Nancy. We can't do any more here.'

They walked, heads bent against the wind and rain, but were overtaken by a carriage and four.

'Nancy, wait.' Freddie called out to the coachman to stop and the carriage came to a halt. Freddie leaped to the ground and held the door open. 'I'll take you home. Get in, please.'

'Freddie. This is a surprise.' Nancy hesitated, eyeing him warily. His prolonged absence had made her suspect that his mother had exerted her considerable influence on him, and that he had proposed marriage to the heiress.

'When I came to Rockwood last time you had not returned from Barbados. I told Patricia that I would return, but I was unavoidably detained.'

'You don't have to explain, Freddie.'

'You can't imagine how much I wish I'd been able to go with you.'

For the first time since Nancy had known Freddie she was at a loss for an answer. She climbed into the carriage, followed by Tommy, who sat beside her, wiping the raindrops from his face. Freddie took a seat opposite, gazing anxiously at Nancy. 'You're very wet. I hope you don't catch cold.'

'You sound like Hester,' Nancy said, laughing. She glanced at Tommy, who was glowering at Freddie. 'It was lucky that Freddie was passing, wasn't it, Tommy?'

'No one just passes through Rockwood,' Tommy said drily. 'I suppose he was on his way to the castle. You seem to drop in as and when you please, Ashton.'

'Tommy!' Nancy frowned at him. 'I'm always delighted to see Freddie. We're still friends, and we decided it was better to keep it that way.'

'It wasn't my choice, Nancy. I've been battling with Mama, who is determined to see me married to Letitia Barclay.'

'Then why are you here?' Tommy demanded. 'Aren't you afraid of upsetting your mama?'

'That's not fair, Tommy.' Nancy gave Freddie an encouraging smile. Her own emotions were so raw that she needed to avoid any arguments. Tommy was only trying to protect her from more heartache, but this was something she needed to sort out for herself. She laid her hand on Tommy's arm. 'Give Freddie a chance to speak, please.'

Tommy sat back in his seat and turned his head away, staring out of the rain-spattered window. 'Just pretend I'm not here.'

'I wanted desperately to talk to you, Nancy,' Freddie said apologetically. 'I t-told your s-sister, P-Patricia.'

'I know, Freddie. But I don't know what there is to say. You and I were not meant for each other.'

'You sh-shouldn't take any notice of my mama. She is ambitious but I am not. I mean, I just want to live like a country squire. I don't care about society and g-gaining more l-land. You and I need to have a proper conversation, on our own.' Freddie sent a meaningful glance in Tommy's direction.

'Yes, I agree,' Nancy said softly.

'You are the one I need to convince, Nancy. You seem to think your history is a barrier between us. I can tell you it isn't.'

'Nancy is the best person I know,' Tommy said, scowling. 'She could do better than you, Ashton.'

'Tommy, that's not fair.' Nancy frowned at him. 'Really, Freddie, we've had this conversation before and, as it happens, I agree with your mama. You need to choose a bride who is worthy of you.'

Freddie shook his head. 'I don't know what I can do to convince you, but there is someone who might be able to help.'

'Who is that?'

'You'll find this very odd, but I'm staying at Grey-stone Park.'

'With Gervase?'

'Good Lord! Are you off your head?' Tommy demanded angrily. 'You know the fellow is a jackass.'

'I'm not so sure,' Freddie said slowly. 'From what he told me when we met accidentally in the Black Dog some time ago, he really believes that Nancy is related to the Greystone family. I called on him last evening on my way here and he showed me the piles of old documents he's sifting through to prove his own identity, and yours as well, Nancy.'

Nancy held up her hand to prevent Tommy from saying anything. 'We've been doing some investigating along those lines, Freddie.'

The carriage drew to a halt in the bailey and James emerged from the castle to open the carriage door.

Freddie laid his hand on Nancy's arm as she was about to alight from the vehicle. 'Give me a day or so to find out exactly what Gervase has discovered, Nancy.'

She sighed. 'To what end, Freddie? I need to know my roots for my own peace of mind, not as a means of claiming a fortune or taking away someone else's inheritance. I don't want to get involved with Gervase and his wild schemes.'

'I agree entirely, which is why I want to do this for you.'

'Freddie, no matter if I turn out to be related to the Greystone family, your mama is set against me and your papa follows her guidance. I cannot and will not do anything to cause a rift in your family.'

Freddie cast an anxious glance at Tommy, who had alighted and was waiting impatiently for Nancy to join him. 'You know that I love you, Nancy. It wouldn't matter to me if you were a washerwoman's daughter, but I know it means a lot to you to know who your parents were.'

Tommy leaned into the carriage. 'We've probably found that out for ourselves, Ashton. It seems that Nancy is Sir Oliver Greystone's daughter. Gervase told her as much himself.'

'Is this true, Nancy?'

She met Freddie's earnest gaze with a wry smile. 'It appears to be, but it's almost impossible to prove. In any case, if I were related to the infamous Sir Oliver, I dare say that would go against me just as much as if I were a washerwoman's daughter. You will never persuade your mama to think of me differently.'

'Give me a day or two. I am gaining Gervase's confidence. Let me see what I can find out from the Greystone papers and we'll talk more then. My mama doesn't rule my life and I'll prove it to you, no matter what it takes.'

22

'You don't believe him, do you, Nancy?' Tommy took off his hat and overcoat and handed them to James. 'The chap is terrified to do anything to offend his mother and father.'

Nancy shook raindrops from her bonnet and slipped off her cape, handing it to James. 'I think you're being unfair, Tommy. He hates to upset people, but that doesn't make him a bad person.'

'You need a better man than Freddie Ashton. If you marry him you will be bullied by his mama for the rest of her life.'

'He hasn't asked me to marry him, not in so many words, and I am not so feeble that I would allow her to make my life a misery.'

'They are one of the wealthiest families in England. You would be treated like an upstart pauper.'

Nancy laughed. 'Tommy, you have a wonderful imagination. Stop worrying about me. I can look after myself. Now I'm going to change out of my wet garments. I'll see you at dinner.'

'Yes, of course. Anyway, we need to find someone who can corroborate Mrs Betts' statement that Lady Greystone gave birth to a child before she drowned herself in the lake.'

'Do you know, Tommy, I think I would almost rather remain in ignorance. I'm not sure I want to believe that my real mother was so ill and distressed that she took her own life, and that my father was a libertine.'

'There's one place we haven't visited,' Tommy said thoughtfully.

'Where is that?'

'The orphanage where you were left on the steps. Maybe they could tell us something.'

'I don't even know which one it is. The vicar and his wife took me on from there.'

'Then Louise should know. Ask her when you see her tomorrow.'

'I will, but I doubt if anyone at the orphanage could tell me anything more than we know already.'

'But, Nancy, if it were true, you would be the one to inherit Greystone Park.'

'I'm a girl, remember, Tommy? It would go to the nearest male family member, which would have been Sir Michael.'

Tommy paused at the foot of the stairs. 'But he's passed away, so perhaps Gervase is the rightful heir?'

'All I know is that Patsy couldn't inherit the estate when her husband died because he had willed it to his daughters. I think Gervase would have a lengthy and expensive court case if he tried to overturn the will.'

Hester came bustling towards them. 'Where have you been? You are both soaking wet again. It's like looking after two children. Go and change immediately. I don't want to have you both sick with chills and fever.'

Nancy and Tommy exchanged amused glances but they did not argue, and they went their separate ways to their rooms to do as Hester commanded.

★ ★ ★

When questioned, Louise was only too pleased to help. She remembered the orphanage where her parents had found Nancy, and it was not too far away. Next morning Nancy and Tommy had their horses saddled and they left for the orphanage. They were riding past the Greystone Park gates when the gatekeeper opened them and Freddie rode out, greeting them with a cheery smile.

'I was coming to see you, Nancy.'

'We can't stop,' Tommy said impatiently. 'We're on an important mission.'

'We're going to make enquiries at the orphanage, Freddie. Tommy thinks they might remember something, but I have my doubts.'

'May I come with you? I fancy a ride after being cooped up with that madman.'

'Why stay there then?' Tommy demanded. 'You could get a room at the Black Dog.'

'As a matter of fact I've decided to stay on in Rockwood for a while. I've found myself a cottage and I'm going to earn my own living.'

Nancy turned her head to stare at him in surprise. 'You don't need to work, Freddie.'

'I know, but that's the whole point. I was fortunate enough to be born into a wealthy family, but had I been a farmer's son or a cobbler's child, I would have been trained to do something useful. I want to prove to you that I am just the same as other men.'

'That's easy to say when you've never had to go without,' Tommy said sarcastically. 'You won't impress Nancy by pretending to be independent of your family.'

'Maybe I want to impress myself.'

'I've never heard anything so ridiculous, Freddie.

344

You don't need to prove anything to anyone, least of all me. And you can stop baiting him, Tommy. It isn't funny.' Nancy urged her horse to a trot, leaving Tommy and Freddie little alternative but to encourage their mounts to follow her.

★ ★ ★

The orphanage was situated in its own grounds a couple of miles from Greystone Park. It had the forbidding exterior favoured by the architects who designed workhouses. They were not meant to be welcoming establishments. Nancy's heart sank as they rode up the carriage sweep to the front of the red-brick building. A small boy ran up to them, offering to hold their horses. Freddie tossed him a penny and the child beamed from ear to ear. However, the welcome from the woman who answered their knock on the door was not so friendly, and Nancy had to use all her powers of persuasion to gain admittance.

They were led down dark corridors to a small office where they waited for twenty minutes or more until the assistant matron came to speak to them. Nancy put her case briefly, but the woman shook her head.

'I am afraid all our records for that period of time were lost in a fire.'

'A fire?' Nancy raised her eyebrows. 'It doesn't seem to have done much damage.'

'It did at the time, but we have devoted supporters who carried out the repairs. However, I'm very sorry, Miss Sunday, I cannot help you.'

There was little they could do other than leave the premises, but Nancy was not satisfied. She waited until they were outside. Freddie tossed some coins to the child who had been taking care of their horses. The boy dived for them and ran off shouting excitedly for his mother.

'I think that woman was lying.' Nancy shuddered, remembering her early days in the institution. She had successfully blocked them from her mind until now, but they came flooding back.

'Surely she would tell the truth. Why would she lie?' Tommy looked from one to the other, but Freddie shook his head.

'I agree with Nancy. I think that woman knows more than she was prepared to admit. Tommy, hold my horse. I have an idea.' Freddie handed the reins to Tommy and strode off to knock on the orphanage door.

'What the devil is he doing?' Tommy demanded. 'That fellow thinks he's so important.'

'That's not fair, Tommy. I do wish you'd try to like Freddie. He's a thoroughly nice person.'

'Maybe, but he's not good enough for you, Nancy. He's convinced that money can buy him anything he wants.'

'I'm sure that's not true.' Nancy walked the horses as they became restive while they waited for Freddie.

Eventually, after about half an hour, when Tommy was beginning to lose patience, the metal-studded oak door opened and Freddie emerged from the building.

'Well?' Nancy said eagerly. 'Did you uncover any mysteries?'

'After a great deal of persuasion and a generous contribution to their funds, I was given this.' Freddie produced a small bundle of cloth from his coat pocket and unfurled it like a flag.

'What is that?' Tommy demanded.

'It looks like a swaddling cloth,' Nancy said slowly.

'The matron didn't want to admit anything at first, but greed won in the end. She had seen the crest and had hidden it away, keeping it to bargain with, should the occasion arise. Today was that day.' Freddie pointed to a monogram embroidered in the corner of the fine cloth. 'Do you recognise it, Nancy?'

She looked more closely. 'It's the Greystone family crest.'

'Exactly. This is the swaddling cloth wrapped around the baby girl who was abandoned on the steps. She remembers it was the thirty-first of March because it was her own birthday.'

'I don't know what to say.' Nancy dashed her hand across her eyes. 'It's such a tragic tale. I almost wish we hadn't come here today.'

'But we did, and this corroborates what Gervase told you. He repeated the story to me several times last evening, although he's convinced that Sir Oliver was his father, which would make you brother and sister, instead of cousins.'

'He's obviously mad.' Nancy turned away, over-come by a maelstrom of emotions. She could only think of her poor mother, sick and alone, who had lost all hope and walked into the dark waters of the cold lake.

'Let's leave it for now, Freddie,' Tommy said abruptly. 'Can't you see you're upsetting Nancy? I've had enough of this place. Let's go home.'

'You're right. We should go now.' Freddie lifted Nancy onto the saddle. 'I'm sorry, but at least you know who your parents are. It is a sad story, but they would be so proud if they could see you now.'

'It's one thing to suspect I was related to the Grey-stones, it's quite another to have proof. I'm truly overwhelmed.'

Tommy vaulted onto his horse. 'I can't wait to see Hester's face when we tell her. She had you down for a housekeeper or a farmer's wife. She'll have to eat her words when she finds out that you are Sir Oliver and Lady Greystone's only child. Let's go home and tell everyone.'

'No, Tommy.' Nancy shook her head. 'I want to get used to the idea before we put it to the family. Rosie and Alex should be coming home soon. I'd rather tell everyone together. It's such an extraordinary story.'

'You do realise that this would make you the heir to Greystone Park?' Tommy said triumphantly. 'Christina won't like that.'

'Gervase is convinced that he can prove he is the true heir.' Freddie mounted his horse. 'I suggest you keep this from him, Nancy. He acts like a fool, but he's not a man to cross.'

'I don't want to take Greystone Park from Christina and Sylvia,' Nancy said firmly. 'They grew up there and their papa left it to them in his will. I'm happy to go on as I am. In fact, I'm not sure whether I want everyone to know the truth. Perhaps the secret should not be shared after all.' Nancy flicked the reins and rode off.

Freddie caught her up on the outskirts of the village. 'Not so fast, Nancy. Don't you want to see my new home?'

She reined in, staring at him in disbelief. 'I didn't think you were serious.'

'Follow me and I'll show you.' Freddie led the way to the old keeper's cottage, where Abe Coaker had once lived. He dismounted and tethered his horse to the fence. 'Bertie has let it to me at a nominal sum in return for work on the estate.'

'What sort of work could you do, Freddie?' Nancy gazed at him in surprise. 'I mean, you aren't used to manual labour.'

'I can chop wood and scare off poachers. I am actually a very good shot.'

Nancy allowed him to help her from the saddle just as Tommy reined in his horse beside them.

'What's going on? Why have we come here, Freddie?' Tommy leaped to the ground and secured the reins around an overhanging branch.

'Freddie says he's going to live in the keeper's cottage,' Nancy said, laughing for the first time that day. 'It's a really silly idea, Freddie. You don't need to do this.'

'I think I do. Despite what you say, I believe you are all under the impression that I'm a rich man's son who is incapable of doing a day's work. I intend to disprove that and earn your respect.'

'What work are you proposing to do?' Tommy stared at him in amazement. 'I doubt if you've ever lifted anything heavier than a cup of coffee.'

'I know a surprising amount when it comes to managing the land. Bertie has offered me the position of gamekeeper and Abe Coaker is going to make sure that I do everything as it should be done.'

'For how long?' Nancy was suddenly serious. 'You surely don't intend to carry this out for very long?'

'I'm not needed at Dorrington Place. Papa has land agents and bailiffs to manage the estate. I will stay for as long as it takes to show you that I am sincere, Nancy. Everything I do is for you. I want you to believe that. I don't care if you are a pauper's child or a member of the aristocracy. I love you for what you are and what you mean to me.'

'I'll bet you ten guineas that you give up after a fortnight,' Tommy said, grinning.

'I'll accept the wager. You'll see.'

Nancy gazed at the tiny cottage on the edge of the wood. It looked dilapidated and in need of someone to bring it back to life. She made her way up the overgrown path and, finding the front door unlocked, she went inside. The ground floor was both kitchen and parlour with a black-leaded range and a clay sink. The well in the small back garden provided water, and at one time Abe had a productive vegetable garden, which was now lost beneath a cloak of nettles and brambles. Upstairs were two small bedrooms, both unfurnished. Nancy descended the narrow staircase to where Freddie and Tommy stood in the middle of the kitchen.

'There isn't even a bed, Freddie. How are you going to manage here? Have you ever lit a fire or cooked on a range?'

He shrugged. 'I can learn. As to furniture, Bertie has been very generous with items consigned to the cellars at the castle.'

Tommy climbed the stairs and his footsteps echoed as he explored the first floor.

Nancy turned to Freddie with a smile. 'You seem to have thought it all out, Freddie. I don't know what to say. Today has been quite extraordinary so far. I feel dazed by it all.'

Freddie nodded. 'I understand. You need time to think things through. I will be here if you need to talk to me.'

'Thank you, Freddie. I appreciate all you've done and I admire what you are trying to do, but I must insist on one thing.'

'Which is?'

'That you dine with us tonight and tomorrow night. In fact, I hope you'll come for dinner until you have mastered the range, otherwise you might starve to death and I don't want that on my conscience.'

'So you do care for me a little, Nancy?'

'You know I do. Just give me time to adjust to all the changes that have happened. I have to get used to being a different person, and I don't think it's going to be easy.'

Freddie took both her hands in his. 'You are still the same sweet, brave, caring Nancy I fell in love with. Don't change, just try to believe in me. I want to be worthy of you.'

Tommy came thundering down the stairs, leaping the last three steps. 'I wouldn't mind living here myself. If you want some help to rescue the garden I'll volunteer, Freddie. I used to help Abe Coaker in the grounds when I was a boy.'

'What about our bet?' Freddie said, laughing.

'That still stands, but I can move in when you leave in a week or so. I could invite some of my friends from university down to stay. We'd have wonderful parties here.'

Nancy grabbed him by the arm. 'Come on, Tommy. It's time we went home. They'll be wondering what happened to us.'

Freddie put his hand in his pocket. 'Do you want to take your swaddling cloth with you, Nancy?'

'No. Please keep it for me. I'll take it if and when I decide to tell the family.'

Nancy hurried from the cottage. She knew that Freddie was sincere and believed he was doing the right thing, but it seemed doomed to heroic failure. He had not spent a day doing manual work in his whole life, let alone fending for himself. At home he had servants to tend to his every whim and she doubted if he had the slightest idea how to make the simplest meal, or how to wash his clothes. His determination to prove his love for her by going to such extraordinary lengths was touching but idiotic. And now she had to deal with the fact that in all probability she was a member of the Greystone family. As she mounted her horse she had a vision of Christina's face when she found out they were cousins, and that brought a smile to her lips. It was an impossible situation. She needed to talk to Patricia, who might have been the wild one in the family, but she was the one person who might understand the turmoil in Nancy's soul.

'Are you going home, Nancy?' Tommy untethered his horse and mounted. 'I'll race you.'

'No, I think I'll call on Patsy first. You go on ahead and tell Hester I'll be back in time for luncheon. I don't want her prying into where we've been this morning.'

'Am I not to say anything?'

'Not yet, Tommy. Let me think it over first.'

'It's not something you can keep secret for long. I'll wager that Mrs Betts has been tittle-tattling about our conversation yesterday. I expect the whole village is talking about it by now.'

'Don't say that. It would just be gossip and, anyway, she swore she kept her patients' business to herself.' Tommy urged his horse to a walk and then a trot as he set off in the direction of Rockwood Castle.

Nancy had not very far to go to reach the house beside the sawmill. She dismounted and handed the reins to Robbins, who emerged from the mill at the sound of horse's hoofs.

'Good morning, Robbins. Is Mrs Wilder at home?'

'I think so, miss. She hasn't asked for the chaise and the boss says she's not to ride her horse for the time being.'

'Thank you.' Nancy walked up the path to the front door and rang the bell.

Fletcher opened it after a brief wait. 'Good morning, Miss Nancy.'

'Is Mrs Wilder at home, Fletcher?'

'I think she's always at home to you, miss.' Fletcher stood aside to let Nancy into the entrance hall. The house smelled of polish with only a faint hint of sawdust from the mill.

Patricia was seated on a chaise longue, stabbing a needle into a piece of embroidery stretched over a hoop. 'Nancy, you're a godsend. I am so thoroughly bored.'

'I had to come and see you, Patsy. I have something to tell you, but it must be kept secret for a while. Don't even tell Leo.'

Patsy dropped the embroidery hoop, her eyes alight with interest. 'Go on, do.'

Nancy took off her cape and gloves and laid them tidily on the sofa as she sat down. 'I've just come from the orphanage where I was raised until the vicar and his wife took me on as one of their servants.'

'Oh, Nancy. Do you think that was a good idea? They didn't know whose child you were then, so I doubt if things will have changed in the last nineteen years.'

'That's where you're wrong. I went with Tommy, but Freddie joined us. He seemed to sense that the matron wasn't telling us the truth and he went back inside to speak to her privately.'

'Don't tell me she knew all along?'

'She had kept the swaddling cloth that was wrapped around the baby. It had a crest embroidered in one corner and she thought it might be worth something to someone one day.'

'Let me guess. That someone was Freddie, who bribed her to give it to him.'

'Yes, that's exactly what happened.'

'Go on, don't keep me in suspense. Whose crest is it?'

'The Greystone family. It corroborates the story that we gathered from the midwife, Mrs Betts. She remembered delivering Lady Greystone of a baby girl shortly before the poor lady committed suicide.'

'How tragic — but that doesn't mean it was you, Nancy.'

'That's only half the story. Gervase said that he was a child of six or seven when Sir Oliver visited his home in the early hours of Sunday morning at the end of March. The sound of someone hammering on the door had awakened him, and he peeped over the banisters to see his father talking to Sir Oliver, who handed him a tiny squalling bundle. Next morning there was no sign of the baby and Gervase's mother cried all day. She was a devoted churchgoer but that Sunday she remained at home. It all sounds far-fetched, but I believe him, and his story confirms what Mrs Betts told me.'

Patricia stared at her open-mouthed. 'Goodness gracious, Nancy. I can hardly believe it. You are a Greystone! You were related to me by marriage when we were together in London.'

'So you believe the story?'

'Why would I not? You were always different, but in a good way, Nancy. I think Hester sensed it from the moment you came into our home, but she saw you as something of a threat, which I don't understand.'

'Neither do I,' Nancy said sadly. 'I'm in two minds whether to tell everyone. In fact, I've told Tommy and Freddie not to say a word until I've had time to think.'

'My dear, it's up to you. I'll do whatever you say. Although if Gervase knows or is suspicious it might be difficult to keep the truth from others.'

'Gervase thinks he is Sir Oliver's son. He's convinced that he's the true heir to Greystone.'

Patricia frowned. 'I know little about the laws of primogeniture, but I believe if the estate is entailed, Gervase would have prior claim as he is the only existing male heir. Even if you are Sir Oliver's daughter, you would not inherit the estate. It seems that Gervase does have a claim on Greystone.'

'You were married to Sir Michael. Didn't you discuss whether or not the estate was entailed?'

'It never occurred to me, Nancy. I had no intention of producing sons and daughters at that time.' Patricia smiled and patted her swollen belly. 'Today I would think differently. However, the only way to find out is for us to visit Sir Michael's solicitor, Gilbert Selly. He has chambers in Lincoln's Inn.'

Nancy sighed. 'But I can't go on my own, Patsy. He wouldn't be inclined to tell me anything and Leo won't allow you to travel to London.'

'Leo will do as I say.' Patricia rose to her feet. 'I've humoured him so far, but this is something that I need to do for you, as well as for Christina and Sylvia. I know they fell out with me when I married their papa, but we were good friends at one time. Besides which, this is your future we're talking about, and I detest Gervase North. To have him living as master of Greystone Park and our near neighbour would be truly awful.'

'But Leo will try to stop you from travelling, Patsy.'

'When I make up my mind to do something there is no one in this world who can prevent it. You of all people should know that, Nancy. Tomorrow, you and I will go to Exeter and catch the London-bound train.'

'If you are sure, Patsy.'

'I am absolutely certain. We will sort this problem out once and for all.'

23

It was noon next day when Nancy and Patricia finally arrived at Gilbert Selly's chambers in Lincoln's Inn. Nancy was still amazed that they had managed to get away so easily, but they had left very early that morning. Patricia had left a message with Fletcher, instructing her to keep her departure a secret for as long as possible, and Nancy had crept out of the castle without telling anyone where she was going. She had left a note for Tommy, placing it in Tilly's hand, explaining briefly why the trip to London was absolutely necessary. She felt like a naughty schoolgirl as they alighted from the hansom cab outside Selly's chambers, but Patricia was apparently in her element. The pallor had gone from her cheeks, leaving her flushed and her eyes sparkling with excitement.

'It's like the old days, when you and I first came to London so that I could follow a career in opera. Now look at me, a respectable matron, soon to be a mother. Who would have thought it?'

'Who would have imagined that I might be the heiress to the Greystone estate?' Nancy replied. 'I would have laughed in their face if anyone had suggested it to me.'

Patricia paid the cabby and picked up her skirts. 'Come along, we haven't any time to waste. I want to get home before Leo sends the police looking for us.'

They entered the tall red-brick building and Patricia demanded to see Mr Selly. The clerk tried to tell her that Mr Selly had appointments all morning and he was in court later that day, but after travelling all the way from Devonshire Patricia was not in a mood to be thwarted. When all her arguments failed, she sank down on a chair and fanned herself vigorously.

Nancy stepped forward. 'Please, sir, you can see that Mrs Wilder is quite distraught. A few minutes of Mr Selly's time is all we ask.'

The clerk eyed Patricia anxiously. 'All right, miss. I'll do my best. Just wait here, please.'

'It always works,' Patricia said, smiling triumphantly. 'Men hate to see a woman cry — that would have been my next weapon.'

'You are shameless.' Nancy looked up as the door to the corridor opened and the clerk beckoned to them.

'Mr Selly can spare you ten minutes before his next appointment is due. Please follow me.'

Patricia rose gracefully to her feet and walked briskly after him with Nancy following.

The clerk opened a door at the end of the wainscoted corridor and ushered them into the office.

Gilbert Selly rose from his seat behind a large mahogany desk. 'Good afternoon, Mrs Wilder. Although, if my memory serves me correctly, you were Lady Greystone when we last met.'

'You have an excellent memory, Mr Selly.' Patricia settled herself on a chair in front of the desk, but Nancy remained standing.

'What can I do for you, ladies?'

'It might be easiest if I were to tell you, sir.' Nancy glanced at Patricia, who nodded in agreement. 'I was a foundling, left on the steps of an orphanage near Rockwood village.'

'Not far from Greystone Park, my late husband's

estate,' Patricia added hastily.

'Yes, this concerns Greystone Park and the estate.' Nancy sank down on a chair next to Patricia. 'I have reasonable proof that my parents were Sir Oliver and Lady Greystone, both deceased.'

'I'm aware of the circumstances surrounding their deaths,' Selly said gently. 'But why do you think you were abandoned?'

'It's rather complicated. Gervase North has taken up residence in Greystone Park. His mother was Sir Oliver's younger sister, and Gervase said that as a child of seven he remembers his uncle Oliver arriving in the middle of the night. He left a tiny baby in the care of Francis North, Gervase's father, but next day there was no sign of the infant, and Gervase's mother was distraught. It would have been about the time that Sir Oliver fled to Spain and was involved in a fatal duel.'

'It was then that his younger brother, my late husband, inherited the Greystone estate,' Patricia said earnestly. 'As you know, Sir Michael willed everything to his daughters, leaving me with almost nothing.'

'I do remember your misfortune clearly, ma'am. It was quite shocking, in my opinion. But why has Mr North come to the fore at this juncture? Surely the time to claim the estate would have been when Sir Michael passed away.'

'I can't answer that,' Patricia said, frowning. 'However, Gervase has made himself and his intention to claim the property known to everyone who will listen. Do you know if the estate is entailed? If that was so then he might have a valid case.'

'The estate is not entailed, but I did think that Sir Michael's will was unusual. However, I carried out

359

his instructions to the best of my ability.'

'If the estate is not entailed, does that mean I could be the legal heir, even though I am female?' Nancy waited anxiously for his answer.

'You would need irrefutable proof of your birth, but as Sir Oliver's legitimate child you would certainly inherit the estate.'

'That's all we wanted to know.' Patricia rose to her feet. 'Thank you for fitting us in, Mr Selly. I'm very grateful for your help.' She extended her hand and he raised it to his lips.

'As am I,' Nancy said hurriedly. 'It's not that I want the estate, but I would like to have a family background, good or bad.'

'If I might suggest something, Miss Sunday. I suggest you try to get some stronger proof of your true identity. Maybe you were baptised at birth and the priest could be found to verify the story. But if Sir Oliver left a will naming you as his daughter that would be irrefutable.'

'Gervase has all the family papers,' Nancy said thoughtfully. 'He wanted me to help him look for Sir Oliver's will.'

'Then perhaps you had better visit Mr North and hope that he has not already discovered the one document that could establish your right to the inheritance.'

Patricia moved to the doorway. 'Thank you, Mr Selly. We won't take up any more of your time. Besides which, we have a train to catch. I think we're done in London for the moment.'

★ ★ ★

The journey home was uneventful but Nancy did not arrive back at the castle until late evening. Hester made no secret of the fact that she was furious and she stomped off without waiting for an explanation. Nancy made her way to the morning parlour, where she hoped to find a welcoming fire. She was cold and tired and very hungry.

Moments later, before she had even had time to take off her outdoor garments, Tommy burst into the room.

'Hester told me you had come home. You might have told me what you planned to do,' he said angrily.

'I left you a note because you would have insisted on coming with us if you had known.' Nancy sighed wearily. 'It was a brief visit to London, Tommy. Mr Selly, Sir Michael's solicitor, was very helpful.'

'Leo was furious with Patsy. I've no doubt he'll let her know exactly how he feels. If I hadn't shown him your note, he would have caught the next train to London.'

'Well, we're back now and no harm done. In fact, I have the information I need. The Greystone estate is not entailed.'

'I don't know what that means.' Tommy gave her a searching look. 'You're pale as a ghost. Have you eaten today?'

'Yes, I think so. At least, we had a cup of coffee from a stall at the station. There wasn't time to stop for a meal.'

Tommy's angry expression melted into a sympathetic smile. 'I'll go and talk nicely to Mrs Jackson. Maybe she can find you something left from dinner.' He left the room and Nancy shrugged off her cape and untied her bonnet strings. She was suddenly tired and she sank into the comfortable armchair by the fire. She had wanted to know her real identity for so long, and she could never have imagined that she was related to the Greystone family, but it still seemed doubtful.

Tommy returned bearing a tray laden with food and they sat round the fire while she ate. She answered his questions in between mouthfuls of warmed-up beef stew, followed by apple pie.

'So from what the solicitor told you, the estate is not entailed, which makes you the legal heir.' Tommy took a jam tart from the plate of cakes and bit into it.

'That's right. But I have to prove my identity before I can put myself forward. The only way to do that is to find some documentation or someone reliable who would corroborate Mrs Betts' account of the night I was born. Gervase was just a little boy when he saw his uncle hand over a tiny baby. He might have dreamed it or simply been mistaken.'

'He obviously hasn't found proof that he is the legal heir to the estate. I think he would have been crowing it from the rooftop of Greystone Park if he had.' Tommy licked jam off his fingers.

'Yes, I agree. I just don't know how I am ever going to find out whether I am Sir Oliver and Lady Greystone's daughter. I would like to be certain for my own peace of mind. I don't care about the estate.'

Tommy grinned and selected another jam tart. 'You could marry Freddie and be the richest woman in England. It wouldn't matter about Greystone Park then.'

'Freddie hasn't proposed and I don't think he ever will. His mother will see to that.'

'She might change her mind if you were to inherit

the estate. By the way, talking of Freddie, he came looking for you this morning. It was all I could do to stop him from following you to London.'

'I'll go to the cottage tomorrow and explain.'

★   ★   ★

Nancy rose early next morning. She ate a hurried breakfast before putting on her cape and bonnet and setting off for the gamekeeper's cottage. The sound of wood being split made her go round to the back garden, where she found Freddie wielding an axe to chop logs into firewood. His bare torso gleamed with sweat, despite the fact that it was a chilly March day. Nancy averted her eyes but she could not resist the temptation to take another look. Freddie was surprisingly muscular for someone who had never done a day's manual work in his life. His broad, well-muscled chest was as perfect as any of the paintings she had seen of Greek gods and she felt a shiver of excitement. However, it would not do to let him see that she was impressed and she looked away hastily.

'You are a constant source of surprise, Freddie. I never thought of you as a practical man.'

He reached for his shirt, which was hanging from the picket fence. He slipped it on and stood for a moment, doing up the buttons. 'I'm country born and bred, Nancy. I used to spend more time out of doors as a child than I did at my books. My tutor used to get very angry.'

Nancy hesitated. 'Tommy told you why I went to London yesterday.'

'He did, but I wish you had come to me first. I would have accompanied you.'

'Patsy and I decided to do it on the spur of the moment. Leo would certainly have prevented her from travelling had she told him. I dare say he was angry with her but she had to see Sir Michael Greystone's solicitor in person.'

Freddie swung the axe so that it lodged safely in the tree trunk. 'Come inside, it's too chilly to stand out here.'

Nancy followed him into the cottage. 'My goodness! What a difference.'

'I am not the useless person you thought I was, Nancy. Take a seat and I'll make a pot of tea. I know how to do that, and I can make toast. I won't pretend that I can cook.'

Nancy gazed round at the spotless kitchen. The range had been cleaned and a fire burned merrily in the grate. A big black kettle bubbled on the hob and there were a few ill-matched pieces of crockery, including a teapot, neatly arranged on a shelf by the door.

'Where did you get all this stuff, Freddie?' Nancy pulled up a chair and sat down at the freshly scrubbed pine table.

'Mrs Jackson was most helpful. I think she took pity on me. And when the old furniture that Sir Bertram threw out arrived, I found among it a box containing everything I needed to make myself comfortable, including tea, sugar and a large seed cake. Mrs Greep at the farm supplied me with milk, eggs and butter. Although she wanted to know everything about me.'

'I hope you didn't tell her too much,' Nancy said, laughing. 'Mrs Greep is a notorious gossip.'

'I revealed enough to keep her happy.' Freddie made the tea and brought it to the table. 'I was angry yesterday, Nancy — I expect Tommy told you — but I was also hurt that you didn't feel you could confide in me.'

'It wasn't that at all, Freddie. We had to go to London to see Sir Michael's solicitor. Gervase would have a valid claim to the property and the title if the estate was entailed, but according to Mr Selly that isn't the case.'

Freddie poured the tea into two slightly chipped cups. 'So you are the legal heir, if you can prove you are Sir Oliver's daughter.'

'Yes, that's it, exactly. But it needs to be something more than Gervase's vague childhood memory of Sir Oliver handing a baby to his father, and the swaddling cloth.'

'Do you know if there are other Greystone relations who might know something?'

Nancy stared at him in wonder. 'Why didn't I think of that? The dreadful Miss Collins is Sylvia and Christina's second cousin, although she is a lot older than they are.'

'Do you know where she lives?'

'I can find out easily enough.'

'Then I suggest we pay her a visit. I've finished my chores for today, and Bertie hasn't given me any work to do as yet, so I'm free. I have my horse and chaise in one of the Greeps' barns. They were very kind and agreed that I might keep them there.'

'Dora Greep will do anything to be first with the news.'

'Drink your tea and I'll walk over to the farm and collect the chaise. Do you suppose that Mrs Greep would have the information we need to find Miss Collins?'

'I'd be very surprised if she didn't, but don't mention my name or it will be round the village that we are engaged to be married before you can get your horse harnessed.'

★ ★ ★

Martha Collins and her companion, Miss Moon, lived in a tiny cottage on the edge of the Greystone estate. When she saw how Lady Greystone's relation lived in such reduced circumstances, Nancy was not surprised that Miss Collins bore a grudge against anyone connected to the family in any way.

Miss Moon opened the front door and she gave Freddie a blank stare but her expression changed subtly when her gaze travelled to Nancy.

'If he's sent you from the big house to ask more questions, Miss Collins isn't at home.'

'Are you referring to Mr North?'

'He was calling himself Greystone when he came knocking on the door several days ago.'

'We are not here on his behalf,' Nancy said hurriedly. 'May we come in?'

'I don't think she'll want to see you.'

'We need Miss Collins' help, Miss Moon,' Freddie said with a persuasive smile. 'It's most important or we wouldn't bother you.'

Nancy slipped past her. 'This is ridiculous. I just want to ask her a couple of questions.'

'You can't do this,' Miss Moon protested, but she was too late. Nancy had opened the door to the front parlour and she stepped inside.

'I'm sorry to inconvenience you, Miss Collins. But I really need your help.'

'If you're here on behalf of that upstart you can leave immediately.' Miss Collins turned her back on Nancy.

'I am not here for Gervase North. The very opposite.'

Miss Collins glanced warily over her shoulder. 'What then?'

'Did you know that your cousin Helena gave birth to a baby shortly before she died?'

'It was a terrible tragedy. She took the baby to a watery grave. We don't talk about it.'

'I think she drowned herself because her husband took the infant from her. He knew she was dying and there was a good chance that he might not return from Spain. He gave the baby to his brother-in-law.'

Miss Collins faced her with a belligerent stare. 'If that's true, where is that child today?'

'She is standing before you, ma'am,' Freddie said firmly.

'You!'

'I know, I find it difficult to believe.' Nancy took the swaddling cloth from her reticule. 'I was wrapped in this when they found me on the steps of the orphanage.'

Miss Collins took it gingerly between finger and thumb. 'It is the Greystone crest, but this could have been stolen from the nursery. Anyone could have taken it.'

'But you admit that Lady Greystone had a child.'

'Yes, it's no secret. We do not speak of it because of the disgrace. My cousin chose to take her own life and we thought the life of her baby, too.'

Freddie walked over to a rosewood bureau in the corner of the room. He studied a watercolour portrait hanging above it. 'Is this your cousin, Miss Collins?'

Martha gave it a cursory glance. 'Yes, that is my dear Helena. A nicer, kinder person never walked the earth.'

Freddie lifted it off the hook and examined it carefully. 'Who does this remind you of, Miss Collins?'

'It's Helena, of course. A perfect likeness. Put it back at once.'

Freddie crossed the floor to stand beside Nancy, holding up the portrait. 'This could be you, Nancy. Isn't that so, Miss Collins?'

Miss Moon had been standing quietly in the doorway, but she stepped forward, gazing at the painting. 'It is a striking resemblance, Martha.'

'I think you know more than you are telling us, Miss Collins.' Freddie hung the portrait back on the wall. 'You were obviously close to Lady Greystone.'

'We were like sisters.' Martha's voice broke on a sob. 'She was an angel.'

'I think you should tell them about the document, Martha.' Miss Moon moved to the bureau and opened it.

'No, leave it where it is. I was entrusted to keep it until such time as it was needed.'

'Isn't this the time, Martha? I believe this young lady is Helena's daughter. Think what she would want.'

Martha stood up and went to stand by the window. She was silent for a moment and then she turned slowly to look directly at Nancy. 'You do resemble Helena when she was a girl. How old are you?'

'I'm nearly nineteen.'

'All right, Moon. Find the document and give it to her. I don't want it to fall into the wrong hands. Gervase North was here looking for it, having been through all the family papers, but I had no intention of allowing it to fall into his hands.'

Miss Moon handed the sealed document to Nancy. 'This has been waiting to be read for nineteen years.'

Nancy's hand shook as she took it from Miss Moon. She broke the seal and unfolded a yellowed piece of parchment.

'I think I know what it says.' Martha resumed her seat by the fire. 'Tell me anyway.'

'It seems to be Sir Oliver's will,' Nancy said slowly. She passed the document to Freddie.

'Well, what does it say?' Martha demanded imperiously. 'I've kept it all these years so I feel I have a right to know its contents.'

Freddie cleared his throat and began to read.

This is the last will and testament of Sir Oliver Greystone, revoking all other wills. I leave all my possessions, including Greystone Park and the entire estate, to my wife, Helena Greystone, but knowing her delicate constitution I fear her life will be tragically short. In the event of her death I leave everything to my only child, my daughter, who has yet to be named. Due to unforeseen circumstances I am forced to flee the country, but I leave my daughter in the safe hands of my sister, Elizabeth North. Witnessed this day the thirtieth of March in the year of our Lord 1844 by Dr Horace Bulmer and Midwife Violet Betts.

'Is it a legal document?' Nancy asked slowly. 'I was left at the orphanage on the thirty-first of March 1844. They chose that as my birthday so I'll be nineteen in just over a week.'

Freddie folded the will carefully. 'It's obvious that

Dr Bulmer and Mrs Betts can testify that this is genuine. You need to take this to the family solicitor, Nancy. Your claim has to be conducted correctly.'

Martha nodded. 'I agree. Take it now before Gervase North finds a previous will. Otherwise you will end up in the Court of Chancery, and that could take years to come to a satisfactory conclusion.'

Freddie took Nancy by the hand. 'If your family solicitor cannot handle the case, I will put it in the hands of our lawyers in London. We'll get this sorted out one way or another, Nancy. I want you to have what's rightfully yours and, more importantly, a family of your own.'

A glimmer of humour lit Martha's eyes momentarily. 'I suppose that means we might be related, Nancy. I suppose that wouldn't be too bad. You have courage, I'll give you that.'

'Thank you, Miss Collins.' Nancy held her hand out to Miss Moon. 'And thank you, Miss Moon. We might never have seen this if it hadn't been for you.'

Miss Moon blushed scarlet, eyeing Martha as if she expected her to erupt in anger, but Martha merely smiled.

'Credit where it's due, Moon. I should have thought of it myself.'

'We should leave now, but thank you both so much,' Nancy said, smiling.

Freddie held the door open. 'Good day, ladies. My thanks also.'

★   ★   ★

Nancy could hardly contain her excitement when they reached home. She could not find Bertie and Wolfe, but Walter was at home in the wing of the castle where he and Louise now had an apartment. He cast his eye over the scrawled writing on the parchment.

'It looks genuine. I haven't seen Sir Oliver's writing so I can't judge it on that, but I'd say this would stand up in a court of law, especially if the two witnesses were persuaded to come forward. Why don't you take it to Herbert Mounce in Exeter? He's getting on a bit in years but he has vast experience in dealing with family matters.'

Nancy nodded in agreement. She shot an apologetic look in Freddie's direction. 'I know you offered to put it to your London lawyers, but perhaps local knowledge is more important here. I'm going to ride to Exeter this afternoon.'

'I'll take you in my chaise,' Freddie said firmly. 'I promise I won't interfere, Nancy. You can talk to your solicitor and give him instructions. I'll just see you safely there and back again.'

'Good man.' Walter slapped him on the back. 'Now, if you don't mind, I have a whole chapter to write by the end of the week. My publisher is getting restive. Anyway, isn't it time for luncheon? I'm feeling peckish.'

'Heavens, yes. I don't want to upset Hester by being late for a meal.' Nancy tucked the document into her reticule. 'I don't think I'll say anything about this as yet. I want to be sure myself before I tell the family.'

'Quite right,' Walter said, smiling. 'I've already forgotten what you just showed me. Are you staying for luncheon, Freddie?'

24

Mr Mounce had been suitably impressed by the evidence that Nancy presented and he agreed to send off the will, advising her to say nothing until probate was granted. However, on her nineteenth birthday, when the family were gathered in the castle dining room for a special luncheon in her honour, Nancy could resist the temptation no longer. She stood up to thank everyone for their gifts and good wishes.

'It's a shame that Freddie can't be here because he had an urgent summons to return to Dorrington Place, but it was he who helped me to find Sir Oliver's last will.'

'What are you talking about, Nancy?' Hester demanded irritably. 'This is supposed to be a cheerful occasion.'

'Yes, I know that and I wasn't going to say anything until after probate was granted, but it seems that I have an identity after all. Moreover, I am an heiress.'

Tommy jumped to his feet. 'You have final proof? How did you get it Nancy? Why didn't you tell me?'

'I shouldn't be saying anything now,' Nancy said, laughing. 'But Miss Collins, Lady Greystone's cousin, had Sir Oliver's will all the time.'

Bertie frowned. 'Are you telling us that you are Sir Oliver's daughter?'

'I always knew you were someone special, Nancy,' Walter said, smiling. 'It doesn't need a piece of paper to prove.'

'Great heavens!' Bertie stared at her in astonishment. 'I mean, if it's true I'm more than happy for you, but I don't remember hearing that Sir Oliver had a child.'

Hester pursed her lips. 'How could you be his daughter, Nancy Sunday? You were abandoned on the steps of the orphanage.'

'I know. I've heard that so many times, Hester, and I've said it myself. But I am Sir Oliver and Lady Greystone's daughter. We visited the orphanage and they had kept the swaddling cloth wrapped around me. It was embroidered with the Greystone crest.'

'Which could have been stolen by a maidservant who had been wronged by some man,' Hester said grimly.

'I seem to have heard that story before.' Nancy met Hester's angry look with a challenge. 'It happens in domestic situations, as you well know, but in this case it was not true. There are two very reliable witnesses to the will, both of whom were present at the birth.'

'But Lady Greystone took her own life,' Louise said gently. 'Why would a new mother do that?'

'She was dying of consumption, and she knew her husband was about to flee to Spain in an attempt to avert a terrible scandal.' Nancy sighed. 'It's a tragic story.'

'It seems you have conclusive proof,' Leo said, smiling. 'Congratulations, Nancy. You deserve to have some luck.'

'I agree.' Patricia reached for her husband's hand and held it to her cheek. 'When I think what I went through before I met Leo, it makes me thank the stars for allowing our paths to cross.'

'I just wish that Rosie and Alex were here,' Nancy

said, sighing. 'I don't suppose you've heard from them, Patsy?'

Patricia shook her head. 'Not for a week or so. They must be finding it more difficult to secure Trevenor and the business than they thought it would be. I wonder if Rupert Charnley has been able to give them any advice.'

The words had barely left her lips when the door burst open and Tilly entered, clearly agitated.

'I'm sorry, my lady. They wouldn't wait.' She stood aside as two men strode into the dining room.

'Piers!' Patricia half rose to her feet, but sank back on her chair.

'I gather I am to offer you congratulations,' Piers said smoothly. 'Tobias has been kind enough to tell me something about what has been happening in my absence.'

'Tobias. This is a surprise.' Hester stood up, staring at her son in disbelief. 'It's all right, Tilly. Bring two more place settings and tell Cook we have two more for luncheon.'

'Yes, my lady.' Tilly backed out of the room, eyeing Piers warily.

'So you've returned from your exploits abroad, Piers,' Bertie said, drily. 'I suppose you intend to play the part of the prodigal son?'

'You know me, Bertie. We landed at Exmouth and intend to travel on to Cornwall later today.'

Patricia gazed at him, shaking her head. 'This is so like you, Piers Blanchard. You are absent for years and years and then you turn up unannounced and act as if nothing has happened.'

'Well, you're here now.' Walter pushed back his chair and stood up, holding out his hand. 'You must have some tales to tell after all your experiences in the penal colony, let alone the blockade running.'

Piers shook his hand. 'Thank you, Walter. Not everyone is so magnanimous.' He glanced round the astonished faces at the table. 'You all look so shocked. I am a free man now, not an escaped criminal.'

'Take a seat everyone,' Hester said testily. 'This is supposed to be a civilised family luncheon to celebrate Nancy's nineteenth birthday.'

'I'm sorry, Ma. I'll go to the servants' quarters if that makes it easier.' Tobias backed towards the doorway.

'You'll do no such thing, Toby,' Bertie said firmly. 'You are part of this family whether you like it or not.'

Louise patted an empty chair beside her. 'Come and sit by me, Tobias.'

'Thank you, ma'am.' Tobias glanced anxiously at his mother but she nodded her approval.

Piers pulled up a chair and lowered himself into it. 'I won't be stopping long. I gather I'm needed at Trevenor.'

'You could have returned weeks ago,' Nancy said crossly. 'We travelled a long way to beg you to go home where you were desperately needed.'

'That's right,' Leo added. 'You ignored us when Alex and I tried to persuade you to abandon your gun-running and blockading. What changed you mind?'

Piers shrugged. 'Maybe I had an attack of conscience.'

'You were making a fortune out of other people's misery.' Patricia gave him a withering look. 'Shame on you, Piers.'

'Yes, I'll admit all my wrongs. You are quite correct, Patsy, as always. However, I plan to atone, if I can.

375

I'm determined to save Trevenor and the clay mine.'

'How heroic,' Patricia said sarcastically. 'You always manage to make yourself look better than you really are, Piers. I've no doubt Lady Pentelow will greet you like a returning hero.'

Hester turned to her son. 'Well, Tobias, this is a lovely surprise. Will you be staying?'

'I'm sorry, Ma. I have to get back to my ship before dark. I just wanted to see you before we sail.'

'I suppose I'll have to get used to this,' Hester said, smiling. 'I'm proud of you, son.'

'You'll stay for tonight, won't you, Piers?' Bertie asked. 'Another day won't make much difference after so many years abroad.'

'Well, I'm not afraid to ask.' Patricia leaned across the table, fixing her gaze on Piers. 'What changed your mind about returning home, Piers? I don't believe you have a conscience.'

Piers leaned back in his seat. 'You are right, of course, Patsy. I used to take what I wanted without any thought to others. But after Alex and Leo left for home I started thinking, and I realised that if I didn't return to Trevenor soon I might be too late. Grandmama isn't the easiest person to love, but she did her duty by me and Aurelia, as well as Alex. I always pay my debts, that's my one saving grace.'

Bertie eyed him thoughtfully. 'You might find you have competition, Piers.'

'What do you mean by that?'

'Rupert Charnley accompanied Alex and Rosie when they went to Trevenor. Do you know him?'

Piers frowned. 'I know him by sight. His family own one of the biggest sugar plantations on the island.'

'You'd better make haste to return then, Piers, or

you might find you have a rival for Trevenor,' Patricia said mischievously.

'The estate belongs to me.'

'It does,' Patricia said, seriously. 'But Aurelia's late husband was a partner in the mine with Alex. Aurelia will own that share now. She would be a good catch for anyone and Rupert is very handsome as well as being wealthy. The Blanchards might lose their share in the mine and the income from it if she should remarry.'

Nancy could see that Piers was put out by this remark, but Tilly hurried in to lay two extra place settings, followed by Flossie carrying a large tureen of savoury-smelling soup.

Conversation ceased while everyone ate, and at the end of the meal Hester took Tobias to her private parlour, while Piers produced a box of cigars, which he shared with Bertie and Walter. They even allowed Tommy to sample one, although Nancy could hear him coughing and spluttering as she left the dining room. She smiled as she made her way to the drawing room with Patricia and Louise. Tommy was still very young in his ways and she loved him dearly, but perhaps not in the way he wished.

They settled themselves comfortably by the fire and Tilly brought a tray of coffee and some of the little fancies that Mrs Jackson had made especially for Nancy's birthday.

They drank coffee and discussed Nancy's news. There was one thing upon which they were all agreed. Gervase must not be told of the will that had been sent for probate. Even if he had discovered previous testaments, it was obvious from the date that this would have been the last one Sir Oliver had written.

'I'm in two minds whether or not to tell Christina.'

Nancy looked from one to the other but both Patricia and Louise shook their heads.

'Certainly not,' Patricia said firmly. 'She is as bad as Gervase. She'd do anything to keep Greystone Park for herself and Sylvia.'

'Christina is lady of the house at Cottingham Manor now, but I wouldn't want to turn Sylvia out.'

'Of course you'll do the right thing, Nancy.' Louise patted her on the shoulder. 'No one doubts that. They are your cousins, after all.'

Nancy laughed. 'So they are.' She raised her coffee cup. 'I'll drink a toast to that. I just hope Christina sees it in a generous spirit.'

Patricia and Louise exchanged meaningful glances.

'It's Gervase I worry about most,' Nancy said dismissively. 'I don't think it's going to be easy getting him out of Greystone Park when the will is read. The most important thing is to keep him imagining that he is going to inherit until probate is granted.'

Patricia shook her head. 'I don't trust him. Remember Ewart Blaise, Nancy? I think Gervase is very similar in character and best avoided.'

'Yes, don't be tempted to go near him, Nancy,' Louise added earnestly. 'From the little I've seen of him, I agree with Patsy.'

'I wanted to visit Mrs Betts again,' Nancy said with a heavy sigh. 'But Mr Mounce advised against it, and the same for Dr Bulmer. He said it would be better if he obtained an affidavit from them confirming that they attended the birth and that it was their signatures on the will.'

'Best leave it to the experts.' Patricia replaced her cup and saucer on the tray. 'All this excitement has made me weary. I think I'll go home and rest, that's if

I can tear Leo away from listening to Piers's stories of derring-do. No doubt they've started on the brandy.'

'I'll see you home,' Nancy volunteered.

'I would go with you,' Louise said apologetically, 'but I have to rescue Jennet. She's looking after the children and they'll be getting restive. She'll be glad when Rosie returns home. Dolly, Rory and Phoebe really miss their mama and papa.'

Nancy stood up to ring the bell for a servant. 'I'll have the chaise brought to the front entrance, Patsy. I can drive you home. I'd like a breath of air, anyway.'

Patsy smiled. 'Thank you, Nancy. You always did look after me, even when you were just a girl. If I should be lucky enough to have a daughter I will call her after you, although Nancy will have to be her second name. Leo wants a girl to be called after his mother, Rebecca.'

'Rebecca Nancy,' Louise said thoughtfully. 'That's very pretty, but shouldn't you call her after your mama, Patsy? She is a famous opera singer.'

'I haven't seen Mama or Claude for so long that I've almost forgotten their existence. One day Mama will turn up again and expect us to be thrilled to see her, but she's never really been part of our lives.'

'I think that's sad,' Louise said, sighing. 'I would like Charlotte to know her grandmama.'

'Who knows?' Patricia shrugged. 'She could arrive today. That's what she does, and then she'll disappear again when an offer is tempting enough.'

Nancy tugged at the bell pull. 'And if it's a boy? Will he be called Leo after his pa?'

'Of course, but I will choose his second name. However, before you tease me further, it won't be Gervase. That is certain.'

'You rang, miss?' Tilly appeared in the doorway.

'Yes, Tilly. Will you send word to the stables to have the chaise brought to the front entrance? I'm going to take Mrs Wilder home.'

★ ★ ★

The luncheon party had gone on much longer than Nancy had realised and daylight was fading when they left the castle.

'Isn't that the Greystone carriage?' Patricia said as they stopped to allow the vehicle to pass.

'Yes, that's strange. I didn't think Gervase left the estate very often these days. I think he's afraid that Christina will move in at the first opportunity.'

'I expect she would, knowing Christina. She must be fuming to know that he's taken up residence. But she'll be even more furious when she discovers that Greystone actually belongs to you. Gervase will be beside himself, too.'

Nancy encouraged the pony to a brisk walk. 'We'll have to make sure that neither of them finds out until everything is settled legally. Anyway, they don't matter. We have to look after you and little Nancy. I rather like the idea of a baby being named after me.'

'It might be little Leo.'

'Of course. I'll love him, too. We'll be home soon and not before time. Those clouds look ominous to me. I think it's going to rain.'

Patricia wrapped her cape around her swelling belly. 'It feels like thunder. You mustn't stay long when we reach the mill house. I don't want you to get wet and catch a chill.'

'Don't worry. I'll be home before the storm breaks.'

Nancy flicked the reins and the pony obliged by breaking into a trot.

Fletcher let them into the house and she echoed Patricia's concern about the ominous clouds. Nancy shrugged it off but she did not stay long and she left the mill house after a few minutes, having made certain that Patricia was comfortably settled to wait for Leo's return. There was no need to worry when Fletcher was in charge. It would take a brave woman to flout Fletcher's orders. Even Patricia, who had been known as the family rebel, bowed down to commands from the indomitable Fletcher. Nancy set off for the castle feeling satisfied that she had left Patricia in good hands.

However, the weather began to deteriorate before she had gone more than a couple of hundred yards and the sky darkened dramatically as huge drops of rain began to fall. A boisterous wind rushed in from the sea and flashes of lightning preceded loud claps of thunder. The pony shied and bucked in the shafts and Nancy almost lost control, but somehow she managed to calm the animal and keep the chaise upright. They reached the fork where the roads diverged, one way leading to the castle and the other road leading to the Greystone estate. But to Nancy's dismay she found the way home blocked by another vehicle.

A flash of lightning illuminated the carriage door emblazoned with the Greystone crest. Nancy reined in and leaned forward.

'Hey there. Are you able to move?'

Before she had a chance to catch her breath, a clap of thunder made her pony rear in the shafts and the chaise overturned. Stunned and barely conscious, Nancy found herself being lifted from the ground and thrown unceremoniously into the offending vehicle, which started forward at such an alarming rate that she was unable to move.

They were travelling at a spanking pace but eventually she managed to heave herself up onto the seat. She had to hold on for dear life as the carriage slowed down, swerved and then straightened up regaining speed. She peered out of the window and her worst fears were realised as Greystone Park itself came into view.

The carriage came to a halt outside the main entrance, but even as she attempted to escape the door was wrenched open. She was lifted bodily and flung over a man's shoulder so that she hung like a puppet, unable to control her own movements.

'You might as well give up,' a familiar voice said triumphantly. 'You are my honoured guest, Miss Nancy Greystone, if that really is your name.'

'Make him put me down, Gervase.' Nancy could hardly speak as her head was bumped against the man's back. All she could see was a pair of legs and the top of his riding boots.

'Take her to the east wing, Wills.'

Nancy gave up the struggle, concentrating on keeping her head from being pounded as Wills took the stairs two at a time. She was half-winded when he finally set her down roughly on the floor. She scrambled to her feet, glaring at him as he backed towards the doorway.

'Are you one of the Wills brothers who went to prison for smuggling?'

He brushed a stray lock of hair from his lined forehead, glaring at her beneath heavy black brows. 'Mind your own business, miss. Do as the boss says and you won't be harmed.'

'I should think not. Send Mr North to me now, Wills. I want to speak to him.'

'I'm Seth Wills and you will treat me with some respect, miss. I will pass your message on to Mr North but the rest is up to him.' Seth went to the table and took a box of matches from his coat pocket. 'I'll leave you a light. But you'd best be quiet. If you scream and make a fuss, I won't answer for my temper.'

'You have to let me go. My family will notify the police if I don't return home.'

'That ain't my concern, miss.' Seth backed out of the room, slammed the door and Nancy heard the key grind in the lock.

She was sore all over from being thrown from the chaise, although no bones seemed to have been broken. Her head ached and she realised that she was trembling from head to foot. She managed to reach a chair and she slumped down on the seat. The room she had been left in was not one she recognised, but she could tell they were on the second floor, and she had heard Gervase give orders to take her to the east wing. She knew from her time spent with Sylvia this was a little-used part of the mansion and in need of some redecoration. There was a bed in one corner and the furniture looked as though oddments had been thrown together rather than discarded. The Persian carpet was faded and threadbare in parts and a patchwork coverlet on the bed looked as though it had seen better days.

When her head cleared a little, she stood up and went to the window, hoping perhaps she could signal to one of the gardeners or a servant who was loyal to the family and not to Gervase North. The storm was still raging, and flashes of lightning illuminated the grounds. She realised that her room had been chosen well and there was little chance of anyone seeing her. Tall trees behind a high stone wall were an effective barrier, and there was no chance of escaping through the narrow window.

The candle sputtered in the draught and almost went out. The thought of being left alone in the dark was frightening enough without being kept a prisoner by a madman. She was now convinced that Gervase must be a lunatic to think he could kidnap her and get away with it. She searched the room for more candles and found several stubs in candlesticks on the mantelshelf and an oil lamp that seemed to have a little oil left in the font. She had no intention of remaining locked up, but it would be a long night in almost complete darkness should the first candle be extinguished. She rattled the door knob even though she had heard the key turn in the lock, and she knew it was pointless. However, it gave her a sense of at least attempting to escape. She hammered on the wooden panels with her fist and called for help, but again she knew it was useless. The servants' hall was too far away for anyone to hear her cries, and she doubted if anyone would come. Whether it was fear or loyalty to their new master she had no idea, but Gervase seemed determined to keep her prisoner. She sat on a chair at the small tea table, which, she could tell by the ingrained sticky finger marks and scratches, must once have been part of the nursery furniture. Perhaps Gervase would send someone with food or even something to drink. The candle burned down to a stub and she was glad she had lit another to take its place. She was cold, tired and angry, but eventually she was too tired to wait any longer. She took off her boots and climbed into bed, pulling the quilt up to her chin.

Nancy awakened to daylight streaming through the window and a hint of pale spring sunlight filtered through the small panes. She sat up and stretched, wondering what Gervase had planned. She was not afraid but she was furious with him for placing her in such an invidious position, and she really did think that he was quite insane, as Patsy had suggested. The sound of approaching footsteps made her pull on her boots and she rose to her feet, ready to make a dash for freedom should the opportunity arise.

To her surprise it was the parlour maid, Ivy Lugg, who stepped into the room, but any chance of pushing past her was foiled by the presence of Seth Wills, who stood outside in the corridor. Ivy laid a tray of tea and toast on the table and backed away.

'I'm sorry, miss,' she said in a low voice. 'The master's orders.'

Nancy caught her by the apron as she was about to leave the room. 'I thought you had left when the house was closed down.'

'The master needed servants and I had to have work, miss. My ma and pa are poorly and I'm the only breadwinner in the family.'

'I'm so sorry, Ivy.' Nancy moved closer. 'I need to get away from here. Can you help me?'

Ivy's brown eyes opened wide with fear and she glanced over her shoulder. 'I can't. I'm sorry.'

'What's going on there?' Seth demanded. 'Come out, girl. Leave Miss Sunday alone.'

Ivy backed out of the room. 'Sorry, miss.'

'I want to see Mr North,' Nancy said loudly. 'Tell him, please.'

But the door had closed and she was alone again. She was tempted to toss the tray out of the window, but hunger and thirst overcame her principles and she filled a cup with strong tea, adding a dash of milk. She drank thirstily and ate the buttered toast, even though it was cold and not particularly tasty. However, the food and drink made her feel stronger but she could do nothing other than wait.

Eventually, after about half an hour — although Nancy had no way of telling the time — the door opened and Gervase strolled into the room, smiling broadly.

'Good morning, Nancy. I hope you slept well.'

She glanced over his shoulder bracing herself to push past him, but once again his bodyguard was standing outside the door.

'Are you completely mad, Gervase?'

'Not at all, my dear. I am quite sane, as you will discover when we are married.'

Nancy's legs gave way beneath her and she sank down on the nearest chair. 'What are you talking about? You are the last man on earth I would marry.'

'Think it over, Nancy. You have spent the night in my home without a chaperone. Your reputation will be ruined, and the only way to redeem yourself is to marry me.'

'You really are crazy. Why would I do that? I would rather be thought of as a scarlet woman than be tied to you for life.'

'Then you will have to stay here, in this room, until you change your mind.' Gervase turned away and walked to the door.

'Wait a minute.' Nancy took a deep breath. 'Why, Gervase? Why would you want to marry a woman who detests the sight of you?'

He turned slowly to face her. 'You must think I'm a fool, Nancy Sunday. Or should I say Nancy Greystone?'

'What do you mean by that?'

'I've had you followed. I know about the swaddling cloth and the fact that you and Ashton paid a call on Martha Collins. You see, I had already been to visit that lady, to no avail. I didn't believe her when she said she knew nothing about your birth, but on a second visit she was delighted to tell me to my face that you are the heir to Greystone.'

'It's true and there's nothing you can do about it, Gervase. The will has gone to probate and there are witnesses who will testify to the fact that I am Sir Oliver and Lady Helena's child, while you are the son of Mr North and Elizabeth Greystone, Sir Oliver's younger sister.'

'But I am the only male heir, therefore I should inherit. However, to make absolutely sure of my position, I will have to marry you. As your husband, I will own everything of yours anyway.'

'My family will come to rescue me. Freddie won't allow this to happen.'

'I have a guard on the gates and the groundsmen have been told to apprehend any trespassers. And if you think Freddie Ashton will disobey his mama and marry you, you are very much mistaken. He will give in eventually and propose to the heiress.'

'You're forgetting I am an heiress now, Gervase. I have a name and it's one of the oldest families in the county.'

'You have yet to prove that in a court of law, my dear. Admit it, Nancy. I am your best bet of becoming mistress of Greystone Park. You need me as much as I need you. Love doesn't come into it.'

'The pony and chaise will have been found. Patsy saw your carriage and they will soon work out where I am. You might be able to keep members of the Carey family out but you can't do anything if the police are involved. I will be home again by this afternoon.'

'Brave words, but foolish, Nancy. You are ruined, my dear. You have spent the night in my company without a chaperone. I'll leave you to think things over.'

25

Starvation was not apparently part of Gervase's plan. Ivy arrived with a tray at what Nancy assumed must be midday, and the aroma of vegetable soup, hot bread rolls and a plate of apple pie was too tempting to resist. Yet again Seth Wills stood guard outside the door and Nancy did not have a chance to speak to Ivy, who was clearly nervous and distressed by the whole situation. However, when she came to take the tray back to the kitchen, there was no sign of Seth.

Nancy grasped Ivy by the wrist. 'I can speak to you without being overheard. You must help me, Ivy.'

'I daren't, miss. I would lose my position again. I can't afford to do that.'

'All I want you to do is to get a message to Rockwood Castle, letting them know that I am being kept prisoner here.'

'The master would know it was me what done it, miss.'

'Mr North won't be master here for very much longer, Ivy. I have inherited Greystone Park, which is why he's keeping me here. I promise that you will always have employment here with me if you do this one thing. Make an excuse. Tell Cook or Mrs Simpson that you need to visit your parents. Once you're outside the gates you can tell anyone in the village that I'm being kept prisoner here. They'll take the information to Rockwood Castle.'

'The master won't allow any of us to leave the

estate, miss.'

Nancy frowned. 'Then forget to lock the door. Leave the key in the lock and I'll do the rest. Please, Ivy. Your future depends upon this as much as mine.'

Ivy eyed her warily. 'I'll do it on one condition, miss.'

'All right, Ivy. What is it?'

'That you take me with you. The master is known to whip servants who don't obey him. I'm only doing this for you because I remember how good your family was to Miss Sylvia. She's a lovely lady and I am fond of her.'

'Sylvia will return to Greystone even if I am proved to be the rightful heir. She will always have a home here and be taken care of properly.'

'Does that mean you'll take me with you?'

'Of course. We'll wait until after dark. I know a way through the woods where Christina, Sylvia and Patricia used to play. Patricia told me about it. We'll go straight to the mill house, where you will be safe. Fletcher won't allow anyone to harm you, and Patricia will make sure your parents don't go without.'

Ivy's brown eyes filled with tears. 'I don't know how to thank you, miss.'

'Just leave the key in the lock after you collect my supper tray. Meet me in the scullery when Cook and Mrs Simpson are having their dinner in the servants' hall. I'm well versed in their habits since I stayed here to look after Miss Sylvia.'

'You can rely on me, miss.'

★ ★ ★

As Nancy had suspected, Gervase had put a guard at the front entrance, but he had not imagined that anyone would try to escape through the servants' quarters. There was no one about when Nancy and Ivy slipped out through the scullery, and the yard was deserted. Nancy was familiar with the grounds of Greystone Park, mainly from her early days when she and Tommy used to join some of the village children, scrumping apples, cherries and pears from the orchard. They had been expert in evading the groundsmen and gardeners, and Nancy remembered the short cut that would take them to a part of the stone wall that had partly collapsed.

They melted into the darkness and after many stumbles over tree roots and hummocks of long grass, they reached the place where the wall was relatively easy to climb. Once they were in the lane, Nancy led the way to the churchyard, knowing they would be safer there than on the main road. Ivy was terrified of ghosts but Nancy assured her that the dear departed were the least of their worries. It was Gervase's thugs who were the danger.

However, they did not see a soul as they hurried along a short stretch of the main road and it was easy to take a short cut through the field farmed by the Greeps. The lingering smell of smoke from the blacksmith's forge hung in the air as they hurried past the smithy; the wheelwright's shop was in darkness as was the sawmill. Bats zoomed overhead and an owl screeched as it flew low over the bare soil.

They arrived at the mill house and Nancy went to the back door and knocked.

It was opened by Fletcher wielding a wooden rolling pin. 'Good God, Miss Nancy. Where have you been?

The whole village is looking for you.' She peered over Nancy's shoulder. 'Is that you, Ivy Lugg? What are you doing here?'

'Please let us in and I'll explain,' Nancy said urgently. 'I don't think anyone saw us, but it's important for Ivy to be kept safe. I wouldn't have escaped if she hadn't risked everything to help me.'

'Come in.' Fletcher stood aside to let them pass, closing the door firmly behind them. 'You look in a sorry state, the pair of you. Best tidy yourselves up before you see the mistress. She has company.'

Nancy backed away. 'Who's here? It's not Gervase, is it?'

Fletcher rolled her eyes. 'I can see I'll get no sense out of you. Forget what I said and follow me.' She turned to Ivy, holding up her hand. 'Not you. Stay in the kitchen and I'll make you a cup of tea.' She led the way to the drawing room and opened the door without knocking. 'Look who has just turned up.'

Nancy stifled a sudden desire to giggle. Fletcher had never bothered to adopt the polite demeanour of a servant, but it would take a brave person to attempt to change her attitude. Nancy entered the room and came to a sudden halt.

'Freddie! You're the last person I expected to find here! I thought you had urgent family business.'

He crossed the floor in two strides and wrapped her in an embrace. 'Nancy, my darling. What happened? We have the police scouring the countryside for you.'

Patricia rose from the sofa. 'We've been frantic with worry.'

'Indeed we have.' Leo placed his arm around Patricia's shoulders. 'Patsy hardly slept last night for worrying about you, Nancy. We've had the whole

392

village looking for you.'

Nancy felt herself swaying and Freddie helped her to the nearest chair. 'Sit down. Take your time and tell us everything.' He turned to Fletcher. 'Brandy, please.'

'Yes, my lord.' Fletcher bowed out of the room.

'I'm sorry,' Nancy said wearily. 'I felt a bit faint but I'm all right now. It's been an ordeal but at least I'm free.'

Freddie kneeled at her side. 'What do you mean?'

'Gervase sent one of his men to kidnap me. I was locked in a room at Greystone Park.'

'You were taken prisoner? If he's harmed you in any way, he'll have me to answer to.' Freddie took her in his arms and held her so tightly that she could feel his heart beating against her breast.

'I'm not hurt, Freddie. I escaped with Ivy's help.'

'Tell us what happened,' Patricia said anxiously. 'Why would he do such a thing?'

'Start at the beginning, Nancy, my darling.' Freddie released her, brushing a lock of hair from her brow with a gentle hand. 'Tell us how it happened.'

It seemed such an improbable story but Nancy related the events of the previous evening until the moment she and Ivy had walked into the scullery at the mill house.

'Damned man.' Freddie rose to his feet. 'I've a good mind to go to Greystone Park this minute and throw him out. He has no legal right to be there in the first place, and by kidnapping you and keeping you imprisoned he's committed a criminal offence.'

'Then we should let Constable Burton know exactly what happened.' Leo helped Patricia back to her place on the sofa. 'It's no use taking the law into your own

393

hands, Ashton. Although I would like to beat the devil out of that man myself.'

'Why would he do such a thing, Nancy?' Patricia asked tiredly. 'What good did it do him to keep you locked up?'

'He wants to marry me,' Nancy said with a wry smile. 'Not because he loves me. He just wants to ensure his right to the estate. I think he's realised that Sir Oliver wasn't his father, but if he married me everything that I own would become his property. We are cousins if I can prove my identity, but that doesn't worry him.'

'Unspeakable.' Leo clenched his fists. 'Perhaps you and I ought to go there and teach him a lesson, Ashton.'

'You'll do no such thing,' Patricia said hastily. 'Leave it to the police.'

'Yes, I don't want either of you to get into trouble on my behalf.' Nancy looked up as Fletcher marched into the room with a tray laden with a decanter and four glasses.

'Brandy for all.' She placed the tray on a side table. 'What shall I do with Ivy Lugg? I have her sobbing in the kitchen. She thinks her ma and pa will starve to death because she's lost her position.'

'I remember Ivy. She is a good servant.' Patricia smiled up at Leo. 'We will need a nursemaid soon, my love.'

Leo nodded. 'Of course. Anything you want, Patsy.'

'She's terrified of Gervase,' Nancy added anxiously. 'She says he whips servants.'

'His days of bullying are almost over.' Freddie accepted the glass of brandy that Fletcher gave him and he handed it to Nancy. 'Take a sip of this. It will make you feel a bit better, and then I'll take you home.'

Nancy sipped the brandy. The strong spirit warmed her and she stopped shivering, but she refused a second drink. 'I'd like to go home now, Freddie. I came here first because I was afraid that we were being followed. I thought that Gervase would think I'd gone straight home and head for the castle.'

'You did exactly the right thing,' Patricia said firmly. 'You are safe here with us and so is Ivy.'

'There's something else.' Nancy took courage from the brandy warming her veins. 'Gervase said I would have to marry him as my reputation will be ruined by spending a night in his company.'

'As if anyone would believe that you were with him by choice.' Patricia shook her head. 'The man is deluded.'

Freddie downed his drink in one swallow. 'I really want to lay my hands on that fellow. I'm n-not n-normally a v-violent man, but he's g-gone too far.'

'Take Nancy home, Ashton,' Leo said angrily. 'I'll alert Constable Burton. You and I will accompany the police when they raid Greystone Park. We'll make sure the bastard doesn't get away.'

'Agreed.' Freddie helped Nancy to her feet. 'Are you all right to walk to my carriage? I'll carry you, if not.'

'I'm not a weak little woman, Freddie. But I would like to go home and let everyone see that I'm unharmed, even if my reputation has been damaged.'

'Everything you tell me about him makes me want to choke the life out of him.' Freddie turned to Leo with a grim smile. 'I'll meet you at Greystone Park. Make sure that Constable Burton knows what he's up against.'

'I'd like five minutes alone with him,' Fletcher said, cracking her knuckles. 'Me and Wolfe could make him cry like a baby.'

'I'm sure you're right.' Leo patted her on the shoulder. 'But I need you to protect my wife and Ivy, should Gervase happen to show his face here.'

'You can trust me, boss.' Fletcher puffed out her chest. 'The missis and young Lugg are in safe hands.'

Freddie proffered his arm. 'Are you ready, Nancy?'

She nodded. 'I'm coming. I'll see you tomorrow, Patsy. I'm so sorry you were upset.'

'It's not your fault, my dear. If it weren't for my condition, I would be the first to storm the gates of Greystone Park. I would have things to say to Gervase that he wouldn't wish to hear.'

Nancy managed a weak smile as she took Freddie's arm and allowed him to lead her outside to where his horse was tethered. He helped her into the chaise and took the reins.

'Why were you at the mill house, Freddie?' Nancy studied his profile as he guided the horse into the lane. 'You never said what brought you there.' Nancy wrapped the woollen rug round her legs as the cold night air nipped at her face and fingers.

'I returned to Rockwood to find that you were missing. I went to see if Leo had any idea what might have happened to you.'

'But you were summoned home by your papa. Why did he need to see you so urgently?'

'It was an excuse my parents used so that they could have a last attempt to change my mind about marrying their choice of bride. I told them in no uncertain terms that there is only one woman for me and nothing will alter that.'

'I dare say they were a bit put out.'

'I don't care, Nancy. I love you and it doesn't matter if you are rich or poor. You are the only one for me.'

'Oh, Freddie. I don't want to set you against your family. I know you love your mother and father, and I love you, too.'

He turned his head to give her a wide smile. 'That's the first time you've told me that.'

'It's true, Freddie, but I won't be responsible for breaking up your family. It would come between us eventually, and I couldn't bear that.'

'But if you and I were married my parents would grow to love you as I do. There would be no question of a rift.'

'You can't be certain of that.'

'When I arrived at Rockwood and they told me you had been missing all night I thought I would go mad. I've been to practically every house in the village asking if anyone had seen you, including Greystone Park.'

Momentarily diverted, Nancy turned her head to gaze at his profile. 'Did you speak to Foster or any of the house servants?'

'I didn't get past the gates. I was turned away by a rough-looking fellow who swore that Mr North had gone away.'

'Gervase said he had hired ruffians to protect his privacy. I think you will have a fight on your hands if you challenge them.'

'A fight is just what I want now. I'm opposed to violence, but Gervase has gone beyond what can be considered civilised behaviour. I'll see you safely home, Nancy, and then I'm going to join the others and we'll have Mr North out of Greystone Park and in prison where he belongs.'

'Please don't do anything silly, Freddie,' Nancy said anxiously. 'Leave it to the police.'

'I'll do whatever is necessary. I won't allow anyone to harm you in any way, Nancy.' Freddie pointed ahead. 'We're almost home. I'll leave you in Jarvis's safe hands, but I will be back as soon as possible.'

★ ★ ★

Freddie left her in Jarvis's care before driving off into the darkness. For a moment Nancy thought that Jarvis was going to hug her, but he limited himself to a wide smile and a nod of his head as he welcomed her home. She found the family assembled in the drawing room and was overwhelmed by the genuine warmth of their greeting, and the relief on all their faces to see her safely home. Even Hester was moved to give her a peck on the cheek, although she tempered her unexpected show of emotion by scolding Nancy for driving on her own after dark, giving Gervase the opportunity to abduct her. However, Hester's was a lone voice criticising Nancy's actions. Bertie was furious and Walter left the room declaring his intention of joining Freddie and Leo in helping the police to storm Greystone Park if they were denied access. Tommy had apparently been the first to volunteer and had gone with Constable Burton.

'I can't sit here doing nothing,' Bertie said at last. 'Wolfe, have my carriage brought to the front entrance. You and I will go to Greystone Park. I might not be able to do anything, but you can offer your services to Constable Burton.'

A slow smile spread across Wolfe's face. 'Aye, sir.

That's what I've been waiting to hear.' He loped off, leaving the door to swing shut behind him.

'You shouldn't go, Bertie,' Hester said angrily. 'Leave it to the police, or let Wolfe go on his own.'

'What? And miss a good fight?' Bertie threw back his head and laughed. 'Now that we know Nancy is safe, I want to see Greystone humiliated and arrested. As for him trying to take advantage of Nancy, I'll see him locked up for life if I have anything to do with it. The magistrate is a friend of mine — an ex-army man, who knows how things should be done.'

'You will keep an eye on Walter, won't you, Bertie?' Louise clasped her hands as if she were praying. 'I'm afraid he'll get hurt.'

'Don't worry, my dear. Wolfe won't allow that to happen, and neither will I. It's not as if Gervase has an army defending him. His hired thugs will melt away when faced with the police and the rest of us there to back them up. Gervase will wish he had never started this whole thing by the time we're finished with him.'

'I'm coming with you,' Nancy said firmly. 'I won't sleep if I go to bed.'

Bertie gave her a calculating look. 'All right. I'll take you, but on one condition. You must stay in the carriage with me. Is that clear?'

'Yes, Bertie.'

'Do you promise to do as I say?'

'I promise.' Nancy turned her head at the sound of a commotion outside the room. The door was flung open and Felicia de Marney made a grand entrance, followed by her husband.

'What on earth is going on, Bertie?' Felicia demanded, throwing off her cloak and allowing it to fall to the floor. 'The village is swarming with policemen.'

'Yes, Bertie, old chap. Is there a villain on the loose?'
Claude picked up his wife's fur-lined cloak.

'Well, now. This is a surprise. How long is it since you last graced us with your presence, Felicia?' Hester rose from her chair. 'I suppose this means you are in between engagements. Are you planning to stay for a while?'

'If it's inconvenient we can always book a room at the Black Dog,' Claude said apologetically. 'I realise it's rather late, but we've had a long journey.'

'Have you come far, Mrs de Marney?' Louise asked tentatively. 'I'm afraid your grandchildren are in bed, or I would bring them down to see you.'

Felicia turned to give her a frosty stare. 'Oh, you're still here, are you, Louise? I thought that you and Walter would have found a home of your own by now. And I've told you before that I do not recognise myself as being a grandmother. My public think of me as being eternally youthful.'

Nancy could see that Louise was hurt by this and she stepped forward. 'I know you are angry with me, Mrs de Marney, but there's no need to take it out on your own flesh and blood.'

'Which you are not.' Felicia looked Nancy up and down. 'You seem to have made yourself at home here, too. I thought you would be living with Patsy, or didn't she want you?'

'You are still the same sweet-natured person you have always been,' Hester said drily. 'I'll ring for Tilly. She'll light a fire in your old room. We've had dinner but I expect Cook can make something for you.'

'Please don't trouble her,' Claude said hastily. 'We dined on the way from Exeter.'

Hester beckoned to Louise. 'I expect you want

to check on the children. I'll made sure that proper arrangements are made for Mr and Mrs de Marney.' Hester sailed out of the room, followed by Louise.

Wolfe put his head round the door. 'The carriage is waiting, boss.'

'Carriage? Where are you going at this time of night?' Felicia demanded, sinking down on the chair nearest to the fire.

Nancy took the handle of the Bath chair. 'We are on a mission to catch a criminal, Mrs de Marney.'

'Yes, Mama. You'll have to excuse us and entertain yourselves for the rest of the evening. We'll tell you all about it at breakfast.'

Nancy pushed the wheeled chair out into the hallway and Wolfe took it from her.

'That gave me a great deal of pleasure,' Bertie said, grinning. 'My mother loves to make an entrance but this time we've stolen her thunder, so to speak, Nancy. I'd rather we didn't have to do this but . . .'

Wolfe growled with laughter. 'Don't lie, boss. You're enjoying every minute of it.'

'I suppose I am,' Bertie said cheerfully. 'Forget my mother and her husband. We've got more important matters on hand. Remember that you are under orders to stay in the carriage no matter what, Nancy?'

'I haven't forgotten.' Nancy patted Sir Denys's visor as she walked past the suit of armour. 'We need your spirit on our side, Sir Denys. I hope you will come with us and bring Gervase to justice.'

26

Nancy, Bertie and Wolfe arrived at the gates of Greystone Park in time to see Gervase escorted out of the estate by two burly police constables. Gervase was protesting loudly and he made an attempt to escape but was met by Freddie's fist, which felled him to the ground.

'You deserved that, North,' Freddie said, rubbing his knuckles. 'The law will punish you for what you've done, but that was from me for putting Nancy through such an ordeal.'

Gervase was hauled to his feet by the constables. 'I'm bleeding,' he bleated. 'You've broken my nose.'

'You fell while attempting to resist arrest,' Constable Burton said severely. 'Tie his hands and put him in the wagon. He can rest in the cells tonight.'

'I want him charged with abduction and imprisonment,' Bertie said firmly. 'Miss Sunday is my ward and I am responsible for her.'

Nancy did not argue. Greystone Park might belong to her when probate was granted and Mr Mounce had made a case to prove her identity, but at the moment she had no desire to enter the grounds. She watched Gervase being hustled into the police wagon with a feeling that justice was being done. Gervase had tried to walk over everyone in his chosen path to become the owner of Greystone Park, but he had been found out and would pay the price. She turned to see Freddie walking purposefully towards her, and she leaned out of the carriage.

'You were magnificent, Freddie.'

He smiled ruefully. 'I'm ashamed to say I rather enjoyed punching Gervase on the nose. He deserved it for what he put you through.'

'Are you coming back to Rockwood with us?'

'Not tonight. Leo invited me to stay at the mill house, and I think that might look better, but I'll come round to see you first thing in the morning.'

'Tell Patricia that her mama has descended upon us,' Bertie said, grinning. 'No doubt, when she hears Patricia's news, our mother will be overjoyed at the prospect of becoming a grandmama yet again.'

Freddie laughed. 'I'm well acquainted with Mrs de Marney. I will pass on your message.' He turned to Nancy, reaching out to clasp her hand. 'I'll see you in the morning. Try to get some rest, my darling.'

She raised his hand to her cheek. 'I'll sleep better knowing that Gervase is locked up safely. Good night, Freddie.'

Wolfe glanced over his shoulder. 'Shall I take you home now, boss?'

'Yes, Wolfe. We've seen enough.' Bertie leaned back against the squabs. 'I didn't do anything myself but it was very satisfying to see North receive his just deserts. Drive on.'

Nancy blew a kiss to Freddie as the carriage moved off in the direction of Rockwood Castle. She knew that Freddie loved her, but if they were to have any future together she still had to overcome his parents' prejudice, and that was not going to be easy.

★ ★ ★

Next morning, the first visitor to arrive was not Freddie but Herbert Mounce, who had driven himself from Exeter in an eccentric curricle that had seen better days, as had the old horse that was harnessed between the shafts.

Nancy happened to be passing the window and had seen him draw up at the front entrance and hand the reins to Pip, the under groom. She hurried to greet him as Jarvis ushered him into the entrance hall.

'Good morning, Mr Mounce. You are up and about early.'

'Good morning, Miss Sunday, or should I say, Miss Greystone?' A slow smile crossed his stern features.

'Do come into the parlour, Mr Mounce. I'll send for some refreshment.' Nancy beckoned to Flossie, who was trying to look inconspicuous as she dusted the oak coffers. 'Ask Cook to make up a tray of coffee and sandwiches for Mr Mounce. He's come all the way from Exeter.'

Flossie bobbed a curtsey and flitted off in the direction of the back stairs. Nancy led Mr Mounce to the morning parlour and motioned him to take a seat.

He placed his leather document case on the tea table, and sat down. 'You are well, I hope, Miss Greystone?'

'I am indeed, but why are you calling me Miss Greystone. Has probate been granted?'

'It has, and I have your father's will here, as well as signed affidavits proving that you were born on the day before you were found on the steps of the orphanage. Dr Bulmer says he remembers attending your mother soon after the birth, but shortly after that he was told that mother and child had both drowned in the lake. Moreover there were no other births around that date that he knows of. I had the same story from Mrs Betts, the midwife.'

'Did she mention the swaddling cloth with the family crest?'

He nodded. 'Yes, she did. That's exactly how she left the baby in her mother's arms.'

'Is that enough proof, Mr Mounce?'

'I have another person who will confirm the details. The present vicar, Mr Shaw, was not ordained at the time, but his predecessor, who retired many years ago, was called upon to baptise the infant. Apparently Lady Greystone knew that she had not much longer to live and was racked with fears for the safety of her baby. It seems that the poor woman was in a bad way, due to her advanced illness.'

'Do you know what name the child was given?'

'I do, and it was Nancy. I have the baptismal certificate for you.' Mr Mounce opened the document case and produced a yellowed slip of paper. 'The vicar had kept it out of respect for the family, and as the baptism was not conducted in church you could find no record of it.'

'It's hard to believe, but how did the orphanage come to give me that name?'

'Sir Oliver must have told his brother-in-law that you were to be called Nancy. Perhaps Mr North left a note with your name on pinned to your garments. Someone would have seen it and probably discarded it as being unimportant. The women who work at the orphanage are well-meaning souls, but unlikely to have paid much attention to a slip of paper. Probably many of them are illiterate anyway, so it would mean little to them.'

Nancy shook her head. 'So I am Nancy after all. I

can hardly believe it. Thank you so much, Mr Mounce. You don't know what this means to me.'

'I'm delighted to have been of service. Now all we have to do is to register you and apply for a birth certificate. With all the evidence we have I hope it will be a straightforward case. Would you like me to do that for you?'

'Yes, please.' Nancy jumped to her feet and opened the door. 'Come in.'

Flossie staggered in and placed the heavy tray down on the tea table.

'Thank you, Flossie.'

'Mr Jarvis told me to tell you that Lord Ashton has arrived, Miss Nancy.'

'Just in time to thank you for all your hard work, Mr Mounce,' Nancy said delightedly. 'Show him in Flossie.' She waited until Flossie had left the room. 'This is so exciting, Mr Mounce. I can't wait to tell Freddie. Do help yourself to sandwiches.' She passed him the plate and was about to pour the tea when the door opened and Freddie strode into the room. He crossed the floor in long strides and kissed Nancy on the cheek.

'Good morning, Mr Mounce. Judging by Flossie's agitated state, you must have news for us. I hope it's not bad.'

Mr Mounce swallowed a mouthful of food. 'Not at all, my lord. It's very good.'

'Enjoy your sandwiches, Mr Mounce.' Nancy filled a cup and passed it to him. She stood up and took Freddie aside. 'I can't wait to tell you what I've just learned. Your mama and papa won't be able to look down on me now, Freddie. I am indeed an heiress, although maybe not as wealthy as the one they chose for you.'

Freddie seized her round the waist and kissed her soundly on the lips. Nancy was too shocked and excited to protest. She allowed herself to savour the embrace before drawing away. 'Freddie, you're embarrassing Mr Mounce.'

'No, really, please pay no attention to me.' Mr Mounce selected another sandwich. 'These are delicious, Miss Greystone. Just what I needed after an early morning start.'

'If we leave you to enjoy your meal, would you be prepared to tell my family in person what you've just told me?' Nancy asked eagerly. 'I'm afraid if I do it myself they'll think I'm imagining things.'

'Certainly. I will be happy to oblige. I don't suppose your cook has any cake, has she?'

Nancy rang the bell and moments later Flossie bustled into the room. 'Mr Mounce would like some cake.'

'Yes, Miss Nancy.' Flossie was about to leave the room when Nancy called her back.

'Have you seen Mr and Mrs de Marney this morning?'

'They are at breakfast with Sir Bertram and Master Tommy, miss.'

'Thank you, Flossie. That will be all for now.' Nancy turned to Mr Mounce, who had just finished off the last sandwich. 'Mr Mounce, would you be kind enough to accompany us to the dining room? I want you to tell my family exactly what you told me.'

He rose to his feet, wiping his lips on a clean damask table napkin, which he then abandoned reluctantly. 'I will have some cake?'

'Of course. It will only take a few minutes of your

time.'

He followed Nancy and Freddie to the dining room where Felicia and Claude were just finishing their meal. Wolfe was about to push Bertie's chair out into the hallway but Nancy stopped him.

'This won't take long, but I want you to hear what Mr Mounce has to say. It's very important.'

Felicia rolled her eyes. 'Nancy, dear, we have only just finished eating.'

'Let the man have his say, Felicia,' Claude said gently. 'It's obviously important to Nancy.'

Mr Mounce cleared his throat. 'Some time ago, Miss Nancy came to me asking for help to discover her true identity.'

'Get on with it, Mr Mounce,' Felicia said impatiently. 'We haven't got all day to sit here listening to you go on as if you are in the courtroom.'

'My apologies, ma'am. I'll try to be brief and succinct.'

'Good man,' Claude said appreciatively. 'What was it you wanted to tell us?'

'After a lot of serious investigations, we have discovered that Miss Sunday is really Miss Nancy Greystone, the legal heir to the Greystone estate and family fortune, which was left to her by her papa, Sir Oliver Greystone.'

Felicia choked on her coffee. 'You are telling fibs, Mr Mounce.'

'On my honour, ma'am, it is the truth. I have affidavits from the doctor and midwife who delivered Lady Greystone of a baby girl on the day in question, and a copy of the baptismal certificate that the vicar wrote shortly after the birth.'

Tommy leaped from his seat at the table and rushed

round to give Nancy a hug. 'We knew it all along, didn't we?'

'Well, I thought it was true, but now I know it is and the will has been probated. All that Mr Mounce has to do is to register my birth, a little late, but it can be done.'

'Most certainly,' Mr Mounce agreed. 'Now may I return to my tea and cake, Miss Greystone?'

'Of course,' Nancy said happily. 'Please do.'

He backed out of the room, nodding to Bertie. 'Sir Bertram.'

Felicia stared at Nancy in disbelief. 'Who would have believed it? I certainly would not.'

'We should travel to Dorrington Place to let my parents have the good news,' Freddie said, smiling. 'I don't care if you are an heiress or a beggar maid, but unfortunately they do, and you said last night you didn't want to go against them.'

'Most certainly not. I won't come between you and your family, Freddie.'

Felicia turned to them, her eyes wide with curiosity. 'Excuse me, Nancy. Did I hear you correctly? Are Freddie's parents being difficult?'

'You've met my parents, Mrs de Marney,' Freddie said warily. 'You know that they are a little old-fashioned in their outlook.'

'Old-fashioned or not, I won't allow them to cast aspersions on anyone from this family. If you are going to Dorrington Place then I am going also.'

Claude laid his hand on her arm. 'Felicia, my love, this really isn't our business.'

'Of course it is, Claude. Nancy is like a daughter to me and a sister to Rosalind and Patricia. Remember the time in London and that trouble in Paris? Nancy helped us to avoid a dreadful scandal. We owe her this.'

Nancy turned her head away to hide a smile. Felicia had changed her tune now that she knew Nancy was of genteel birth.

'It couldn't be that you want the Dorringtons to offer you work, would it, my love?' Claude said wryly.

'Certainly not. The thought never entered my head, although I know that Lord Dorrington is a patron of the arts. We will go to Dorrington Place today.'

'But, my love, we've only just arrived here. We've been travelling for months.'

'You are my manager as well as my husband, Claude. You did the bookings, now it's my turn to choose where I wish to perform. Not, of course, that I am doing this for selfish reasons, but my public always wish to see me and hear me sing.'

'Yes, my love,' Claude said with a sigh. 'Of course.'

'You will put a carriage at our disposal, Bertie.' Felicia met his baffled look with a hard stare.

'Yes, if you so wish, Mama. I doubt if it would make much difference if I refused.'

'Precisely.' Felicia rose gracefully from the table. 'What are you waiting for, Nancy? Go and pack a few things. I need to tell Violet to stop unpacking. How long do you think we will be away, Claude?'

He shrugged and shook his head. 'It was your idea to visit Dorrington Place, my love.'

'You are no use. As always it will be up to me to make the necessary decisions.' Felicia brushed past Nancy and Freddie. 'Don't stand there staring. Go and change into something more suitable for travelling, Nancy. You don't want to arrive at Dorrington Place looking like a peasant, do you?'

'My parents have no say in this, Nancy,' Freddie said firmly. 'I will marry you whatever happens. But we will go to Dorrington Place today, if that makes you happy. We will face them together.'

'I don't want to lose you, Nancy,' Tommy said firmly, 'but I can see the way things are with you and Freddie. You can hold your head up no matter whether you are just Nancy Sunday or Miss Nancy Greystone. Don't allow anyone to make you feel inferior.'

'Well said, Tommy.' Freddie gave him a friendly pat on the shoulder.

'There's just one thing,' Bertie said plaintively. 'If you marry Freddie, you will have to move far away. We've been a family for so long, Nancy. I, for one, will miss you very much.'

Freddie shook his head. 'Don't worry, Bertie. I won't take her away from the people who love her. I don't care if we live in a shepherd's hut just so long as Nancy is happy.'

Hester appeared in the doorway. 'I don't know what is going on but Christina Cottingham is here and she demands to see you, Nancy. I don't know how the news has spread so fast but it seems that everyone in Rockwood village knows who you really are.'

'Where is she, Hester?'

'I left her in the music room. She doesn't look happy.'

'I'll come right away.' Nancy turned to Freddie. 'Please will you go and keep Mr Mounce entertained? I might need him to speak to Christina before he leaves.'

Freddie raised her hand to his lips. 'Of course. Don't allow her to bully you, Nancy.'

'Certainly not. I must remember that I am Miss

Nancy Greystone. I am not afraid of Christina; after all, she is my cousin.' Nancy giggled at the thought as she made her way to the music room.

Christina stopped pacing the floor to face her with a belligerent frown. 'So you are claiming to be the rightful owner of Greystone Park. My papa left it to me and to Sylvia. I suppose that imposter Gervase North put you up to this.'

'Won't you take a seat, Christina?'

'No, I am not staying long. I just came to tell you that Greystone Park belongs to me and my sister. I heard that Gervase has been arrested, which is right and proper, but don't think you can take advantage of his absence.'

'Christina, please stop a minute and allow me to explain.' Nancy sank down on a damask upholstered piano stool. 'My solicitor is here if you wish to speak to him. He has proof that I am Sir Oliver and Lady Greystone's daughter. It was Gervase who told me that he saw Sir Oliver place an infant in his father's care, but Gervase was convinced that he himself was Sir Oliver's son, which is untrue.'

'What proof could your solicitor possibly have after all this time? How old are you, Nancy? Seventeen, eighteen?'

Nancy smiled. 'I was nineteen on the thirtieth of March, Christina. Mr Mounce, our solicitor, has the documents. I'll ask him to show them to you before he applies to register my birth.'

Christina gasped as if all the air had been sucked from her lungs. 'You're lying. Just like Gervase, you will say anything to cheat Sylvia and me out of our birthright.'

Nancy rose to her feet, holding out her hand. 'You

have Cottingham Manor, Christina. If your sister wishes to live at Greystone Park, I will take care of her, although I haven't yet decided if I will live there myself. Come with me, and speak to Mr Mounce.'

'If you're lying you will look very silly when I tell the world that you were in league with Cousin Gervase.'

Nancy walked to the door. 'You may do as you wish, but I suggest you see Mr Mounce first.'

★ ★ ★

It was late afternoon by the time Nancy and Freddie arrived at Dorrington Place. It had taken Mr Mounce a long time to convince Christina of the facts, but eventually she had flounced out of the room and Mr Mounce had finally been able to leave for his office in Exeter. Felicia, Violet and Claude had travelled in Bertie's carriage, driven by Ned Hudson, as Jim Gurney was getting too old to handle the reins on long journeys.

Pickering showed them into the drawing room where Lady Dorrington was dozing over a piece of embroidery. Her lapdog, a small pug, jumped up and barked shrilly, and Lady Dorrington awakened with a start.

'Freddie? You've returned.' Her smile faded as she recognised Nancy and her jaw dropped at the sight of Felicia and Claude. 'I don't recall requesting the entertainers?'

'Mama, Mr and Mrs de Marney are our guests, as is Nancy. You remember her, of course.'

'Yes, how could I forget the little foundling?'

'Mama, that is v-very impolite.' Freddie faced her angrily. 'If that is how you feel, perhaps we ought to leave right away instead of tomorrow morning.'

Nancy laid her hand on his arm. 'Lady Dorrington, might I speak to you in private, please?'

'I don't know what you could have to say to me, but yes, I suppose so. Freddie, take these people to the conservatory and give them tea, or whatever they wish for.'

Freddie leaned towards Nancy. 'Are you sure about this?'

'Yes, of course. Please do as your mama asks.'

'I will, but I trust you will treat Nancy with the respect she deserves, Mama.' Freddie ushered Felicia and Claude out of the room, closing the door behind them.

'Well now, miss. What is this all about? I believe you know my opinion on your relationship with my son.'

'Yes, my lady. You made that very plain at our last meeting. I am not here to beg for your approval. I want to tell you that I love your son more than I could ever imagine loving anyone, which is why I won't allow him to propose to me unless you and Lord Dorrington approve.'

Lady Dorrington's eyes narrowed. 'Are you trying to blackmail me into saying something that I will regret?'

'Of course not. I respect the bond between parents and children. I was denied that myself because I was a foundling, but that doesn't mean that I have no respect for the feelings of others. I've recently discovered who my parents were and where I belong, but the truth is that my real family are the people who took me in as a child and brought me up. They have shown me love and understanding. Things that are sometimes missing in people who are actually related.'

'Are you saying that my husband and I lack empathy with our only child?'

'No, but perhaps you are not listening to Freddie. He is a wonderful person and I love him dearly, but I also love him too much to break the bond he feels for you and his papa. I might not be good enough for him in your eyes, but I am no pauper and I find I have a family pedigree just as good as your own. Not that it matters to Freddie, but he does care what you think.'

'Do I understand you properly, Miss Sunday?'

'Actually my name is Greystone. Nancy Greystone of Greystone Park in the county of Devonshire.'

'Really?' Lady Dorrington eyed her thoughtfully. 'Well, Miss Greystone, would you be willing to give up all claim to my son's affections if I told you that he must choose between you and his family?'

'It would break my heart, but yes, if you and Lord Dorrington cannot accept me as being part of Freddie's life, then I will tell him that we can never be together.'

Lady Dorrington leaned towards Nancy with a hint of humour in her smile. 'Are you sincere or are you just saying that?'

'On my honour, I mean every word.'

'I admire honesty and courage. I can see that you have both, Nancy Greystone, and you have my blessing, but there is one condition.'

'A condition, my lady?'

'That you take the singing woman home with you when you return to Rockwood Castle. I will allow her to entertain us after dinner this evening, but tomorrow you will take her away from here. Do you agree?'

'I do, my lady,' Nancy said, smiling.

That evening after dinner, Lady Dorrington went out of her way to make Nancy feel at home, although Lord Dorrington remained slightly aloof. However, Felicia was invited to sing, which she accepted graciously, and everyone made their way to the music room. Nancy took her seat at the pianoforte, flexing her hands nervously. She had not played for a while but when she began the music came back to her fingers and they flew over the keys.

Felicia sang three arias and accepted the applause as if she were on the stage of the grandest opera house in the world. Claude proffered his arm and led her to her seat where she was plied with glasses of port wine and praise for her wonderful voice. One of Lord Dorrington's guests happened to know Mr Chart, the manager of the Theatre Royal in Brighton, and he promised to recommend Felicia for the leading role in their next opera.

Nancy left Felicia, Claude and their new friends drinking champagne. Freddie took her hand and tucked it into the crook of his arm. 'Let's go for a walk in the orangery. It's more peaceful there.'

Nancy leaned against him as they walked through the elegant corridors to the orangery at the side of the great house. It was lit by hundreds of candles and the aroma of the hot beeswax mingled with the exotic scent of the orange blossom so carefully cultivated in the heated greenhouse.

'I don't know what you said to Mama,' Freddie squeezed Nancy's hand, 'but she's a changed woman. Papa will come round to her way of thinking when he realises that we are in earnest.'

'I was totally honest with your mama, Freddie.'

'Well, it certainly worked. They know that I love you more than life itself and I would do anything to make you happy.'

'I am happy just being with you, Freddie.'

He led her to a seat secluded by palm trees. A small table was set with a bottle of champagne resting in an ice bucket and two glasses.

'I've been waiting for this moment for a long time, Nancy. I loved you from the first moment I saw you and nothing will ever change that.'

'I love you, too, Freddie. But I meant what I said to your mama.'

'She believed you, as I do. You are so honest it shines out of your lovely face and I want to spend the rest of my life with you. We can live here or at Greystone Park or in the treehouse in the castle woods. I don't care. I just want you to marry me. Will you, Nancy? Will you marry me?'

She answered by giving him a fleeting kiss on the lips. 'Yes, Freddie. I will.'

He enveloped her in his arms and this time the embrace was fierce with longing and pent-up passion. He released her reluctantly. 'I have something for you. I had it with me the other night but it wasn't the right time or place.' He took a small velvet box from his pocket and opened it. A diamond and emerald ring winked in the candlelight. He slipped it on her finger.

'Now you can't run away ever again, Nancy.'

She smiled. 'As if I would want to. I will always be by your side, Freddie. For good or ill, I'll be with you.'

We do hope that you have enjoyed
reading this large print book.

Did you know that all of our titles
are available for purchase?

We publish a wide range of high
quality large print books including:
Romances, Mysteries, Classics
General Fiction
Non Fiction and Westerns

Special interest titles available in
large print are:
The Little Oxford Dictionary
Music Book, Song Book
Hymn Book, Service Book

Also available from us courtesy of
Oxford University Press:
Young Readers' Dictionary
(large print edition)
Young Readers' Thesaurus
(large print edition)

For further information or a free
brochure, please contact us at:
Ulverscroft Large Print Books Ltd.,
The Green, Bradgate Road, Anstey,
Leicester, LE7 7FU, England.
Tel: (00 44) 0116 236 4325
Fax: (00 44) 0116 234 0205

Other titles published by Ulverscroft:

RUNAWAY WIDOW

Dilly Court

London, 1859. When Lady Patricia Greystone's husband dies suddenly, she is left with nothing. At twenty-four, she finds herself a penniless widow. Determined not to return to her family cap in hand, she strikes out on her own.

Patricia's voice is her only hope. She makes her living singing at inns and on the streets. But a dangerous figure from her family's past is lurking in the shadows, and before long she finds herself fleeing the city.

Without her family around her, will Patricia lose her way?

WINTER WEDDING

Dilly Court

Christmas is coming. But the happiest time of the year is marred by a cruel twist of fate. Rosalind Blanchard's husband Piers is gravely wounded in a shipwreck, and she finds herself head of crumbling Rockwood Castle once more. Pregnant with his child and alone, she turns to the only man who has ever made her heart sing — Piers' brother Alex.

However, though Alex was her old love, Piers must be her future. Until shocking news changes everything. As the first snowflakes begin to appear, so too does another chance of happiness for Rosalind. One that might just include her beloved home and true love Alex by her side . . .

RAG-AND-BONE CHRISTMAS

Dilly Court

London, 1865. Snow is falling fast, and Sally Suggs is working tirelessly to bring in enough money to keep bread on the table. Her father, a skilled rag-and-bone man, has fallen ill — and now Sally has taken up his trade. But this is a man's world, where competition is fierce, and Sally's rival Finn Kelly always seems to be one step ahead. With no-one to protect the Suggs family, the black-market traders of London's underbelly circle closer. Sally needs to find help in the most unexpected places if they are to survive . . .